Introduction to Anthropology

SALZWASSER
VERLAG

Theodor Waitz

Introduction to Anthropology

Reprint of the original, first published in 1863.

1st Edition 2022 | ISBN: 978-3-37500-092-9

Verlag (Publisher): Salzwasser Verlag GmbH, Zeilweg 44, 60439 Frankfurt, Deutschland
Vertretungsberechtigt (Authorized to represent): E. Roepke, Zeilweg 44, 60439 Frankfurt, Deutschland
Druck (Print): Books on Demand GmbH, In de Tarpen 42, 22848 Norderstedt, Deutschland

INTRODUCTION

TO

ANTHROPOLOGY.

BY

DR. THEODOR WAITZ

LONDON

1863.

CONTENTS OF VOLUME I.

	PAGE
Dedication	xi
Editor's Preface	xiii
Author's preface	1
Introduction	

DEFINITION AND SCIENTIFIC POSITION OF ANTHROPOLOGY.

Definition; Naturalist's view; Theologian's view; Philosopher's view; Position of Anthropology in Germany; Division of Anthropology into two parts; Physiology and Psychology of Man; History of Civilization; Scope of Anthropology; Question of Species; Position of Ethnology; Latham's definition of Anthropology . 3

ON THE UNITY OF MANKIND AS A SPECIES, AND ON THE NATURAL STATE OF MAN.

Man to be studied in aggregate; Individual and social life of Man; Unity, or Plurality of Species; Limited view of Mankind; Plurality of Species and Race-Antagonism; Parallelism of physical and psychical qualities of Man; Psychical life; Cuvier's view; Bory de St. Vincent on the Negro type; Division of the question 10

PART I.

PHYSICAL INVESTIGATION.

The notion of Species; Its application to the organic and inorganic kingdoms of Nature; Definition of Species discussed; Cuvier's definition; Prichard's definition; Unity of Species resulting from

Unity of Origin; Agassiz, Vogt, Giebel, and De Candolle, on Species in Animals; American School; Fecundity as a criterion of Species, Buffon; Hybridity as a criterion of Species, F. Müller; Desmoulins on Hybridity among Cattle; Fecundity of Hybrids; Nott and Gliddon on definition of Species; "Race" as applied to Mankind and Dogs; Inferences from the foregoing; Reversion; Cases of Mongrels, Mestizoes, Mulattoes, etc.; Opinion of Geoffrey St. Hilaire; Blumenbach on Reversion; Geographical distribution of Species; Range of Variation; Species and Race; Application of these terms to domestic animals,—Nott; Application to Mankind; Variations peculiar to each Species; Agassiz's application to Man and Ape; other Writers referred to; Retrospect 17

SECTION I.

ON THE MODE AND MAGNITUDE OF THE PHYSICAL CHANGES TO WHICH MAN IS SUBJECT.

1. *Climate.*—Influences of Climate stated; Correspondence of Climate with physical organization; Effects of the hygrometric state of Atmosphere; Effects of the barometric state; Müller's explanation of black skin of Negro; Berthold's explanation; Foissac's explanation; Godron on climatic influences; Heusinger's observations; Facts by D'Orbigny; Volney on Negro physiognomy; Blumenbach's views; Influence of Climate on stature; Views of Lauvergne, Zimmerman, Geoffroy St. Hilaire; Influence of Climate on the sexual organs; on the intellect; on fecundity; on colour of skin, hair, and eyes; Influence of geographical conditions on the human frame; Different Races compared; Pruner-Bey on climatic influence; Complexion in different Climates; Effects of American Climate on German, English, etc.; the genuine Yankee; Australian Climate; Influence on Character 34

2. *Aliment.*—Effects on Body and Mind undoubted; Influence of Wealth and Poverty; Degenerate Irishmen of Ulster; the Bosjesmans; Rice-consuming peoples; Flesh-Eaters; the Fiji Islanders and other Vegetarians; American tribes and their various dietary; the Yakuts; the Arabs, Bedouins, etc.; Milne-Edwards on Nutrition; French military standard; Effects of mode of life on the skeleton; Hunters and Fishers; Malay, Japanese, and Chinese women, effects on them of sedentary or active habits; Social relations and castes, how they act on the Body; Change of habit and its effect on the Portuguese settler; the Barabra, Kordofanese, etc. 57

3. *Mental Culture.*—Mental influence favourable or unfavourable to the physical development; Low development subject to external influ-

ences; Uniformity of uncivilized peoples; Old Germans; Aboriginal Americans; Uniformity of Character among the Negroes; Individuality of the Fijians; Effects of imitation; in Clans of Scotland; on the individual resident abroad; The free-born and slave Negro; asserted change of features in the former; Superiority of Creole Negroes; Causes of this difference; Effects of social intercourse on American Negroes; Greatest change in the Northern States; Mental Culture in the physiognomy of all nations; Effects of Cultivation on the English and German physiognomy; on the Sikhs; Change in the Magyars; the Finns and Lapps; Shape of Skull no criterion of Race; Skull varies most in civilized peoples; Modification in the same people; Abbé Frère and Huschke on cranial development; the slow change of physical peculiarities; Importance of the mental influence; Retrospect 67

4. *Hereditary Transmission.*—Spontaneous origin of new peculiarities; how rendered permanent; Breeding of domestic animals; Breed of Otter Sheep; Hungarian cattle; Mental peculiarities hereditary; Transmission of accidental peculiarities; Mutilation; Change in the dog; Origin of Races; Morbid peculiarities; Family peculiarities; House of Hapsburg; Lambert family; Six-fingered peculiarity; Albinism; White Negroes; White individuals among the Blackfeet and Mandans; Hereditary deformities cited by Gosse and Wagner; European and savage Children compared; Psychical peculiarities transmitted; Children of Polynesia; of South America, Arabia, South Africa, etc.; Evidence of Incas; Nott and Gliddon on innate and inherited instincts; Mechanical and artistic talent transmitted; Hereditary aristocracy of the Mind; Transmission of innate and organic individual peculiarities; Retrospect and results 80

SECTION II.

THE CHIEF ANATOMICAL AND PHYSIOLOGICAL DIFFERENCES WHICH DISTINGUISH THE VARIOUS RACES.

Man and Ape compared; Traditions in India of ape-like Men; Nott and Gliddon on Negro and Orang-Utang; the Negro type of the Soudan, Kordofan, etc.; their thickness of Skull; Duncan, Sömmering, Pruner-Bey, Tiedemann, Blumenbach, Lawrence, Morton, Huschke, and others, on Negro Anatomy; Negro features described; Hair of the Negro, Hottentots, Bushmen, and Austral Negroes; The beard; Vrolik on the limbs of Negro; The hand and foot of Negro, according to Burmeister, Sömmering, and Dutenhofer; The blood of Negro; His skin described, and the effects of age and climate thereon; Peculiar exhalation from the Negro skin; Skull of Negroes, Australians, Americans, New Zealanders, and other types described; Teeth; Proportions of the limbs; Deficiency of calf; Burmeister on the feet of Negro and Ape; Use of the foot among jugglers of America; Disagreeable odour of the Negro and other Races; Differences between African and Austral Negroes; the head of the Negro type; the Hottentot Venus; Circumcision of Women in Egypt, in Abyssinia, in the countries of the Nile, among the Hottentots, etc.; Cranial deformation; Situation of the Ear; Egyptian Mummies; Abnormities of anatomical structure; Physiological peculiarities; Animal heat; Rate of pulse; Age of puberty and marriage; Proportions of male to female births; Congenital deformities; Mortality; Signs of age; Sustentation of pain; Physical endurance; Amount of food; Bodily strength; Results of Freycinet's experiments with the dynamometer; Results of Buckton; Endurance of savage nations; Muscular weakness of the Americans; Endurance of the Negro; of the South Americans, etc.; Duration of life; Diseases; Vital energy of savage and civilized peoples compared; Healing power; greater among savage than civilized nations; Human parasites; Acclimatization; Superiority of the White Races in this capacity; Cause thereof; the English in India; Whites in West Indies; Negroes in West Indies; conflicting evidence on Acclimatization; Capacity of blushing; not confined to the White Races; Formation of speech-sounds; Use of the hands; Perfection of the senses; Sense of sight in savage nations; its cultivation by Europeans; Sense of taste; Effects of music; Sense of smell; in Negro and other savages; Negro music; Retrospect 90

APPENDIX TO SECTION II.

ON THE ASSERTED INVIABILITY OF THE AMERICANS, POLYNESIANS, AND AUSTRALIANS.

Rapid decay of American tribes; by small-pox and fevers; by tribal wars; by spirit drinking; by loss of territory; by scanty prolificacy; by abortion and infanticide; through early marriages; Prolificacy of North American women; of South Americans; Decrease of population in Polynesia; Statistics thereon; Causes; Drunkenness; Infanticide; Abortion; Sexual excesses; Internal wars; Human sacrifices; Cannibalism; Famine; Venereal diseases; Sterility; and psychical causes; Decrease of the Australians; Diseases; Drunkenness; Sexual excesses; Infanticide; Negligence; Want of nourishment; Invasion of Europeans; Injustice done to the natives by the English official 144

SECTION III.

THE RESULTS OF INTERMIXTURE OF DIFFERENT TYPES, AND THE PECULIARITIES OF THE MONGRÈLS.

Difficulties of the question; Influence of the parents on the offspring; Conflicting opinions; Burmeister; Buffon's views; Mestizoes; Mulattoes; Quadroons; Quintroon; Tschudi and Pöppig; Danes and Hindoos; Opinions of Geoffroy St. Hilaire, Nott and Gliddon; American Mongrels; Castelnau's statement of various cross-breeds; Zamboes and Cabourets; Different degrees of constancy in intermixture; Effect of different impregnations; Tertroon, Quadroon, Quintroon; Transition of Mongrels to higher races; Value of Mongrels in the States; Qualities of Negro in the Quintroon; Mental and physical characters of the Mongrels; Gobineau on the effects of crossing; Nott's theory objected to; Mongrels of Europeans and Australians; Effects of intermarrying; Nott on sterility of Mulattoes; Inviability of Mulattoes; Nott on the confusion of terms; Cross-breeds of Mexico and the Phillipines; Permanence of type; Mixed populations of Europe; Evidence in favour of unity 167

SECTION IV.

REVIEW OF THE PRINCIPAL THEORIES REGARDING THE UNITY OF MANKIND.

Great improbability of permanence of type; Wide limits of variation in Man; Views of Blumenbach and Prichard; Views of Hamilton, Smith, and Lawrence; Hombron's theory of centres of creation; Human fossils; Wilson on antiquity of Man in Scotland; Theory of Agassiz; His Zoological provinces; Difficulties of his theory; His change of opinion; New division; Objections raised, and his theory discussed; Latham on original migrations; Descent from a single pair improbable; Unity of Indo-Germanic peoples; The most probable theory of descent; Climatic influence on Man and Animals; Natural origin of Man; Affinity between Man and Ape; Fossil Apes; Relation of Negro to White Race and Apes; Negro type described at length; Forms intermediate between White and Negro; Lucæ and Pruner-Bey on race characters; Other deviations from typical forms; Hair and eyes; Grounds for Classification; Type unchanged, as shown by Egyptian monuments; The Jews, "white" and "black"; Jewish crania; Cranial variations; Blumenbach, Retzius, Weber, Engel, Desmoulins, and others on Classification; Lesson, Pickering, Hamilton Smith, Hartmann, D'Omalius d'Halloy, W. F. Edwards, on Constancy of type; Retrospect and results 190

SECTION V.

ON THE CLASSIFICATION OF MANKIND.

1. *Anatomical View.*—Division of the section into three parts; Natural division according to external variations; D'Omalius D'Halloy's basis of division; Blumenbach's cranial division; Lacépède and Duméril's addition; Cuvier's three types; Pickering, Prichard, Latham, Bory, Desmoulins, Agassiz, Nott and Gliddon on Classification; Hombron on Australian and Negro type; Vater, Morton, and Tschudi; Retzius' system of Craniology; Zeune's cranial types; Disagreement of Authors on Classification; Difficulties of the Cranial Classification exposed; Value of Phrenology; Quetelet's measurements of the skeleton; Reference Table of measurements of various parts of the human frame 230

2. *Linguistic View.*—Importance of Philological investigations; Insufficiency of the comparison of vocabularies; Importance of grammatical structure in the transmission of a Language; Analysis of a sentence in illustration; The structure of a perfect Language; American Languages Polysynthetic; Agglutinated Languages of Asia; Inflected Languages; Monosyllabic and Polysynthetic Languages compared; Change in Structure of a Language; Original Unity of Language improbable; View of Humboldt; Max Müller's theory; Balbi's Summary of the Languages of the Earth; Arbitrary division; Crawfurd on the Malay Languages; Relative value of the Physical and Philological investigations in determining the Unity or Plurality of Origin; Positive principles of Philology and negative principles of Naturalists; Objections to Nott and Gliddon; Philology alone inadequate for the determination of Race; Loss of Languages in American Races; Change of Language: instances cited; Absorption of small by greater Nations; Romans, Arabian, Normans, Longobards, Greeks, etc.; Parallelism between loss of Language and the Extinction of a People; Preservation of Languages 238

3. *Historical View.*—Reason given for this division; History founded on traditions; Tradition of the Noachian Deluge; Analogies between Mongolian and American Peoples; Delafield, Humboldt, Squier hereon; Tradition of destruction of the Earth; Zodiacal signs of the old and new worlds; Conformity of Customs in Nations widely separated; Examples cited; Conformities of Customs no basis for Classification 254

PART II.

Psychological Investigation.

Introduction; Importance of Psychology to the study of Mankind; Our fragmentary knowledge of uncultivated Peoples; Tendency to undervalue such knowledge; Too much reliance put upon Cranial development; Morton's theory; Views of Engel, Lawrence, and Prichard on Cerebral structure and Cranial form; Parchappe's measurements of the various types; Tables of Tiedemann; Discrepancy between his theory and his facts; Morton on Cranial capacity; Nott and Gliddon on Peruvian Skulls; Morton on North American Tribes; Huschke's measurements and comparisons; Size of Skull no criterion of mental power; Meaning of mental "capacity"; No grounds for Psychical specific directions among Mankind; Gist of the Psychological question; Method of investigation to be pursued in following sections 259

SECTION I.

THE SPECIFIC CHARACTERS OF MAN.

The psychical differences between Man and Brute not apparently so great as the physical; Importance of this inquiry; "Perfectibility," and its application; The Brute capable of improvement; Teaching of experience, and its limit in the Brute creation; Instinct: its intellectual nature; Cases of its cultivation; Its cultivation in Man; Language a specific human peculiarity; Language in the lowest Races; Grammatical structure the distinguishing feature between Man and Brute; Homogeneousness of human nature; Obscurity of psychical life of Animals; Characteristics of Man; External psychical manifestations; Personal ornamentation; Social character of Man; Ethical importance of property; Human society; Sensuality of the Negro; Religious notions universal; Religion in the lowest Races; Moral ideas; Distinct sources of Religious and Moral ideas; Origin of Religions explained; Superstitions; Distinctions between Man and Brute; Use of the senses; Power of speech wanting in Brutes, and reason thereof; Individuality of Man; Language a test of Civilization; Sense of the beautiful; The lower senses of Animals, and their limited influence on character; Psychological value of the action of the senses 269

SECTION II.

PRIMITIVE STATE OF MAN.

Value of psychological facts in determining the Unity of Mankind; Differences in Mental Development among civilized and savage nations; The possible high Antiquity of Man as indicated by Geology; Man nowhere found in a Primitive State: Slow growth of Language discussed; same argument applied to Physical Changes in Man; Parallelism of Infancy and Savage Life; Difficulties in the way of a Scientific Investigation of the Primitive State; the Primitive State cannot now be represented; First Efforts of the Primitive Man dependent on External Nature; Natural Indolence of Man; Indolence characteristic of all uneducated persons; Vanity and ambition the levers of Civilization; Peyroux de la Condrenière, Klemm, and Wuttke on the Psychical Superiority of the White Races; Psychical effects of Cultivation; Self-control an acquired faculty; Barbarism not Degeneracy; Attachment to country among uncultivated nations; Inhabitants of the Darfur; Congo-Negroes, Kru-Negroes, Fuegians, Hottentots, etc.; Motives for action and physical indulgences, social enjoyment and habit; External life of Primitive Peoples; Individuality of character not so common; Vices of Primitive Peoples; Cannibalism; Revenge; Social relations: marriage among the barbarous; Polygamy; Polyandry; Chastity; Sense of shame; Examples quoted; Marital rights; Influence of habit and custom; Social conditions; Societies: clanship; Primitive religions; Uniformity of religious conceptions; Note on "Le Peuple Primitif" of Rougemont; the Symbolism of Colour among Primitive Peoples; their ideas of human beauty; Courtesy and manners; Uncleanliness of Primitive Peoples; Man's nature unchangeable; Uncultivated White races; Compared with savage races; Degenerate Irish; White settlers of Buenos Ayres; Creoles of La Plata, of California, of Brazil, of Goyaz; Portuguese in Africa; White people in Banda Islands, of the Mauritius, etc.; Objections met; Cases of relapse into savage life; Atrocities committed by Whites, by Hindoos against English, by American settlers; The slave trade; Moral sense; Drunkenness; Position of woman: among savage peoples, among the old German, in Greece, in Rome, among Chinese, Hindoos, Mohammedans; Habits of so-called savages to be found among civilized nations; Differences of mental power in individuals of same races; Asserted relapse of some savage nations from an ancient civilization; Natural state of man not that of original purity; Psychical unity of mankind; original disposition and external circumstances, and their influence on the development of a people; Inconstancy of mental power; Civilization the work of individuals, not of the whole nation; Mental endowment changes with the history of a people; Obstruction to civilization among Fuegians, Australians, etc.; Among the Berbers, Guanches, Abyssinians, Egyptians; Race ascendancy; Retrospect; Theories of Klemm, Wuttke, Eicthal, and Nott and Gliddon "On Psychical Distinction" . . 284

SECTION III.

ON THE VARIOUS DEGREES OF CIVILIZATION, AND THE CHIEF CONDITIONS OF ITS DEVELOPMENT.

Further arguments necessary to maintain the theory of the specific unity of mankind; Influence of surrounding nature on development of man; Effects of climate; Reluctance to labour in hot climates; not confined to natives; Physical precocity; Abundance of natural food in torrid zone: its paucity in the frigid; Effects thereof in the development of man's civilization; The temperate zones; Temporary energy exhibited in the tropics; Endurance of Negro; Mental characteristics of tropical peoples; Americans of the States; Obstructions to progress; Hunting life; Characteristics of the hunter; The fisher; Agricultural life; Reasons for the stationary position of the Negro; Nomadic life; Pastoral life in North and South America; Cattle breeding in America, in Africa; Influence of climate on the temperament; Influence of geographical conditions; Coast line, tidal rivers, mountains, etc.; Negroes of the interior and of the coast; Advantages of a long coast line in the progress of civilization; the Polynesians; Migrations, and their effects on progress; Great importance of migrations in creating competition; Effects of intermixture; War, and its civilizing power; Intermixture; Density of population: its influence on progress of civilization; Agassiz; Morton on the mission of the "higher" races; their doctrines opposed; Humboldt on the unity of mankind; The theological view of the origin of civilization; Impediments to the progress of a nation; Effects of agricultural pursuits; their influence on the national character; Political conditions; Law and government: Barthez and Passy thereon; Acquisition of private property, and its retention among primitive peoples; Advantages of a despotism; Brooke on Chinese and Malay peoples; Necessity of despotism to the progress of primitive peoples; Absence of free governments in tropical climates; Unequal distribution of property: its importance to progress; Comparison of the various classes of society; Greater psychical differences among the cultivated; their importance to progress; Highly-gifted individuals; Genius existing in every race; Productive countries, and the stimulus they give to civilization; Importance of trade; Value of international commerce; injurious to the savage people; Exceptions quoted; Creation of new wants; Barter; Religion—conditions of its advantage or disadvantage; The origin, development, and nature of primitive religions; Religions of savage nations impede their progress; Intensity of religious convictions in American tribes; Erection of temples; Meaning of immortality among primitive religions; Hero-worship; Legend of Fohi; Great founders of religions; their influence an element of civilization; Natural religions inadequate for progress; their superstitious tendency; Religion the work of individuals; The greater success of religions of native origin; Mohammedan religion: its limited usefulness; Influence of art on civilization; The power of knowledge; its influence on religion; Knowledge the chief lever of civilization; Motives for its development; Tendency to progress not innate in man 328

Civilization dependent more on historical events than on original mental endowment; National character—not determined by Race alone; nor by Religious or Political institutions; Differences in state of Civilization only those of degree; The general value of Civilization; Enjoyment; Labour; Happiness without culture—Cases cited; Improbability of a uniform Civilization; A high state of culture, morals, and religion incompatible with a tropical life; Christianity; Conclusion 380

DEDICATION.

To

The Founder of the Anthropological Society of London,

JAMES HUNT, Esq., Ph.D., F.S.A.,

F.R.S.L., F.A.S.L.,

FOREIGN ASSOCIATE OF THE ANTHROPOLOGICAL SOCIETY OF PARIS,
HONORARY FELLOW OF THE ETHNOLOGICAL SOCIETY OF LONDON,
CORRESPONDING MEMBER OF THE UPPER HESSE SOCIETY
FOR NATURAL AND MEDICAL SCIENCE,

UNDER WHOSE ABLE PRESIDENCY THE AFFAIRS OF THE SOCIETY
HAVE BEEN CONDUCTED WITH UNEXAMPLED SUCCESS,

THIS WORK IS INSCRIBED,

WITH FEELINGS OF THE HIGHEST REGARD AND ESTEEM,

BY HIS SINCERE FRIEND,

J. FRED. COLLINGWOOD.

EDITOR'S PREFACE.

The Anthropological Society of London was founded early in the present year, and in its first general Circular announced that it contemplated publishing the present volume as the first of a long series of standard works on Anthropological Science. After the preliminary arrangements had been made, the Council and Publishing Committee of the Society conferred on me the honour of entrusting the superintendence of this work to my hands. My duty is accomplished, and I have now the pleasure of introducing Dr. Waitz to the English reader.

It will be advisable, in the first place, to record here the object of the Society in undertaking to publish translations of works on General Anthropology. The publication of a series of works on the Science of Man forms an integral part of the object for which the Society was established: as its programme sets forth, "The publication of a series of works on Anthropology will tend to promote the objects of the Society. These works will generally be translations; but original works will also be admissible." The Society regards this measure as an important means by which it proposes to encourage "all researches tending to establish a *de facto* Science of Man."

The responsibility of recommending Dr. Waitz's *An-*

thropologie der Naturvölker for translation rests with the Council and Publishing Committee of the Society. I may briefly explain the reasons which tended to its selection. The question arose, "what continental work best represents the present state of Anthropological Science?" The unanimous reply of the Council was, that no modern work has so well epitomised the present state of our knowledge on the subject as the first volume of Professor Waitz's *Anthropology of Primitive Peoples.* The President of the Society thus spoke in his Introductory Address:*

"In selecting works to be translated, we shall be guided by a desire to introduce books into this country, which, while being useful to the student and teacher, will at the same time help to give the reading public a better appreciation of the object and extent of anthropological science. The Council will not simply favour the translation of works, in the opinions of which they agree, but will aim at introducing those works which best represent the prevailing opinions respecting Anthropology on the Continent. The importation of foreign ideas and modes of treating our science cannot fail to produce beneficial results."

It is not necessary to insist here on the unsatisfactory nature of every systematic work on Anthropology that has yet been published, for the infancy of the Science of Man is a sufficient explanation. It is, however, advisable to have the latest authorities collected in a handy volume, which may serve as a basis for future research. The personal opinions of an author are only of secondary value in all systematic works, for the facts are not yet collected so as to enable anyone to pronounce decisively on some of the vexed questions of Anthropological Science. To the student of the Science of Mankind this work will be invaluable. Nothing can better illustrate the present con-

* See "Anthropological Review," i, p. 15.

dition of the science than the contradictory statements contained therein; but in the hands of travellers it may greatly help to rectify much of our present confusion.

There has hitherto been no work in the English language on Anthropology which could be recommended as a text-book for travellers and students generally. Since the time of Prichard no work has issued from the press of this country of general utility. There have been many special treatises, but none at all comparable to the present volume. In America, the important and comprehensive works of Nott and Gliddon have helped to supply a want; but they are so violent in opinion, and there is such a universal impression that they were written "with an object," that their value as text-books is very much lessened. Dr. Waitz shares with many authors, a suspicion that these works were written to prove the distinct origin of superior and inferior races of mankind, and at times, perhaps, he fails to do the American authors justice.

The present work has rarely been noticed in this country; but in France it has been freely criticised. It has also been well received in Germany, and Dr. Waitz's firmest theoretical opponents have willingly admitted the zeal, immense research, and erudition he has shown in the collation of his materials. Neither is it written in a narrow party spirit, but the author is candid and impartial, and the whole tone of his work is characteristic of a truly philosophical mind.

With regard to my own duties as editor, I have only to explain that the original has been followed as closely as possible consistently with rendering a readable translation of language so thoroughly idiomatic as are the writings of Professor Waitz. The great number of references which the work contains has led me to depart from the original in their arrangement: for the greater comfort of the reader I have placed them at the foot, whereas in the German they appear in the text.

The present edition has been enriched by numerous additional notes and references from the pen of the author, the former, as a rule, having been incorporated in the text. I have, partly on that account and partly from the character of the work, refrained, with two or three exceptions, from encumbering its pages with additions of my own. But this course will be no precedent for the editors of future publications of the Society. In many cases it may be the special duty of the editor to bring the work of which he has charge up to the science and knowledge of his day.

The table of contents has been somewhat amplified, and a copious index added. This was required, inasmuch as the time when the work will be continued has not been determined on by the Society, and the present volume is complete in itself, forming one of the most valuable contributions, that has yet appeared, to general Anthropology.

J. F. C.

4, St. Martin's Place, London,
October 14th, 1863.

AUTHOR'S PREFACE.

The questions raised in this work—which have for a considerable time been discussed in America rather as party questions, but have in England, since the emancipation of the negroes, become subjects of unprejudiced, serious inquiry,—have been scarcely touched upon in Germany, until recently a controversy arose, the politico-theological rather than the scientific tendency of which, created for them a transitory attention, without, however, leading to an exhaustive treatment of the subject, or exciting that deep interest which it deserves. Scientific problems, which seem to lie between or to embrace the several branches into which we are accustomed to divide human knowledge, are, amongst us, not favoured by fate. If formerly, philosophy took charge of such orphan problems, they are at present no longer considered, since philosophy is gone out of fashion; and consequently in our universities there is neither a faculty nor a professor who takes charge of them.

I have, nevertheless, ventured to treat upon this subject, though I cannot justify my act by the consciousness of possessing a competent knowledge in all the sciences bearing upon its investigation. Led to it by psychological studies, I had from the beginning no hope of arriving at a perfect solution of a question which it were desirable should be treated by the united powers of the zoologist and geologist, the linguist, historian, and psychologist. But as such a happy combination may be long in occurring, there remained but the alternative either to leave the question in abeyance, or to try its solution with insufficient means.

I may be blamed for having chosen the latter course; the more so, as with my limited means and the want of useful authorities, there was no hope of an exhaustive employment of existing materials. I must, under these circumstances, leave the book to answer for itself. If it succeed in arousing an interest for general questions concerning man, in advancing the knowledge of human nature, of which still, here and there, curious notions prevail, and thus laying the foundation for future and better works, its object will be attained.

With regard to the plan of the work, I have only to say, that the succeeding volumes will contain ample proofs in support of the general principles advanced in the first volume. These proofs will be found in the special descriptions of the life of the peoples inhabiting Africa, America, and the South Sea. The description of their external life will, as being less characteristic and important, and also from being better known, be treated less prominently; whilst greater attention will be devoted to the description of the psychical, moral, and intellectual peculiarities of these nations.

An accurate citation of authorities seemed to me indispensable, both for control and for my justification. I have therefore added the year of publication to the titles of the works quoted, so that there may be no doubt as to the editions I have consulted. Where Prichard is mentioned, without any addition, the third original English edition of his large work is alluded to.

Th. Waitz.

Marburg, 30th October, 1858.

INTRODUCTION.

ANTHROPOLOGY, as yet, occupies but an uncertain and indefinite position among the various sciences relating to man. According to its name, it aspires to be the science of man in general; or, in precise terms, the science of the nature of man. To the zoologist, and to naturalists in general, Man seems to be neither more nor less than the most organized parasite of the earth,—the highest mammal; to the theologian he appears as a being, by his mortal body belonging to nature; by his spiritual endowment rising far above, standing in strict contrast to it, and occupying, by the Divine breath which has animated him only, a privileged position between God and nature. Whoever acknowledges in nature a spiritual power and an inconceivable wisdom to which he turns with a certain religious worship, might feel inclined to designate one part of the conflict between these two views as a mere logomachy, but only one part of it; for the question, whether man—at least in one aspect of his nature—stands beyond and above, and not in nature, would still be left in doubt, as well as the other question allied to it with reference to the priority of spirit or of matter.

A third view, which, in a certain sense, endeavoured to reconcile both the above theories, has only contributed to expose the conflict between them,—it is the theory according to which the spirit of humanity is the spirit of God himself, the same one and absolute spirit which, unconscious of itself, creates the world, and only reaches the end of its development in man as the sole agent of divine self-consciousness. A self-evident sequence of this conception is, that knowledge of God and knowledge of human nature (Anthropology) are identical, since God, according to this theory, can have no other attributes than those which present themselves in the history of the mental development of man as purely human attributes, acting, at the same time, as divine powers in the history of civilization. We thus perceive the striking contrast between these three conceptions relating to the human being; for the first places man altogether in nature; the second does so in part; the third places him entirely *above* nature.

In this conflict of opinion—one side of which humbles the self-esteem of man as much as another flatters him—and considering the intrinsic interest of the subject, one might expect anthropology to be an industriously cultivated field, and that especially the faculties of those who assign to man so peculiarly sublime a position, not merely upon the earth, but in the whole universe, should be zealously directed to it. Yet such is not the case. In Germany it is at present a common case, that in the fields of various sciences, and even within the same science, opposite theories grow up, without their respective propounders taking any notice of each other, or even endeavouring to consolidate their doctrines. The strength of party supplies the strength of argument; the trouble of giving scientific proofs seems unnecessary where such value is attached to the judgment of those who, by agreeing in some fundamental points, represent each other with the instinctive force of an *esprit de corps*. With the same kind of tact, all that has grown upon a foreign stock is silently passed over or eliminated, whilst that which seems homogeneous is assimilated; and thus scientific life moves in individual separate small spheres, whilst the more comprehensive and fundamental questions are no longer discussed.

This applies also to the question of the nature of man; but here another circumstance occurs which has essentially contributed to prevent Anthropology from acquiring its rights,—this is, the peculiarly limited conception formerly attached to it. The old treatises on this subject make it appear merely as an aggregate of materials which already belong to other branches of science, and are in Anthropology only arranged and popularly expounded. The most important and interesting facts which comparative Anatomy, Physiology, and Psychology have pointed out with regard to the differential character of man from the animals nearest to him, constituted the chief portion of Anthropology. Some other subjects were added, of which either nothing is known, or which do not admit of a scientific exposition, such as investigations into the origin of mankind, animal magnetism, mysterious solar, lunar, terrestrial influences, partly a heritage of the old philosophy of nature which has succumbed to the progress of natural science. Thus Steffens distinguished a geological, physiological, and psychological anatomy. Latterly, this mode of expounding Anthropology has been abandoned; for though the present time is by no means quite adverse to the belief in the supernatural and improbable reciprocal relations between natural objects, admissions of this kind are very sparingly made; hence works on Anthropology in this direction have disappeared. Moreover, they could not, as mere aggregates of materials belonging to other sciences, claim an independent interest; and the superficial phrases in which they indulged on a variety of subjects, such as dancing, declamation, poetry, and love, for the purpose of embracing, according to the German custom, every human peculiarity, were not calculated to supply the requisite interest. One great reason why Anthropology could not sustain itself in this form, is owing to the awkward position in which it was placed by being considered and treated at one time as an empirical, and at another time as a philosophical science; thus assuming an undefined and fluctuating character: here, it appeared with abstract deductions, without any experimental basis; there, as a mere collection of interesting experimental details, arbitrarily changing the mode of treatment. In opposition thereto, it is requisite to declare in this place, once for all, that Anthropology is to be considered as an empirical science, because its subject, *Man*, is only known to us empirically, and hence it is requisite to study man by the same method which is applied to the investigation of all other natural objects.

In attempting to limit the sphere of Anthropology, and to

assign to this science a proper and well-defined position among other allied branches of human knowledge, our attention is first directed to two departments of study, differing greatly in matter and method, but which, nevertheless, in spite of their external dissimilarity, possess this in common,—that they both make Man the exclusive subject of their consideration, in the investigation of his nature; we allude to the Anatomy, Physiology, and Psychology of man, on one part; and to the History of Civilization, on the other. Our task, therefore, is to inquire into what has been accomplished in these fields, as regards the nature of man, and whether the results obtained form such a complement that from their combination the desired knowledge may be obtained.

Anatomy, physiology, and psychology consider man as an individual being, not indeed (like the practical physician and pedagogue), as an examplar, but as the representative of a genus: not with regard to particular accidental peculiarities by which he is distinguished from other individuals of the same genus; but in so far as the common or generic character of all similar individuals is represented in him, and the laws to which, externally and internally, all these individuals are subject, appear manifested in him. But the consideration of man, in his social relation, is foreign to these sciences; the whole sum of mental performances, which proceed only from a multifarious reciprocal action of individualities, and which in the course of centuries essentially transform the external and inner life of society, lies beyond its sphere. And if Psychology does not altogether desist from casting a glance at this sphere, it feels obliged to remain at the gate, and to rest satisfied with an historical description of certain facts, as the concatenation of the acting causes is too great to enable it to reduce the course of events to psychological laws, thus finding its progress obstructed just where the proper field of the History of Civilization commences. The latter directs its attention exclusively to social life and its development; and the contribution which, from this point of view, it renders towards the knowledge of human nature, is doubtless as essential as that contributed by the natural sciences. There remains, unfortunately, a considerable gap in our knowledge; for these different branches of science stand yet, side by side, unconnected, whilst they should, by combination, assist each other.

This is first shown by the relation of Physiology to Psychology. Both these sciences are usually so limited that the first treats of physical, and the second of psychical life; hence, the reciprocal actions of the physical and psychical organization remain unexplained, for an investigation of this subject fits neither in the frame of physiology nor of psychology. And yet, as regards the question of the nature of man, the modes and peculiar form of this reciprocal action are of the greatest importance. The obscurity as regards the essence of the soul, and its connexion with the body, is not a sufficient excuse. The disputed points might, without any great loss, remain untouched, if the task proposed were merely to investigate the amount of the influences of the physical organization, with its peculiarities and periodical changes, upon psychical life; and the kind of reaction the body experiences from psychical activity; to what extent they take place, and what are the proximate and remote results.

Still larger than the gap subsisting between physiology and psychology, is that obtaining between the physical and historical parts of our knowledge. The History of Civilization is unquestionably developed by the collective action of four connected groups of causes. The first is the physical organization of man. The second presents itself in the form of the psychical life peculiar to each people, which appears developed in all individuals belonging to it in a world agitated by various interests, views, and feelings. Surrounding nature forms the third. The fourth is the sum total of social relations and connexions of individuals and circles of society, internally and externally. The History of Civilization by itself has only for its object the representation, to the fullest extent, of the origin and the decline of each civilization, and the ascertainment of their causes. Here it becomes evident how unconnected the physical part of the science of man stands beside the historical part; for we are as yet very far from being able, by a philosophy of history growing out of physiology and psychology, to indicate why and wherefore the history of one people has undergone a different process of development from that of another people; why one people has no history at all, and in another the sum of mental performances never exceeds a certain limit; and yet in every case it is the aggregate of the physiological and psychological facts alone which contains the essential conditions of the historical facts.

In assigning to Anthropology the task of mediation between the physical and historical portion of our knowledge of man, it will not merely be delivered from the reproach of being a mere collation of borrowed materials, and thus unjustly claim the position of an independent science; but it will acquire a better right to its name, inasmuch as the nature of man mainly rests upon this,—that he steps out of his individual life, and enters into a social connexion with others, by whom he himself arrives at a higher and truly human development. It is at the point of his transition from isolation into social life that Anthropology must lay hold of man, and investigate the conditions and results of his further development.

Let us endeavour more closely to examine this task of Anthropology in its relation to history. In the historical consideration of man, the differences of physical organization and the influences of surrounding nature, stand in the background; the former, because the development of civilization is, with some few unimportant exceptions, limited chiefly to the Caucasian race; the latter, because the conformation of the human race, however dependent it may originally in pre-historic times have been on surrounding nature, has gradually, with progressive civilization, by division of labour, intercourse and trade, art and science, greatly emancipated itself from this dependence. Whilst History endeavours to represent the various phases of civilized life to the fullest extent, the interest of Anthropology rests chiefly upon the general features and the greatest differences in the various forms of human life; for as regards the latter science, these diversities form the most important and characteristic part, and we should have but a one-sided conception of man, if our notion of him were only derived from the history of civilization without taking into consideration the requisite supplement arising from the study of uncivilized nations, and of man in a primitive state. It is just this point which anthropology has to keep in view. History only begins where reliable traditions or writings exist,—where a beginning of civilization has been secured,—where certain objects are rationally pursued,—where a people by the force of historical conditions, either influenced by the genius of individuals arising among them, or by external causes, arrive at a certain development. Anthropology, on the other hand, embraces all the peoples of the earth, including those who have no history, in order to acquire the largest possible basis; and endeavours partly to sketch an ante-historical picture, and what may, in contrast to the historical development of peoples, be termed the natural history of human society, namely, its necessary natural formation upon a given soil, and under given stationary external conditions.

As man appears in history neither as a living body, such as physiology describes him, nor as a spiritual being, as conceived by psychology, but as a combination of physical and psychical life, he must be considered as a whole in the reciprocal action of his physical organization and his psychical life; for it is only as a whole that he appears as the elementary basis of history. There arises in the interest of history another question, as to the extent to which the notion of man should be applied,—whether all individuals and peoples, usually comprehended under that term, are of one and the same nature,—whether they belong to *one* species, or whether there be not such specific differences in the physical and psychical endowments of individual stocks as would justify history in excluding them, assigning them to zoology, and defending their employment as domestic working animals by higher organized beings, properly called *men*. To this question there is another closely allied, which attracted considerable attention during the last century, but which seems now almost neglected; namely, the question as regards the primitive or natural state of man (*Naturzustand*). On glancing at the mode in which it was formerly treated, its present neglect can scarcely surprise us; for in the absence of empirical materials requisite for the solution of this problem, recourse was had to mere rhetoric of a political and religious nature, in order to establish certain favourite notions with regard to the primitive man. Yet it is this point which is of such great importance to the student of the history of mankind; and it is the very last which should be neglected in laying a foundation for the history of humanity, bearing always in mind that this investigation must be conducted in an empirical method, and not by a deduction from abstract notions.

The fourth theme of Anthropology is that of Ethnography or Ethnology, the object of which is an investigation into the affinities of various peoples and tribes. Closely allied with it is the History of Mankind; and it seems arbitrary whether this branch of knowledge be considered as a separate part of Anthropology, or belonging to Ethnology. The important results to which, in modern times, German philology has led, caution us against the errors still committed in determining affinities of nations, and grouping them in families or races, by viewing them exclusively from an Ethnological stand-point, and neglecting the historical and other evidence.*

ON THE UNITY OF MANKIND AS A SPECIES, AND ON THE NATURAL STATE (NATURZUSTAND) OF MAN.

Whosoever would arrive at a just conception of Man must not consider him exclusively as an individual being, for man is, as was well observed by Aristotle, a social being; as an

* That the definition which Latham ("Man and his Migrations," London, 1851) has recently given of Anthropology, is confined within too narrow limits, requires, after what has been stated, no elucidation. He distinguishes the natural history of man from the history of civilization: the first considers man as an animated, the second as a moral, being. The natural history of man he divides into Anthropology, treating of the differential characteristics of man in contrast with the brute; and Ethnology, the doctrine of races or varieties of mankind. By the first, the peoples are to be classified according to their physical resemblances, and hence Hottentots, Esquimaux, the population of Tierra del Fuego, are to be grouped together, in order to deduce the effects of external influences; in Ethnology, on the other hand, the peoples must be grouped according to their affinities.

individual being he cannot be fully understood. Anatomy and physiology have therefore by themselves no claim to determine the nature of man; nor can they do so in combination with psychology, which being chiefly founded on self-contemplation, carries us but a few steps beyond the individual man. There is no doubt that the social life into which he enters, contributes much towards teaching the individual what passes within him, as in a mirror, and exhibits to him sensually what he would never have been able to comprehend by mere self-contemplation. Nevertheless, this enlarged field of observation is still too confined to enable us to deduce from it alone the notion of Man.

In order to extend our horizon we must direct our attention to the history of a people, and from it to the whole history of civilization. Yet even this basis is not sufficiently comprehensive. We require, in order to have a just conception of the nature of man, a knowledge of all mankind; but this knowledge cannot be obtained nor even thought of, if it is not preceded by defining the limits of mankind, and determining the question whether all men are of one species, or if not, within what limits the notion of species is to be confined.

The question whether the individuals which we are accustomed to call human beings, are all of *one* stock, or whether there are between them permanent specific differences, is important to all sciences. Whether the knowledge of which man is capable, is absolute for all thinking beings, or is only relative to his peculiar stand-point, still all his thinking and knowing is specifically human, and his only concern is that it should be universally valid among human beings; for every endeavour in our researches to rise above the sphere in which nature has confined us, resembles the attempt to fly with imaginary wings, when it is inconvenient to put the legs in motion. All the truths which are brought to light necessarily relate to the nature of man, partly, since all knowledge comes of him, and partly because all recognized truths lay claim to general assent, requiring confirmation, not by individual and merely subjective, but by universal human conceptions and notions. We may, therefore, as a necessary pre-supposition of all sciences, assume that there is a universal and unchangeable human nature; unless we place ourselves upon a purely empirical stand-point, from which "universal" signifies nothing more than a relatively high degree of probability, because at different times and under different circumstances it is acknowledged as true by men of different degrees of civilization.

The question of the unity of species and the nature of man specially belongs to those branches of knowledge which treat of the intellect. These sciences usually make the abstract ideas on mental life, its signification and connection which they find prevalent among peoples of different degrees of culture, the basis of their deductions. And whence should these sciences take their starting points for logical, psychological, ethical, religious, and æsthetical considerations, if not from the ideal sphere of the people from which they have proceeded? The inquirer will certainly, in the reception of these ideas, not proceed without discrimination, but he will compare the history of the development of one people with that of his own people. This leads him finally to draw all mankind into the circle of his investigations, since having once entered the wide field of the history of the development of human conceptions, he cannot avoid the conviction, that a too limited notion of man and his intellectual nature must obstruct many of his scientific views.

Though it has hitherto not been doubted that the same laws of thought are applicable to all men (which is only rendered certain by the assumption of their specific unity), it has been frequently discussed whether all of them are capable of the same intellectual and moral development, whether conscience speaks to all in the same manner, whether the same religion is adapted to the intellectual and moral conception of all. Whosoever denies both this and the unity of the human species, generally acquires his notion of human nature from the study of the Caucasian race, and places his theoretical views on right, morality, and religion, upon quite a different basis from the disciples of the opposite theory. He obtains thus a code of laws and morals which is only binding for one part of humanity;

for whether among the other species of man which he assumes, there are conditions analogous to our ideas of justice and morality, and if so, of what quality, would require a separate investigation, which would also apply to religious and æsthetical notions, etc. If there be various species of mankind, there must be a natural aristocracy among them, a dominant white species as opposed to the lower races who by their origin are destined to serve the nobility of mankind, and may be tamed, trained, and used like domestic animals, or may, according to circumstances, be fattened or used for physiological or other experiments without any compunction. To endeavour to lead them to a higher morality and intellectual development would be as foolish as to expect that lime trees would, by cultivation, bear peaches, or the monkey would learn to speak by teaching. Wherever the lower races prove useless for the service of the white man, they must be abandoned to their savage state, it being their fate and natural destination. All wars of extermination, whenever the lower species are in the way of the white man, are then not only excusable, but fully justifiable, since a physical existence only is destroyed, which, without any capacity for a higher mental development, may be doomed to extinction in order to afford space to higher organisms.

To such or similar conclusions, the theory of specific differences among mankind leads us. Thus there are different and more comprehensive interests attached to the question of the unity of the human species, than to the probably unsolvable problem of descent from one pair or several pairs, or the contest about permanence or mutability of races.

On these grounds it would be an erroneous conception, which, however, is not rare among naturalists, to think that on physical considerations alone, for or against the permanence of types, we can decide on unity of species; for whatever side we take on the question of the mutability of the external man, we should have to declare against specific differences, if it were to turn out that they all possess the same qualities which arrived at different degrees of development, determined only by external circumstances and mode of life. Though some external and internal differences may in certain tribes present themselves as constant—which can scarcely be denied even in people originally of the same stock—if it cannot be shown that there is a difference in the form and mode of development of intellectual life, if it cannot be shown that some, under equally or still more favourable external conditions of development, are detained in a lower scale than others by original weakness, the proof of specific difference is not complete. We do not mean to assert that whatever great and constant external diversities may prevail among mankind, it still would, from a similar mental endowment, follow that they belong to the same species: we acknowledge in this respect the equal rights of physical and psychological proofs, but we cannot, as is often done, deem the latter of less importance than the former, as a mere secondary consideration of not much account. The question whether we have to decide for or against unity of species, where there is a considerable constant physical difference combined with equal mental endowments, or physical equality with psychical dissimilarity, may be left in abeyance, as it has no practical signification. Nature has seemingly relieved us from this embarrassment, in combining almost everywhere the same pyschical endowment with the same physical characters, without, however (in individuals as little as in whole nations), adopting a strict parallelism of external and internal development as a fixed law. If such a parallelism, as some modern authors have indicated,* cannot be shown to obtain generally in the animal kingdom,—since the development of the organization does not always correspond to that of the intellect, and though even in the human race it is still doubtful whether the degrees of intellectual development correspond to those of the body, and specially of the brain,—there has, as yet, neither in animals nor in man been found an instance of a combination of specific physical equality, with a specifically different psychical endowment.

Though we may be justified in classing animals, of whose psychical life we know so little, according to their external

* Compare Volkmann, Art. "Gehirn," in "Wagner's Handwörterb. der Physiol."

organization, we cannot, in man, make our ignorance of his inner life the ground for considering him merely in his physical aspect. It is a distorted view which Cuvier takes* in order to keep psychological arguments at a distance in the classification of animals, when he says that all vital manifestations which occur only periodically are useless in classification. The psychical life of every species of animals is no doubt as constant as physical life, though certainly less accessible to investigation. This should, however, not make us forget that all classifications of animals which rest exclusively on their organic peculiarities are only provisional, and can have no absolute and universal value, since, owing to our necessarily imperfect knowledge, they cannot be subjected to exhaustive investigation. But with regard to man, the mere physical organization and its mutatability is insufficent to enable us to decide the question of unity of species, since the character of humanity consists, first and foremost, in the specific development of psychical life, and only secondarily in the physical organism as the embodiment of this spiritual essence. Hence it is inappropriate to treat man merely as an object of natural history, and to divide mankind into races or species, according to external forms, without taking into consideration that the most striking distinctions between individuals and peoples are to be found in mental qualifications. When, for instance, Bory de St. Vincent† considers it as undoubted that the Negro, in spite of his comparatively smaller brain, possesses the same mental capacity as the Austrian, whom he foolishly enough calls the Bœotian of Europe, and the same capacity as four-fifths of Frenchmen; and when he ascribes to all his species of mankind the same degree of perfectibility, and attributes to nine Europeans out of ten no higher mental endowments than to the Hottentots, it may be considered as a complete recantation of his theory with regard to specific differences existing among mankind. Van Amzinge‡ appears, up to this period, to have been the first author who considered a classification of mankind, founded on

* Thierreich übersetz (Animal Kingdom, translated), by Voigt, 1, p. 5.

† "L'Homme," 2nd edit., 1857, ii, p. 62,

‡ "Investigation of the Theories of the Natural History of Man," New York, 1848.

mere physical character and irrespective of psychical endowment, as unscientific.

For the above reasons our investigation respecting the unity of mankind is divided into two parts; the first has to examine whether all human beings are to be considered of the same species on physical grounds; the second, whether or not they are so on psychological grounds.

PART I.

PHYSICAL INVESTIGATION.

THE notion of species is founded upon the fact that the typical similarity of natural objects is preserved throughout all their changes. Between the inorganic and organic kingdoms of nature, there obtains in this respect only this difference:—that the sphere of action is larger or more manifest in the organic world, the natural laws leaving a wide margin for the production of individual varieties, and further that the preservation of types can only be effected by the propagation of individuals belonging to them. Apart from this, the signification of the term species applies equally to organic and inorganic objects; it designates the constancy of the assemblage of characters occurring, regularly combined, in nature.

Without entering into any details with regard to the abuse made of this term in philosophy, it may be sufficient to observe, that species are neither mere subjective abstractions formed only to classify the innumerable natural objects, nor are they exemplars, which, as active principles, form the foundation of all natural objects. They are, in fact, nothing else than empirical laws of natural production; for the constant coincidence of similar characters must have as its fundamental cause a corresponding constant assemblage of natural conditions.

So long, therefore, as by the term species nothing more is designated than the typical similarity of natural phenomena, the regularly recurring complex of characters, and the regular recurrence of the same complex of causes by which that typical similarity is maintained, the term expresses, to the exclusion of every hypothesis, merely the fact as observed, and presents no difficulty whatever. But if it be requisite, since differential characters between individuals are nowhere wanting in nature, that in the notion of species there should be included a criterion according to which we might decide as to the range of variation for each type—that is to say, to determine the limits of each, or what magnitude or qualities of the differences between individuals might justify us in including them in the same type or not—then the definition of the term species becomes difficult, or rather not the definition itself, but the laying down of a rule as to the extent of the variation for each type to which the term is to be applied. The only positive and valid proof that a certain number of individuals belong to the same species, proceeds from the demonstration that they have descended from the same original stock; and in all doubtful cases, the question of unity of species can only be decided by analogy with those cases in which unity of stock has been amply demonstrated. But as the extent of this range of variation, and consequently unity or diversity of descent can, in comparatively few cases, be decided by direct evidence, there remains a wide room for doubt as regards unity or difference of species. This is the more the case, as on the one hand within the very same stock later generations exhibit considerable deviations from the preceding, and, on the other hand, these deviations, arising in the course of time, may be so constantly transmitted that it cannot with any certainty be maintained, that they do not possess the same absolute constancy as that attributed to specific characters. These actual phenomena are designated by the term *varieties*, which are partly individual, or merely transitory, or more or less permanent, in which case the term *race* is used. The difficulty consists in determining the difference between species and permanent variety, or race.

We purpose reviewing the principal attempts made in this direction, in order to pave the way for our investigation of the specific unity of mankind, and learn what weight is to be attached to arguments derived from natural history.

The definition of species, as given by Cuvier,[1] seems to have been generally accepted in natural history. "To the same species belong all such individuals which have descended from each other or from common parents, and from those who resemble them as much as they resemble each other."

Prichard's definition that the term species includes separate origin and constant transmission of organic peculiarities, is identical with that of Cuvier. Though this definition is theoretically unquestionable, it contributes little or nothing to the solution of the practical question with regard to the characters by which individuals of the same species may be distinguished from others belonging to a different species; for the difficulty to be solved is, to establish a decisive character for the great majority of cases in which we know nothing of descent, and in which the resemblance of the individuals is less than that generally subsisting between parents and children, and individuals of the same stock. For such a character, definitions are required which can be confirmed or refuted by experience; but this, as regards common descent, excepting individual instances, is not the case, for in respect to remote generations more or less probable suppositions are only possible. To this defect may be added another of still greater importance.

Though we may readily grant that unity of species results from unity of descent, and though in the study of zoology and descriptive natural science unity of descent is chiefly considered, as it treats of the propagation and history of organized beings, still it is a confusion of terms to identify the notions of unity of species and unity of descent, which according to the above definition is frequently done even by Prichard, who considers separate descent and original differences of character as convertible terms. In spite of this frequent confusion of terms, he observes, very justly, that the term species should only be applied to an aggregate of individuals, where nothing intervenes to consider them as the descendants from the same stock: that is to say, when we are not obliged to reduce them

---

[1] "La réunion des individus descendus l'un de l'autre ou de parents communs, et de ceux qui leur ressemblent autant qu'ils se ressemblent entre eux." —Règne Animal, 2nd edit., i, p. 16.

to different stocks, although for these, we must add, it remains as yet undecided whether they have descended from one or several, and in the latter case again, whether from perfectly similar, or not perfectly similar pairs. Should we be inclined to assume or consider as possible, that all, or but a few species of animals, have descended from several protoplasts, we are already cautioned not to confound the notions of unity of species and unity of descent. If, then, the notion of species and the whole sphere of its applications is not, at the outset, to be placed on a fluctuating basis, it will be requisite to keep the reference to unity of descent separate from it, which is necessary in order that every thing merely hypothetical should be excluded therefrom. The notion of unity of species of a number of individuals rests, as we have seen, in the organic and inorganic world, solely upon the similarity of their external and internal nature, upon the regular coincidence of the same essential characters, by which, however, nothing, either in animals or plants, is yet decided as to community of origin. This community of origin is merely a probable deduction from the actual similarity of their nature, because propagation and transmission seem to be the only way of its preservation. It is on this ground alone, that organic beings, belonging to the same species, should not exhibit greater differences than such as can be traced in individuals of the same stock; and yet there remains, in spite of this, a possibility that individuals whose differences do not exceed the limits of variation of the same stock, are not descended from the same parents, nor from perfectly similar parents; notwithstanding which there would be a sufficient justification for including them in the same species.

We shall, therefore, adopt the first proposition that unity of species results from proved unity of origin; but not the second, which has often by zoologists been considered as inseparable from it, namely, that separate descent, wherever it can be traced, is a sufficient proof of difference of species. In cases of the latter kind the process in modern times has usually been to declare similar types, which hitherto had passed as mere varieties, to be different species, if these types belonged either to certain definite regions, or if apparently unsurmountable obstructions prevented their migration from one region to another.

Thus, Agassiz and others cite the Asiatic and African lion;[1] Vogt, the chamois of the Pyrenees and of the Alps; the mouflon in Sardinia and Asia Minor, which though they differ very little from each other, cannot be considered as belonging to the same stock, and are consequently not of the same species. Giebel,[2] especially, has quoted a large number of examples which seem to prove that the assumption of single prototypes for individual species of animals, is in many cases untenable, partly because an existence in masses is in many cases requisite for the nutriment of others, partly because the migratory capacity of many is too limited to admit of their gradual propagation over the whole regions which they at present occupy; such is the case as regards the mole, the beaver, many snails, and most fresh-water animals. Gregarious animals can scarcely be considered as having descended from a single pair. Hence, several centres of creation have been assumed, at least for some genera. Here it is especially necessary to distinguish unity of descent from unity of species. This may, perhaps, be done by assuming, whenever the facts require it, that a species consists of "homogenous species," "sub-parallel species," or "stocks," namely, where in individuals of an ascertained or strongly presumptive different stock, the usual limits of variation within the same stock are not passed, and the physical and mental development is essentially the same; so that according to Prichard's expression, "there is nothing in the way to consider them as the descendants of the same stock." And when he further agrees with De Candolle, that it does not unfrequently occur that two individuals who really belong to the same species, whose common descent is incontestible, yet differ more in their external aspect than others of a different species, we are reminded of the uncertainty of all conclusions as regards unity of stock if inferred alone from similarity of type.

---

[1] Swainson ("Treatise on the Geography and Classification of Animals," p. 284, 1835) is inclined to assume five distinct species of lions, and quotes other similar instances.

[2] "Tagesfragen aus d. Naturgesch.," p. 69, 1857.

In itself, it is of little importance what signification is given to the term "species"; but so much depends upon it, that unity of descent, which requires a separate proof, should not be included in the notion of typical equality of beings. The conception of species does not merely belong to zoology and botany, but to all sciences; the former must, therefore, if necessary, give it a more precise definition; but, at the same time, should keep it free from theoretical assumptions, as it is merely intended to designate the actual facts. If in modern times there prevail an inclination to designate every variety as an original species, "which despite of all external influences remains permanent," and to consider this character of permanency of type, even under unfavourable circumstances, as the sole criterion of species,[1] a definition is then given, which, in itself, is not objectionable; but there is then danger to overlook or altogether deny the actually existing variability of type, so that the conception of species (as is the case in Morton and his disciples, of the American school), is in fact a mere definition prepared in order to arrive at the intended result of a plurality of the human species.

Like separate descent, so also has fecundity been considered as a criterion of difference of species, founded chiefly upon the following facts:—

In a state of perfect liberty, and under normal conditions, animals of the same type not only pair with each other, but usually select, by preference, such individuals of the same type as resemble them most, especially as regards colour. Crossing of different types and the production of hybrids, occur in the free state only under abnormal circumstances, and if intentionally occasioned by man, they succeed only by the agency of artificial means. The mare must be blindfolded if she is to be covered by the male ass; the ass must be painted over like a zebra to couple it with that animal, and even such means succeed only when the individuals belong to nearly allied species. The produced hybrids are in most cases sterile, or if

[1] So Agassiz, in Nott and Gliddon, who defines species as the sum of individuals which, since it has been known to man, has always retained the same peculiarities.—Desmoulins, "Hist. Nat. des Races Humaines," p. 194, 1826.

not, as frequently is the case with sheep and goats, the cross breed is not permanent, like the original types. This equally applies to plants, though in them the return to the original type may only occur after a series of generations, namely by intermixture of the hybrids with individuals of the original type. Induced by these phenomena, Buffon[1] includes in the same species, all individuals which in the free state produce young possessing between themselves an unlimited prolificacy.

This criterion of species, although approved of by F. Müller and others, has recently been much canvassed. It was already contested by Rudolphi,[2] who asserted that not only were there many hybrids produced in the natural state, but that prolificacy was the rule as regards the hybrids of mammals. Though this assertion is manifestly far beyond the truth, still there stands the remarkable fact that crossings between remote species, and even between different genera, are frequently prolific, (ass or horse with horned cattle, stag and cow, bear or buck with a bitch, dog and cat, roe and sheep, swan and goose), whilst the hybrids of more proximate species are not so: jackal and dog, ox and buffalo, hare and rabbit,[3] (as asserted by some), resist all attempts at crossing them. We are certainly yet a long way off from concluding, from the above individual phenomena, the unlimited prolificacy of cross-breeds; they serve only to draw our attention to the fact that we are, as yet, entirely ignorant of the law upon which the success or failure of cross-breeding depends; but this has not deterred some writers from the attempt to clear this gap. Thus, Bory assigns to the hybrids of the sheep and wild ass (*onager*), of wolf and dog, siskin and linnet, unlimited prolificacy, though he cannot assert the same as regards the mule.

Desmoulins declares the herds of cattle of the United States, beyond the Alleghanies, to be the progeny of the American bison and European cattle, the former having a differently formed skull and two ribs more than the latter; and he con-

---

[1] Œuvres in 4to, iv, p. 386: Succession constante d'individus semblables et qui se reproduisent.

[2] Beiträge zur Anthropol., 1812.

[3] The *Leporine*, a hybrid of hare and rabbit, may now be seen in the gardens of the Zoological Society.—Ed.

siders that the hybrids form a new permanent species.[1] This is said also to apply to the domestic dog in relation to the wolf, fox, jackal; and also to the mulattoes, who always preserve the same type, and should therefore be considered as a new species; whilst mongrels of tribes of the same stock (for instance, of different Indo-Germanic peoples), preserve no fixed type, but exhibit variable forms. In opposition to this, it is necessary to state, that no reliable instance can be adduced of the permanency of a hybrid race by in-breeding, least of all in mammals; that the production of new independent types in this manner is as yet extremely doubtful; and that the adduced examples, so far as they have been confirmed, can only be considered as individually extraordinary facts, which have but little value in the attempt to lay the foundation of a new theory of the laws of nature in the preservation of types, and so to place the conception of species upon a different basis.

All the examples which are usually adduced to prove unlimited fecundity of hybrids, admit of a twofold interpretation. If (according to Vogt) wolf, dog, and fox are prolific among themselves, and if propagation is so much easier the nearer we approach the highest animals, it may—apart from the problematical second part of this proposition and of the doubtful cases of dog and fox, the successful pairing of wolf and dog, the hybrids of which propagated, in one instance, during four generations—(A. Wagner)—be maintained that dog and wolf do not belong to different, but to the same species. R. Wagner accordingly lays down the proposition,[2] "that where an intermixture of hybrids is observed (which can only with certainty be asserted of wolf and dog, camels, goat, and sheep,) the specific differences of the parent animals is, at least with regard to mammals, doubtful." From his collection of hybrid cases in the animal kingdom, it appears that in point of fact there is no certain example of fecundity (not to speak of *unlimited* fecundity) of hybrids between themselves, and only individual instances of prolific intermixture with one of the

[1] Morton ("Hybridity in Animals and Plants," p. 6, New Haven, 1847) considers this as doubtful.

[2] Prichard, Uebers, i, 449.

parent stock. What, indeed, would be the signification of specific differences in nature, and how objectless would be their permanence, if their obliteration were rendered possible by continued production of hybrids!

Morton, the predecessor of Vogt, in this respect has endeavoured to show that hybrids of different species are the more prolific between themselves, the greater their capacity to become domesticated. His examples refer chiefly to the horse, the ass, the zebra, the wolf, dog, jackal, fox, the swine, fowls; and it cannot be denied that, according to his examples, the phenomena of hybridity possess a greater extension than was formerly admitted. He concludes therefrom that, as regards man—pre-eminently a domestic animal,—the inference from unlimited fecundity to unity of species is not applicable; and his successors, Nott and Gliddon, distinguished accordingly, among the various species of animals, those which by intermixture produce none, or unprolific, or prolific hybrids as remote, allied, and proximate species. The so-called races of mankind are said to stand in the latter relation, as the permanence of their organic peculiarities, as well as those of the races of dogs, is ascertainable from the ancient Egyptian monuments. As this last assertion leads us to the notoriously erroneous proposition, that there is, properly speaking, no alteration of type, the question of hybridity itself is placed upon very slippery ground, since the majority of domestic animals have ever been subjects of contention as regards unity or difference of species, and are consequently least adapted to lead to a decisive solution.

There certainly prevails in modern times an inclination to assume a plurality of species, where formerly races only were distinguished; and in proportion as this has been done, fecundity alone as a decisive mark of unity of species has lost its weight. We must not omit to state that this is especially the case if unity of species is considered as identified with unity of descent, in which case fecundity affords no absolute proof for common origin, if stocks originally distinct prove themselves productive between each other. The question would, however, still remain, whether by distinguishing stock from species there may not have been originally distinct parallel stocks of the same species, which in their essential character, as well as in respect of the range of variation through which they pass, may exhibit an unlimited fecundity between each other.

However decidedly we may oppose a theory of the origination of new species by the production of hybrids, this much must be admitted, that from unlimited prolificacy alone the unity of species can hardly be inferred. On the other hand we can scarcely agree with Holland,[1] when he asserts that the theory that individuals, however much they may differ, belong to one species if they prove to be of unlimited prolificacy, moves in a circle, and assumes what remains to be proved: for it is an empirical fact that a really unlimited prolificacy nowhere occurs where important differences of organization prevail; and an essential feature of the character of fecundity as a mark of species lies in this, that it does not involve the unsolvable doubt of common or separate descent, but ignores it.

Notwithstanding the variety of objections which may be raised against unlimited fecundity as a decisive character of species, it cannot, as has recently been said,[2] be considered as of merely secondary importance. It retains its importance, though it is not ascertained how many generations have proved prolific in order to arrive at the conclusion that they belong to the same species; and further, sterility not only occurs between individuals of the same stock, but the extinction of some races is as clearly demonstrated as the extinction of whole species. If recent experience has shown in the breeding of domestic animals that different races are some-

---

[1] "De l'Homme et des Races Humaines," p. 213, 1853.

[2] Giebel (loc. cit.) has misrepresented this point, by stating, what no one has asserted, that fecundity has been considered as the only criterion of species; hence he requires from the adherents to this doctrine that they should only count such individuals to be of one species whose unlimited fecundity is experimentally proved. It is a further misrepresentation, when he says, that difference of species cannot be inferred from sterility, for however correct this may be, it does not follow that fecundity should be neglected as a criterion; for it is only contended that, where minor differences of organization exist, the specific nature of which is doubtful, sterility or prolificness may afford important assistance in deciding the question; though it may be granted that the decision obtained in this way is not absolute and final, it is certainly not valueless and unimportant, unless the capacity of reproduction is not considered as an essential character of the animal world.

times not indefinitely prolific, or produce malformed, defectively organized young—parallels of which are found in the intermixture of different human races—the objection is not of any weight against unlimited prolificacy as a specific character; for whenever this is held out as a criterion it is not asserted that it occurs without exception among all individuals and races of the same species, but expresses only the fact of a merely limited prolificacy between individuals of specifically different types. It may, however, be considered as an unavoidable defect in this criterion, that it cannot decide whether there be within the same species varieties which, between themselves, possess only a limited prolificacy, or none at all.

On casting a retrospective glance at our investigations we arrive at the important proposition, that inferences from common descent to unity of species have an absolute certainty, those from unlimited fecundity have a high degree of probability, whilst the conclusions as to differences of species from separate descent or limited prolificacy are less safe.

A further mark of distinction between race and species is also afforded by the so-called *reversion;* that is to say, by the return of individuals prolific between themselves to the original type of the parent stock, which thus proves itself permanent. As the hybrids perish, the mere varieties revert, under certain circumstances, to their original types, and thus show that they have no specific existence. In cases of mongrels of two doubtful types, though proving indefinitely prolific (*e. g.* Mulattoes or Mestizoes), should they, by continued intermixture with each other, return to one of the parent stocks (Negro, white, or American), one would feel inclined to assume a difference of species of the latter, because the transformation into a different type failed; we should then have obtained a better definition of one of the criteria, fecundity; but such a case seems not yet to have occurred. There would still remain some doubt as to the correctness of the conclusion, whether new characters arising in the course of time may not under circumstances become so fixed as to acquire a permanence equal to specific characters, though it is a probable, but by no means proved, supposition that all characters arising in the course of time possess but a small degree of constancy.[1] Where mongrels intermix not among themselves but with one of the parent type (*e. g.* Mulattoes with Negroes), and revert to it, it is no proof for the specific difference of the parent stocks, since it is a well known fact that in the intermixture of races the more numerous race absorbs the less numerous.

This reversion represents only a special application of the general rule, according to which Blumenbach has endeavoured to determine the distinction between species and race, namely, that all differences between individuals or groups of individuals which may be considered as having been produced by external influence, or have arisen in the course of time, do not constitute specific differences.

Though the general validity of this rule may be readily admitted, still its application is often very difficult and uncertain. When, as mentioned by Wagner (in Prichard), the same species of animal is met with in Sumatra, Java, Borneo, Timor, Celebes, and even in the Philippines, or in the Asiatic continent, exhibiting in all these countries constant variations, it might be difficult to decide whether in such cases we should assume different species or races. The fact is, that the axiom that all individuals which only differ in variable pecularities, belong to the same species, is only a different version of the notion of species as an assemblage of constant characters, and presents nothing new in relation to the distinction between species and race. This conception of species possesses, nevertheless, the advantage of fixing our attention on the point from the investigation of which, the definition of species, in doubtful cases, may be expected, namely, the range of variation for every species.

It may also be observed with regard to this last mark of distinction, that the inferences drawn therefrom to unity of species have greater value than when applied to difference of species. The former must be considered proved as soon as it is demonstrated that the greatest variations in the respective individuals are still within the limits of those differences which

[1] I. Geoffroy St. Hilaire thinks that the characters of a race are the more constantly transmitted the older the race is.

arise and disappear in the course of time, or which may be found in several generations of the same stock. The argument, on the other hand, for difference of species in any case, has but little to support it, if the variation of the respective types, leading to an alteration of type, cannot be demonstrated. The proof would only be perfect if we succeeded in positively demonstrating the immutability of the pure types after they have for a sufficiently long time been subjected to the most various external influences, and have given rise to a relatively large number of mongrels of these types and their varieties, to establish the fact that the hybrids ultimately revert to their respective original types. If they prove prolific between themselves without the mongrels exhibiting a tendency to reversion, the fixity and, consequently, the specific difference of the latter can only be considered as doubtful. In the same manner the continuance of the pure types under unchanged external circumstances, even if it has lasted for several thousand years, as the Negro type in north-eastern Africa, is by itself alone insufficient to establish them as specifically different.

The last argued criterion of species and race has been used by Blumenbach (and by Prichard after him) to found upon it a long series of conclusions drawn from analogy. They chiefly directed their attention to the question, whether the greatest differences exhibited by human beings are only so great and no greater than those presented by known races of animals, so that we might be justified in considering them as differences of race, or whether they are analogous to specific differences among animals. Blumenbach, who may still be considered as a chief authority, and a cautious observer, shows plainly[1] that if the same laws determine the variability of types in animals and man, the latter necessarily constitutes but one species, since animals of the same species exhibit, as regards colour, hair, size, cranial form, no greater differences, produced by climate, food, etc., than are presented by human beings. Essentially, Blumenbach has never been refuted, though he is now ignored by those who find his arguments inconvenient; for

[1] "De generis humani varietate nativa," 3rd ed., p. 75, 1795.

it cannot, for instance, be refuted that the domesticated swine, in spite of the different cranial form, belongs to the same species as the wild boar, since in many parts of America the imported swine have again returned to the type of the wild boar. The considerably larger alimentary canal of the domestic cat, compared with that of the wild cat, has, by some, been considered as a probable consequence of their food being more of a vegetable kind, whilst others claim it as a proof of difference of species. De Salles[1] expresses the argument of Blumenbach in the following terms:—"La domestication de l'homme, oscillant perpétuellement entre les extrêmes de la civilisation et l'état sauvage, doit avoir modifié l'homme encore plus profondément que les autres animaux domestiques." Man is certainly, zoologically considered, pre-eminently a domestic animal, and we cannot escape the conclusion that if the laws of variation in animals also apply to him, the changes exhibited by domestic animals in the torrid and frigid zones must, by analogy, extend to man.

On account of this analogy Nott and Gliddon (and recently Giebel), following Morton, have endeavoured to prove that the various canine races must be considered as specifically distinct: and if this be conceded (as proved by the ancient Egyptian monuments, in which the permanence of character is exhibited,) the prolificacy of these between themselves weakens the dogma of the unity of the human species; for, "zoologically speaking, mankind and *canidæ* occupy precisely the same position." Although this proof can hardly be deemed sufficient to shake the conclusions from the great number of examples adduced by Blumenbach, it has this opposed to it:—that others include all the *canidæ* in the same species because there exists between them no fixed line of demarcation, the transitions of their characters being manifold and perceptible, and their prolificacy increasing by cross-breeding.[2] Nott, moreover, weakens his own argument from analogy, by observing:[3] "Again and again, in previous publications, I have alluded to the fallibility

---

[1] "Hist. Générale des Races Humaines," p. 265, 1849.
[2] Godron, "De l'Espèce et des Races," p. 64, Nancy, 1848.
[3] Loc. cit., p. 402.

of arguments drawn from analogy alone, while insisting that no true analogies can be said to exist. *Every animal, from man to the worm, is governed by special physiological laws.* . . . The rules current among breeders of domestic animals have been considered as applicable to man, but the notion itself is very unphilosophical and could never have originated with any intelligent naturalist of thorough experience."

This analogy has, nevertheless, been generally recognized as a legitimate mode of argumentation. Even in the same work from which we have quoted, Agassiz declares that it must be considered as proved that the laws which govern the variation of type in animals are "in the same limits and the same degree" applicable to mankind. If we were to ask for the proofs of this, and why the inferences of Blumenbach are rejected, it may be long before we receive an intelligible answer.

However clearly it may be demonstrated that the differences between the various types of mankind are not greater than those produced in animals by the influences of climate, food, etc., this circumstance in favour of the unity of mankind should not be over estimated, because the justification for such a parallel is doubtful. Not only is the comparison of differences found in specifically different individuals uncertain, but it is inadmissible, because it includes the assumption that the range of variation for all, or not very remote species, is nearly the same. De Candolle, as quoted above, has shown that sometimes individual varieties within the same species exhibit more considerable diversities than different species themselves; to which may be added the remarks of Swainson* on the diversities which establish specific differences, that there are constant specific differences which seem much less marked than many diversities of race. If the latter were really confined to narrower limits than specific differences, we might possess a pretty certain and convenient distinctive mark between race and species; but such is not the case: *e.g.*, the variability of the ape, so closely approximating man, is far from being so extensive as that possessed

[1] Loc. cit., pp. 275, 35.

by domestic animals and man. The range of variation of every species seems to be peculiar to each, and governed by special laws. Hence, it proves nothing when Agassiz says, the chimpanzee and the gorilla differ no more from each other than the Mandingo and the Guinea Negro, and both do not differ more from the orang than the Malay or European from the Negro: if the former are to be considered as belonging to different species, the latter should be considered equally so. That particular laws of formation govern individual species of animals is indicated by their different capacity for the production of hybrids. This would be certain if Desmoulins were right in his assertion that the diversities of various species, and their sphere of variation, diminishes the more they approach man. The fallaciousness of drawing conclusions from the analogy of one species to another has recently been pointed out by Lucas,[1] who proves, by many examples, how extremely different, quantitatively and qualitatively, is the power of resistance in different races to external influences in regard to the transformation of races. Some other instructive examples are furnished by Giebel.[2] They show that similar deviations in different genera of animals are of very variable importance, "as in one family or genus one or another organ has obtained a particular significance for the whole organism," so that frequently characters or groups of characters which are essential to one constitute in the other no fixed specific characters, but vary greatly.

In condensing the results of our investigation regarding the definition of species, we have found that it designates those types permanent which are transmitted by propagation. We were induced to separate the questions of unity of species and unity of descent on the ground that the same assemblage of constant characters may belong originally to distinct stocks; and we could not, therefore, consider unity of descent as necessary to our definition of species. If, thus, separate descent was no valid proof for difference of species, unlimited prolifi-

---

[1] "Traité philosophique et physiol. de l'hérédité naturelle," ii, p. 116, 1857; and Nusard, *ibid.*, ii, p. 452.

[2] Loc. cit., p. 45.

cacy proved an important, but not a decisive mark of distinction between species and race, and could only be considered as a probable sequence.

Finally, reversion and its allied phenomena appeared insufficient to furnish an undoubted criterion of species and race. And as it became apparent that such a criterion could not be established, we hoped that the defect would be supplied by the conclusions of analogy furnished by the comparison of various species. This expectation was also doomed to disappointment, as the limits of variation in different types seem to be of a greatly diversified extent. The result, therefore, of our investigation (which is scarcely surprising in an entirely empirical subject), is this: that the general question as regards a decided mark of distinction between race and species can only be answered by the particular study of the extent of variation in individual types; that is to say, that in every question of unity or difference of species we are referred entirely to the study of the individual phenomena themselves.

The investigation of the unity of mankind as a species can only be finally completed, when the results of long continued influences of all possible external conditions in which man is able to live, are as fully and clearly ascertained, as the results of all possible crossings of various human types after a long series of generations. But as our experience in this respect is very far from being perfect, we are compelled to stop at some more or less probable propositions, which must proceed from the solution of the question, whether a gradual alteration of types belonging to the same stock can be proved, and whether it be sufficiently extensive in order to show that the greatest differences prevailing among mankind are merely variations. Next to that the question will be, whether the cross-breeds of the various types, by limited prolificacy, or by constant reversion to the parent type, resemble more the hybrids or mongrels of different races.

SECTION I.

ON THE MODE AND MAGNITUDE OF THE PHYSICAL CHANGES TO WHICH MAN IS SUBJECT.

ALL permanent changes, apart from morbid phenomena, produced on man in the course of time, may, with regard to their origin, be divided into four classes. I. Climate; II. Aliment and mode of life; III. Psychical influences, growth and decline of mental culture; IV. Deviation from the original type, resulting from unknown causes and transmitted more or less permanently.

In many cases it cannot with any certainty be determined to which of these four classes certain phenomena belong, and whether they may not be the results of a combination of causes. It is still less possible exactly to ascertain in what manner such causes have produced these changes; which is specially the case with regard to climate.

What is termed the influence of climate, consists of the direct and indirect influences of the temperature of the air, its degree of moisture, pressure, and chemical composition (malaria); the frequency and variations of winds; rains, their periodicity, etc. Though it is undoubted that a long continuance of such influences produces certain changes in the human organism, but little is known in what mode they are effected. Nothing remains then, but to state, as an ultimate fact, the coincidence of climatic influences with certain differences in the corporeal organization. The reason of this uncertainty is, that the effect of the climate cannot easily be separated from that produced by alimentation and mode of living, which generally act in combination. It is known that the hygrometric state of the atmosphere influences respiration and perspiration, and that the absorption of oxygen by the lungs is in inverse proportion to the temperature of the air, and in direct proportion to the barometric state; it is further known that the barometric state reaches its maximum under 32-33° lat., and is, under the equator, subject to daily regular oscillations; but all this only enables us to say that, in consequence of such circumstances in different climates, various changes are produced in the animal economy, without our being able exactly to trace out their origin.

These circumstances, in combination with other causes which J. W. de Müller[1] has treated of, lend at first sight a certain probability to the explanation of the black skin of the Negro, namely, that in hot climates the amount of oxygen inspired is insufficient to change the carbon into carbonic acid, and that the unconsumed carbon is deposited in the pigment-cells of the skin. Berthold[2] gives a similar explanation, namely, that in spite of the great development of the liver in hot climates, and a diminished activity of the lungs, a sufficient quantity of carbon is not removed from the body; hence the vessels carry a large quantity of carbon which, with an increased perspiration is retained beneath the epidermis. It is, however, difficult to admit that the browning of the skin in our climate in summer, is produced by the same causes as the black colour of the Negro, and that it would only require a greater intensity and a longer duration to become so entirely. Nor can it be admitted, that the tawny skin of many pregnant women and the examples quoted by Blumenbach,[3] of the black spots on certain parts of lying-in women, as well as the tawny colour of such women who have never menstruated, prove in any way that the colour of the Negro is not owing to specific causes ; for the objection would still remain, that under the tropics in East India, South America, and one part of Africa, there live no blacks, and that neither as regards Negroes nor other peoples, the colour of the skin is exclusively determined by the absorption of oxygen. Those who insist upon an explanation must rest satisfied with that given by Foissac,[4] who attributes the colour of the Negro to the predominant vegetable diet containing much more carbon than animal diet. This explanation offers the same difficulties as the former, and is open to similar objections, as is also

[1] "Causes de la Coloration de la Peau," p. 24, Stuttg., 1853.
[2] "Lehrb. der Physiol." 2 Aufl., ii, p. 325.
[3] "De generis humani var. nat.," 3rd edit. p. 156.
[4] "Ueber den Einfluss des Klimas auf den Menschen," p. 67, Gott., 1840.

another opinion of Foissac, which attributes the tawny colour of the Polar nations to the diminished absorption of oxygen, their blood being charged with carbon, owing to the hot summers and the heated and smoky winter habitations. Though some of these circumstances may have their share, it cannot be ascertained to what cause the colour of the Polar tribes is chiefly due. Hence, the assumption of specific peculiarities is still permissible. We are, therefore, obliged to rest satisfied with a mere probability regarding the causal connexion of climatic influences and alimentations, with physical peculiarities; and frequently even probability fails us.

It is this impossibility to analyze the effects of climate and nutrition which has induced Godron[1] to assert that climate has but a superficial influence on plants and animals and could have contributed but little to the differences of human races; and that the causes of the latter lie rather in the differences of nutrition and modes of life: for whilst some plants and animals thrive unchanged in different climates, the wolf and the fox retain the same characters in the torrid or the frigid zone, like the wild horses in South America which possess the same characters as those of the Crimea and Ukraine.

The influence of climate as a general agent cannot, however, be called in question. We may quote the well known facts mentioned in detail by Heusinger,[2] that in cold climates, the size, growth, sexual development, and prolificacy of animals diminish, whilst hair and feathers grow more abundantly; fatty deposits are found, and the colour becomes white, whilst the contrary occurs under the tropics. Many of our domestic animals which thrive in different climates, present the most evident examples of these influences.

How much the human economy can adapt itself to climatic conditions, is proved chiefly by climatic diseases and the morbid predispositions peculiar to every climate; and though the consequences are not always a visible change of the external form, the modifications in the vital process are undeniable. It fre-

[1] "De l'Espèce et des Races," p. 16 and 70, Nancy, 1848.
[2] "Grundzüge der Vegl. Physiol.," p. 211, 1831.

quently occurs that strangers rapidly die in a country where malaria prevails, whilst the natives live and apparently thrive—facts we shall presently mention—and it seems to make no difference whether the strangers belong to the same type or not as the natives. We may instance the fact that the native Peruvian thrives and remains free of pulmonary complaints at an altitude from 7000 to 15000 feet above the level of the sea, which, as in Quito, is frequent destructive to the white.[1] Setting aside extreme cases, such as a sudden change of all essential conditions of life, nothing justifies the assertion that man transplanted into a foreign clime *must* either die or remain as he is. If man can bear the transportation into an essentially different climate, his organism will experience certain modifications, and it is not to be expected that the change should not be as externally perceptible as it is in many animals. D'Orbigny[2] goes so far as to assert that, in Peru, at the altitude above mentioned, the trunk is changed by the influence of respiration, the body is short but compact, whilst the inhabitants of the damp lowlands are more slender in form. Without entirely assenting to this view, we must admit that external conditions, especially such as approach the limits beyond which man could not exist, considerably alter the physiological process; and we must not wonder if, in the course of several generations, a corresponding change is effected in the external form. It is as yet uncertain whether such alterations occur within a comparatively short period and are arrested at a certain point,[3] or whether, like some wild plants changed into varieties by cultivation, the change proceeds at first slowly and afterwards with great rapidity—both may possibly occur under different circumstances.

Volney[4] says, that the Negro physiognomy resembles a face acted upon by the light of the sun and heat, exhibiting overhanging eyebrows, half-closed eyelids, raised cheeks, and projecting jaws. We cannot subscribe to the explanation given

---

1 "Stevenson, R., in Arauco," ii, p. 174, 1826.
2 "L'Homme Americain," i, pp. 96, 113, 1839.
3 "Lyell, "Elements of Geology," 7th ed., ch. 37.
4 "Voyage en Syrie et en Egypte," i, p. 70.

by Stanhope Smith[1] of the peculiarities of the Tatar, namely, that severe cold had the effect of contracting the eyebrows and eyelids, closing the mouth, and raising the cheeks, which has produced the short broad face, and the harshness of features.

Blumenbach[2] has cautiously admitted an influence of climate upon the features but not upon the facial bones, and maintains that the latter become modified by the activity of the facial muscles, as shown lately by Engel.[3] We do not, therefore, agree with the censure pronounced on this work by Barthes.[4]

Much less doubtful is the influence of climate on stature, and the more rapid or slower development of the body. Many travellers have compared the Esquimaux with the inhabitants of Tierra del Fuego and found them resembling, though they live at such a distance from each other. This external resemblance has induced many to assume a special race of "Hyperboreans," which includes all the Polar nations of the northern hemisphere.[5] We must, from the as yet unproved relationship of many of these peoples, infer a certain levelling influence of climate, as all of them are of short massive stature. This applies also to the Peruvians inhabiting high altitudes, who are, moreover, distinguished, as has been often observed in other nations inhabiting cold climates, by a considerable size of the head. Thus, the Hindoos inhabiting the hot plains are distinguished from those of the mountainous regions by smaller, less-projecting foreheads, without, however, exhibiting any intellectual inferiority.[6] Lauvergne,[7] on the other hand, incorrectly asserts, that in families who, from mountainous countries, migrate to the plains, the head becomes after a few generations

---

1 "On the Causes of the Variety of Complexion and Figure," p. 106; New Brunswick, 1810.

2 "De gen. hum. var. nat.," p. 212.

3 "Das Knochengerüst des Menschlichen Antlitzes, 1850; Untersuch. über Schädelformen, 1851. L. Fick ("The Causes of the Forms of the Bones," 1857), has endeavoured to prove that muscular activity has no such influence upon the shapes of the bones, though the growth of the bones depends upon the forms of the soft parts surrounding them.

4 "Nouv. Elemens de la sc. de l'Homme, ii, p. 132, 1806.

5 Lacépède, Duméril, Virey, Bory.

6 Broc. in Lucas, ii, p. 465.

7 "Les Forçats," p. 315.

more developed, which is generally the case with the progress of civilization.

Zimmermann[1] concludes, from the high stature of the Patagonians and the old Germans, whose country was then colder than now, that the highest stature belongs to the colder regions of the temperate zone, whilst Blumenbach[2] thinks stature increases on approaching the tropics. To both these assumptions it may be objected, that the short inhabitants of Tierra del Fuego live very near the Patagonians, the Laplanders near the Fins and Swedes, and similar examples shew that in this respect all that can be asserted is, that the greatest development of man and domestic animals seems to occur in the temperate zone.

I. Geoffroy St. Hilaire, who shares Zimmermann's opinion,[3] mentions as a known fact, that the peoples possessing the shortest stature inhabit nearly all the most northern part of the northern hemisphere. His own tables, however, which must not be altogether confided in, as is plainly shewn from his numerous exceptions, indicate the nature of this assumed fact. Since (as he himself observes) near such peoples of high stature there live other peoples of short stature, we must admit that descent is of more decided influence than climate, though the latter is not without its due effect. The animals, about the size of which in relation to climate Geoffroy lays down a series of axioms,[4] differ in this respect. Some species grow smaller in warm climates, others in cold climates.[5]

A sufficiently well-known and constant effect of climate (in support of which, we shall quote a number of facts), is the rapid or tardy development of the sexual organs. This development is, like stature, also dependent upon nutrition and mode of life; whence many deviations may be explained from the rule that sexual maturity occurs earlier in warm, and later in cold climates. This influence also extends to the intellect.

---

[1] "Geogr. Gesch. des Menschen und der vierfüss. Thiere," 1778.
[2] "De gen. hum. var. nat.," p. 93.
[3] "Ann. des Sci. Nat.," p. 702, 1832; Froriep's Notizen, No. 818, p. 54, 775, 1833.
[4] Froriep's Notizen, 1832.
[5] Swainson, p. 275.

Among the Arabs, the boys exhibit the same demure behaviour as adults.[1] Little children are more intelligent than those of the same age amongst us, though probably not for the reason given by Brehm,[2] that they are entirely left to themselves and that in their helplessness they learn early to use their physical and mental powers. Negro children learn to run about much earlier than the children of Europeans.[3] The children of the natives of Nukahiwa swim alone in the water when they are scarcely a year old;[4] and in Tahiti they often learn earlier to swim than to run.[5] R. Schomburgh equally found that the children of the Zuramatas in Guiana, learn to use their physical and intellectual powers much earlier than European children. That this precocity is no peculiarity of the race is proved by its being also found among the white Creoles in the West Indies, and among the Brazilians.[6] In the same latitude and climate, the time of puberty occurs earlier among Negros and Mongolians than among Europeans;[7] this is partly the result of mode of life, and partly an inherited peculiarity which changes but slowly in the course of several generations. A well-known instance of the permanence of race peculiarity is afforded by the Jewish girls in Central Europe. They arrive at maturity, and grow old, at an earlier period than the daughters of the peoples among whom they live.

A similar influence of climate is assumed with regard to fecundity. That it must be very great among the Negroes in Africa, may be inferred from the enormous losses which Africa has suffered (without any perceptible diminution of its population) by the agency of the slave-trade. On the other hand, the extinction of the aboriginal Americans has been attributed to deficient fecundity of the race, a subject we shall treat of in the sequel. In this place we may observe, that Quêtelet[8] has some

---

1 Hoskin's "Travels in Ethiopia," p. 179, 1835.
2 "Reiseskizzen aus Nordöst Africa," i, p. 56, 1855.
3 Des Marchais, "Voyage en Guinée," p. 282, Amst., 1731.
4 "Wise Los Gringos," p. 138, 1850.
5 Tyermann and Bennett, "Journal of Voyages and Travels," i, p. 360, 1831.
6 Rendu, "Etudes sur le Brésil," p. 19, 1848.
7 Lacépède, "Hist. Nat. de l'Homme," p. 109, 1839.
8 "Ueber den Menschen," p. 67, 1838.

doubts whether, under similar circumstances, the North or the South is more favourable to fecundity. The greatest fecundity known, combined at the same time with great demoralization, is that of Guanaxuato in Mexico,—in the year 1825, it exhibits the proportion = 1 : 16·08.

Macauley[1] speaks of a Negress at Santiago, in Haiti, who produced seven children in three years, and thirteen in six deliveries. Twice she gave birth to triplets, and three times to twins. Another Negress was surrounded by two hundred descendants. To have one hundred grandchildren is not considered extraordinary.

The influence of climate upon the colour of the skin is not contested, but in many respects is yet unexplained. That it does not alone depend on geographical latitude and the mean temperature, has been often observed and proved by Humboldt as regards the population of America; nor are the blackest people of that continent found under the equator.[2] This holds equally good with regard to the Polynesians, of whom Beechey says, that the blackest people inhabit the Vulcan, and the lighter the Coral Islands. The inhabitants of the Marquesas, Navigation, Friendly, and Society Islands form a series, varying from light to dark shades. The inhabitants of New Zealand and the Sandwich Islands are still darker;[3] also the inhabitants of Easter Island.[4] But in the same latitude with the Polynesians as well as at a little distance from them, there live large numbers of tawny dark-brown peoples, among whom, again, the natives of Van Diemen's Land are darker than the New Hollanders, who live nearer the equator (Peron). The inhabitants of the East and West coast of South Africa are very dark. Three hundred English miles in the interior, there are on both sides of this part of the world two regions inhabited by lighter coloured peoples. The natives of the central part are,

[1] "Haiti, ou, Renseignements authentiques sur l'abol. de l'esclavage," pp. 167, 171, 176, Paris, 1835.

[2] This had already been noticed by Columbus, who was surprised to find the colour of the native Americans under the equator lighter, than in the northern regions.—Herrera, Hist. General, xiii, p. 12, 1730.

[3] Hale, "Ethnography and Philol. of the United States Expl. Expedition," p. 9, Philadelphia, 1846.

[4] Forster, "Bemerk. auf seiner Reise um die Welt," p. 211, 1783.

however, again perfectly black.[1] The dark colour of the Ainos on the Kurile Islands, is in remarkable contrast to the climate they inhabit.

From these and similar facts, it may be inferred that the colour of the skin is not so much owing to climate as to descent. Humboldt,[2] who found no difference in Peru among the inhabitants of the Cordilleras and those of the hot plains, ascribes to it, like Ulloa, great durability among the Americans, and considers the influence of climate in this respect, as trifling. This is also the case with regard to the colour and the quality of the hair; and, although less constantly, as regards the iris, between which the parallelism is unmistakable, inasmuch as the dark tint of the skin is accompanied not merely with a dark iris and dark hair, but also with a proportionate tendency in the latter to curl, which circumstance had already been pointed out by Blumenbach. The white race alone contains peoples of florid complexion, light hair and iris, and in this lies a proot for the greater influence of descent over climate.[3]

One of the most interesting examples of this kind is exhibited by the Berbers in North Africa—blue eyes, fair skin, and red beard, are very common among some Kabyles;[4] high stature, white skin, and light hair, are especially found among the Chaouias in Auras.[5] These characters, by which they were often considered as the descendants of the Vandals, are possessed by them chiefly in the mountainous parts; it therefore again becomes doubtful, what in this case belongs to climate and what to the purity of blood. Several instances in favour of the theory that the colour of the skin is more determined by descent than by climate, may be found in Humboldt.[6] The

[1] Livingstone, "Missionsreise u. Forschungen," 1858.

[2] "R. in die Aequinoctialg. ed. Hauff," ii, p. 55.

[3] The author of an interesting article on "Human Hair in Morgen-Blatt, 1855, No. 14, says,—"The dark colour of the hair of the Irish and Celts must long ago have vanished, in consequence of intermixture with the neighbouring fair-haired tribes, or the dark-coloured Celts must have become fair, since they inhabit parts of Europe which contain the light-haired nations, namely, those north of 48° latitude.

[4] Prévost, "Nouv. Ann. des Voy.," i, 126, 1848.

[5] Guyon, *ib.*, ii, p. 390, 1848; compare also M. Wagner, "Reisen in Algier," ii, p. 56, 1841.

[6] "Neu Spanien," i, p. 117.

Mexicans, for instance, are much darker than the aboriginals of the hottest parts of South America; and the Guaicas[1] are much lighter than the Indians by whom they are surrounded, although they seem to share the same mode of life. Maehlenpfordt[2] observes with regard to the Mexican Indians, that they are as brown in the cold mountainous regions as in the south and hot valleys, and that the covered parts of the body are frequently of a darker colour than the unprotected parts. The only parts which are constantly of a lighter colour, are the palms of the hand, and the soles of the feet. Desmoulins[3] supports his theory, that the pure races retain their peculiarities, by the Rohillas, a colony of the Affghans north of the Ganges, who are said even now to possess the same physical characters as the Icelanders—white complexion, blue eyes, fair hair, European physiognomy. His authority for this is Niquet, who adds, that they see badly in bright day light, which creates the suspicion that he speaks of Albinos. Moreover, the Affghans exhibit all shades of colour; in the western table-land, they have an European clear complexion; in the east of the Indus, they are darker, and even black.[4] The colour of the skin cannot in some cases be satisfactorily explained either by reason of descent or the influence of climate; it must then be dependent on other influences. The Portuguese Creoles, in Java, *i. e.*, the cross-breds of the Portuguese and natives, who have propagated on the Island for centuries, are much darker in colour than the Javanese themselves.[5]

Uncivilized nations preserve, at least under common conditions, not only the type generally, but also the colour of their skin and hair. This is specially shown by the Fulahs, who, though of a different stock, have preserved their peculiarities among the Negroes. Thus Burckhardt[6] was able to recognize the descendants of the Bosnian soldiers, who, sent by Sultan Selim (1420), settled in Nubia, and who by their brown colour

---

[1] Humboldt and Bonpland, "Reise," iv, p. 495.
[2] "Schilderung der Rep. Mejico," i, p. 204, 1844.
[3] "Hist. Nat. des Races Humaines," pp. 21, 162, 168.
[4] Prichard, iv, p. 91.
[5] Pfyffer, "Skizzen v. d. Insel Java," p. 67, 1829.
[6] "Reisen in Nubien, p. 194, 1820.

and features betrayed their northern origin. Rafalowitsch[1] also asserts that he recognized them by their fair skin in Derr, lower Nubia. But when Duprat[2] asserts that Berbers, Arabs, Turks, and Jews in North Africa have perfectly preserved their characters in spite of the perfect equality of the conditions in which they live, we must observe that this is scarcely correct, and that there is no general equality of conditions, in as much as Duprat considers the Moors who chiefly inhabit cities to be unmixed Arabs. That upon the Mauritius, as D'Unienville asserts,[3] the Creole- and Mozambique-Negroes, Malgasches, Malays, Telingas, Malabars, and Bengalese, are easily to be distinguished as they have preserved their peculiarities, does not prove anything against the influence of climate, since it differs but little from that of their native country; and from the constant renewal of all slave populations, climate has hardly been of sufficiently long continuance to have produced a change in them, whilst, on the other hand, every individual tribe is distinguished from the others by language, manners, and modes of life.

No doubt many instances furnish us with evidence that peculiarities of bodily formation which have persisted through many generations are but very slowly altered; but they are not sufficient to invalidate the opposite doctrine, that in several peoples of the same origin the physical characters have altered by the influence of climatic conditions in combination with extensive changes in diet and mode of life. Though there is no regular increase in the darkness of the skins on approaching the equator, still it can be proved that colour, like many other physical peculiarities, depends partly on local conditions besides geographical latitude. The facts, however, are not altogether free from contradiction, so that definite rules on the effect of climate can only be obtained from more extensive observation.

Mountaineers are usually of a lighter colour and more vigorous than those of the same tribe inhabiting the valleys. The

---

[1] Erman's "Archiv. f. wiss. Kunde v. Russl.," xiii, p. 114.
[2] "Essai sur les races de l'Afrique," Sept., 1845.
[3] "Statistique de l'Ile Maurice," i, p. 276, 1838.

Hindoos in the cold mountainous regions, especially in the Himalayas, are white and have frequently blue eyes, the beard and hair of the head are sometimes curly, brown, or red. The Siah-Posh, or Kaffirs of Hindukuh, who speak a language allied to the Sanskrit, are of European whiteness; the inhabitants of Cashmir are brown.[1] The Hindustani are tall, vigorous, warlike, light coloured; the Bengalese in their damp and mild climate, short, weakly, timid, and black.[2] Those who consider the colour of the skin as permanent, must attribute it, in regard to the Hindoos, to intermixture with the dark aboriginal inhabitants of India.[3] The institution of castes may, perhaps, support this explanation. A remarkably striking contrast is exhibited by the fine vigorous Tudas in the high healthy parts, in comparison with the miserable Curumbars, inhabiting the unhealthy lowlands. If the Abyssinian, whose olive coloured skin becomes usually lighter during the rainy period, approaching that of the European, descend from the highlands into the valleys, he becomes of a dark brown. Analogous changes are observed in the hair and wool of animals.[4] The inhabitants of Enarea in the low and marshy parts are perfectly black, and have the features and the woolly hair of Negroes, whilst those of the mountainous parts of Enarea and Kaffa are not even so dark as the Neapolitans;[5] and though this may, according to Combes et Tamisier,[6] be going too far, there still exists an important difference. The natives on the banks of the Zambesi are very dark and negro-like, but the colour of the mountaineers is like that of coffee and milk mixed. In harmony with these facts is the remarkable circumstance that the proper and well-marked Negro type is only found in hot low countries, whilst the inhabitants of highlands mostly deviate from it, and are both physically and intellectually superior. Hombron (p. 282) endeavours to prove that the Polynesians become in• unhealthy

---

[1] Elphinstone, Alex. Burnes, Prichard, iv, pp. 91, 209.
[2] "Lassen Ind. Alterthumsk.," i, p. 404.
[3] Hombron, "Zoologie. zu D. d'Urville Voy. au Pole Sud," 164. Omaluis d'Halloy.
[4] Lefebvre, "Voy. en Abyss.," iii, p. 299, 1845.
[5] Bruce, "Quellen des Nils," ii, p. 309, 1790.
[6] "Voy. en Abyssinie," iv, p. 285, 1838.

parts uglier and more like the Malays. Winterbottom,[1] who asserts that lean people of dark colour become of a lighter colour on growing fat, found the inhabitants of the unhealthy coasts of Sierra Leone, darker than those who live inland. Thus we also hear of the Arowakas, in Guiana, that whilst some of them resemble in complexion the Spaniards and the Italians, those living in the unhealthy low parts near the sea are nearly as dark as the lighter coloured Negroes.[2] In this way it may, perhaps, be explained why the Chiriguanas, in the old missions of Piray, are of dark brown colour (color morenos), but those who remained heathens, their women specially, are nearly as white as the Spaniards.[3] The former may, under the direction of the missionaries, have cultivated the soil, the latter may have lived in the forests protected from the sun.

From these and other instances it has been inferred that hot and damp countries favour the darkening of the skin.[4] The frequency of bilious diseases, which occur on changing the residence from high dry lands to low marshy grounds, has been often observed. Further confirmations of the fact are found when we notice the change of colour which Europeans experience in other parts of the world, and especially under the tropics. Even the traveller who remains there but a short time loses his colour. "When I arrived at Ghadames," says Richardson,[5] "I had a rosy colour, now I am like these yellow men." The covered parts, however, preserve their original colour, as has been proved in the case of the French soldiers in Algiers. On the other hand, it is stated of the North-American Indians that the covered parts are not lighter in colour than the naked.[7] This is also asserted of the natives of Mexico and Peru.[8]

---

1 "Nachr. v. d. Sierra Leone," p. 240, 1805.

2 "Journal of the Royal Geogr. Soc.," ii, p. 229, according to Hilhouse.

3 "Viedma in de Angelis, Coleccion de Obras y Documentos," B. Aires, iii, § 9, ad. 50, 1836.

4 Jarrold, "Anthropologia; or, on the Form and Colour of Man," p. 188, 1838. Heusinger, "Grundriss der Anthropol.," p. 87, 1829.

5 "Trav. in the Great Desert of Sahara," i, p. 265, 1848.

6 Lay, James, "Account of an Exped. to the Rocky Mountains under M. Long., Philad.," i, p. 285, 1823.

7 Humboldt and Bonpland, "Reise," ii, 250.

These cases can, however, hardly be considered as peculiarities of race; for the European in Java, as well as in the West Indies and Africa, soon loses his red cheeks, and experiences other changes if he remains for a long time exposed to a tropical climate. Whoever lives for a long time in Guinea, and is much exposed to the sun, becomes almost copper-coloured.[1] Raffenel[2] goes so far as to assert that people of the Caucasian race who are for a considerable time exposed to a tropical sun gradually assume the colour of the Negro, there being well-authenticated instances of pure Arabs who had become under such circumstances blacker than those accounted very dark among Negroes. And if, as we are informed, the Portuguese colonists of Cachaux, in West Africa, have become black mulattoes,[3] and those of Cape Verd, the coast of Guinea, in Quilimane,[4] in Batavia, Ternate, Bombay,[5] in Larentuka (Flores), and in Dilli (Timor),[6] have after a series of generations become black or nearly so, it cannot altogether be ascribed to intermixture with the natives. Even Pruner,[7]—who is not partial to the doctrine of the great influence of climate on the organization of man, and who considers the structure of the skeleton in the various races as unchangeable,—states from his own observation, that the European acclimated in Egypt, acquires after some time a tawny skin, and in Abyssinia a bronzed skin, he becomes pallid on the coast of Arabia, cachectic white in Syria, clear brown in the deserts of Arabia, and ruddy in the Syrian mountains; whilst the hair does not merely become darker, but acquires a softer texture, with a tendency to curl. An interesting gradation of all shades down to the negro-black is exhibited by the Jews. West of Tomsk, in the Barabinsky Steppes, they have a clear skin and light hair,[8] which is uncommon in England and Germany. In Spain, Portugal, Syria, the East Indies, and Congo, they exhibit

---

[1] Monrad, "Gemälde der K. v. Guinea," p. 371, 1824.
[2] "Nouveau Voy.," i, p. 272, 1856.
[3] Durand, "Voy. en Sénégal," an. x, i, p. 169.
[4] Owen, "Narr. of voy. to explore the shores of Africa," i, p. 290, 1833.
[5] Forrest, "Voy. to New Guinea," p. 36, 1779.
[6] Olivier, "Land und Seereisen in Niederl. Ind.," ii, p. 266, 1829.
[7] "Die Krankheiten des Orients," p. 83, 1847.
[8] Simpson, "Narr. of a Journey Round the World," ii, p. 410, 1847.

different shades.[1] Though it may be that the Jews, banished by John II, 1492, from Portugal, may, as Sprengel[2] asserts, have intermixed with the Negroes of St. Thomas, this must not be considered as the sole cause of their altered complexion.

Though it appears that in the same people, if they live in various degrees of latitude, the colour of the skin usually increases in darkness on approaching the Equator, *e.g.*, in the Chinese, who from Pekin to Canton present all shades from light to deep copper colour; the Arabs, from the Desert to Jemen, from olive colour to black; the Australians about Moreton Bay, coal black; but 10° south copper coloured:[3]—still, we must not lose sight of the important exceptions, lately also pointed out by Livingstone, to the assumption that the blackness of the skin increases with heat and moisture. An apparent exception is offered by the white race in South America: the Europeans near to the Equator in the hot and damp Guayaquil, have a fair complexion, clearer even than that of the Spaniards in their native country, and blue eyes and light hair are common among the women. This may perhaps be explained by the ladies taking particular care of their complexion. In the unhealthy spots of these parts, as Panama, Portobello, Carthagena, the Spanish Creoles do not present the fair hair and fresh colour so frequently seen in Guayaquil.[5] It may also be observed, that the Spaniards in Chili are white, and of a fresher colour than in their own country, but the Portuguese in Brazil are of a lead colour or yellow.[6] It is still more striking, that whilst in Carthagena there may yet be seen fair or red-haired women, in Santa Fè, which is much colder, only dark complexions with black hair are found.[7] The same condition with regard to colour is stated of the Indians of Peru, by Tschudi.[8] Zarate[9] also

[1] "Prichard," iv, p. 597.
[2] "Vom Ursprung des Negerhandels," p. 32, 1779.
[3] Dunmore Lang, "Cooksland in N. E. Australia," p. 380, 1847.
[4] Stevenson, ii, 108. Basil Hall, "Extracts of a Journal written in Chili, Peru, and Mexico," 3rd, Edit., ii, p. 109, 1824.
[5] Ulloa, "Voy. de l'Am. mérid." l, 145, Amst. 1752.
[6] Frezier, "Reise nach der Sudsee," p. 88, 1718.
[7] Mollien, "Voy. dans la rép. de Colombia," ii, p. 132, 1824.
[8] "Peru Reiseskizzen," ii, p. 359, 1846.
[9] "Hist. de la Découverte du Pérou," i, p. 41, 1724.

asserts that in Peru, mountaineers possess a lighter colour than the lowlanders; whilst Tschudi says, the colder the climate the darker the colour. In Puna dark red-brown; in Sierra considerably lighter, nearly of a rusty red; darker on the coast, and straw-yellow in the forests.

The example of the native Peruvians, who are dark brown in the Andes, though they have but two rainy months in the year, has induced D'Orbigny to declare a hot and moist climate, provided the country affords sufficient shade, as favourable to whiteness of skin; and he cites, as a proof, the light-complexioned Yuracares (Antisana) compared with the Quichuas and Aymaras. Thus Dobrizhoffer[1] saw in the forests of Paraguay, Indians of European white colour, whilst the Payaguas, who live almost entirely upon the water and are much exposed to the weather, are darker at least than the Guaranis.[2] Gumilla[3] has made the same observation, which is confirmed by Humboldt and Bonpland.[4] To these may be added Eschwege,[5] who says that the lower classes of Portugal and Spain, especially the fishermen, who are much exposed to the weather, possessed the same colour as the Indians of Minas Geraes, which is deepened in the latter by their uncleanliness. Hence A. de St. Hilaire[6] declares that the colour of the Brazil Indians is merely the result of the climate and their uncleanliness. Hombron again states, that the mountaineers of New Guinea and the Philippines, although living in damp, thick forests, are not less black than the New Hollanders; but he also observes, that the blackest negroes somewhat lose their black colour after a few years' residence in warm and damp colonies. That heat and moisture alone do not produce a yellowish brown skin, is shown by several Polar nations, and the majority of North American Indians, among whom again the natives of the greater part of the north-west Coast exhibit a remarkable exception in their white skin.

---

1 "Geschichte der Abiponer," ii, p. 18, 1783.
2 Demersay, "Bulletin Soc. Géogr.," i, p. 17, 1854.
3 "Hist. nat. civ. et g. de l'Orénoque," i, p. 2, 1758.
4 "Reise," iv, p. 495.
5 "Journal v. Brasil," i, p. 85, 1818.
6 "Voy. dans l'intérieur du Brésil," i, p. 426, 1830.

As in many of these instances there exists such a striking and unexpected diversity of colour, which is not to be accounted for by any great difference either of diet or descent, there are no means of explaining the contradictions, excepting by the different modes of life, and the modes of protection against the influence of climate.

This is of special importance in countries where great heat is combined with sudden alterations of temperature, or of dampness and dryness. Want of protection against the influence of climate in such cases appears greatly to favour the darkening of the skin. Continued confinement to the house, as is well known, blanches the skin. This also takes place in healthy persons in winter, whilst the warm sun in the spring, combined with out-of-door exercise, darkens the complexion. Numerous instances, both in Europe and in other parts, show that fishermen and navigators exposed to all changes of the weather, are always of darker complexion than the rest of the population. If Belcher[1] observed the contrary in the Canary Islands and among the Malays in the Bajows, and that the Sandwich Islanders and the Tahitians had been of a lighter colour before the missionaries forbade them to fish (?) and to bathe, he stands alone in the erroneous assumption, just as D'Orbigny and Troyer,[2] who assert what has not been confirmed by any voyager, that among nations of brown or dark brown skin, the exposed face is of a lighter colour than the protected parts, and that the higher classes in the Sandwich Islands have a darker complexion than the lower classes. There are, no doubt, peoples among whom the males differ in colour from the females, without our being able to trace a difference in descent or in mode of protection. Among the natives on the Pilcomayo, the females are said to be as white as the Spanish women;[3] among the Coroados and Puris, the males have a much darker colour, while the females are yellow and capable of blushing.[4] But though such instances are at present in-

[1] "Narr. of the Voy. of H.M.S. Samarang," ii, p. 94, 1848.
[2] "Bullet. de la Soc. Ethnol.," 22 mai, 1846.
[3] Erbaul, "Geschichten der Chiquitos," Wien, p. 447, 1729.
[4] Burmeister, "R. nach Brasilien," pp. 246-260, 1853.

explicable, they do not invalidate the general rule, that the colour of the skin and the whole external aspect are essentially influenced by habits of life, comfort or misery, and particularly by the want or sufficiency of protection against heat, cold, and moisture. This is confirmed among all races.

Though we find among all the castes of the Hindoos light and dark individuals of all shades, the lower castes are mostly darker, the Brahmins mostly of a lighter colour, so that in comparison with the rest of the population they appear white even in Mahratta, the Deccan, and Calcutta. A wandering tribe of Rajpoots, the Bengari, who travel through the country as corn merchants,[1] are much darker and more vigorous than the rest of their tribes (Lassen). The women and girls of the Hassanieh Arabs in East Africa, who are very careful of their complexion, are of a light bronze colour, and differ in this respect so much from their dark-brown husbands, that one is inclined to consider them of a different tribe.[2] Many women in El Obeid (Kordofan) who protect themselves from the sun, are not darker than brunette European women. Among the yellow-brown Mongolian race in China and Japan, the workmen are brown; high-born ladies nearly white; and upon the Luchu Islands the colour alternates from dark brown to white.[3] In Bony (Celebes), many women are very white.[4] The most striking diversities of colour and hair are found among the Fins, unless we are able to explain it by intermixture. The black-haired dark Laps and Woguls are nearly allied to the fair Fins, the black-haired but clear complexioned Magyars, and the red-haired Ostiaks. L. v. Buch considers the protection against the influence of climate, wholesome food, warm clothing, and good habitation, among the Fins, and the want of them among the short Laps, as the chief causes of these phenomena. Many peoples of the South Sea, especially of the Society, Sandwich Islands, and New Zealand, offer so considerable a difference in complexion, that one is often inclined to assume a mixture of different races; which supposition is

---

[1] Ritter, "Erdk.," v, p. 687.
[2] Brehm, i, p. 331.
[3] Prichard, iv, 519.
[4] Olivier, "R. in Niederländisch Indien," ii, p. 175, 1829.

not supported by linguistic data, and has been generally abandoned. At any rate, such a theory must be much limited, and is in Polynesia only applicable to the Tonga and Samoa Archipelago; hence the great differences of colour and physical conformation upon most of the above groups of Islands must be considered as the result of external conditions.

From the preceding facts there seems to result, that the colour of the skin, though not always in proportion to latitude and mean temperature, is essentially influenced by climate; that the extent and mode of this influence is chiefly regulated by habits and mode of life; that next to these, descent has the greatest influence; and that food has also its share in the production of colour, though in a subordinate degree. It is further shown that hot and damp countries, unprotected by forests, and a mode of life which exposes the organism to climatic influences, strongly favour the darkening of the skin. Frequent and great alterations of temperature, especially sudden changes from wet to dry, brown the skin in every climate and in every race, if the body is much exposed and unprotected.

We must not, however, expect that the European in America or Africa, or the Negro in America, should, after a few centuries, or perhaps ever, assume the type of the aborigines; for where diet and habits of life, and the whole care for body and soul differ so essentially between immigrants and aborigines, the former can only very gradually approach the latter, specially where there is a constant influx of immigrants. This assimilation can only be effected as far as the influence of climate is alone concerned. The following observations are interesting in this respect.

The Germans who in the last century emigrated to Pennsylvania, and to the banks of the Mohawk, differ at present considerably from the German type; and, between the Yankee and the Englishman the difference is said to be still greater. "Pale, a somewhat darker colour, smoothness and softness of features, strike the stranger. The effect of the climate is more decided in the central and southern than in the northern parts, and more striking in the plains near the sea than in the vicinity of the Appalachian mountains, and also among the working classes more than among the higher classes. The colour of the inhabitants of New Jersey below the cataracts, is much darker than that of the Pennsylvanians, as their country is flatter and covered with stagnant waters. Along the south coast of Maryland and Virginia, the colour is deeper. The inhabitants of the lowlands of Carolina and Georgia, especially the poorer and working classes, are but little lighter than the Trokeese. They are mostly so thin and lean that their limbs appear disproportionately long. The hair is thicker and stiffer than in the European, and does not readily curl. The stiffness increases with every generation."[1]

The American as compared with the Englishman is lean, although he grows fat after a long sojourn in Europe. There obtains, however, in this respect, a difference between north and south. The Virginian (the West Virginian excepted)[2] is tall, slender, and lean; the New Englander shorter, and has mostly a round face; both, it must be observed, are of the same stock. "The genuine Yankee," says Carpenter,[3] "may be distinguished from the Englishman by the sharpness and angularity of his features. There is an excess of breadth between the rami of the lower jaw, giving to the lower part of the face a peculiar squareness in contrast to its oval form in the Englishman, and which tends to assimilate the Anglo-American to the aborigines of the country." It has long been observed that the English immigrants in North America are more vigorous workmen than their descendants.[4] It may be observed that the flesh of our domestic animals seems there to be less nutritious and of less flavour, and that the breed of cattle is inferior.[5] Beside, the leanness, the stiff shaggy hair are also characteristics of the American; the curly hair of the European becomes straight in America (Jarrold), so that the American is, gene-

---

[1] Stanhope Smith, "On the Causes of the Variety of Complexion and Figure," p. 68, New Brunsw., 1810; and Imlay, "Nachr. v. d. west Lande der N. A. Freistaaten," im Magaz. der Reisebesch., ix, p. 126: Vater, "Unters. über Americas Bevölkerung aus. d. alten Continente," p. 71, 1810.

[2] Kriegk in "Luedde's Zeitschrift für Erdkunde," i, p. 484.

[3] Todd's "Cyclop. of Anat. and Physiol.," p. 1330.

[4] Johnston, "Notes on North America," 1851.

[5] Franz, "Anweisung zur Vervollk. der Viehzucht, p. 105; and Clemens, in der "Deutschen Vierteljahrschrift," ii, p. 78, 1849.

rally, in caricature, represented with a long neck and long hair. The latter is, in comparison with the soft silky hair of the Englishman, evidently an approach to the American Indian. The long neck is connected with a weaker development of the glandular system, to which must be added the nervous irritability of the American. These peculiarities have been connected with the dry west winds which predominate in the United States; notwithstanding nearly double the quantity of rain which falls there, in comparison with most European countries, drought frequently injures the harvest.[1] Other causes contribute to this change, such as the restless activity of the Yankee, and his love of spirituous liquors. The American is also said to have a voice of less metal, and his eyelids are said to be shorter, than those of the European.[2]

Whilst in New South Wales, as in North America, the children of European parents are apt to become tall and lean,[3] there is a tendency among the European colonists at the Cape to grow fat;[4] which reminds us of the large fat tails of the Cape sheep, and the fat hips of the native women. The white creoles in the West Indies, have also a disposition to grow fat; they are tall and well-made, and distinguish themselves from the Europeans by the flexibility of their limbs. Their pale yellow complexion and their precocity have already been mentioned. Their eyes are deep-seated, usually of grey, black, or dark-brown colour. The skin generally feels cool.[5] Some authors (Vater), mention the prominency of their cheek-bones, which is denied by others. Nott ascribes to them, besides their pale complexion, no peculiarities which distinguish them from the whites. With regard to this assertion, it must be considered that most Europeans, the English especially, only go to the West Indies to acquire wealth and then return to their native country. Joseph Brown[6] mentions that the same parents, who,

[1] Williamson, "Observations on the Climate of America," New York, 1811.
[2] Jarrold, p. 135.
[3] Lesson, "Voy. Médical autour du M., 1829," p. 110; and Majoribanks, "Travels in N. S. Wales, 1847," p. 217.
[4] Barrow, "R. durch die inneren Gegenden des Südlich. Afr., 1801-55," ii, p. 121.
[5] Bryan Edwards, "Hist. des Colonies Anglaises dans les Indes occ." p. 175, Paris, 1801.
[6] "Cyclop. of Pract. Med.," ii, p. 419.

in the West Indies produce children of West Indian colour and physiognomy, produce in Europe, children of European colour and physiognomy. The white creoles in Peru originating from the North of Spain lose their ruddy complexion in the second generation, the whiteness of the skin becomes sallow.[1] Red hair and blue eyes disappear from the family in succeeding generations. (Sucle retroceder en las generaciones siguientes sacando el pelo roxo y ojos azules del tronco de su familia. Uanne, obser. sobre el clima de Lima. Madrid, 1815, p. 106.)

The changes which the Negroes undergo in America will be treated of in the sequel, as they are not so much owing to the climate as to the change of habit, diet, and their intercourse with a more intellectual race. Here it may be merely observed that though some instances have been quoted[2] of Negroes who, transplanted to the north, have become gradually lighter, and ultimately white, they are isolated cases, like that mentioned by De la Salle,[3] of a French lady whose hair changed in the East Indies from dark brown (perhaps dyed?) to a bright red. As regards the Botokudes, among whom in their own country there are white men with red cheeks, although they live under 20° south lat., it scarcely can excite surprise that they become in Europe white in winter, as mentioned by Prince Max.[4] Blumenbach, and Hunter before him,[6] believed that it takes a longer time for a Negro to grow white than for a European to become black. Skin affections must be taken into consideration before admitting the above cases as proofs either way. A morbid affection was probably the cause in an instance related by Anderson,[5] of a Negro whose black shining skin became in a very cold night of a pale ash-grey colour. Prichard[7] speaks of Tuaryks, who, when living alone in an oasis, became gradually, as regards hair and features, negro-like; but the metamorphosis has been lately invalidated by Barth,

---

1 El blanco algo se quiebra.
2 Blumenbach, "De gen. hum. var. nat.," p. 60.
3 Voy. autour du M. sur la Bonito," ii, p. 281, 1845.
4 "R. nach Brasil," ii, pp. 4, 66.
5 "Diss. de Hominum Variet.," p. 38, 1775.
6 "R. in Südwest-Afr.," 1858.
7 Chap. iv, p. 600, according to Hodgson.

in as much as the Negroes were in former times much more numerous in North Africa than now, and that intermixture between Negroes and Tuaryks occurs frequently in the southern districts of the latter.

The influence of climate upon temperament and character has been as much exaggerated as that upon the physical constitution. According to Falconer,[1] a hot climate greatly increases sensibility, and predisposes to sensual excesses, revenge, thoughtlessness, inconstancy, and cowardice; whilst a cold climate produces the opposite qualities. He also endeavours to show that climate has an influence upon laws, religion, and politics. Travellers, Werne for instance, have observed in themselves and other persons that the temporal residence in a tropical climate produces a great irritability of temperament which disappears again in Europe. Something similar is also found here and there among immigrants who are already acclimatized. "A morbid irritability is general in this country (Port Natal); this is more the case in the bay, that is, around d'Urban, than here (Pietermaritzburg), so that the more sober Maritzburgers are astonished at nothing that happens down the country, unless something rational is effected."[2] These effects appear, however, to be merely transitory and of a local nature. Generally we may assume that the continued influence of a hot climate produces a relaxed state, diminishing bodily and mental activity, or, as Pöppig says,[3] that it leaves man physically and morally more inert than a temperate climate. It is not always the case that people living under a serene sky are more joyous and more inclined to sports and dancing than those enveloped by mists and clouds. In North and South America, as well as in the South Sea, there are found under the same climatic conditions, unsocial and morose nations, as well as cheerful and social peoples. While Egyptians and Hindoos are patient and unimpassioned, the Esquimaux and Tschuktch are of an irritable, cheerful, and elastic nature. The present Chileno (says Pöppig) does not possess that characteristic irritability

[1] "Remarks on the Influence of Climate," 1781.
[2] Bleek, in Petermann's "Geogr. Mittheil." p. 369, 1856.
[3] R. in Chili, Peru, and the Amazon River, ii, p. 180, 1835.

and inconstancy which the prejudice of the north ascribes to the south, but he appears calm and discreet.

The important influence of diet upon the body, and indirectly upon the mind, has never been doubted (a resumé of the varieties of food used by many nations may be found in Foissac).[1] Besides the quantity and the quality of the articles of diet, there must also be taken into consideration the amount of labour requisite to procure them. It is only when man can procure digestible food in sufficient quantity without too much physical exertion that the body can become properly developed. Hence alimentation is closely connected with habits of life.

That wealth and poverty exercise a decided influence upon growth and mortality has been proved by Quetelet. Geoffroy[2] has endeavoured to show that generally among the mammals there is a remarkable harmony between bodily size and the food assigned to them by nature. The consequences of hunger and of the consumption of large quantities of food not sufficiently nutritious by itself, potatoes specially, may be ascertained in the large towns and manufacturing districts of our modern civilized states. Ireland offers the most striking example of this kind. In 1641, and following years, Irishmen were driven out of Ulster and the south of Down into the forest by the English. When they were again found, at a later period, they seemed quite altered, only five feet two inches high, big bellied, bandy legged, features distorted, open mouthed, and projecting teeth.[3] Similar instances are found in other parts of the world, showing the effects in whole tribes.

The Bosjesmen are, as is proved by their language, a Hottentot tribe driven by their enemies into a stony, sterile tract, and kept confined to it. Their country is even deficient in spring water and rain. If the chase with bow and arrow is unproductive they search for roots, ants, locusts, snakes, and lizards to satisfy the cravings of hunger. The degeneracy of

---

[1] "Ueber den Einfl. d. Klimas," p. 20, 1840.

[2] Edin. New Philos. Journal, April to July 1833; Froriep's "Notizen," No. 818, 1833.

[3] Prichard, "Uebers," ii, p. 373; Dublin Univ. Mag., No. 48, p. 658.

their bodily condition, as compared with that of their allied tribes, and their approximation to the brute creation, which Lichtenstein has so vividly described, justifies us the more in attributing it to their miserable mode of existence, since the Bosjesmen on the Zuga river, and in the north-east of the Ngami lake, who do not suffer from want, are strong and well made, looking much better than those of the south in the desert who speak the same language.[1]

In the same manner it can be shown that all peoples which we find physically and morally in the lowest scale of humanity, live in the deepest material misery. To this class belong the aborigines of Tierra del Fuego and Australia. The former inhabit a wild and rocky mountain-coast, which even obstructs free motion, so that they are obliged to pass the greater portion of their lives in their huts or in their boats; hence their crooked thin legs.[2] They suffer much from hunger and cold. Notwithstanding their miserable appearance, it is highly probable that they belong to the powerful tribe of the Araucanians, with whom, in respect of their bodily formation, D'Orbigny classes them, whilst in their manners they resemble the Patagonians, so unlike them in body. Attention has been directed to the external resemblance of the people of Tierra del Fuego to the Esquimaux, so that it may be imagined that climate and mode of life induce a certain resemblance of physical formation. Australia is deficient in water and large wild animals. Among the tribes of the natives those who are badly nourished stand physically and mentally lowest. On proceeding from Port Jackson northwards to Port Macquarie, Clarence, Moreton, and Rockingham Bay, Port Essington, the natives are found to be physically and mentally superior.[3] Those who live in the eastern part of the interior are frequently exposed to hunger, and feed but sparingly on kangaroos, whilst those who dwell on the banks of the Lynd and Mitchell rivers, and near the

---

[1] Livingstone, Journal of the Royal Geog. Soc., xxi, p. 23, and xxii, p. 164.
[2] Wilkes's "Narrative of U. S. Expedition," i, p. 124, Philad., 1845.
[3] Hodgson, "Reminiscences of Aust.," p. 254, 1846; King, "Narrative of a Survey of the Intertropical and W. Coasts of Aust.," i, p. 1827, 203; Leichardt, "Tageb. einer Landreise in Aust.," p. 415, 1851.

gulf of Carpentaria, have fish in abundance, and are not so timid as the former, being more inclined to trade.[1] The aborigines of Australia Felix are physically and intellectually superior to those of New South Wales.[2] Though it has hitherto not been doubted that the peoples of Australia are all of the same stock, there are great differences found among them, which must chiefly have been produced by food and mode of life. The disproportionately long arms and legs of the natives of New South Wales are not general; in the north-west tall muscular men are found.[3] There exist, especially on the Darling, great differences in features and colour.[4] Among some the hair is straight, among others curly or woolly.[5] Besides the commonly small forehead, there are observed in the west and the interior, receding foreheads.[6] In the region of Port Stephens foreheads of European shape are sometimes seen.[7] Similar differences are observed with regard to the shape of the nose.

It has been asserted that a nation feeding much on animal food is more vigorous, and bolder, more passionate and less docile, and becomes physically and mentally better developed than by a vegetable diet. This general assertion has been refuted by Foissac,[8] and it must not be forgotten, that the primary condition of bodily and mental health is not merely the nutritious quality of aliments, but their suitableness to the wants of the organism, which depends partly on the climate. If for the preservation of the same physical force in winter, and in cold climates, a rich substantial animal diet is requisite, the inhabitants of the torrid zone preserve the same force with a small quantity of vegetable food. Even the workman in Benguela is satisfied with a handful of Maniok meal;[9] the

---

[1] Leichardt, p. 250.
[2] Byrne, "Twelve Years Wanderings in the British Colonies," i, 365, 1848.
[3] Grey, "Journal of Two Expeditions in Australia," i, p. 232, 1841.
[4] Mitchell, "Exped. into the Interior of Eastern Australia," i, p. 211, 1838.
[5] Hale, Wilkes, Hodgson, Dampier, "Nouv. voy. autour du m. 1701," ii, p. 141.
[6] Stokes, "Discoveries in Australia," i, p. 89, 1846; Sturt, "Narr. of an Exped. into Central Aust.," ii, p. 135, 1849
[7] Dawson, "The Present State of Australia," p. 339, 1830.
[8] "Ueber den Einfl. des Klimas," p. 197, 1840.
[9] Tams, "Die Portugies. Besitzungen in Südwest Afr.," p. 36, 1845.

Kru-negro remains muscular in his laborious exertions, with a purely vegetable diet, chiefly rice, which is also the case with the inhabitants of Yarriba.[1] The English are less able to bear the moist heat of tropical climates than the Portuguese, Spaniards, and even the French, because they cannot easily give up their animal diet and spirituous liquors. In Brazil alone the Portuguese seem to form an exception; they live there on meat, fish, and spirituous liquors, apparently without injury. The Esquimaux requires for his meals considerable quantities of animal food, fat, blubber, etc.; but a large consumption of indigestible aliment gives so much work to the digestive organs as to interfere with the development of the intellectual faculties, though it may not be so injurious as the consumption of large quantities of non-nutritious aliments.

However true it may be that the desire for a quantity of substantial food prevails more in cold and temperate climates, there are still exceptions to this rule. The Negroes of the Gold Coast are great gluttons, and even Europeans who visit this region preserve their good appetite.[2]

If the comparison be confined to the English with the Irish, the European with the rice consuming Hindoo or Japanese, or even with the Chinese who eat flesh sparingly, it certainly would appear that an animal diet is favourable to the development of the character and the intellect. The case, however, is altered if a more comprehensive view be taken. The South-African nations cannot do for any length of time without animal food.[3] The Hottentots and Kaffirs, who, like the peoples of cold climates, consume fat and tallow in large quantities,[4] differ a good deal in character and activity. On the arrival of the Dutch at the Cape, in the seventeenth century, they found the Hottentots peaceable, intellectually inert, but good-natured, and yet they were then like the warlike Kaffirs of the present day, a pastoral people, living chiefly on the milk of their cattle.

[1] Köler, "Einige Notizen über Bonny," p. 57, 1848; Lander, "R. zur Erforsch. des Niger," i, p. 81, 1833.

[2] "Allg. Historie der Reisen," iv, p. 127.

[3] Lichtenstein, "R. im Südl. Africa," i, p. 110, 1811.

[4] Thunberg, "R. durch e. Theil v. Europa, Afr. u. Asien," i, p. 175, 1792; Gardiner, "Narrative of a Journey to the Zulu Country," p. 175, 1836.

The Buraets, and many other Siberian nomadic tribes, are short and weakly through living entirely on animal food (Pallas). On the other hand, the greater portion of the South Sea islanders, living almost entirely on vegetables and fish, are intellectually gifted, and many of them very warlike.[1] The most savage, and at the same time the most gifted people, the Fiji islanders, live almost entirely on vegetables, chiefly yams. The inhabitants of New Caledonia are large, well-proportioned, and more vigorous than those of the New Hebrides. The Mohav-Indians, on the Colorado, in North America, are of athletic structure, though living exclusively on vegetable food.[2] From these examples, which might easily be multiplied, we are not inclined to consider with Lesson (128), the vegetable diet of the inhabitants of Ualan (Micronesia) as the cause of their effeminacy and peaceful disposition, nor to consider any necessary connexion of that kind, as do Gerdy and Lucas.[3]

The capacity of thriving on any kind of sufficient alimentary substances appears, besides the climatic conditions, to depend on the habitude of the organism which seems to be transmitted to the offspring. It may further be observed, that the European is, with regard to vegetable food, more favourably circumstanced than the inhabitants of other quarters of the globe, in as much as proper preparation renders his vegetables more nutritious and digestible than the maize of the native American, the millet of the African, and the rice of the Asiatic, which, to afford the same nourishment, must be consumed in large quantities, producing a less advantageous effect on body and mind.

Further proofs of the great influence of aliment and mode of life on man are furnished by the American Indians. Though it is undoubted that the Indians west of the rocky mountains belong to the same stock as those in the East (the Indian tribes in the interior of the Oregon region resemble very much those who formerly were in possession of the eastern part of the United States); yet, both mentally and physically are they

---

[1] Moerenhout, "Voy. aux Iles du gr. Ocean," i, p. 120, 1837.
[2] Sitgraves, in "Bullet. Soc. Geog.," i, p. 379, 1855.
[3] Loc. cit., ii, p. 474.

inferior to the Indians of the East. Their resources are more limited, and their diet poorer.[1] All fishing peoples of these parts are weaker than their allied tribes; less enterprising, as they have not the habit of sustained activity requisite for hunting. The Takhalis or Carriers in the north of New Caledonia; the fishing tribes on the Columbia; the Upper Californians on the coast, are shorter and more delicate than the inhabitants of the interior living by the chase.[2] Among the weakest and most miserable human beings may be enumerated the Paiuches, on the northern Colorado and in the region of the Salt Lake.[3] The Schoschonies live in an almost desert tract, with but little game; (buffaloes are only found in the neighbourhood of the Rocky Mountains) they grow fat at the time of salmon fishing, but become again emaciated in winter and spring.[4] The size of the Esquimaux differs according to the richness of the tract they inhabit.[5] The American Indian seems generally to have no tendency to grow fat; there is, however, an exception as regards the Moxos in South America, who lead a more protected and secure life, being agriculturists and navigators besides fishers and hunters. (D'Orbigny.)

There is scarcely a people among whom more striking differences are found accordingly as they are nourished, than among the Jakutes. Those who live in the meadows on the south side of the mountains are five feet ten inches to six feet four inches in height, well-formed and vigorous; whilst those in the north are only of middle stature, and of an unhealthy aspect.[6] A similar difference is found among the nomadic people, the Reindeer-Tschuktsh and the Tschuktsh tribe settled on the coast, above whom the former claim a superiority.[7] The Arabs differ much in their habits, and their physical peculiarities vary accordingly, as shown in Egypt. In the colder regions they are clear complexioned (yellow in the Hedschas, white in

---

1 Hale, p. 199.
2 Farnham, "Travels in the Californias," p. 364, New York, 1844.
3 Ibid., p. 376.
4 Wyeth, Schoolcraft, "History of the Indian Tribes," i, p. 206.
5 Seemann, "R. um d. W.," ii, p. 53, 1853.
6 "Billings, R. nach d. Nördl. Gegenden v. russ. Asien, n. Am.," p. 122, 1803.
7 Ibid., p. 233; Wrangell, "Statist. und Ethnog. Nachrichten über d. russ. Besitzungen im Am.," p. 59, Petersburg., 1839.

Algeria and Aleppo, says D'Escayrac,[1]) in Mecca yellowish-brown, and have neither the eagle nose nor the fine features of the Bedouins; in Jemen the noses are straight like the Greek nose. In Hauran (south of Damascus) the Arabs are mostly of short stature, small face, thin beard; whilst the Fellahs are taller and more robust, beard strong, but their eyes are less piercing. This difference must be considered as the effect of mode of life, as it was not appreciable before the sixteenth century.[2] The Bedouins in the middle of the desert have, Negro-like, almost woolly hair. In Nubia, south of Dongola, there are Arabs of a shining black colour, who do not intermix with the Negroes.[3] The Sheighias in Nubia, are of a shining black,[4] and considered to be the finest men in the East, not excepting even the Turks.[5] Hoskings,[6] however, calls them dark brown, and observes, that they have sometimes larger nostrils and thicker lips than Europeans, perhaps the result of intermixture with the Negroes.

That the size of the body depends essentially on nutrition has been proved by various instances quoted by Milne Edwards.[7] This is shown by the statistical information on stature, furnished by the districts of Paris and the various departments of France. The French military standard confirms the results obtained. Before 1789, the standard was five feet one inch, for cavalry five feet three inches. Though, from 1816 the mean height of the French was somewhat raised during the peace, still the standard had to be lowered in 1818 to four feet nine inches; in 1830 and 1848 it was again lowered, as the requisite number of recruits could not be obtained of the legal standard.[8] That the development of the trunk is essentially affected by the activity of the muscles, is shown by the measurements of Quêtelet, of Europeans, Kaffirs, and Ojibbeways, compared

[1] "Die Afric. Wüste u. das Land. d. Schwarzen," p. 185, 1855.
[2] Ritter, "Erdk.," xv, p. 990.
[3] Prichard, iv, p. 590.
[4] Waddington and Hanbury, "Journal of a Visit to some parts of Ethiopia," p. 122, 1822.
[5] Ibid., p. 194.
[6] "Travels in Ethiopia," p. 128, 1835.
[7] "Elémens de Zoologie," p. 254; compare also I. Geoffroy St. Hilaire, "Ann. des Sc. Nat.," 1832; Froriep's "Notizen," 1833.
[8] "All. Zeitg.," No. 22, 1852.

with those of Negro slaves.[1] The mode of life has also an important influence on the form of the pelvis. Whilst the Malay and Japanese women have a comparatively large pelvis and parturiate with facility; the Chinese women have often a narrow pelvis, which may perhaps be ascribed to their sedentary life, as, even among the neighbouring Japanese and Malay ladies of high rank, difficult labours occur.[2] Whether there obtains in Europe a similar difference, as a rule, between the inhabitants of cities and of the country, might not be an uninteresting subject of inquiry.

The influence of aliment and mode of life is more strikingly exhibited where, in addition to a difference of habit, there obtains a difference of social relations, and a separation of the various classes of the population. By their combined action, they produce among men originally from the same stock, a gradual inequality both in their internal and external characters. To this may be ascribed the striking differences among the Finnish nations, as well as those existing between the castes and ranks in India and Polynesia. We have already spoken of them, but they deserve repetition, since besides aliment and mode of life, social relations combine with them. On one side, there is the nobility in the consciousness of superiority; in Polynesia, from a belief of their being in direct communication with the gods, the aristocracy are almost worshiped: on the other side, the people are conscious of having been born to servitude, or as is the case with some castes, are reckoned unclean during their whole existence. Similar relations existed in the old Inka Empire. The aristocracy were as in Polynesia, and as the highest caste in India, in possession of all knowledge, which, on their being exterminated by the Spaniards, disappeared with them. Analogous differences between the aristocracy and the common people are found everywhere. Among the Kurds along the Turco-Persian frontier, the traveller easily distinguishes the caste of peaceable agricultural labourers by their nearly Grecian physiognomy, from the higher caste of warriors.[3] The latter

---

[1] "Bullet. de l'Acad. des Sc. de Belgique," tome xx.

[2] "Allg. Medic. Centralztg.," No. 6, p. 37, 1853.

[3] Prichard, iv, p. 68.

have stern angular features, and staring grey or bluish eyes. There exist also linguistic differences between the two castes—that of the labourers approaches more the Persian dialect than that of the warriors; hence, a diversity of stock is not improbable.[1] Among the Bechuanas of Littaku, the higher ranks are distinguished by a clearer complexion, higher stature, and European features.[2] Among the Chinese who have for several generations lived in affluence, the peculiarities of the Mongolian race grow fainter and the features become nobler.[3] The free Indians of Ecuador are mostly better made and have finer features and a lighter colour than those employed by the whites as shepherds and agricultural labourers. The former are, in many parts, so white and have such good features, that they seem only by their dress to differ from the Europeans.[4]

How much the necessity of adopting different habits of life influences the development of internal and external characteristics, is shown by the inhabitants of Wojjerat in the south-east of Tigre. They are said to be the descendents of Portuguese soldiers, who settled there in the sixteenth century. Combes and Tamisier[5] doubt it, but Poncet in his travels, in 1698, say's of them, they are easily known, and they were the so-called white Abyssinians.[6] In the temperate climate of this mountain region, surrounded by many savage nations, and forced by them to many wars in order to preserve their independence, they have become a proud athletic race, more powerful than the majority of the aborigines. They form, in this respect, a contrast to the Portuguese descended from merchants, who, in the East Indies, in unhealthy regions, have by a dissipated life, become weaker even than the natives of these parts.[7] The Fulahs in the south of Bornou, surrounded by natives who are less civilized, are still herdsmen, without that desire for conquest and reform which distinguishes the

---

1 Ritter, "Erdk.," ix, 570.
2 Philip, "Researches in South Africa," ii, 128, 1828.
3 Epp, "Schilderungen, aus Holländisch-Indien," p. 168, 1852.
4 Villavicencio, "Geogr. de la rep. del Ecuador," p. 167, New York, 1858.
5 "Voy. en Abyss.," iv, p. 319.
6 "Allerhand lehrreiche briefe v. d. mission de ges. Jesu ad. d. neue Welt-Bot.," iii, p. 100, Augsburg, 1726.
7 Salt, "Voyage to Abyssinia," p. 274.

western Fulahs, and have, excepting their small features, hands and feet and the high forehead, little resemblance to the Fulahs of the west.[1] Generally speaking, the different aspect of the Fulahs in the interior of Africa corresponds closely with the degrees of civilization and the social relations in which they live, and cannot be explained by an assumed intermixture with the Negro-race. Between the inhabitants of the southern and northern King's-Mill-Islands (Mikronesia), there exists equally a great difference both externally and in character, and there is no reason to suppose that they are of different stocks. The latter live in peace, and have abundant food, which is not the case as regards the former.[2]

The argument in favour of the power of such conditions furnished by the Barabra in Nubia, is however exposed to many objections, the Barabra are described as of a shining black, but otherwise not at all negro-like. They have thin, curly, but not woolly hair, a pointed nose with large nostrils, a large mouth, and but moderately thick lips. Nevertheless, they speak, according to Rüppel,[3] a Negro language, which with its dialects extends over the whole country from Dongola to Kordofan. This language prevails also in Darfur;[4] and it seems, therefore, as Cooley,[5] following Ibn Khaldun, observes, that the people of the Barabra are of Negro descent, like the native population of Kordofan and Darfur; but that in consequence of agriculture, trade, and a higher civilization, the features have gradually improved, which is also asserted of other negro tribes as the effect of the introduction of Islamism.[6] Opposed to this view, is the circumstance, that the Nubians have been described by the ancient Arab geographers as a fine race of men, not at all negro-like;[7] and that particularly the present province Berber had been conquered under the fourth Kalif after Mohammed by Abadja Arabs, who came from Jemen, and the present Barabra are said to

---

1 Barth., "Reisen u. Entdeckungen," ii, p. 476.
2 Wilkes, "Narrative of the U.S. Explor. Exped.," v, p. 107, Philad., 1845.
3 "R. in Nubien, Kordofan," p. 126, 1829.
4 Burckhardt, "R. in Nubien," p. 486, 1820.
5 "Negroland of the Arabs," p. 118, 1841.
6 Compare Prichard, ii, p. 342.
7 "Isthakri," p. 21.; "Cod. Goth. Idrisi trad. p. Jaubert," i, p. 25.

have descended from intermixture.[1] Their country manifestly is one of those where an extended intermixture of Negroes with Abyssinian and Arabs took place.

Finally, it may be noticed that Lepsius[2] designates the Kundschara language as predominating in Darfur and the greater part of Kordofan, a language which is a foreign Negro-idiom, while the Nuba language may perhaps be considered as belonging to the Caucasian (Semitic?) language. Russeger,[3] and also Brehm,[4] appear to be of the same opinion in considering the Barabra as belonging to the Ethiopian (Abyssinian) peoples from their linguistic similarities.

Many of the preceding instances have taught us what important changes in the organism may be effected by a combination of diet, physical culture, and social condition. But as these are chiefly connected with an entire change in habits, there occurs in most cases a corresponding change in *mental development*. In now considering the effects of psychical influences, it must be observed, that a separation of the particular influence which each individual agent exercises is impracticable; for in the great majority of physical changes produced by the continued action of psychical influences, nutrition and mode of life are acting in the same direction. An abundance of the necessaries of life, combined with a feeling of security and a permanent social condition, are usually connected with a relatively high degree of mental culture, which reacts favourably on the development of the body. On the other hand, hunger, uncleanliness, and misery, produce gradually an obtuseness of intellect, loss of energy, and when combined with an oppressed social condition, may contribute to arrest bodily development in a people.

The lower the mental development of a people, the more subject is it to external natural influences. These may act directly upon the organism, or indirectly. If all conditions of

[1] Hoskins, p. 200.
[2] "Bericht über d. verh. der Preuss. Akad.," p. 382, 1844.
[3] "R. in Europa, Asien, u. Afr.," ii, p. 192, 1843.
[4] Chap. i, p. 72.

life are of a simple kind, and if activity is exclusively directed to satisfy physical wants, there will be a great external resemblance in individuals; for a feeble exertion of the mind, and a uniform expression of mental emotion, impress upon the physiognomy and the whole body the stamp of uniformity, exhibiting but little variety. A greater difference between individuals is only found in more highly developed nations.

Just as the Romans found the old Germans very much like each other, so it is with the civilized European who looks at so-called savages for the first time. This, no doubt, may in most cases arise from merely taking a superficial view. Thus Kendall[1] says of the Mexican women, that they appear to strangers very like each other, because they wear the same dress, have black hair, dark piercing eyes, and very regular features. The expression of Ulloa,[2] that he who has seen one American has seen them all, has been much criticised. Molina considers it as a great exaggeration, and observes, that the error arose from similarity of colour; that all the tribes he had seen exhibited different features, and that a Chilese, for instance, was not less distinguishable from a Peruvian, than a German from an Italian. Hale also observes, that no two European nations differ from each other, in external aspect, so much as the Indians above, from those below the great Cataracts of Columbia. It is unnecessary to accumulate proofs that great differences between various tribes of America do exist. The fact, however, stands thus: that whilst peoples may be easily distinguished from each other, there exists a very great resemblance between the individuals belonging to the same people. The great uniformity of external aspect of the aboriginal Americans has also been noticed by Humboldt and Morton, the latter excepts only the Esquimaux. The features of the Botokudes are as various and diversified as among Europeans.[3] The Indians on the Orinoco form another exception.[4] It has been observed by many travellers, that it

[1] "Narrative of an expedition across the Prairies," p. 11, 1845.
[2] "Physikalische u. histor. nachrichten," ii, p. 92, Lpz., 1781.
[3] Prinz Maximilian zu Wied. "R. nach Brasil," ii, p. 4, 1820.
[4] Humboldt und Bonpland, "R. in d. Aeq.," iii, p. 493.

is difficult to distinguish in America males from females by the features of the face. Pickering[1] asserts this of the Mongolian race in general. This applies also to many Negro tribes. Huschke[2] observes, that the differences in the capacity of the cranium between the sexes is least in the Negro, and increases gradually up to the European. De Hell[3] found a great resemblance in the individuals of the Mongolian tribes on the Caspian Sea. D'Orbigny, as Humboldt did before him,[4] says the same of the aboriginal South Americans; thus permanence of type is, according to them, partly owing to the non-intermixture of the various tribes. It cannot be doubted that this great physical resemblance chiefly arises from deficient expression of psychical individuality, owing to the low state of mental culture. Among barbarous nations, says Humboldt,[5] we find rather a tribal than an individual physiognomy. Though these phenomena may perhaps not exactly be considered as a brute resemblance, still it has been remarked that even among our domestic animals there is a greater difference in external expression than among the same animals in a savage state. This difference may be the consequence of psychical development acquired in their relation and dependence on man. Köler, it is true,[6] ascribes to individuals of a Negro tribe the same diversity of features as among Europeans; but this is, excepting in mixed nations, incorrect, as there is no doubt that a uniformity of mental qualities exists among the same tribe. The slave dealer in Upper Egypt (Schendy) merely inquires after the native place of the slave, and not after his character, because long experience has shown him the importance of descent to be greater than that of individual character; thus, the Nubas and Gallas are considered as very faithful, those of Northern Abyssinia as treacherous and malicious, those of Fertit as savage and revengeful.[7] Though

1 "Races of man," p. 15, 1849.
2 Schädel, Hirn u. Seele, p. 48.
3 "Trav. in the steppes of the Caspian."
4 "R. in die aequinoctialg.," ed. Hauff., ii, p. 15.
5 "Neuspanien," i, p. 116.
6 "Notizen über Bonny," p. 91, 1848.
7 Katte, "R. in Abyssen.," p. 131, 1838; Burckhardt, pp. 423, 447.

Burmeister[1] speaks of great individual differences of physiognomy among Negroes, this is to be understood chiefly of national features, as individuals of different Negro peoples came under his inspection in Brazil. Among the Polynesians, and especially among the most gifted of them, the Fiji Islanders, the individuals of the same tribe exhibit as great differences in features as the inhabitants of any part of Europe.[2]

Though the uniformity of external aspect, which predominates among uncultivated nations, must be considered as partly owing to the influence of the mental state upon the body, we must not lose sight of another source from which such a uniformity arises. An assimilation of features and movements from involuntary imitation may arise, not only among single families, but among large communities, just like many linguistic expressions and other habits, and such will be especially the case if they lead a more secluded life. In the clans of Scotland, for instance, these family resemblances are very striking.[3] An assimilation may also be observed in a single individual who has lived for a series of years among a foreign tribe, and having adopted their manners and mode of life, has, to some extent, become one of them. Something of the kind was observed in Gützlaff, when he returned after a long residence in China. In America, especially, Europeans have been found among the Indians, whom they greatly resembled after a long residence among them. Similar cases have also occurred in New Zealand and Australia.

An analogous effect of the reaction of intellectual life is also seen in the circumstance that the free-born Negro children in Sierra Leone have better features, more intelligent eyes, and a nobler deportment and form than their liberated parents.[4] The same difference has been observed between the maroon and slave Negroes in Jamaica.[5] "The blacks cannot now be treated as formerly; they now think, hear, and see as well as

[1] "Geol. bilder.," ii, p. 101.
[2] Hale, loc. cit., pp. 10, 48.
[3] Jarrold, "Anthropologia; or, Diss. on the form and colour of man," p. 112, 1858.
[4] Norton, "A residence in S. Leone," p. 278, 1849.
[5] Dallas, "Gesch. der Maronen neger auf Jam.," p. 148, 1805.

the white, they have become more intelligent than they were, and will soon become still more so," said a Negro of Jamaica to Lewis.[1] The same difference between the free and the slaves among the Guaranis in Paraguay, Corrientes, and Bolivia, has been observed by D'Orbigny and Broc.

It is asserted that whenever in the West Indies a Negro is found occupying a superior position, he generally presents some Caucasian features, such as a longer or more hooked nose, resembling the Jewish physiognomy.[2] In whatever way these cases may be explained, they, at least, show that the bodily formation of the Negro has not that absolute permanence which some would ascribe to it; and though one might be inclined to confine their change of type within narrower limits than higher races, those who, like Nott, deny any change of the Negro in America, are evidently in the wrong.

Concerning mental qualifications we possess some sufficient and confirmed data. Stevenson[3] observed several times that the Negroes born in Peru possessed better mental capacity than those newly imported from Africa. He says nothing of physical differences, excepting that the Creole-Negroes are stronger and more athletic. According to Tschudi,[4] the newly imported Negroes are less lively than the Creole-Negroes, but patient and more faithful than the former. The greater capacities of the Creole-Negroes have been confirmed by the documents which the Commission of the French Chamber of Deputies received from the colonies in 1839. De Lisboa[5] agrees in this view, adding the observation, that these higher capacities must not be considered as a consequence of education, in which the Creoles are entirely deficient; hence the low state of mental capacity in Africa must be the result of social condition. Froberville also,[6] who considers the physical and moral sensibility of the Negro as considerably more obtuse than that of the white, speaks of the striking intellectual difference between the African parents and their children born in the colonies.

---

[1] "Journal of a resid. among the negroes of the West Indies," p. 84, 1845.
[2] Day, "Five years residence in the West Indies," i, p. 141, 1852.
[3] Loc. cit., pp. 179, 198.
[4] Loc. cit., i, p. 154.
[5] "Bullet. de la soc. Ethnol." p. 54, Janv. 1847.
[6] "Bullet. de la soc. Geogr.," ii, p. 326, 1847.

It is, besides, well known that Negroes born in America fetch higher prices than those newly imported, a fact which speaks plainly in favour of the superiority of the first. Such differences of mental capacities cannot be entirely unaccompanied by external changes, there being such a parallelism between physical and psychical life, that no great change can take place in the latter without re-acting upon the former, and giving it expression. Though such physical changes may not be demonstrated to any extent in the Negroes of America, it must be taken into consideration that it required a constant new importation of African Negroes to supply the slave population, and that comparatively there are but a small number of slaves whose ancestors have lived for many generations in America. The cases in which the latter circumstance exists belong mostly to the South of the United States, West Indies, and South America; as statistics have shown that Negroes thrive less in the New England states, though it may be going too far to maintain that climatic conditions render it impossible for them to perpetuate themselves in that quarter.

D'Orbigny[1] maintains that the type of the Negroes born in America is easily distinguished from that of the newly imported in whom it is more pronounced. Lyell (second journey) learned from many physicians in the slave states of North America, that the Negroes who had much intercourse with Europeans (independent of sexual intercourse), approach them gradually in shape of skull and form of body (in the course of several generations), and connects this with Dr. Hancock's observation, that even among the Negroes of Guinea a greater mental cultivation changed in course of time the general physiognomical expression, that the lower jaw and the shape of skull became modified. That such a difference is observed between the domestic and the plantation slaves (the latter preserving their original type), has already been observed by Prichard, who quotes Wisemann to that effect. Supported by such cases Ward[2] asserts that the Negroes in the course of 200 or 300 years had in some parts of America, without inter-

[1] Loc. cit., p. 143. [2] "Natural hist. of mankind," p. 157, 1849.

mixture with other races, partially lost their thick lips and projecting lower jaw, and their original peculiarities had been lessened under the influence of improved physical and moral conditions. Williamson[1] confirms this improvement of the Negro character, specially as regards the Negroes of Long Island; and Lavayssé[2] speaks of a better physical and intellectual condition of the Creole-Negroes, as founded upon the general experience of the planters. Stanhope Smith[3] says expressly that he does not speak of Mulattoes, but of pure Negroes, and observes that the well cared-for domestic slaves in America lose gradually their specific disagreeable odour; that their hair becomes less crisp, and grows in the third generation to the length of several inches. He states an instance, confirmed by many observers, of a Negro who without any disease had become white and straight haired. In New Jersey specially there are Negroes to be found with straight noses, well-formed foreheads, and straight incisors.[4] These instances, although they may not be considered as perfectly impartial observations, are too numerous, too definite, and too free from any suspicion as to their sources, to be rejected off hand. Two other circumstances are noteworthy; first, that the greatest changes in the Negroes occur in the North of the United States, whence it follows that the climatic conditions have not been without their influence; secondly, that just the third generation is mentioned as that in which the metamorphosis becomes appreciable, the same generation of which Philip[5] maintains that in the South African missions the shape of the crania of the children deviates from its original form, and commences to improve; and also Mallat[6] asserts, that in the third generation the tamed Negrito, of Manilla, becomes modified, and approaches in form and character the Tagales. Whether we are sceptical or not as to these instances, their coincidence is remarkable, and worthy of further investigation.

[1] "Observations on the climate of America," p. 42, New York, 1811.
[2] Loc. cit., pp. 139, 141.
[3] Loc. cit., p. 265.
[4] Loc. cit., p. 91, 115, 170
[5] "Researches in S. Africa," ii, p. 129, 1828.
[6] "Les Philippines," i, p. 45, 1846.

Similar instances of a greater or less metamorphosis of the physical type by altered conditions of civilization, occur also among us; only that in many of such cases it cannot be shown with certainty how far intermixture between several peoples has occasioned it; and this uncertainty becomes greater, inasmuch as the variations in civilization occur in consequence of the intercourse of these peoples.

If we were in possession of exact representations of the physical aspect of individuals of the same people at different periods, we might, by comparison, infer how far the external characters of a people correspond to the progress or retardation of its intellectual culture. De Salles remarks very justly, that all uncultured nations possess, in comparison with civilized nations, a large mouth and somewhat thick lips. Zimmermann[1] has directed attention to the great differences between the ancient and modern Germans, and endeavoured to explain them from changes of the climate and mode of life; but their spiritual culture must also have greatly contributed to the physical changes. The high stature, the light or red hair, the blue eyes, and the clear complexion which they possessed at the time of the Romans, have not, it is true, been lost by them, but have become less general. We find in Jarrold[2] the analogous assertion, that in the time of Henry VIII, red hair predominated in England, and that at the commencement of the fifteenth century, grey eyes were more general, and dark eyes and hair unfrequent. He also mentions, that the cheek bones of the English were then more prominent, as they are at present towards the north. This reminds us of the strong features presented by the old German painters, showing that our own physiognomy has not always been the same. More refined manners, mental emotions, and a diminished firmness of character appear to have softened the rigid, hard, and angular features.

As a further proof of the influence of intellectual culture on physical form, may be quoted the instance of the Sikhs, a religious sect, formed in 1469 by Nanaka, and which has since

---

1 "Geogr. gesch. des Menschen," i, p. 54, 1778.
2 Loc. cit., pp. 155, 216.

lived in an isolated state. Originally Hindoos of the Punjab, they are now strikingly distinguished from their nearest allied tribes, somewhat in the same degree as the Hindoos from the Chinese, by extremely regular features and an oval face.[1] They wear long beards,[2] and are said to resemble in face and deportment, more than any other Asiatic people, Europeans, with the single exception of the inhabitants of Cashmeer.[3]

The cases of the Osmanli-Turks and the Magyars are more difficult to deal with. The improved shape of the skull and of the features of the former in comparison with their allied tribes in Asia, has been ascribed to the handsome women of the harem; and the physical improvement of the Magyars, who at their arrival in Europe were of extreme ugliness, to their intermixture with Germans and Sclavonians. There are in European Turkey, about 700,000 Turks scattered among 15,000,000 of other tribes (Schafarik); and as the influence of the harem cannot have extended to the whole people, it is very probable, as is proved by historical evidence, that intermixture has largely taken place, less among the lower than among the higher classes, the language of the former containing less Arabian, Persian, and European elements than the written language and that used in conversation among the higher classes.[4] That theory has most in its favour which assumes that both intermixture and intellectual progress have contributed to improve the physical conformation of the Osmanlis. This, perhaps, is also the case as regards the Magyars. They differ at present very much from Finns, yet their language is Finnish, though some Indo-Germanic elements are found in it (Pott). Where they have remained less mixed and less cultivated, in some remote, chiefly mountainous parts, they possess the ungainly primitive type. The flat lands exhibit the transitions to a nobler type; they are conjoined in Szegedin. The peasants in Cumania and Jazygia are specially distinguished by handsome regular features.[5]

---

1 Prichard, iv, p. 240.
2 Malcolm, "Asiatic Researches," xi, p. 259.
3 Pavie in "Mém. de la soc. Ethnol.," i, p. 263.
4 Schleicher, "D. Spr. Europas," 1850.
5 Rey in "Nouv. ann. des voy.," ii, p. 113, 1849.

W. F. Edwards[1] describes, as peculiarities frequently occurring in Hungary—globular head, low receding forehead, oblique eyes, short flat nose, thick projecting lips, flat occiput, weak beard,[2] short stature. This form is manifestly very different from that of the Finns, nor can it be compared with that of the Lapps. It is almost a caricature of the Mongolian type; for the Finns have short conical crania, flat temples, and globular occiput; the skull of the Lapps is smaller and thinner.[3] One is certainly inclined to doubt the theory of the absolute permanence of types, and to adopt rather an extensive change in the form of the crania by climate and intellectual pursuits, when it is seen that Retzius is obliged to deny the affinity between Finns and Lapps, on account of the difference in shape of skull. The Finns were, in former times, the free owners of the soil; their monuments and their poetry testify of a high culture in past times; while the Lapps ever have been, and still are, miserable nomads. Might not the physical differences be considered as having gradually arisen? The Karele has an oval skull; the Savolax, a round one. The Tavastlander, a squarish-round skull, and yet the Finnish speaking Karele, we are told, is no Finn, but has lost his own language and appropriated another, merely because his head is oval.[4] Yet the Croats and Dalmatians do not show the Sclavonian type; whilst the old Egyptian type is still detected in the Fellahs; and the Greek type has been preserved in Greece, specially in the Morea (Pouqueville), notwithstanding the great admixture of foreign blood.[5]

There are other instances, very difficult to be explained from intermixture alone. We do not, therefore, consider that the linguist is justified in conceding so much in this respect to the anatomist and zoologist as Pott has done, who assumes[6] that intermixture has produced an essential change in physical

---

[1] "Des caractères phys. des races hum.," p. 73, 1829.
[2] The Magyars at this time have fine long beards, which are the objects of particular care.
[3] Retzius in "Müller's archiv.," p. 109, 1845; compare also Hueck, "De craniis Estonum," p. 10, 1838.
[4] Retzius, loc. cit., p. 394, 1848.
[5] Edwards, loc. cit., p. 101.
[6] "Die ungleichheit menschl. Rassen," p. 147, 1856.

formation among the Magyars, Osmanlis, Finns, and Samojeds, while they have preserved their language—that "an exchange of body" with foreign tribes has taken place without an exchange of soul; whilst on the other hand, the Romanic nations were compelled to adopt the Latin as their language without any great injury to the essential peculiarities of their corporeal structure. Without considering such a theory as absolutely impossible, we should still require more stringent proofs to support it; for intermixtures of great extent which alter the physical type of a people can scarcely be thought of, unless the language should experience a corresponding change. Where foreign races, as the Chinese in the East Indian Archipelago, bring no women with them, and can only ally themselves with native women, it cannot be wondered at that the mongrels belong to one type according to language, and to another according to race (at Java for instance, according to De Jong);[1] but such instances are among the rare exceptions. Though it is plainly shown, how among the Romanic nations the language of the conquerors replaced that of the conquered, the change which the Latin underwent corresponds to some extent with the physical metamorphosis by which the Celts in Gaul became the French of the present day, and the Iberians became Spaniards. How much must be ascribed to intermixture, or to many other causes, can be hardly ascertained. We are far too ready to ascribe it to the first cause simply because it affords a convenient explanation. When, for instance, the Finns are considered as originally a Mongolian people, which has improved its physical type by intermixture with the white race (Castren), the theory is objectionable on account of the linguistic development and its inflections, which certainly cannot be ascribed to the engrafting of Indo-Germanic elements upon a Mongolian foundation. With regard to the Magyars and Osmanli-Turks, it must be admitted, that the admixture of foreign elements has contributed to the change of their physical type, the extent of which

[1] "Reisen nach dem Vorgeb. der guten Hoffnung," ii, p. 373, 1803.

always depends on the degree of resistance to external and internal influences possessed by various races.

The shape of the cranium is now by many naturalists considered as an infallible criterion of race, and yet those who have devoted the greatest attention to the subject admit that the individual differences in the form of the cranium become greater in proportion to the higher intellectual development of a nation.[1] According to Engel,[2] there are but few deviations in the cranial structure among uncultivated nations, but many among civilized nations. We have already stated that this fact is, with some exceptions, generally correct; and if we repeat it here it is on account of the admission that the form of the cranium is liable to changes. Though Edwards[3] is of opinion that the effect of civilization amounts to very little as regards its influence upon physical development, because among the same people the most different degrees of culture are found in connexion with the same physical type—an axiom which denies that mental capacities are indicated by the shape of the cranium—we must bear in mind that to support such an opinion we would require a more exact division of national types than we at present possess. We find, however, instances which seem to prove that the form of the skull is by no means as constant as is usually asserted. Retzius, himself, found that the female skulls belonging to the higher and middle classes in Sweden are generally smaller than those of country people, and he considers this to be the consequence of a different mode of life and occupation. Latham[4] inserts a table from Wilson's "Archæology and Pre-historic Annals of Scotland," in which it is shown that the cranial capacity of the ancient Scots was less than at a later period, which he is inclined to consider as the result of civilization. With regard to Negroes, the old skulls of Negroes dug out in New York were, according to Dr. Warren, much thicker, and betrayed, phrenologically considered, much less mental capacity than the skulls of a recent date.[5] All this leads us to the view taken by Müller

[1] Retzius, loc. cit., p. 205, 1848.
[2] "Unters über schädelformen," p. 121.
[3] Loc. cit., p. 30.
[4] "Man and his migrations," p. 63, 1851.
[5] "Quarterly Review," June 1851.

and Engel, that the shape of the skull is everywhere essentially dependent on mental culture, and changes with it.

We may also mention, as bearing upon the investigation of this subject, the theory of Abbé Frère, who believes that the more original a human type is the more developed is the occiput and the flatter the forehead, whilst with the progress of civilization the forehead becomes more arched and the occiput flatter.[1] Huschke[2] observes that in the Negro the posterior lobes of the brain predominate, in the Mongolian race the middle lobes, and in the European the anterior lobes. Such assertions resemble, however, too much a phrenological scheme to be adopted without reserve.

The changes which physical peculiarities undergo, proceed as slowly as the progress of cultivation, hence they cannot be easily traced within historical times, especially as investigations on this subject have only been commenced in recent years. Though we may agree with Prichard, that the physical characters of nations correspond to their social and intellectual condition, we must take care not to go so far as to maintain with Courtet de l'Isle,[3] that the capacity for civilization and the intellectuality of races corresponds with their physical beauty. It is true that among nations, as among individuals, the intellectual faculties and performances give rise to corresponding expressions in the body; but if we were to admit that regular beauty is the natural expression of regular mental cultivation, and that nations approach this type in proportion to their mental development, it would follow that a one-sided development only in one direction or an imperfect development, however important otherwise, could not always produce a corresponding beautifying of the body.

On taking a retrospective view at the changes to which the external aspect of man is subject, we must, among the causes which produce them, consider those treated of last as not less influential than geographical and climatic conditions, to which too much importance has been attached. The phenomena which

---

[1] Serre's "Gazette médicale de Paris," 31 Juillet, 1852.
[2] Schädel, Hirn und Seele, p. 100.
[3] "Bullet. de la soc. Ethnol.," 1847.

we have learned to regard as the results of different degrees of mental culture, warn us not to under-estimate the latter. In confining ourselves here to the physical changes to which man is exposed, in order to show the exaggeration of the influence of climate and soil upon psychical life, we must first consider that a perfect dependence of man upon surrounding nature only occurs when he is in a primitive state; no sooner does he rise to a higher state of culture, than he ceases entirely to correspond to the natural conditions. There is another important circumstance which must be borne in mind, that no people can exactly in its external aspect correspond with surrounding nature, inasmuch as, probably without exception, all peoples have only arrived at their present localities after more or less extensive migrations. Hence, it is explicable how, from the various crossings and differences of direction which the peoples have taken in their migrations, we should find nations of such various types under the same degrees of latitude and under similar climatic conditions; for in consequence of these migrations, there must have been for them an accumulation of climatic influences, as Latham calls it.[1] By successively settling in different latitudes, they have for a shorter or longer time experienced various external influences, and have passed through different modes of life and degrees of culture.

Besides climate, physical and mental culture, there is another source whence arise the changes to which the organism is subject in the course of many generations: namely, the *spontaneous origin of new peculiarities*. This can only be reduced to a predisposition in certain individuals to deviate from the physical form of their parents without our being able to explain the how and the why these deviations occur, and whence they arise in those who first exhibit them. It is for this reason that we term such peculiarities *spontaneous*, and consider them specially, although it can scarcely be doubted that they are owing to the same causes which have occupied our attention hitherto.

[1] Latham, "Nat. Hist. of the varieties of man."

It is a well known fact, that neither any two individuals nor children of the same parents are perfectly like each other, but that sometimes there exist considerable differences. Under favourable circumstances these characteristic differences are permanently transmitted to the offspring, whence may arise the changes to which individuals of the same stock are subject, which may contribute to an explanation of the differences existing in the physical organization of mankind. The differences originating in this way become only permanently fixed, if such individuals as possess them intermarry: cases which, in modern civilized states of Europe, with its abundant population and the separation of the various ranks of society, but rarely occur, but which happened more frequently in primitive states of society, when families lived in a comparatively isolated state without much intercourse with foreign tribes. It has been objected to this theory of the differences exhibited by the races of mankind, that such spontaneous deviations from the type of the primitive stock are not permanent, but disappear again after a few generations (Morton). This objection, however, loses its importance on casting even a superficial glance at our domestic animals, among whom it is shown that the breed may be permanently improved.

With regard to plants, it is now generally assumed that the seed propagates the species only, but not always the variety. In the animal world, deviations from the original type arise and disappear more easily in some species than in others, and, according to Prichard,[1] are more permanently transmitted, if the deviations have arisen from pre-disposition rather than from external circumstances. The breeding of domestic animals is founded on the transmission of such spontaneous, and not easily explicable, peculiarities, namely—colour and quality of skin and hair, tendency to become fat, strength, size and shape. Even mental qualities are improved by the pairing of corresponding individuals.[2]

The transmission of physical and mental qualities has been

---

[1] Loc. cit., i, p. 374.

[2] Many examples of this kind of individual peculatities having become hereditary, may be found in Heusinger, "Anthropol.," p. 98, and "Lucas, Traité de l'hérédité," i, pp. 239, 291, 1847.

specially observed in domestic animals; and though in most cases of this kind there is only a disposition to propagate new races, which soon disappears,[1] it may be owing partly to the discontinuance of favourable circumstances, and partly to the deficiency of individuals distinguished by similar characteristics which can be paired, to fix the deviation as a permanent character of a new race. That new races really originate in this way is proved by many instances. One of the best known examples of this kind is the so-called Otter-Sheep, bred from a sheep of peculiarly long body and short legs, in Massachusetts (1791), which propagated rapidly in North America, and the breed was liked on account of their inability to surmount the fences.[2] This race appears to be permanent, so that on being crossed with the common sheep, the mongrel resembles either one or the other race.[3] In a similar manner the uncloven hoof has become hereditary in the Hungarian cattle. A bull without horns in Paraguay produced only calves without horns (Azara); a buck goat with cartilaginous prominent nasal organs, transmitted these peculiarities to its offspring (Pallas). Similar instances are found in Jarrold, Foissac, Knight.[4] That temperament is equally transmissible is shown in the docility, or restiveness, and biting and kicking propensities, of horses.

Still more important than the transmission of innate individual peculiarities, is the inheritance (by no means rare) of such qualities which have only accidentally arisen. To this belong the successful cases of acclimatization, which tell at first much on the physical organism, whilst the succeeding generations find themselves as well off in their new home as their parents in their old climates. At a height of 9,000 feet above the level of the sea in Mexico, harriers were found useless, but their offspring are now well fitted for coursing (Lyell). The

---

[1] Lucas (ii, 896) arrives at the conclusion, that the pecularities arising in the course of time, are so much less permanent in proportion as they deviate from the species, and have only lasted for a few generations, especially when the favourable circumstances which gave rise to them cease to exist.

[2] "Philos. Trans.," 1813.

[3] Bachman in Smith, "Unity of the hum. races," p. 310.

[4] "Philos. Transact., 1837."

geese introduced in Bogotá laid at first but few eggs, only one fourth were hatched, and half of these perished. In the second generation the geese began to thrive. Mutilations also are sometimes transmitted. Williamson[1] saw in Carolina, dogs which have been deficient in tails for three or four generations in consequence of one of their ancestors having accidentally lost it. A cow, three years old, which had lost by suppuration her left horn, produced three calves, which instead of the left horn presented only a small protuberance on the skin (Thär). Dogs and horses whose tails or ears are clipped, as the draught dogs in Kamtschatka,[2] often transmit these deficiencies to their offspring (Blumenbach). This can scarcely surprise us when we consider that even psychical qualities, which have only been acquired in the course of life, are equally transmissible. Wherever oxen have not been used as draught animals, it is much more difficult to accustom them to it, than where the custom has existed for some generations (Sturm). This applies also to horses, milch cows, the barking of dogs, and the mewing of cats. Dogs who return to a wild state no longer bark, and cats are said not to mew in America. It is further known that docility is hereditary in dogs, especially in shepherd and hunting dogs. Where fox-hunting is usual, the young foxes are, even without any previously acquired experience, more timid and cautious (Leroy). Other instances of transmission of acquired instinct may be found in Lucas.[3] In many of these cases we must certainly not be too hasty to ascribe to nature what may perhaps be owing to the instinct of imitation, as in the instance cited by Carpenter,[4] that some dogs do not attack the Pecári singly but in packs, whilst others choose the less advantageous mode of attack. That acquired psychical qualities are capable of transmission, by producing a corresponding disposition in the offspring, cannot be doubted.

It would be premature to explain the origin of human varieties from these observations made on animals; it must, however,

---

[1] Loc. cit., p. 40.
[2] Langsdorff, "Bemerk. auf e. R. um d. Welt," ii, pp. 236, 1812.
[3] Loc. cit., ii, pp. 479, 482.
[4] Loc. cit., p. 421.

be admitted, that they are more to the purpose than those given in favour of the theory of a specific difference between human races—a theory chiefly supported by the assumption that the same peculiarities have been transmitted through an indefinite period of time. If we are justified from the few instances of prolific hybridity, in contesting the law that unlimited prolificacy only occurs within the species, we might be equally justified in explaining the origin of races from the exceptional transmission of deformities. At any rate, the cases of transmission of individual peculiarities are sufficient to point out the way in which the origin of various races was possible, though we may not be able to learn how it actually occurred. The facts of the transmission of acquired physical or mental qualities to the offspring, present very interesting psychological phases in their progressive transformation and development of a people. In turning now our attention to man, we must remind the reader that we do not require the analogy presented by animals, since hereditary transmission in the human race can be proved by many instances. Although we shall here only enumerate those cases in which deformities have shown themselves hereditary, they cannot be considered as invalid; for though it may be objected, that the physical differences of mankind are not to be considered as morbid deviations from a normal type, this fact may be admitted without any weakening of the argument. In the first place, it is not only in many instances impossible to decide whether an inherited peculiarity is a morbid one or not, but the fact itself of the transmission of deformities can also be looked upon as a special case of the general rule, that, deviating peculiarities of the organization are frequently transmitted to the offspring, so that each instance yields a new contribution to the proof of such transmission.

That family peculiarities of various kinds are regularly transmitted, is a well-known fact. The most frequently quoted instances of this kind are, the thick lip of the House of Hapsburg since its alliance with the Jagellones; the tall life-guards of Frederic I. of Prussia, who produced a large sized progeny. Colour and quality of the skin are also transmitted, and so are temperament, acuteness, idiocy, or deficiencies in the organs of sense. Instances of hereditary blindness and deafness, and of alternating dumbness, so that every second or third child was deaf, are given by Lucas. Harris[1] communicates a case of hereditary blindness in one eye, and of a double thumb on the right hand. The so-called porcupine men of the family Lambert, with their excrescences on the hands and feet, have often been quoted. Thomson has endeavoured to prove that the peculiarities of the skin are transmitted in the male line, which he supports by many illustrative cases.[2] In Birmah, remarkably hirsute men have been met with, to whom the peculiarity was transmitted through three generations.[3] There are also instances recorded of six-fingered, six-toed, and of web-footed individuals who transmitted these peculiarities to their offspring. The frequent tendency of succeeding generations to reproduce deviations presents itself also in the hereditary transmission of a number of diseases, such as goître, cretinism, and mental affections.

Albinism may also be mentioned, which in some parts, especially in the Isthmus of Darien, is so prevailing that the Albinoes have been considered as a distinct race. Coreal heard them thus described.[4] At a later period Wafer gave an account of these Albinoes.[5] Blumenbach[6] has already shown that it occurs sporadically in man and animals in every part and in every race. Though we cannot altogether agree with Prichard, who denies that there is anything morbid in Albinism, and only ascribes to Albinoes a more delicate organization than that of the white, the supposition of G. Forster,[7] that light-complexioned men, when they exist among dark races, have frequently, but erroneously, been described as Albinoes, is probably correct. From the looseness of descriptions, this cannot always be decided, which is the less surprising as skin diseases have frequently been mistaken for Albinism. Blumenbach has pointed out that white-spotted Negroes must

1 "The Highlands of Ethiopia," 2nd edition, i, p. 286.
2 "Edinb. Med. Journal," Dec., p. 501, 1858.
3 "Ausland," p. 461, 1858.
4 "Voy. aux Indes occ.," ii, 140, Amst., 1772.
5 "Merkw. R. nach Darien," p. 117, Halle, 1759.
6 "De. gen. hum. var. nat.," p. 278.
7 "Sämmtliche Schriften," iv, 231.

be distinguished from such as have become spotted from disease, which frequently occurs also among Malabars and Tartars. When, therefore, Bennett[1] speaks of an Australian with flaxen hair, light-blue eyes, and a white skin covered with small brown spots; and Raffenel,[2] of a Negro whose skin was as white as that of sunburnt Europeans, whose beard and hair were red, the iris greenish; and when Proyart[3] describes a similar case, reminding us of the well-known portrait in Blumenbach, these instances relate to Albinism.[4] This, however, does not apply to the instances mentioned by Lander,[5] of a light-brown man of Negro descent with Negro features, brown eyes, and white eyebrows; and also of a "coal-black" man with light-brown eyes. Mollien[6] found among the Fulahs men nearly white, who, he expressly declares, were not Albinoes; and Prichard cites similar instances.

We shall, in the sequel, cite many cases exhibiting individual deviations from the national type. These, however, can but rarely become permanent, as the national type is always that which harmonizes with the soil and the climate, and the external relations in which the respective peoples live. There are, however, among the Black-feet and Mandans of North America, some who have an almost white skin and ruddy cheeks, and whole families with grey or mixed grey hair;[7] and among the Chaouia-Berbers in the Auras Mountains the absence of the lobule of the ear, which also occurs among the Cagots in Spain, has doubtless become general from an accidentally-arisen peculiarity.[8]

Instances are not wanting of mutilations that have been transmitted from parents to children; such, however, occur less frequently, according to Blumenbach. The children of an officer whose little finger had been cut across and become

---

[1] "Wanderings in N. S. Wales," i, p. 437, 1834.

[2] "Voy. dans l'Afrique occ.," p. 228, 1846.

[3] "Hist. de Loango," p. 196, 1776.

[4] Details on its occurrence in Africa may be found in Raffenel, "Nouv. voy.," i, p. 227, 1856.

[5] "Reise zur Erforschung des Niger," i, p. 124, 1833.

[6] "R. in d. Innere von Afr." p. 57, 1820.

[7] Prinz Max. zu Wied, "R. in N. Am.," ii, p. 106, 1839.

[8] Guyen, in l'Institut, ii, p. 92, 1848; and "Nouv. ann. des voy.," ii, p. 398, 1848.

crooked, possessed an analogous defect. Gosse[1] cites the case of an officer wounded in the battle of Eylau, who transmitted to his offspring a scar on the forehead. Other instances of inherited deformities are found in R. Wagner.[2] It has not been established that, among peoples who give an artificial form to the skull, succeeding generations exhibit a similar shape. Pöppig considers it probable, and Rathke[3] is inclined to believe it from the shape of the skulls (macrocephalic) found near Kertch, in the Crimea: Tschudi and Morton maintain the contrary. Gosse[4] cites several instances in which irregular cranial shapes, originating in families hitherto strange to it, were transmitted by the parents; but he adds, very justly, that a regular transmission of artificial cranial shapes is not to be expected when, as is usual, the heads of the boys only and not of the girls, are artificially deformed.

European children, compared with those of savage nations, show that the form of the toes in the new-born is affected by the habits of the parents of wearing boots and shoes. It seems not yet to have been investigated how far this is the case in the girls of the higher classes in China. On directing our attention to psychical life, we meet with an hereditary transmission of character in many instances. Among uncultured nations we find first an instinctive use of the senses, independent of all education and imitation, and which differs from that of the civilized man. The Polynesian throws his children, who have not yet attempted to swim, into the water, apparently without any injury; the mountaineer allows his infant to play near declivities, dangers to which the citizen would scarcely expose his children. Children of the natives of Pitcairn (mongrels of the White and Tahitians) swam when but two or three years old merrily about in the surf.[5] The three year old children of the Choños, in South America, throw themselves into the water to swim.[6] It does not, therefore, seem to be a

[1] "Essai sur la déform. art. du crâne," p. 7, note, 1855.
[2] "Naturgesch. des menschen," ii, p. 245, and Lucas, ii, p. 490.
[3] Müller's Archiv, p. 147, 1843.
[4] Loc. cit., pp. 134, 138.
[5] Bennett, "Narrative of a whaling voy.," i, p. 35, 1810.
[6] King and Fitzroy, "Narr. of the surveying voy. of the Adventure and Beagle," append., p. 127, 1839.

great performance that the Arab children, from seven to eight years, in Lower Mesopotamia, cross the stream.[1] The four year old children of the Gauchos in South America are perfectly skilful horsemen.[2] Among the Bushmen babies creep about, children not one year old walk about boldly, whilst those a little older dig out the onions in the fields.[3] As the child of the civilized man instinctively adopts the habits of his parents, so does the child of the uncultured, which is moreover with difficulty civilized, and always retains a tendency to return to the mode of life of the parents. Supported by such and similar facts, which we shall investigate hereafter, Rush, Girou, Spurzheim, Burdach, and others, have maintained that acquired mental development is transmitted just as is physical development. Lucas especially has given many instances to that effect. Nott and Gliddon maintain that the development of civilization among peoples does not depend so much upon the mental effort to attain certain objects, nor upon the concatenation of external circumstances, as upon innate and inherited instincts, which are nobler among nations capable of cultivation than among uncivilized peoples, where the instincts are more of an animal nature. This opinion has been expressed by others in different terms, namely, that the lower a people stands in the scale of civilization, its mode of life is more instinctive; the more the people becomes civilized the more the instincts are replaced by a conscious mode of life.

How frequently mechanical and artistic talents, and even the predilection for certain kinds of occupation, are transmitted from the father to the son and grandson is well known, and may be explained by a particular capacity for a peculiar use of the limbs and a higher perfection in the employment of the senses, having its origin in organic causes. But the extent of such hereditary transmission is not only limited to qualities of psychical life depending on physical conditions, but also to what is the proper source of it, for there is no doubt that we find a higher mental activity and capacity among some tribes

[1] Ritter, "Erdk.," xi., p. 970.
[2] Scarlett, "South Am. and the Pacific," 1838. Head, "Rough notes taken during journies across the Pampas," p. 20, 1826.
[3] Lichtenstein, "R. im Südl. Africa," p. 376, 1811.

than among others, just as we find differences in this respect among individuals of the same tribe. Thus the missionaries in Hindostan found that the children of the Brahmins possessed greater capacities, and were generally more gifted, than those of the lower castes. The history of artists, scholars, and of reigning houses shows that great mental power, energy, and a capacity for mental development continues in the same family sometimes for several generations, whilst others exhibit just the contrary, which is proved by the histories of families in common life. In such cases we must be careful not to ascribe to natural disposition what may perhaps be the consequence of imitation and education. Admitting all this, we still find such a similar development of mind and character as cannot be explained otherwise than by hereditary transmission.

However little we may be inclined to assume an hereditary aristocracy of the mind, and though we admit that if it existed it would not be permanent, the fact still remains that there are, not only with regard to mental capacity, men of coarser or more refined organization, but families, castes and tribes who are preferentially distinguished by such peculiarities, and in whom they are for a long time transmitted.

The gist of all these facts lies in this, that under favourable circumstances there is regular transmission of original and merely individual peculiarities, and that this transmission may also occur as regards not merely innate, but also acquired, characters. Even where community of descent is unquestionable among a people which we have no reason to suppose of mixed origin, and among families, we observe individuals of different physical and mental capacities transmit their special qualities to succeeding generations, among whom they become more or less permanent. If we take into consideration the great variety of characters which families and classes of every population present, we recognize in this difference of individuals upon which the formation of races is founded, an important law of nature, apparently destined to be a counterpoise to the law of permanence of species, and the constancy of the transmission of its characters.

In concluding our observations on the causes upon which, by their combined action, the changes in the physical organization of man depends, we arrive at the following results.—The assertion that the physical type possessed by the respective races remains entirely permanent is erroneous; it is only as to the limits of certain changes that doubts exist. It is impossible to determine the exact influence of each individual agent, or to point out its limits. The theory which has most in its favour is, that mental culture possesses the greatest influence, climatic conditions alone have the least, diet and mode of life hold an intermediate place. Finally, the spontaneous origin and transmission of new qualities appear among the most influential agents in the production of differences among mankind. Still it must be borne in mind that it can only become extensive in its effects among a people where cultivation has obtained a firm soil, or where the original uniformity of individuals, both externally and internally, no longer exists, and where the acquired qualities are transmitted externally to succeeding generations.

SECTION II.

THE CHIEF ANATOMICAL AND PHYSIOLOGICAL DIFFERENCES WHICH DISTINGUISH THE VARIOUS RACES.

In the preceding section we have investigated the nature and the extent of the changes to which the human frame is subject, and traced them to their causes. If we are to arrive at any conclusion on the question whether all the peoples of the globe belong to one species, or whether specific differences exist among them, we must study the anatomical and physiological facts. By doing so we may learn, whether the extent of the existing differences is within the sphere of physical change, the causes of which are traceable.

If we must, on the one hand, examine the differences among mankind with regard to bodily shape and physical life, and the changes to which they are subject, it is not the less necessary, in order to arrive at any result, to compare these changes with those which occur among animals standing next to man in organization. We shall therefore examine the characteristics of the ape. In doing so we shall not enter into any minute details, but simply point out the main differences, which are as follows.—The brain of the ape[1] is considerably smaller in volume and inferior in development to that of man. The face is distinguished by a flattened nose and a projecting lower jaw, small chin, the lips deficient in fulness, facial angle small (30-33° in adults). The external ear is, compared with the human ear, of a very rude form, and without a lobule. The teeth are unequal and distant from each other. The size of the canine teeth is considerable compared with the rest, and the first premolar is of a conical form and larger than the second premolar tooth. The ape has an inter-maxillary bone, which is however absent in some species, and the occipital foramen is situated considerably backwards. The pelvis is of small extent and narrower laterally than it is in its antero-posterior diameter, contrary to its shape in man. The vertebral column has a single curve, which is concave towards the abdomen. The upper extremities and the hands are longer than in man; the foot is in fact a large curved hand, the ape having four opposable thumbs, those of the forehands being small, and only capable of motion together with the other fingers. The thighs are also curved; the heelbone directed upward, so that the ape approaching nearest to man cannot without difficulty walk upon the sole, but does so upon the edges. These circumstances, and the position of the occipital foramen, render the ape fit to climb, whilst the anatomical structure of man proves him to be intended to walk upright. The hair, the length of the body, the limitation as to climate and food, and the duration of life, are also important distinctions between the ape and man. The slow growth, the protracted childhood, and late appearance of puberty, the deficiency in instinct, menstruation, special diseases, the power of language, of laughing and crying, are other physiological marks which distinguish man from the ape.

The chimpanzee and the recently-discovered tschego[2] on the Gaboon river, belonging to the genus *Troglodytes*, approach

[1] "On the differences between man and the ape in osteological respects." See Owen in "Transact. of the Zool. Soc.," i, 343.

[2] Prof. Waitz here alludes to the *Troglodytes tschego* of Duvernoy ("Archives du Muséum," vol. viii, 4to, Paris).—ED.

nearest to man, but they still exhibit the above differences. The gorilla[1] presents as regards the form of the hand a greater resemblance to man than the chimpanzee, orang and gibbon. It has only eight carpal bones; flattened nails; the length of the hand is less, the breadth proportionally greater than in other apes.[2]

There are many narrations of past and modern times of men who were said to resemble apes. Thus, their existence in Tschittagong is still believed in India; they are said also to inhabit the region between Palmo, Tschumbulpur, and the sources of the Nerbudda.[3] We cannot be surprised at such a belief, since the ape appears as a caricature of man. Some negroes consider apes as men, who will not speak in order not to be compelled to labour. It is scarcely necessary to add that hitherto all stories about ape-like men have come to nothing. The truth is limited to the known fact, that the negro most resembles the ape; here we intend to compare their typical peculiarities. Assertions like those of Nott and Gliddon,[4] that the Hottentots and Bushmen are morally and physically but little distinguished from the orang-utang, and do not differ more from it than the former from the European, are shameless exaggerations,[5] which need not occupy us, being advanced in the interest of the slave-holder and slave-dealer, and accepted only in America. Thus it will probably be with the tails (of 1½ to 2 inches in length) which lately Koegel[6] asserts to have seen on some inhabitants of the Sunda Islands, specially among the Dajaks, and also in the Moluccas. Should this be confirmed, it may perhaps be nothing more than an abnormal elongation of the os coccygis. Ehrenberg[7] treats of the frequency of confounding apes with men, and of the cynocephalus of the Egyptians.

---

1 "Gorilla gina," Geoff. St. Hil.

2 "Comptes rendus, xxxvi, p. 925, 1853.

3 "Ausland," p. 1200, 1855.

4 "Types of mankind," pp. 182 and 457, 1854.

5 Many other exaggerations are found in that work. Thus, it is asserted that Africa south of 10° N., is only inhabited by men whose intellect is as dark as their skin, and whose cranial formation renders every expectation of a future improvement an Utopian dream.

6 "Ausland," p. 1103, 1858.

7 "Abh. der K. Akad., der Wiss.," 1833.

The most distinctly-marked Negro-type is, as Prichard justly observes, found only between the tropics, especially in the interior of the northern half of that region, the so-called Soudan, and on the western coast of Africa. According to Latham,[1] the Negro region extends only from the Niger to Senegal, and a portion of Senaar, Kordofan, and Darfur. The anthropological peculiarities found there are the following:— The skeleton of the Negro is heavier, the bones thicker and larger in proportion to the muscles than in the European.[2] This is especially the case with regard to the skull, which is hard and unusually thick, so that in fighting, Negroes, men and women, butt each other like rams[3] without exhibiting much sensibility. Among some of them, the temporal bone is immediately connected with the frontal bone, as in the *simia troglodytes*; this however is not constant, and is sometimes found among Mongols.[4] Duncan[5] says that in Dahomey skulls without any longitudinal or transverse sutures are by no means rare. According to Sömmering,[6] the capacity of the skull is absolutely less, and all the dimensions of the head smaller, than in the European; the efferent nerves are thicker and the brain harder and smaller in proportion (Monroe, Pruner,) decidedly as in apes. This has been generally denied by Tiedemann,[7] but has in other respects been confirmed by him in his representation of the cerebrum (Tab. v.) of a Bushwoman, which in regard to development and convolutions is not less inferior to that of the Negro than that of the latter to the European. That the convolutions in the Negro brain are less numerous and more massive than in the European (in whom they also vary) appears certain.[8] The similarity of the Negro brain to that of the ape is limited to this; for the cranial capacity of the Negro is not (as Blumenbach, Lawrence,

---

1 "Nat. hist. of the var. of man," p. 471, 1850.
2 Pruner "Die Krankheiten des Orients," p. 64, 1847.
3 Hamilton Smith, "Nat. hist. of the human species," p. 190.
4 Hollard, "De l'homme et des races hum.," p. 251, 1853.
5 "Journey in West Africa," ii, p. 246, 1848.
6 "Ueber d. körperl. Verschiedenheiten des Negers vom Europäer," p. 51, 1785.
7 "D. Hirn des Negers," 1837.
8 "Burmeister Geol. Bilder," ii, 123.

and Morton, in Cran. Amer., have maintained) less than that of all other races.[1] The coronal region is arched in the Negro, but the forehead is often less developed than in the European woman (Huschke). The Negro brain thus possesses the type of the female and the child's brain, and approaches that of the superior apes. This does not agree with what Sömmering states, viz. that the transition from the occiput to the back is flatter in the Negro than in the European, nor with Burmeister, that the Negro possesses a shorter and less projecting occiput. The latter has endeavoured to explain from this circumstance the backward position of the occipital foramen, which is denied by Prichard, and declared by Latham as not constant, whilst Hollard admits a slight difference in this respect, and so does Arnoux,[2] observing, however, that the particular form of the Negro required such, but does not in any degree prevent the erect posture of the head.

The superficies of the face, which is usually described as small, is nevertheless, in proportion to the surface of the cranium, larger than in the European (Sömmering, Lawrence). Whilst in the European the forehead, the nasal region, and mouth and chin, form equal sections of the face, there is in the Negro a considerable increase in the lower part (Burmeister). The facial angle is little above seventy degrees, and the projecting jaw gives to the face a snout-like appearance. The small laterally-compressed skull gives ample space to the temporal muscles, from the great development of which in length and breadth the lateral compression of the skull has been explained. The forehead is small and globular, its surface uneven and knotty (Blumenbach). The eyes,—the sockets of which, according to Prichard, are not larger than in the European, but described as larger by Sömmering,—are narrow, black, and protuberant, mostly with a yellow conjunctiva (Pruner), frequently exhibiting blood-vessels.[3] The cheek-

---

[1] See Tiedemann, W. Hamilton, Parchappe, "Rech. sur l'encéphale," and Huschke, Schädel, Hirn, und Seele, 1854; the latter of whom gives 37·57 ounces of brain in 54 cases; for the Malay, only 36·41 in 98 cases.

[2] "Bullet. Soc. Ethnol.," 1847.

[3] Clapperton "Tageb. der zweiten R. ins innere v. Afr.," p. 184, 1830.

bones are prominent, and the thick flat nose, with wide nostrils, projects, together with the jaws, from the face. The ethmoid bone is much developed. To this has been ascribed the great development of the sense of smell in the Negro, but it must be remarked that this occurs only exceptionally among Negro people. The nasal cavity is like the buccal cavity, more spacious than in the European; the nasal cartilage is deficient in development.[1] The lips (especially the upper lip) are puffy, and on that account very different from those of the ape; their colour varies from a dirty rose colour to that of cherry red, and from dark red to tawny (Sömmering), or is brown externally and red internally. The upper jaw is stretched, directed forwards, the tongue thick and large, the palatine arch larger and longer than in the European. The space for the teeth is said to be very large, so that the hindmost molar tooth can be more developed. There are sometimes six molars, the incisors are not perpendicular, the superior especially are long and inclined forwards. The whiteness of the teeth, which has been considered as a peculiarity of the race, appears to be produced by rubbing them with vegetable fibres, chalk, etc.[2] There are also regions where many bad and decayed teeth are seen, for instance, in Nyffe. The Negro has no inter-maxillary bone, but only, as the European in childhood, a rut which marks it. The chin is small, but broad and receding. The masseter, as well as the temporal muscles, are much developed. The external ear projects out of the head, is small, but not, as in the monkey, broad and flat (Burmeister); it is more equally rounded than in the European (Pruner), and as generally among the inferior races the *helix* is said to be flatter, but the *tragus* and the lobule smaller (Vollard, p. 99). The voice of the Negro is low and hoarse in the males, but acute and shrieking among the women (H. Smith).

The hair of the Negro, which does not gradually, as in the European, diminish towards the temple and the neck, ceases

---

[1] Dutenhofer, "Ueber die Emancip. d. Neger.," 1855.

[2] W. Müller, "Die Afr., Landschaft Fetu," 1676; Lander, "Reise zur Erforschung des Niger," iii, p. 94, 1833; Raffenel, "Voy. dans l'Afr. occ.," p. 198, 1846; Hecquard, "R. a. d. Kuste u. in d. innere v. West-Afr.," 1854.

abruptly like a wig (Sömmering). In some spots it is entirely wanting, so that among the Hottentots, Bushmen, and Austral Negroes of the South Sea, it grows in separate tufts. Although essentially differing from the wool of animals, it much resembles it. Its curl is, according to Henle, owing to its elliptic form. It is harder, more elastic and shining than that of the European. It is usually not longer than three inches, which is not owing to being cut, for all Negroes in Brazil like long hair (Burmeister). This natural shortness of the hair is said not to be general. Many Negro tribes regularly cut their hair, and, if frequently combed, it is said to reach, on the coast of Guinea, the length of a foot.[1] Dandolo[2] saw among the Bakkara on the White Nile a couple of very black Negresses with enormous heads of hair like a wig, half a metre in circumference. It seems however doubtful whether in these instances, pure Negroes are meant. The beard is mostly very scanty, and grows only in advanced age; whiskers are generally wanting, hence the pride of the Moors living among the Negroes, who by their beards exhibit their Arab descent,[3] and the high value put, in Ashantee, upon a strong beard.[4] Chest and body are but little, arms and legs not at all, covered with hair.

The relatively thick and strongly developed neck of the Negro, shorter by an inch than that of the European, combined with a less curved vertebral column, enables him to carry easily burdens upon the head, so that the Fantis for instance prefer, in carrying stones, to place the wheelbarrow upon the head.[5] The chest is larger and more arched than in the European. The pelvis is narrower, more conical, all its diameters are smaller, hence the belly is more pendulous. Vrolik[6] has shown its similarity to that of the ape. With regard to the limbs, White has drawn attention to the greater relative length of the forearm in the Negro. In the European

---

1 Isert, "Neue R. nach Guinea," p. 164, 1790.
2 Viaggio in Egitto, "Nel Sudan e Mil.," p. 271, 1854.
3 M. Park, "Voy. dans l'Intérieur de l'Afr., Paris," an viii, i, 247.
4 Bowdich, "Mission von S. Coast nach Aschante," p. 391, 1820.
5 Duncan, loc. cit.
6 "Consid. sur la diversité des bassins," 1826.

the proportion of the female arm is =12 : 9 : 6; in the male =12,5 : 10,5 : 7; in the Negro woman =12 : 10 : 7; in the Negro =12,8 : 9,6 : 7,5; hence the hands appear in the Negro as long drawn with a relatively small breadth. The Negro has fine white nails, but which feel hard like wood (Burmeister). Daniell[1] says on the other hand that, according to his measurements, the fingers and the hands only are longer than in the European, but not the arms.

The skin between the fingers reaches higher up in the Negro than in the European.[2] The leg is, on the whole, longer, but the flat foot, which is but little arched, the ankle being but one and one-third by one and a half above the ground, reduces it in such a manner, that the leg appears short. The upper part of the thigh is not full, the Negro generally being not prone to become fat. The knees are somewhat bent, the calves weak, as if laterally compressed. Bandy-legs are frequent, probably in consequence of the mode in which the mothers carry their children on the back. On account of the weakness of the legs, the Negro is said to be very sensible to a blow on the shinbones.[3] The heel of the Negro is longer and broader and the foot longer than in the European, a peculiarity which is also said to belong to Mulattoes even after they have become white.[4] The toes are small, the first smaller than the second, and separated from it by a free space (Burmeister). The sesamoid bones are more numerous in the Negro than in the European (Sömmering). Duttenhofer[5] states that a Negro can stand for hours upon the extreme edge of one or both feet, a task we should imagine most painful for him considering the flatness of his feet.

As regards the *blood* of the Negro, various statements are to be found in Sömmering. Pruner describes it as black and pitchy; Foissac[6] and Omboni[7] deny a difference in colour of the

---

1 "L'Institut," ii, p. 88, 1846.
2 Van der Hoeven.
3 Day, "Five years resid. in the W. Indies," ii, p. 98, 1852.
4 Day, loc. cit., i, p. 51.
5 Loc. ct., p. 83.
6 Loc. cit.
7 "Viaggi nell. Afr., occ. Mil.," p. 159, 1845.

Negro blood from that of the European. T. W. de Müller[1] observes that in hot climates the arterial blood of white and coloured men also resembles venous blood, in consequence of the greater quantity of carbon contained in it; and it has been asserted that the predominance of the latter induces mental indolence. The choleric and phlegmatic temperaments only are said to prevail among Negroes. The greatly developed genitals exhibit frequent turgescence. The glandular system is much developed (Pruner). The stomach has a rounder shape (Sömmering).

The *skin* affords to the Negro a greater protection against the rays of the sun than to the European, as, exposed to the sun for a longer time, it is not blistered; it is also perceptibly thicker on the whole body than that of the European; it is always cool and velvety to the touch. With regard to the latter point, the savage natives of Central Africa are said to form an exception, as their skin becomes wrinkled and chapped.[2] It is more or less black according to the deposition of the pigment, which (according to an analysis not entirely to be relied upon), consists of nine-tenths of carbon to one-tenth iron and fat (De Müller), and is found in the common cells of the mucous layer of the epidermis, and not in special pigment cells, whilst the dermis of the Negro is like that of the European.[3] This pigment, which is wanting in the Negro fœtus, is also deposited in the mucous layer under the nail,[4] and in the membranes of the brain (De Müller), exceptionally, though rarely, also on the gums and the velum palati,[5] and upon the tongue (Pruner). The palms only, and the soles of the feet, are of a lighter colour, the first, frequently of European whiteness (Burmeister). According to Flourens' former opinion there was said to exist between the epidermis and dermis an organ absent in the white, which contained the colouring matter; he has, however, now adopted the prevailing opinion that there is no difference in

---

[1] Loc. cit., p. 45.
[2] D'Escayrac die Afr. Wüste und das Land der Schwarzen, p. 186, 1855.
[3] Kölliker, "Microscop. anat."
[4] Beclard, "Anat. générale," p. 309.
[5] Arnoux, "Bullet. soc. ethnol.," p. 52, 1847.

the structure of the skin between white and black men, a deposition of pigment also taking place in the former, though in lesser quantity. Kölliker observes that no microscopically visible pigment is found where the skin is white; but he adds that it can be detected in the skin of Europeans of brown or dark complexion. Krause[1] says that freckles and brown moles in the skin of Europeans are in structure like the epidermis of the Negro;[2] and that the skin of the white in hot climates experienced an analogous change. The colour of the Negro differs in various nations; further, that the colour of the skin can therefore not be considered as a specific difference from other races, as it is chiefly dependent on external conditions. This is supported by other considerations, chiefly by the fact, that the Negro becomes lighter in advanced age;[3] and that the women, during the years of menstruation, when the carbon is removed by other means, are said to be lighter than the men (de Müller). It is finally also to be borne in mind that new-born Negro children are of a light grey colour, and that in the northern parts of the Negro region the children become only perfectly black in the third year (Pruner). Camper[4] saw a Negro child that at birth was of a reddish colour, then became first black around the nails and the nipples, on the third day the genitals became coloured, and on the fifth and sixth day the whole body. Children born in the cold season take a longer time in becoming black. The children of the Arabs in the south, even where they have not intermixed with the Negroes, but have their colour, exhibit at birth a copper colour;[5] whilst those of the American race are at birth of a yellowish-white or reddish-brown colour.[6] Those of the native Australians in the environs of Adelaide are immediately after birth of a yellowish-brown, and only become dark at a later period.[7]

---

1 Art. Haut., in Wagner's handwörterb., p. 15, 123.
2 Compare Simon in Müller's "Archiv.," p. 167, 1840.
3 Carne's "Journ. of a voy. to the West Coast of Africa," p. 372, Boston, 1852.
4 "Kleine Schriften.," i, p. 24, 1782.
5 D'Escayrac, loc. cit.
6 Prinz Max., loc. cit., p. 103, 1839.
7 Koeler in monatsb. der ges. f. Erdk., iii, 44.

The frizzly hair developes itself as gradually as the colour of the skin. In the suckling the hair is of a chestnut brown, and of a silky texture (Burmeister). The skin exhalation has in the negro a peculiar, disagreeable odour, which, however, is but little perceptible in some individuals, whilst in others it is smelt at a distance. This odour is particularly strong among the Balantes and Bissagos,[1] and among the Negroes in the south of Sierra Leone, the Ibos, Papaws, Mokos, etc.[2] It corresponds to the odour emitted by the black feathers of birds and the black hair of the dogs in Guinea (Foissac).

From the preceding description of the Negro-type, in which we have preferred to let every author speak for himself, it cannot be doubted that there is a certain resemblance between the Negro and the Ape, although the distance between them is sufficiently great to discard any idea as to their relationship. We must add here a few more observations to shew that the differences between the Negro and European are less important than they appear at first sight.

The singularly thick skull which is considered as one of the characteristics of the Negro race is not exclusively peculiar to it. We need not mention that it is frequently occurring in mental diseases, and Herodotus ascribes such thick skulls to the ancient Egyptians. The natives of Van Diemen's Land break wood on their heads (Labillardière).[3] This is also the case among the Penhuenches in South America, and many Indians in Brazil.[4] The skulls of the Australians are said to be much thicker than those of Europeans.[5] Herrera mentions that the Spanish conquerors were not able to split the skulls of the aborigines of Cuba and Haiti with one stroke of the sword. Ulloa[6] says that the skulls found in old American graves are about six to seven inches thick. Polack[7] found the

---

[1] Arnoux, loc. cit., p. 215.
[2] R. Clarke, "S. Leone," p. 51, 1846.
[3] Labillardière, "Rel. du voy. à la rech. de la Pérouse," An. viii, ii, p. 54; Melville, "The present state of Australia," p. 348, 1851.
[4] Pöppig, "Reise," i, 466; Spix und Martius, "Reise," p. 696.
[5] Dawson, "The present state of Aust.," p. 66, 1830.
[6] "Physikal. und hist. Nachr.," ii, 99, 1781.
[7] "New-Zeal., being a narrative of travels," i, p. 214, 1838.

same thickness in a New Zealand skull. The remarkable thickness of the skulls of the Zulu Kaffirs, who do not properly belong to the Negro tribe, is considered by Delegorgue[1] to be the consequence of exposing the unprotected head to the heat of the sun. In France also, remarkably thick skulls were dug out in many places,[2] and the Bretons are distinguished by the same peculiarity, and frequently fight with their heads like Negroes.[3]

Oblique prominent front teeth do not, according to Sandifort,[4] exclusively occur among Negroes, but are seen, though in a less degree, among Kaffirs, Aboinese, Cingalese, Japanese, etc. Even among Europeans, laterally compressed skulls with oblique incisors, are not so very rare.[5]

With regard to the length and proportions of the arm: Jarrold[6] has proved by measurements that the forearm of the Scotch (twelve inches to six feet length of body) is intermediate between the Negro (twelve and a half inches to six feet length of body), and the Englishman (eleven and a half inches to six feet length), and that the length of the hand is proportionately large in the former; hence also in this respect the resemblance of the Negro to the monkey is not specific.

The deficiency in the calves are in Sennaar and Taka as often found among the Arabs as among the Negroes.[7] Brehm[8] has observed the same among the Nomades of East Sudan, and assigns as a cause that they are accustomed to sit on the heels, by which the thigh rests on the calves. Moreover the peculiarity is not general among the Negroes.

Burmeister has pointed out the resemblance of the foot and the position of the toes of the Negro to that of the ape.

It has indeed been often noticed that the large toe is frequently used by Negroes as a thumb; but however seductive it

---

[1] "Voy. dans l'Afr. australe," ii, p. 219, 1847.
[2] Serres, in "l'Institut.," ii, p. 123, 1853.
[3] Lenormant, "Nouv. ann des voy.," i, p. 110, 1848.
[4] "Tabulæ craniorum," Lug. Bat., 1838.
[5] Loc. cit., p. 62.
[6] R. Wagner, "Naturgesch. des Menschen," ii, p. 219, 1831.
[7] Werne, "Feldzug von Sennaar nach Taka," p. 58, 1851.
[8] Loc. cit., p. 76.

may be to dwell upon this point, it can easily be shown that there is not much in it after all, for the same peculiarity has been observed not merely in the Australians,[1] who often, to conceal their spears, drag them along between the toes,[2] but also in the Indian on the Orinoco[3] and in Yucatan, where the natives pick up money with their feet, and throw stones with them.[4] The jugglers at the court of Montezuma performed their extraordinary tricks with the feet: some of these performers Cortez took to Spain, where such feats are only performed with the hands.[5] The Marquesas islanders, the Malays of Luzon and Samar, and some inhabitants of Sumatra, also use their feet, and specially the first and second toes, to raise light objects.[6] Such facts may have induced Bory[7] to maintain that the opposable thumbs on the lower extremities of the ape cannot be considered as a specific difference between it and man, mentioning at the same time that this peculiarity is possessed in the same, or even in a higher, degree by the gum-gatherers of Marrensin, (Dep. des Landes), in consequence of much climbing. At any rate, the resemblance in this respect of the Negro to the ape must be abandoned. How much the use of the limbs is due to training is shown by the Bayadères in the East Indies. Already in the course of the first year the mother of the future Bayadère at Java bends the limbs of her child cautiously in every direction. The Bayadère is able to bend the last phalanx of the fingers separately, forwards and backwards, to make the back of the hand as concave as the palm, and even to place the whole hand back upon the forearm. Her toes possess the same flexibility and capacity for grasping as the fingers, and the vertebral column is flexible in every direction.[8]

---

1 Mitchell, "Three Expeditions, i, p. 303, 1838; Howitt, "Impressions of Austr. Felix," p. 284, 1845; Hodgson, "Reminisc. of Austr," p. 245, 1846.
2 King, "Narr. of a survey of the coasts of Austr.," i, p. 370, 1827.
3 Gillii, "Nachr. vom Lande Guiana," p. 252, 1785.
4 Waldeck, "Voy. dans la prov. d'Yucatan," p. 65, 1838.
5 "Gomara in "Historiad. prem. de Ind.," p. 342, Madrid, 1852.
6 Langsdorff, "Bemerk. auf einer Reise um die Welt," i, p. 151, 1812; Mallat, "Les Philippines," ii, p. 38, 1846; de Pages, "Reise um die Welt," p. 175, 1786; Marsden, "Sumatra," 1788; Rengger, "Naturgesch. der Säugeth von Paraguay," ii, p. 376.
7 "L'Homme," i, p. 45, 1827.
8 Gumprecht, "Ztschft. f. allg. Erdk.," ii, p. 118, 1854, nach dem Tageb. eines officiers.

The disagreeable odour of the Negro has also been considered as a specific peculiarity. But besides the great differences existing in this respect among the Negroes themselves,[1] the native American also emits a peculiar though not so strong an odour (Catinca), as Blumenbach has also mentioned with regard to the Caribs and other natives. It is transmitted by the Negro and American to the Mulatto and Mestizo.[2] The Araucanians especially, who live on animal food, have an extremely disagreeable odour, which is in Chili known by the name of "soreno."[3] Hearne, on the other hand,[4] assures us that nothing of the kind is perceived in the North Indians, with proper cleanliness, and Oviedo y Valdes[5] says of the Indians of Panama, that they only smell disagreeably like the Negro when they omit washing for a couple of days. Say[6] attributes the odour of the skin exhalation of the Indians chiefly to the substances which they rub in, observing at the same time that the odour of the white is disagreeable to them. If, as is asserted, the natives of Luzon can distinguish the clothes of their masters by their smell[7], and the Australians are equally able to do so,[8] it results that not only has the skin exhalation of the white race, but that every individual has a specific odour, which is in fact proved by the capacity of the dog to trace his master. A practised dealer in hair is said to be able to distinguish German hair from French hair, and even Irish, Scotch and English hair.[9] Though it may be incorrect what Kretzschmar asserts[10], that whilst the Hottentots emit an intolerable odour, the Bushmen and the Kaffirs are free from it, it still results that the disagreeable odour of the Negro is not to be considered as a specific

[1] The skin exhalation of the Huallenga in Taka, who belong to the Bischaris, is equally disgusting (Werne, "Felzug von Sennar nach Taka," p. 228, etc., 1851).

[2] Humboldt, "Neuspanien," i, p. 192.

[3] Lesson, "Complément des œuv. de Buffon," ii, 163.

[4] "R. von Prinz Wallis fort. z, Eismeer," p. 257, 1797.

[5] Ternaux, "Recueil de docum. sur l'hist. des possess. espagnoles dans l'Am.," p. 130, 1840.

[6] In James, "Acc. of an exped. from Pittsburgh to the Rocky Mount., Philad.," i, p. 285, 1823.

[7] Mallat, loc. cit., ii, p. 38.

[8] "Australia felix," p. 127, Berl., 1849.

[9] Morgenblatt, no. 110, p. 316, 1855.

[10] "Südaffr. Skizzin," p. 207, 1853.

peculiarity. A good authority, Rengger,[1] states that he has many times observed, that Europeans acquire on their acclimatization in Paraguay a stronger, more disagreeable and negro-like odour, and that in consequence of this change in the activity of the skin, they are, like the Indians and the Negroes, less molested by the mosquitos. They attack, indeed, according to Humboldt and Bonpland, equally Indians and Europeans, but the consequences of the stings, and the swellings which ensue, as well as the pain, are slighter in the former.

According to Unanue[2], the sweat of the European and African is an alkaline reagent, that of the aboriginal Indian, acid; but this acid reaction, he adds, may be removed by a continuous animal diet, just as the alkaline peculiarity of the sweat of the Negro may be reduced by vegetable diet. The sweat of the Spanish Creoles is either alkaline or acid, according to their diet.

It cannot be our intention to deny by these remarks the greater resemblance of the Negro to the ape in comparison with the European, but simply to point out that the resemblance has been greatly exaggerated. Sometimes, peculiarities which he shares with the higher races merely in a higher degree, have been pointed out as specific animal resemblances, at other times our ignorance of the physical characters of the other races has been used at the expense of the Negro, for it is as yet quite undecided whether among the peoples of the Malay, American races, &c., there may not prevail similar proportions in the forms of the pelvis, hands and arms. The necessary measurements to decide these points are yet wanting.

In further considering the most striking anatomical differences between peoples and races, we would also observe that the Negroes of the South Sea (Austral Negroes, Negritos, Negrillos) are distinguished from African Negroes by a more striking negro-physiognomy (it has been designated as an exaggerated or caricatured negro-physiognomy), and by a shorter stature. They are on the average about four feet eight

---

[1] "R. nach Paraguay," p. 244, 1835.

[2] Loc. cit., p. 108.

or nine inches high, without our being able to assign want of food or misery as the cause of it. They are, excepting the Bushmen (which, on the average, are about four feet high) (Lichtenstein), the shortest race on the globe. The giant and pigmy races of which old travellers speak have vanished, and thus it will probably be with the tailed men.[1] The appendages having, as in Sumatra, proved to be pieces of dress made of bark or skins, which were hanging down behind.

The Hottentots and Bushmen, though differing from the Negroes (especially in the form of the head and physiognomy), possess the chief peculiarities of the Negro type. Thunberg[2] describes the vertebral column of the Hottentots as strongly curved inwards. The upper thighbone of the Bushmen resembles more that of the ape than that of Europeans. Cuvier, in his minute description of a Bushwoman, has, independent of other peculiarities belonging to the negro-type, drawn attention to the smallness of the ear, and a deficiency in the posterior edge, resembling the ear of the ape, and compares the fat cushions upon the hips of the Hottentot women to similar formations in some female monkeys, as in the Mandrill and Pavian, whilst Desmoulins combats this analogy. Fatty cushions upon the hips are also observed in Negresses (Pruner) in Congo, Mandara, among the Makuas and Kaffirs, and even among the women of the Southern Tuaryks, where they have intermixed with the blacks.[3] This peculiarity is also met with among the Nubian and also the Somali females.[4] Among some Negroes these appendages are considered a particular beauty. The women about Cape Coast wear cushions[5] on this part, which reminds us of a recent European fashion. Finally, we may mention the much talked-of Hottentot apron,

---

[1] Compare Castelnau, "Renseignements sur l'Afr. centrale," 1851, and Trémaux in "Bullet. soc. geogr.," i, p. 139, 1855.

[2] "R. durch eines Theil. v. Eur., Afr., und As.," ii, p. 168, 1792.

[3] Omboni, p. 161; Denham, Clapperton, and Oudney, "Narr. of trav. in Afr.," 2nd ed., p. 201, 1826; Bunbury, "Journal of a resid. at the Cape," p. 159, 1848; Barth, "R. und Entdeckungen," i, pp. 328, 599.

[4] Burton, "First footsteps in East Afr.," p. 108, 1856; Comber, "Voy. en Egypte, en Nubie, etc.," ii, p. 215, 1846.

[5] Cunka—Huntley, "Seven years service on the Slave Coast," i, p. 70, 1850.

which however cannot be described as a monkey formation. It consists of a prolongation of the *præputium clitoridis* and of the *nymphæ*, which has first been described as peculiar to the Bushwomen, in a memoir by Peron and Lesueur, 1805. Observations on this subject by Müller may be found in his Archiv., 1834, p. 319. A similar excrescence has been noticed by Sonnini,[1] and before him by Thevenot in Egypt and Abyssinia, where girls are circumcised. This certainly cannot be considered as a proof, for although the circumcision of girls prevails among many tribes in Africa, especially in Sennaar and the surrounding regions[2] in Congo, among some of the Betschuana tribes,[3] it probably refers only to the clitoris, which, according to Werne,[4] is completely extirpated in Bellad-Sudan.

That this operation should be exclusively confined to the Mohammedans in East Africa (as stated in "Nouv. ann. des voy.," 1835, iii, 172), is scarcely probable. It is also practised among the Susus and Mandingos in the West.[5] The women of Patagonia are said to have an uncommonly large clitoris (Foissac), but no circumcision is practised. Nor can we, from the circumcision of the nymphæ (which is common in the countries on the Nile from the first cataract), conclude that there exists a similar formation in these parts as in the Hottentot women. Bosmann[6] however relates of the women of Wydah, that they can be circumcised like the Hottentot women; and Adams[7] reports that in Dahomey the nymphæ are artificially elongated. Clarke also[8] observes that the women of Popo are distinguished by uncommonly large nymphæ and a large clitoris. A similar artificially-produced deformity among the Mandan women is described by Prince Max.[9] Among the women of the Bushmen,

---

1 "R. in Ober und Nieder Æg.," p. 300, 1800.
2 "Bellad Sudan."
3 Cailliaud, "Voy. à Méroe," ii, p. 278, 1826; Donville, "Voy. au Congo," i, pp. 66, 108, Stuttg., 1832; "Delegorgue," ii, p. 561.
4 Feldzug von Sennaar, "Nach Taka," p. 201.
5 Matthews, "R. nach S. Leone," p. 72, 1784.
6 Viaggio in Guinea, trad. dal Franz., Ven.," iii, p. 88, 1752.
7 "Remarks on the country east from C. Palmas to the R. Congo," p. 15, 1823.
8 "S. Leone," p. 49, 1846.
9 "R. in N. Am.," ii, p. 107.

a double membrane, as above described, is sometimes seen; two cases of this kind are reported in Meyer.[1]

As one of the most important deviations from the normal form may be mentioned the *os incæ* on the occiput of the old Peruvians, discovered by Tschudi, which, in form of a rectangular triangle, occurs in ruminants and carnivora.[2] It appears however not to be a fixed peculiarity of race.[3] Zeune[4] saw such a bone in the skull of an adult Kalmuck woman and on that of a Java woman. Hence it appears only to be an individual abnormal formation. Before the times of the Incas there existed, according to Morton,[5] in Peru, a half civilized people with long and narrow skulls, with a low receding forehead and a facial angle of sixty-seven degrees, and a capacity of only seventy-five cubic inches. Though the American race is, independent of artificial pressure, distinguished by a low forehead,[6] still the above description of the form of the skull, if it were natural, as Morton originally considered, would be a most remarkable abnormity; but Morton himself has given up that notion.[7]

It is further noteworthy that in the old Egyptian monuments, as Winckelmann has pointed out, the ear is situated rather higher up than usual. Dureau de la Malle thought recently that he could detect the same peculiarity in several mummies and in some Jews.[8] Czermak[9] found nothing of the kind in the mummies examined by him. Morton's investigations[10] led also only to a negative result. He considers the difference as unimportant, and that the cartilage merely may have been larger and reached higher up. Nott and Gliddon consider it as founded on error. Though this deviation is as yet undecided, that, observed by Blumenbach, that the incisors of the mummies resembled in shape the molar teeth, is not considered

[1] "R. in Süd-Afr.," pp. 116, 164, 1843.
[2] Müller's Archiv., p. 107, 1844.
[3] Blake on "Peruvian skulls," Ethno. Trans., 1862.—ED.
[4] "Ueber Schädelbildung," p. 15, 1846.
[5] "Cran. Am.," 102.
[6] Humboldt, "Neusspanien," i, p. 154, 1809.
[7] "On the Ethnography and Archæology of the Am. Aborig." p. 18, 1846; and Schoolcraft, "Hist. of the Ind. tribes," ii, p. 325.
[8] "Revue Encyclopédique" and Lit. Gazette, June 23, 1832.
[9] "Sitzungsbericht d. Wiener Akad.," ix, p. 427, 1852.
[10] "Cran. Ægypt.," p. 26.

as a peculiarity of the race, but the consequence of their mode of living.

There must yet be mentioned the natural foramen in the humerus, or intercondyloid perforation which receives the olecranon, in the extinct inhabitants of the Canary Islands (the Guanches). It occurs also among the Hottentots, but is not a constant character.[1] This abnormity is not unfrequently found in Germany. We must not therefore put the same high value upon this as Desmoulins,[2] who considers the union of the nasal bones of the Bushmen as a specific quality.

From the preceding synopsis of the greatest deviations which can be found in the anatomical structure of the various races, it is clear that we may confine ourselves to the comparison of the Negro with the European in fixing the maximum of the differences existing between the races as regards bodily structure; but the case is altered when we institute a similar comparison from a physiological point of view.

In reviewing the physiological peculiarities of the various human races we must bear in mind the known axiom, that all beings belonging to the same species present the same arrangement of the animal economy. This harmony extends to animal heat, the frequency of the pulse, the commencement of puberty and the duration of sexual capacity, the duration and frequency of gestation and the number of young, the mean duration of life, the periodical changes of the organism, bodily strength and diseases. On instituting a comparison between the white and the other races with regard to physiological functions and qualities, it will be easily shown that there is no question here of permanently specific, but merely of acquired, differences, which are explicable by external or internal conditions, arising from civilization, more or less refined modes of life, exercise, intelligence, and the nature of surrounding media. The greatest energy of physical life is generally found, as indeed may be expected, among peoples in a primitive state; but the longer duration of life, a more extended power

---

[1] T. Müller, "Archiv.," p. 336, 1834; De Salles, "Hist. gen. des races hum.," p. 204, 1849; Hollard, "De l'homme et des races hum.," p. 251, 1853.
[2] Pp. 297, 303.

of acclimatization, a lesser destruction of life by diseases, and greater muscular strength, is found among civilized nations, owing to their protecting themselves from injurious influences of all kinds, in combination with superior nutrition and regular exercise.

The mean animal heat and the frequency of respiration do not materially differ under the tropics and the polar regions. Some indeed have maintained that the first is in the torrid zone less by 2—3°; others (Davy) that in Ceylon it is higher by 2°; this however has not been confirmed. Gmelin, Ross, and Parry found under 74° N. lat. no difference in this respect.[1] That Livingstone[2] found the thermometer under his own tongue rise to 100°, and among the natives only 98°, affords no certain proof of a constant difference between the blood heat of the Negro and the European. The difference may have been the sequel of his fever or the effect of other circumstances. Nor has the pretended quicker pulse of the Southerns been confirmed. Among some North American tribes the pulse is only 64, which is perhaps connected with the rarity of fevers among them.[3] Prichard[4] refers this circumstance to a deficient energy of the animal functions, since also the menstruation of the women among many Indian peoples is said to be but scanty,[5] and puberty of the girls occurs later, from the eighteenth to the twentieth year, the capacity to produce children ceasing with the fortieth year. These phenomena are however far from common among the American race, for the period of puberty among girls commences in the fourteenth year among the Potowatomis, in the fifteenth and sixteenth among the Sioux.[6] Among the Delawares and Iroquois the girls marry at fourteen,[7] and in the torrid zone, marriages are earlier effected among the natives of

---

1 Foissac, p. 15.
2 Loc. cit., p. 166.
3 Say in James, loc. cit., p. 260.
4 Chap. i, p. 133.
5 Lahontan, "Nouv. voy. dans l'Am. sept.," ii, p. 154, La Haye, 1703; and Rengger, "Natgesch. der Säugeth v. Paraguay," p. 11.
6 Keating, "Narr. of an exped. to the source of St. Peter's R.," i, p. 434, 1825.
7 Loskiel, "Gesch. d. Miss. unter den Ind.," p. 72.

America than elsewhere, namely from ten to thirteen years.[1] In ancient Mexico, however, the girls used to marry when sixteen to eighteen years old, and the men from twenty to twenty-two,[2] the law of the old Inca empire prescribing for the former the age of eighteen to twenty, and for the latter from the twenty-fourth year.[3] If, despite the cold climate, the puberty of the girls commences among the Mongols, Kalmucks, Samoieds, Lapps, Kamtschatkals, Jakutes, Ostiaks, etc., about the twelfth or thirteenth year,—(it may be of interest to ascertain how this is among the Magyars,)—the animal diet of these peoples and the heat of their huts may perhaps contribute to it, as in those of the Esquimaux it is said to rise to 28 degrees, whilst in the open air it sinks to —28 degrees.[4] Puberty occurs rather late in the Fiji Islands, namely, in girls about the fourteenth, and in boys about the seventeenth or eighteenth year.[5] Uncommonly early, on the other hand, in the temperate region of New Zealand, where the girls frequently marry when eleven years old.[6] Among the aboriginal Americans the period of puberty seems, as among other races, essentially to depend on climate and mode of life. This circumstance has however, among others, been used to support the assertion that they are a weakly race, deficient in vital power, and that they would have become extinct even if the white immigrants had not contributed to their destruction.[7] This renders necessary a closer investigation of an assertion assuming such an essential difference of organization between the American and other races; but in order not to interrupt our investigation too much by details, we shall treat of it in an appendix to this section.

It has been statistically proved that in Europe the proportion of male to female births is =106 : 100, and there seems in all climates to prevail a similar preponderance of boys over

---

1 D'Orbigny, Strangeway's "Sketch of the Mosquito Shore,", Edin., 1822.
2 Clavigero, "Hist. of Mex. translated by Cullen," vi, p. 38, 1787.
3 Garcilasso, "Hist. des Yncas," iv, c. 8, Amst., 1737.
4 Parry "Second voy.," p. 502.
5 Wilkes, iii, p. 93.
6 W. Brown, "New Zealand and its aborigines," p. 38, 1845.
7 De Pauw, "Rech. sur les Américains," Martius and others.

girls, excepting under particular circumstances. Hofacker[1] ascribes it to the preponderating influence of the male, who in Europe is, on the average, five to six years older than the female. It is also said that the number of male births increases with the advancing ages of both parents. A regular preponderance of female births, which Quetelet[2] quotes of the white population in the Cape of Good Hope, is rare. Nothing of the kind exists among the same stock in Europe, a fact which proves that such proportions are not fixed peculiarities, but depend on particular local influences.

Among the Indians in Central America male and female births nearly balance each other, but among the Whites and Mulattoes of these parts, among the Ladinos, the former are exceeded by the latter in the proportion of 2 : 3, or at least of 4 : 5.[3] In Yucatan the proportion of women to men is, according to some authors, =2 : 1;[4] in Cochabamba, in South America, the number of women to that of men is said to reach the incredible proportion of 5 : 1.[5] In Granada, the capital of Nicaragua, even the casual observer is struck with the numerical preponderance of the females over the males.[6] The same proportion, though in a lesser degree, is found in Goyaz, a city in Brazil,[7] and is said to prevail throughout Venezuela, and particularly in Cumena, where, it is asserted, there are seven females to one male.[8] The preponderance of the female population of Buenos Ayres, as asserted by some authors, is, according to Caldcleugh,[9] unfounded. Elsewhere it is asserted, that in Buenos Ayres the male births outnumber the female births by twenty-three per cent., which seems equally erroneous. Immigration only appears to cause in that

---

1 "Ueber die Eigensch. welch s. b. Menschen und Thieren vererben."

2 "Ueber den Menschen," German by Rieke, 1838; "Journal Asiat.," Jul., 1828; and Sadler, "The law of population," ii, 371.

3 Galindo, "Journal R. Geogr. Soc.," vi., p. 126.

4 Stephens, "Begebenh. auf. e. R. en Yucatan," p. 171, 1853.

5 "Bullet. soc. geogr.," i, 209, 1855.

6 Reichardt, "Nicarag.," p. 88, 1854.

7 Castelnau, "Exped. dans l'Am. du Sud," i, 328, 1850.

8 Otto, "Reiserrinnerungen in Cuba," p. 237, 1843.

9 "Travels in S. Am.," London, i, p. 184, 1825.

region a preponderance of males.[1] According to Castelnau,[2] the males preponderate among the Whites, the reverse being the case among the Indians, Mulattoes and Creole Negroes. With regard to Mexico, Franz Mayer[3] states, from recent official sources, that more girls than boys are born in Vera Cruz, Oajaca, Puebla, Mechoacan, Guanajuato, Jalisco, the preponderance diminishing gradually in the order cited. On the other hand, there are more boys than girls born in Upper California, New Mexico, Sonora, Chihuahua, Cohahuila, New Leon. Hence he lays it down as a general proposition, that away from the equator the preponderance of girls gradually declines, and altogether ceases further North, when there is a turn in the contrary direction. Tamaulipas specially exhibits a constant preponderance of male births. In Africa, on the Gold Coast, the females preponderate only on the coasts, not in the interior.[4] There are also numerous instances to the contrary.

The excess of males over females occurs more frequently than the reverse. Among the Jews in Berlin the proportion of female to male births is =100 : 208; among the Jews in Livorno =100 : 120; and in the Prussian dominions generally =100 : 111.[5] A similar striking excess of male births, =4 : 3, occurs in New Russia, in the governments, Jekaterinoslanw, Cherson, Bessarabia, and Tabriz.[6] In Galega, north-east of Madagascar, the French Government has authorized polyandry among the Negroes, the number of male births being too large.[7] In Tahiti there is equally a preponderance of males.[8] In Upper California a much less number of girls is born than boys, or the mortality must be greater among the former than amongst the latter. This preponderating number of males has for its consequence the decrease of the population, with the exception of the Mission San Luis-Rey.[9] The same cause has

---

1 "Zeitsch. f. allg. erdk. n. folge," iv, p. 143.
2 Loc. cit., i, 138.
3 "Mexico," ii, p. 46, Hartford, 1853.
4 Wilson, "Western Afr." p. 181, Lond., 1856.
5 Burdach, "Physiol.," i, p. 532; Hoffman in Quetelet, p. 56.
6 Fechner's "Centralbl.," p. 368, 1853.
7 Laplace, "Voy. aut. du monde," ii, 119, 1833.
8 "Journal R. Geogr. Soc.," iii, p. 174.
9 Coulter, in "Journal R. Geogr. Soc.," v, p. 67.

partly effected the depopulation of Australia, though it cannot be considered as the only one, and can hardly be looked upon as a sign of deficient vitality in the organization of the natives. The number of females still decreases in Australia.[1] In the known districts of Australia the proportion of males to females among the natives is =3 : 2; that of adults to children, only =5 : 2. The mortality among the children is enormous, the greater proportion of them do not outlive the first month.[2] Sturt, however,[3] observes, that among the smaller tribes in the interior, there is an excess of women in the proportion of 2 : 1, or even greater. This has also been asserted by others.[4]

Congenital deformities are rarer among most savage peoples than among civilized nations; and it is now generally acknowledged that the views of Ulloa, Robertson, and others, who would explain this fact by infanticide, are erroneous. At the time of the conquest there were already in Peru, in regions subject to sudden alterations of temperature, many cripples and blind.[5] In the environs of Leon there were observed many one-eyed individuals—ostensibly in consequence of the great dust. Such persons were rarely met with in Nicaragua.[6] Captain Landolphe[7] saw, during his lengthened travels on the African coasts and in America, only one deformed Negro. Brehm also has confirmed the rarity of deformities among Negroes in East Sudan; but singularly enough, he considered it as a resemblance to brutes, since more refined and intellectual labours are the source of many diseases. Ellis[8] observes of Tahiti, that deformities had been rare in former times, but are more frequent now; there are specially many hunchbacks in the Society Islands.[9] Pickering[10] speaks of

---

1 Eyre, "Journals of exped. into Central Austr.," ii, p. 417, 1845.

2 Fechner's Central blatt., pp. 29, 208, 1853; Westgarth, in "Journal of the Ind. Archipelago," Dec. 1851.

3 "Narr. of an exped. into Central Aust.," ii, pp. 77, 136, 1849.

4 D'Urville, "Voy. de l'Astrolabe," i, p. 495, 1830.

5 Gemara, p. 276.

6 Oviedo, "Hist. gen. y nat. de Ind.," xlii, c. 4.

7 "Mem. cont. l'hist. de ses voy. p. Quesné," i, p. 137, 1823.

8 "Polynes. Researches," i, p. 80, 1832.

9 "Lesson Compl. des Œuvr. de Buffon," ii, p. 214.

10 "The races of man," 1849.

many innate deformities in Polynesia. New Zealand, however, seems to form an exception.[1] In North America, also more rarely in Brazil, cripples were in modern times found in greater numbers.[2] The natives there are said to be now more subject to diseases than formerly.[3] It seems, therefore, that the sanitary condition of savage nations has deteriorated by their intercourse with civilized nations, partly in consequence of new diseases, and partly from changes in dress and mode of life which they gradually adopted, especially where missionaries effected such a transformation of their habits.

The signs of age generally, though not always, present themselves later among savage than among the civilized nations. As deficient protection against the influence of climate and hard work depress the body, we cannot wonder that, for instance, the North-American Indians look old at 40, and their women, who perform most of the labour, present the look of old age even at an earlier period.[4] Similar instances are found among all races.

But it says much for their vital energy, that grey hair and baldness, though they occur, appear but rarely, and only in old age.[5] The teeth also remain sound until old age; they become worn, but rarely carious. Thus it is among the aboriginal Americans, among the New Zealanders, and other Polynesians[6] and among the Bushmen.[7] Teething does not seem to torment the children. Marco Polo wondered at the enduring power possessed by the Tartars in sustaining bodily labour. Similar descriptions have been given of the aboriginal North Americans, who in their hunting and war expeditions support hunger, thirst, heat, cold, and wet, and the most fatiguing marches, with unexampled endurance. To this must be added continuous fasting, and, among some peoples, self-inflicted pain from reli-

---

1 Polack, "New Zealand," ii, 273, 1838.
2 "Prince Max. R. in N. Am.," i, 461; James, ii, p. 112.
3 Hekewelder, "Nachr. v. d. Gesch. d. Sitten der ind. Völkersch.," p. 388, 1821.
4 West, "Substance of a journal of a resid. at the Red R. Col.," p. 112, 1824.
5 Keating, i, p. 156; D'Orbigny, i, p. 128; Gilii, 247; Tschudi, ii, p. 361.
6 D'Urville, loc. cit.
7 Burchell, ii, p. 221.

gious scruples, during which it is a point of honour not to exhibit the least sign of pain. The women who, in order not to give birth to cowards, sustain the labours of parturition with the same firmness, retiring to the forests when their time approaches, bathe in the river immediately after their delivery, and return to their labour with the new-born children on their backs. Thus it is among the Sioux, whilst the wives of the Potowatomis protect themselves from cold during ten days after delivery;[1] but this, as well as difficult parturition generally, is to be considered as an exception.

This capacity for great physical efforts which we find in such a high degree among the North Americans, is usually combined with great digestive powers, which, owing to continued fasting and frequent over-feeding, acquires among savage peoples an unexampled energy. That this is merely the result of habit and not a peculiarity of race, is proved by similar performances among the ancient Greek athletes and many Arabs. The camel drivers who perform the journey from Cairo to Suez, which lasts above thirty hours, remain without food during all that time, and many an Arab boasts of being able to consume a whole sheep at one meal.[2] The Bedouin Arabs during their journeys through the desert, take only daily two draughts of water and two morsels of baked flour and milk. Six Bedouins are said to consume no more than one European; but when they find plenty of provisions they become voracious.[3] We quote a few examples: Eyre's attendant, a native Australian named Wylie, consumed in one night 6½ pounds of boiled meat (not including the bones), and could on the average consume nine pounds daily.[4] Simpson[5] gives a still more remarkable instance of two Jakutes. A Guarani consumes a small calf in a few hours.[6] Ross[7] speaks frequently of the scarcely credible gluttony of the Esquimaux. Every Green-

[1] Keating, i, p. 130.
[2] D'Escayrac, p. 128; Bayard Taylor, "R. N. Centr. Africa," p. 369, 1855.
[3] Ritter, Erdk., xiii, pp. 315, 525.
[4] Eyre, ii, 34.
[5] "Narr. of a Journey round the world," ii, 309, 1847.
[6] Dobrizhoffer, "Abiponer," i, p. 281.
[7] "Narr. of second voy.," p. 447, etc., Lond., 1835.

lander consumes on the average, besides eggs, mussels, and vegetables, annually about 645 pounds of fish and 784 pounds of meat and lard. Strong young men consume daily, during several months, from 10 to 12 pounds of meat, and a considerable quantity of biscuits.[1] An Arowake, on the other hand, lives in the field for three weeks, or even a month, on 10 pounds of Kassava bread.[2] Lichtenstein speaks of the enormous voracity and power of abstinence of the Bushmen. One of them is said to have lived for a fortnight on water and salt.[3] Like the Kaffirs, they are said to grow fat again in a few days. When a famine threatens, it is usual among the Kaffirs not to eat every day.[4] Richardson[5] relates extraordinary cases of the capacity of the Tibbos to sustain hunger for a great length of time, and then to satisfy their appetite with food scarcely fit to eat. Here may also be mentioned the large consumption of a fatty clay by the Otomaks on the Orinoco.[6] Among other peoples the consumption of large quantities of putrid fish seems to be attended with no injury. Among the Takhalis, or Carriers, in North-West America, such substances form favourite dishes, which are kept until they acquire the desired degree of putridity. The Koujages, of Kadjak, cook their berries with bear excrements, and relish this as a condiment, even when they have a sufficiency of other food. They bury boiled pieces of whale in the earth until it becomes putrid, when it is considered a dainty dish.[7] Such a corruption of taste would lead us to suppose a continuous derangement of the digestive faculty, yet we do not hear that the health of these peoples suffers from it.

With regard to muscular power, Péron was the first who performed experiments with the dynamometer and in wrestling. It resulted therefrom that the natives of Van Diemen's Land were inferior in this respect to the Australians, and these again to

---

1 Etzel, "Greenland," p. 374, Stuttg., 1860.
2 Hilhouse, "Journal R. G. S.," ii, p. 232.
3 Thompson, "Trav. in S. Afr.," i, p. 99, 2nd edit., 1827.
4 Delegorgue, i, p. 134.
5 "Narr. of a mission to central Afr.," ii, p. 45, 1853.
6 Heusinger, "Geophagy."
7 Holmberg, "Ethnogr. skizzen über die Völker des. Russ." p. 89, 1855.

the Timorese, but all of them were considerably weaker than the Europeans.[1] He points out, that though the Timorese are amply provided with food, they lead in a hot climate an inactive life, and become weak from want of bodily exercise, whilst the weakness of the first-named nations arises from want of proper nourishment and a frequent change from extreme physical efforts to an apathetic repose. Freycinet[2] has continued the experiments with the dynamometer, and has arrived at the following results:—

	Kilogrammes.
White Creoles from Ile de France lift on the average	64·4
Frenchmen in the same locality	60·3
Sandwich Islanders	66·2 and 58·3
Mozambique Negroes	57·1
Malgasches	56·9
Natives of the Carolines	54·2
New Zealanders, twenty to twenty-five years old	51·4
Timorese and Papuas	40·0
Australians	45·6

The results communicated by Buckton[3] differ from the above:—

	Mean Strength of the Arms.	Mean Strength of the Hips
12 Tasmanians	50·6 kilogr	— myriagr.
17 Australians	50·8 "	10·2 "
56 Timorese	58·7 "	11·6 "
17 Frenchmen	69·2 "	15·2 "
14 Englishmen	71·4 "	16·3 "

With regard to the New Zealanders, it is stated[4] that they can, on the average, lift 367 pounds avoirdupois. Foissac[5] has justly recommended caution in coming to any conclusion from such experiments, as they can only be decisive when performed on individuals of the same nature and the same practice in physical efforts. This is proved by the fact, that the American Hercules, Cantfield, exhibited with the

[1] Peron, "Voy. de decouv. aux terres Australes," ii, p. 417, 2nd edit., 1824.
[2] "Voy. autour du m.," ii, p. 714, 1827.
[3] "Western Australia," p. 91, 1840.
[4] "Journal R. Geogr. Soc.," xiii, p. 92.
[5] Page 41.

dynamometer no more physical strength than an Ojibbeway chief.[1] We should also require, observes Hamilton Smith,[2] experiments to be performed in running, spear-throwing, etc., to form a judgment on the proportion of bodily strength in different nations.

We should also examine the power of endurance, as well as the amount of individual momentary performances. The materials at hand are not sufficient to come to any conclusion in this respect; still it is not without interest to state some of the more important results obtained.

Péron[3] found that the natives of Van Diemen's Land excelled the Europeans in running. This frequently occurs among savages, since their safety and subsistence in war and the chase often depends on their fleetness. The American deer in the open prairie is sometimes caught by the Indians, which however is rarely the case with the Moose deer and the Bison.[4] Similar fleetness is ascribed to the Lapps and Tunguses. T. E. Alexander[5] speaks of two Namaquas, father and son, who, armed merely with a knife, gave chase to zebras, and outran them. And Moffat[6] asserts that among the Barolongs there are some who on foot can keep up with the giraffe. Hottentot Kaffirs and Bechuanas are less muscular than the English and the Dutch colonists at the Cape, but possess greater endurance.[7] The short thin Hottentot excels, according to Alberti,[8] the Kaffirs in lifting weights, and even a White colonist at the Cape, celebrated for his strength, was not equal to the Kaffirs in running and throwing spears, manifestly the consequence of more or less practice, and independent of peculiarity of race.

Péron has collected many instances to prove the physical weakness of the native Americans. On closely examining them it will be found that they chiefly rest upon the rapid decay of

---

1 Quételet, loc. cit., p. 155.
2 "Natural hist. of the human species," p. 165, Edinburgh, 1848.
3 Loc. cit., ii, p. 85.
4 J. Tanner, "Mémoires trad. p. Blosseville," i, p. 201, 1835.
5 "Exped. of discov. into the Interior of Afr.," ii, p. 261, 1838.
6 "Miss. labours in S. Afr.," p. 260, 1842.
7 Moodie, "Ten years in S. Afr.," i, p. 43, 1835; Burchell, ii, p. 439.
8 "Descr. des Caffres," Amst., 1811.

the Indian population. Under the oppression of the conquerors, the native population rapidly perished, chiefly in South America, where they were forced to work in mines. It became then necessary to import Negroes, who could endure the labour, and hence it was concluded that the American Indian is, compared with the Negro, a weakling. Just the contrary is asserted by Frezier[1] and Helms,[2] that only the Indians, not the Negroes, can support the heavy labour in the mines. Both are correct under proper limitation. Negroes cannot stand heavy work in mountainous regions; their skin becomes discoloured, the complexion assumes an ash-grey tint, they sicken and die.[3] Wilson,[4] by no means an unprejudiced writer, asserts that the sugar planters in the hot regions of the interior of Mexico had found it impossible to have their plantations cultivated by Negroes or Zamboes, as neither of these races were viable in these parts. The power of endurance of the Negro under a tropical sun, without injury to his prolificacy, is a known fact; but it has not been taken into consideration that the Negro easily becomes reconciled to a state of slavery, for which the Indian seems unfit; depressed by it, the latter sinks into a state of melancholy, and thus perishes rather from psychical than physical causes. This opinion has been confirmed by Von Sack.[5] A number of facts proves that the Indian is not deficient in physical power for heavy labour. The South American tribes, especially, exhibit all the characters of physical strength; some of them are of athletic structure (D'Orbigny). Even the natives of Tierra del Fuego have proved to be so physically strong, that one of them is sometimes a match for two English sailors.[6] The Hapiris working in the mines of Chili, who, according to some, are not Indians of pure descent, but are considered as such by Tschudi,[7] possess extraordinary

---

[1] "Neueste R. nach der Südzee," p. 353, 1718.
[2] "Trav. from B. Ayres to Lima," pp. 16, 37, 2nd edit., 1807.
[3] Skinner, "Voy. au Perou," Paris, 1809.
[4] "Mexico," p. 311, N. York, 1855.
[5] "Beschr. einer R. nach Surinam," i, p. 87, 1821.
[6] King and Fitzroy, "Narr. of the Survey. voy. of the Adv. and Beagle," i, p. 415, 1839.
[7] Chap. ii, p. 117.

physical strength. Their usual burden (stated by Tschudi to amount only to 50-75 pounds), which they bring up twelve times daily from a depth of 450 feet, exceeds in weight 200 pounds.[1] The Indian porters in Peru carry on their straps, chests weighing above 100 pounds.[2] The journey from Pasco to Lima, fifty leagues, is performed by the Indian on foot within three days.[3] Tschudi relates similar feats of the march of Indian troops in war. "Wherever the experiment has been made, it has been shown that the Indian is capable of sustaining a higher degree of physical effort than the strongest European."[4] The Indians of Quito can, during the greater part of the day, carry a vessel upon the back containing twelve to sixteen gallons of water.[5] The Indians of Caracas carry on their journeys, burdens of about 200 pounds.[6] Captain Head[7] says, "In the mines of South America I saw Indians work with tools which were too heavy for our miners, and carry burdens which no Englishman could have carried. I appeal to such travellers who have been carried by them across the snow, and ask them whether they could have performed the same service to the Indians, and if not, it seems certainly strange that a civilized man should despise the physical power of a fellow man upon whose shoulders he rides." On proceeding northwards we hear that the Indians in Central America perform five to six leagues with a burden of six arrobes,[8] and that the Indians of Mexico bring up from the mines from 13 to 16½ arrobes upon their shoulders.[9] It must however be noticed that the miners in Zacatecas are not pure Indians but Mestizoes, who

---

[1] Darwin, "Naturalists voyage," ii, p. 113, 1844; Andrews, "Journey from B. Ayres to the prov. of Cordova," etc., i, p. xxi, 1827.

[2] Pöppig, "Reise," ii, p. 313; Weddel, "Voy. dans le Nord de Bolivie," p. 305, 1853.

[3] Proctor, "Narr. of a Journey across the Cordillera, p. 314, 1825.

[4] W. Parish, "B. Ayres and the prov. of the La Plata," p. 291, 1838; and Molina, "Essai sur l'hist, nat. du Chili, p. 314, 1789.

[5] Stevenson, ii, p. 176.

[6] Semplé, "Sketch of the present state of Caracas," p. 79, 1812.

[7] "Rough Notes taken during some journeys across the Pampas," p. 113, 2nd edit., 1826.

[8] Legendre in d'Urville, "Voy. au Pole, Sud.," x, p. 291, 1841.

[9] Ward, "Mexico in the year 1827," ii, p. 201, Weim., 1828.

are more nearly allied to the Whites than the natives.[1] According to Lahontan[2] and Perrin du Lac,[3] the natives of North America are less strong but more enduring in their efforts, than Europeans. Rengger[4] says the same of the Indians of Paraguay, and Weld[5] says that Englishmen excel the aborigines of North America in short races, but are beaten by them in long distances. Individual instances of great bodily strength are found among them. Two Ojibbeways proved themselves considerably more powerful than two Belgians of the same age.[6] The Osages belong to the most powerful tribes of the North Americans; they can perform per day sixty miles on foot.[7] Roger Williams states that the Indians of New England travel in one day from eighty to one hundred miles, and return home the following day.[8] The performances of the runners whom the native rulers of Mexico and Peru employed are well known. The so-called postillions in Peru perform on foot from twenty to thirty Spanish leagues.[9] That the beard is but weak among the Americans proves, after these cited instances, nothing against the physical strength of their constitution. Besides, they share this peculiarity with the Mongols and Negroes, and with many South-Arabs.[10] Among the peoples of the Mongol race, the powerful organization of which has never been doubted, the inhabitants of the island Quelpart are considered the strongest; they can lift heavier weights than the English sailors.[11] Among the Esquimaux there are also instances of great strength; for, to overpower one of them, a number of English sailors were requisite in a case related by

---

[1] Lyon, "Journal of resid. in Mex.," i, p. 87, 1828; Burckardt, "Aufenhalt in Mex.," i, p. 152, Stutt., 1836.
[2] Loc. cit., ii, p. 94.
[3] "R. in den beiden Louisianen," ii, p. 29, 1807.
[4] "Naturgesch. der Säugeth. in Paraguay," p. 12, 1830.
[5] "R. durch d. Staaten, in N. Am. Magazin," xx, p. 470.
[6] Quêtelet, "Bullet. de l'acad. des sc. de Belg., l'Institut.," ii, p. 78, 1846.
[7] Nuttall, "Journal of trav. into the Arkansas territory," p. 821, Philad., 1821.
[8] Hutchinson, "Hist. of Massachusetts," i, p. 411, note, 3rd edit., Boston, 1795.
[9] Temple, "Trav. in Peru," i, p. 269, Lond., 1830.
[10] Pickering, "The races of man," p. 225, 1849.
[11] Belcher, "Narr. of the Voy. of H.M.S. Samarang," i, p. 350, 1848.

Beechey.[1] With regard to the Malays and Polynesians we hear of the Macassars, that they can perform journeys of forty to fifty miles per day with heavy burdens.[2] Labillardière[3] states that the inhabitants of the Friendly Islands (Tonga Archipelago) were inferior to the French sailors in wrestling, but Cook found the Tonga Islanders in boxing and wrestling superior to his crew.[4] Wilkes[5] relates cases of a Tonga Islander who swam about in the sea from noon till the next morning, and of a woman from the Sandwich Islands who remained in the water for thirty hours. Cheever[6] relates similar cases. The great physical power of the Sandwich chiefs is frequently mentioned by Jarves.[7]

It has been asserted that the mean duration of life is longest in the temperate zone, and diminishes on approaching the tropics. As we have no statistical accounts of uncivilized nations we must rest satisfied with some stray notices, from which it would appear that there exists no peculiarity of race in this respect. The mean duration of life may be shorter among the Australians than among Europeans, in consequence of privation, but still they reach frequently seventy years and upwards.[8] It has been frequently denied that the American Indians arrive at a very advanced age, but it is now admitted, as proved by many instances.[9] Amerigo Vespucci relates in a letter in Bartolozzi,[10] that he had seen a family consisting of son, father, grandfather, great-grandfather, and great-great-grandfather. Leri says of the natives of Brazils (Tupinambas, Tamoyos), that they are subject to fewer diseases than the Europeans, and reached an age from 100—120 years, and Pigafetta[11] asserts that they reach 140 years. Prince Max[12]

---

1 "Narr. of voy. to the Pacific," p. 553, 1831.
2 "Rel. de la captivité du Cap. Woodard dans l'île de Célébès," p. 147, 1805.
3 Chap. ii, p. 176.
4 Mariner, "Tonga islands," ii, p. 314, 1818.
5 "Narrat. of the U. S. exped.," iii, p. 31; and iv, p. 45, 1845.
6 "Life in the Sandwich islands," p. 123, 1851.
7 "Hist. of the Sandwich islands," p. 77, 1843.
8 Grey, "Journals of two exped. in Austr.," ii, p. 247, 1841.
9 Burmeister, loc. cit., p. 250, 1853.
10 "Ricorche storiche sulle scoperte d'Am. Vesp."
11 "Premier voy. autour du m.," an. ix, p. 16, Paris.
12 "R. nach Brasil," ii, p. 107.

saw an Indian who could remember 107 years. Stevenson[1] has traced similar cases in the parish registers.[2] Men of dark complexion, Negroes and Indians, reach, in spite of their unwholesome diet, even under the tropics, a very advanced age.[3] Poppig[4] is of opinion that only men of colour and Indians reach such an age. It seems therefore exceptional that in South America the Indians on the Orinoco are described by Gilii (p. 250) as weakly, sensitive to changes of temperature, subject to many diseases, and frequently to an early death. It is very remarkable that on the hot coast of Vera Cruz many instances of extraordinary longevity are met with. In 1831 there were in the village Cosoliacac, among 1,595 souls, 40 whose collective ages amounted to 3,407 years, and in 1830 a woman died aged 136.[5] As regards the Malays, we find that Lichtenstein gives instances of their reaching, at the Cape, ages of 107—120 years. Among the natives of the Philippines there are many centenarians; men 80 years of age are seen working vigorously in the fields.[6] Foissac also has collected instances of old age among Polynesians and Negroes. A woman at Cape Coast Castle lived to see the fifth generation.[7] In the Island of St. Thomas, Negroes have reached an age of 110 years.[8] According to the census of the United States of 1850, instances of advanced age from 80 to 100 occur more frequently among the free coloured population, and still more so among the Negroes than among the White population. Among 3 millions of slaves there were 1,400 from 100 years upwards, while among the Whites there were but 800 instances of the kind among 20 millions.[9] Among the Negro slaves in Cuba grey hair and other signs of age appear very late, and

---

[1] "R. in Arauca, Chil.," i, p. 267, 1826.

[2] Compare also Tschudi, ii, p. 360; Spix & Martius, p. 1152; Dobrizhoffer, ii, pp. 51, 281; Rengger, "Naturg. den Säugeth v. Paraguay," p. 12; Azara, loc. cit.; Clavigero, "Hist. of Mex.," Lond., 1787, Append. v, p. 1; Sigaud, "Du climat et des maladies du Brésil," p. 448, 1844.

[3] Humboldt and Bonpland, "R.," iii, p. 86.

[4] "R.," i, p. 208.

[5] Muehlenfeldt, "Schilderung der Rep. Mejico," ii, p. 47, 1844.

[6] Mallat, p. 114.

[7] W. T. Müller, "Die Afric Landschaft Fetu," p. 280, 1676.

[8] Omboni, p. 262.

[9] Petermanns, "Mittheilungen," p. 134, 1855.

one in 900 reaches the age of 100 years.[1] Even among the Hottentots instances of great age frequently occur. Moody[2] mentions a case of one who, from his recollections of former governors of the colony, could not be less than 150 years old.

It is not our intention to give here a synopsis or history of the diseases peculiar to different tribes and climates. It will be sufficient for our subject to show that there appear to be no diseases exclusively peculiar to either of the races of man, although the frequency and mortality of many of them differ in various nations, according to individual predisposition, diet, climate, and medical treatment. Even Nott, who appears to have availed himself of every circumstance to prove that the various races suffer from different specific diseases, was obliged to content himself with the existence of different predispositions. Thus at first, he thought to find a proof for the specific difference of the Negro from the European in the circumstance that Negroes and the coloured population enjoy almost an immunity from yellow fever, so fatal to the White not yet acclimated in the south-western parts of North America. He has, however, now partly abandoned this opinion,[3] and admits that Indians and their mongrels in New Orleans and Florida are as much subject to the attacks of yellow fever as the Whites from the North of Europe. He still however maintains that the liability to contract yellow fever differs essentially in the Negro and the White. We must object that this does not depend upon a peculiarity of race, but upon the influence of climate, for as regards the acclimated Whites in the West Indies, the French refugees, for instance, who fled from St. Domingo to the Continent, the yellow fever was no more injurious to them than to the Negroes.[4] An opposite example is furnished by the Negroes of the third and fourth generation, who, after having been acclimatized in North America had returned to Africa, when they became subject to the same

[1] Graf Görz, "R. um die Welt," ii, p. 44.
[2] Loc. cit., i, p. 288.
[3] "Indigenous races," p. 392, Philad., 1857.
[4] Stanhope Smith, p. 281.

climatic diseases as other unacclimatized individuals.[1] The Black and the White suffer equally from dysentery and intermittent fevers in the south of the United States. A disease very similar to yellow fever (Matlazahuale) carries off a great number of Indians in Mexico, whilst the Whites and the Creoles suffer little from it;[2] but also in this case we are rather inclined to ascribe it to mode of life and other external circumstances, than to a specific difference of races. That Negroes and American Indians are not less subject to the most various mental diseases than Europeans, is expressly pointed out by Sigaud.[3] That savage nations, exclusive of destructive contagious diseases, generally enjoy better health than civilized nations, has been often asserted. Thus many of the old travellers relate of the North American Indians, that they frequently die only of old age, preserving the full use of their senses, and exhibiting in the most advanced age no signs of decay of the vital functions. This is also reported of the Arabs in Africa.[4] The Congo-Negroes are, according to Cavazzi,[5] more rarely sick than the Europeans. The Kaffirs are described as the impersonation of health,[6] there being but one species of putrid fever which causes great devastation among them.[7] It is to the rarity of disease among savages that we attribute the belief general among them, that maladies are something supernatural or produced by magic. This greater rarity, which however is not so easily proved, may arise from the fact, that savages become by their mode of life more hardened against external influences, and that they instinctively adapt themselves to the natural conditions in which they live, and hence enjoy physical health. The civilized man, on the other hand, follows a great number of pursuits which are not compatible with the preservation of health, and if he remain healthy withal, it is because he economises his strength.

---

1 De Salles, p. 263.
2 Foissac, p. 128.
3 "Du Climat et des m. du Brésil," p. 347.
4 M. Wagner, "R. in Algier," ii, p. 52, 1841.
5 "Beschr. der Königr. Congo, Mat. und Angola," p. 168, 1694.
6 Kretzschmar, p. 188.
7 "Baseler Missions Mag.," iii, p. 72, 1852.

The great vital energy of savage, compared with civilized, nations, is shown by the relatively greater healing power of nature (vis medicatrix naturæ) possessed by the former. The experiments made in this respect extend to all races. Leigh[1] relates the case of an Australian whose temporal bone had been fractured by a blow, and the temporal artery divided, and of another whose ulna and radius had been fractured in a terrible manner, that the first took part on the following day in some public meeting, and that, though worms appeared in the arm of the second, the recovery in both took place without any operation or even dressing. Similar cases are to be found in Barrington[2] and Dawson.[3] Though but one in four recover from the operations of the extirpation of the penis and the testicles, which are performed on Negroes by the slavedealers in East Sudan,[4] many examples prove that nature's healing power is as great here as among other Negroes. This extends also to the white races living in Africa, although Russegger[5] points out that in the hot climate of tropical Africa, wounds heal very slowly in the European, especially during the rainy period. Others however maintain that in the tropics, *e. g.* at Trinidad, wounds heal rapidly even in Europeans.[6] W. Earl[7] ascribes the natural healing power among the Malays to their vegetable diet, which prevents violent inflammation. Petit[8] reports a series of his own observations in Abyssinia, that those who are punished by having hands or feet cut off, as well as the children or adults who are emasculated or have the whole genitals extirpated, do not generally die from the operation, although the wounds are entirely left to the healing power of nature. Parkyns[9] relates similar instances. To the Moors, Chénier[10] ascribes that great innate healing power and insen-

---

1 "Reconnoitering Voy. in S. Austr.," p. 173, 1839.
2 "Hist. of N. S. Wales," p. 250, 1810.
3 "The present state of Austr.," p. 317, 1830.
4 Brehm, i, p. 202.
5 "R. in Eur., As., u. Afr.," ii, p. 2, 1843.
6 Ausland, p. 576, 1858.
7 "Eastern seas," p. 43.
8 Lefébvre, "Voy. en Abyss.," iii, 369, 1845.
9 "Life in Abyss.," ii, p. 268, 1853.
10 "Rech. hist. sur les Maures," iii, p. 205, 1787.

sibilty to pain, which has been so often attributed to the native Americans. Rengger[1] is also of that opinion, whilst many modern observers ascribe to the native Americans a highly sensitive and nervous constitution.[2] The case resembles that of the Bedouin Arabs, who consider it a point of honour to exhibit no sign of pain.

With regard to the native Americans, a relatively greater healing power of nature has been observed among the Blackfeet, the Indians of Paraguay and the Abiponians;[3] and of native Mexicans we hear that they heal wounds which would be mortal to Europeans by merely washing them with brandy.[4] Malays also frequently recover from injuries which would prove fatal to Europeans.[5] Of twelve Tonga Islanders whose arms were cut off in the rudest manner, one only died from loss of blood and another from grief.[6] Similar cases of Marquesas Islanders are reported by Marchand.[7]

These examples prove that the healing power of nature is greater among savage than among civilized peoples. We must not however close these observations without mentioning another circumstance which has been made use of to establish the specific difference between the races of man, especially between the black and the white. It has been asserted that the lice of the Negroes are not only black and smaller than in Europeans, but that they do not exist in the former, whilst the European louse perishes in the Tropics.[8] Both these assertions seem to have been first made by Oviedo,[9] which he qualifies by adding, that European vermin is rarely preserved, whilst that of the Indians only attacks some children of the whites born in America. As Peters[10] proves to a certainty, that the European

---

1 "Naturgesch. d. Säugeth," p. 12.
2 Ausland, p. 1146, 1857.
3 Prince Max., "R. in N. Am.," i, p. 581; Rengger, "Naturgesch. der Säugeth. von Paraguay," p. 12; Dobrizhoffer, ii, p. 54.
4 Heller, "R. in Mex.," p. 58, 1853.
5 Crawfurd, "Hist. of the Ind. Archip.," i, p. 31, Edinb., 1820; Harris, "Collect. of voy.," i, p. 743.
6 Mariner, "Tonga Isl.," ii, p. 251.
7 "Neueste R. u. d. Welt," i, p. 144, Leipzig.
8 Duttenhofer, "Die Emancip. der Neger,," p. 33, 1855.
9 "Sumario de la nat. hist. in Historiad. prim. de Ind.," p. 508, Madr., 1852.
10 "Monat. der Ges. f. Erdk. N. Folge," i, p. 98.

louse does not perish under the equator, there is no occasion to dwell further on this point. It is scarcely necessary to observe, that the domestic swine, though not specifically different from the wild hog, has a parasite which is wanting in the latter: the colour of these animals changes with the colour of the skin, on which account Sömmering[1] did not consider the *pediculus nigritarum* as of a different species from the European louse. It seems also certain that both the head louse and the *p. pubis* of Negro nurses passes to white children.[2] Quandt[3] is at any rate incorrect when he asserts, that the fleas and lice of Indians and Americans did not infest Europeans. Neither do the various species of intestinal worms exclusively infest one race, though one species may more or less predominate in any people. Thus in England, Holland, and Germany the *tænia solium* prevails; in Switzerland and in Russia, down to Königsberg, *bothriocephalus latus*; in the south-east of France both prevail; in Abyssinia and among the Hottentots *tænia* predominates.[4]

Another proof of the physical superiority of the white has been brought forward, namely, their capacity of being acclimatized in every zone. This, however, can only apply to the inhabitants of the temperate zone. If it be confirmed that the Sandwich Islanders, who live under the 20° N. lat., become excellent sailors, and can better support a cold climate than even the sailors of Boston, as mentioned by Duhaut Cilly,[5] then the perhaps merely theoretical assertion of Jarrold, that the Negro is, by the structure of his skin, better protected against climatic influences, and can alike thrive in every climate, is hardly correct. That savages cannot support the influence of climate as well as civilized people is mainly owing that the latter accommodate themselves to the climate by care and corresponding changes in their mode of life, which the uncivilized neglect. Hence it has been asserted that it is merely by the force of his intellect that man can subsist in every clime. This seems to be con-

[1] "Ueber die körperl. Verscht. des Negers v. Europ.," p. 8.
[2] Bachmann in Smith, "The Unity of the hum. races," p. 184, 1850.
[3] "Nachr. v. Surinam," p. 221, 1807.
[4] Owen, "Lect. on Comp. Anat. of the invertebrate animals."
[5] "Voy. autour du monde," ii, p. 302, 1834.

firmed by the fact, that the English who cannot give up animal food and spirituous liquors, are less able to sustain the heat of the tropics than the more sober Spaniards and Portuguese, whose dark skin and general habits render them better adapted to a tropical climate. The circumstance that (according to Ulloa and Humboldt) persons of and above middle age best support transplantation to a tropical climate, and reach an advanced age, of which the Batavia *Courant*[1] cites many instances, may perhaps be explained by greater attention paid in mature age to the general health. Zimmermann[2] has, in opposition to the view, that the capacity of man for acclimatization is increased by his intellectuality, cited the example of the Polar nations, who can sustain themselves, despite the small protection against climatic influences. This, however, proves nothing in favour of their capacity for supporting other climates without injury. We must further bear in mind that the incapacity of bearing a rapid change from one climate into one essentially different, is quite distinct from the incapacity to sustain a gradually progressing acclimatization, which must necessarily have taken place during the migrations of so many tribes through different degrees of latitude.

Though the circumstances above mentioned, contribute in many instances to exhibit the capacity for acclimatization to be less in savages than in Europeans, we must still be cautious in coming to any conclusion in this respect. We cannot, therefore, entirely agree with Humboldt,[3] when he attributes to the American Indians a lesser degree of capacity for acclimatization than to the Europeans, on the ground that the working in mines is so destructive to the former from the great changes of temperature. In some mines the temperature is 6° higher than the mean temperature of Jamaica and Pondicherry, so that we may question whether Europeans could without injury sustain such a heat and a sudden change to a low temperature, without injury. It is besides remarkable, when we learn that the mortality among the miners of Mexico is not much greater

[1] July 13, 1830.
[2] "Geogr. Gesch. des Menschen," i, p. 53, 1778.
[3] "Neu-Spanien," i, p. 161.

than among the rest of the population. Latterly, the opinion has gained ground, that the white races possess no particular privilege with regard to the capacity of acclimatization; but only so far has this view been adopted, that a general capacity to become acclimatized in all zones belongs to no race. The more important facts in support of this view are here subjoined.

The American race which inhabits all climates, refutes the privilege which has been assigned to the white race; but it presents, like other races, the phenomena that sudden transplantation into other conditions, causes mortality, unless proper precautions are taken. It is, therefore, not the absolute adaptation of every race to a peculiar climate or the incapacity of maintaining itself in a foreign climate, which causes its decay, but the abrupt change of external conditions. Thus, the Icelander who settles in Copenhagen, becomes liable to, and frequently dies of, consumption.[1] Indians who leave the mountainous parts of Peru to settle on the coast, or inhabitants of the coast who settle in the mountains, perish.[2] The Indian of the Savannah, when transplanted to the damp air of the primitive forests, dies of pulmonary disease, just as the inhabitants of the forests and the hills when they are obliged to settle in the open Savannah.[3] The mortality attending such forced transmigrations, called forth those edicts which were formerly published against this practice in Spanish America. The European, far from supporting the sudden change from one climate to another, finds the tropics as injurious to his health as the Negro finds the northern regions. The Arab and the Copt sicken like the European, in East Sudan, whilst the black displays there his full vital energy.[4] There are many districts in Africa where strangers, and especially Europeans, can neither live nor become acclimated, whilst the natives enjoy good health. Such is the case in some parts of the Darfur, the greater portion of Kordofan, Fernando Po, and Zanzibar. The military in Kordofan consists exclusively of blacks. It seems, however, from

[1] Clemens, "Deutsche Vierteljahrschrift," ii, p. 89, 1849.
[2] Proctor, "Narr. of a journey across the Cordillera," p. 299, 1825.
[3] Schomburgh, "R. in Brit. Guiana," ii, p. 126, Lpz., 1847.
[4] Werne, "Exped. z. Entd. der Q. des W. Nil," p. 47, 1828.

what Pallme[1] says of their sad condition, that the reason is not so much because of the sanitary state of the troops, but rather that the blacks are more easily managed.[2] In St. Felipe de Benguela all white women either miscarry, or bring forth weakly children who die during the first few months.[3] The country around the N'gami lake seems to be uninhabitable for the white, on account of the fevers; the natives alone can support it.[4] The climate of other countries in the tropics is likewise injurious to Europeans, though in a less degree than the African climate. According to Bryson,[5] the mortality of English soldiers in the East Indies is annually 15. per cent.; in the West Indies 18.1; in Africa 58.4. Of 100 European soldiers in East India there live, if well taken care of, and exclusive of such who are carried off by wars, after 5 years, 70; after 10 years, 45; after 15 years, 25; and after 20 years, only 10.[6] In the presidency of Bengal the mortality of the English European soldiers reaches annually 1 in 13.55; among the natives, 1 in 56; in the presidency of Madras, 1 in 26 of the former and 1 in 47·7 of the latter.[7] To prolong his life in the West Indies, the European requires great care and rest; violent efforts are most injurious there as well as in Guiana.[8] Reichardt, however, maintains that the debility and sickening of the Europeans in many tropical countries, and especially in Central America, are wrongly ascribed to the climate: they are rather the indirect consequences of slavery, indolence, sensual gratification, and an irregular mode of life.[9] The incapability of French soldiers to perform more than half the amount of bodily labour in hot climates, has been established by Coulomb at Mar-

[1] "Beschr. von Kordofan," p. 122, 1843.
[2] Mohammed el Tounsy, "Voy. au Darfour," p. 295, Paris, 1845; Pallme, "Beschr. v. Kordofan," pp. 7, 117, 122, 1843; Guillain, "Docum. sur l'hist. la géogr., et le comm. de Afr. Orient.," ii, pp. 1, 93, 1856; Allen and Thomson, "Narr. of the exped. to the R. Niger," ii, p. 198, 1848.
[3] Spix and Martius, "Reise," p. 669.
[4] Livingstone, "Journal R. Geogr. Soc.," xxi, p. 20.
[5] "Report on the climate and princ. diseases of the Afr. station," p. 178.
[6] Ausland, p. 968, 1855.
[7] Dieterici, Über d. Sterblichkeitverh. in Europa, Abh. d. Berl. Akad. 1851, p. 732: Compare M'Culloch in Quételet, p. 624.
[8] Graf. Görtz, "Reise," ii, p. 290.
[9] Nicaragua, p. 280, 1854.

tinique.[1] In consequence of the enormous mortality among the recruits who descend to the coast from the Mexican plateau (on one occasion there died 272 out of 300 in three months) it was resolved to employ acclimatized Negroes and men of colour for the garrison of St. Juan d'Ulloa.[2] A. de St. Hilaire[3] also observes that the blacks and men of colour supported the climate of Villa Boa much better than the whites. Pruner again (p. 68) assumes it as a fact, that the white race cannot perpetuate itself in the greater part of Negro regions. Without slaves, says Köler,[4] the fertile tropical valleys would be unproductive and deserted, as white men cannot labour there in the open air. Further proofs may be found in Nott and Gliddon,[5] who deny the capacity of the white to become acclimated in all Malaria regions, as well as that of the Negro in the West Indies. Dowding[6] calls attention to the fact, that in the whole of the West Indies the whites constitute at present but five per cent. of the population, and consequently the blacks and men of colour will in a short time be the sole occupants of these islands. We cannot, however, admit that incapacity for acclimatization under the tropics is peculiar to the white race, since individuals of any race seem inviable in regions in which they are not acclimatized, even in those parts from which they originally sprung.

Though the injurious influences of tropical climates affect the Negro less (and as it seems in a different manner) than the European, he is nevertheless not less exposed to injury than the white on suddenly changing his climate. Wilson,[7] who, from a twenty years residence on the Gaboon and in C. Palmas, has arrived at the conviction that the noxiousness of the climate of these regions had been exaggerated, states, that coloured people coming from the United States suffer as much from the climate as the whites, though the former accommodate them-

[1] Péron, "Voy. de découv. aux terres Aust.," ii, p. 427, 1824.
[2] Humboldt, "Neu-Spanien," iv, p. 408.
[3] "Voy. au sources du R. S. Francisco," ii, p. 71, 1847.
[4] "Notizen über Bonny," p. 156, 1848.
[5] "Indigenous races of the earth," p. 357.
[6] "Religious Partizanship, Africa in the West," Oxf. 1854.
[7] "Western Afr.," p. 511, 1856.

selves sooner to its influence. Negroes from dry countries, such as Bornou, Hausa, or the Sahara, die soon after their arrival in Sierra Leone. Their acclimatization seems as difficult as that of Europeans,[1] which is scarcely surprising, when we hear of the winter cold in Bornou, where before sunrise the thermometer sometimes sinks to $+4\frac{1}{2}^{\circ}$ c.[2] In Khartoum the natives are said to suffer as much, and even more, from the climate than Europeans;[3] this is, however, an exceptional case. In Senegambia fevers not dangerous to the natives usually kill the white.[4] In the West Indies the Negro exposes himself without injury to rain, which would cause a fever to the white.[5] The Negro can bear the rays of the sun upon a bare head.[6] It is even said that during the rainy season, which is the most dangerous for the European, he enjoys better health than during the dry season. This is reported of the Negroes in Senegambia, in Ruffi, and on the Niger, of the Ibus and of those in Iddah, on the Prince's Island, St. Thomas and Annabon, on the southern part of the west coast of Africa.[7] The rainy months in Angola, October and November, are for the European the healthy, and for the natives the unhealthy, season.[8] Upon the Island St. Thomas, June, July, and August are favourable to Europeans, and the reverse to the natives, who, though they suffer less from the prevailing diseases, are by no means exempt from them.[9]

On the coast of Guinea, the rainy season so injurious to the white, is, according to Roemer,[10] not less so to the Negroes. In Sierra Leone the month of July is dangerous to the blacks, and

1 Koelle, "Gramm. of the Bornu lang.," p. 8.
2 Barth, iv, p. 12.
3 Russegger, "Reise," ii, pp. 2, 38.
4 Raffenel, "Voy. dans l'Afr. ou.," p. 322, 1846.
5 Day, "Five years' resid. in the W. Indies," i, p. 87, 1852.
6 Werne, "Feldz. nach Taka," p. 134.
7 Brunner, "R. n. Senegambien," p. 111, 1840; Schoen and Crowther, "Journals of the exped. up. the Niger," p. 166. 1842; Allen and Thomson, i, p. 325; Boteler, "Jour. R. G. S.," ii, p. 275; Des Marchais, "Voy. en Guinée," iii, p. 9, 1731; Tams, "Die Portug. Besitz. in süd West Afr.," 1845.
8 Livingstone, ii, p. 65.
9 Des Marchais, loc. cit., iii, pp. 9, 5.
10 "Nachr. v. d. Küste Guinea," 1769, p. 10.

August to the whites.[1] Brehm however denies the different effects of seasons upon different races in East Sudan.[2]

Though, according to the above statements, it is scarcely probable, as asserted by Werne,[3] that Negro soldiers are less able to bear the fatigue of a campaign in hot countries than the white, it is not less certain that Negroes cannot without difficulty support a cold climate. The Negro is sensitive to even moderate changes of temperature.[4] Callié and other travellers relate that on such occasions they complain bitterly of cold; we must, however, bear in mind the scanty covering which they use. This must also be taken into consideration when Richardson[5] mentions that the Negroes seem not so well to support the hot winds in Sahara as the Arabs and the Moors, in addition to the fact, that in North Africa the change of temperature is sometimes very great, being on some occasions so low, that French soldiers have been frozen to death. The Kaffirs, who were some years since exhibited in Europe, did not show any of that sensitiveness to cold which the real Negro is said to possess. This sensitiveness is, however, not exclusively peculiar to the Negro; the Bisharis have the same peculiarity,[6] and the inhabitants of Fezzan, habituated to a high temperature, are accustomed, in inquiring about each other's health, to say, "I trust you don't feel cold."[7] A great susceptibility of change of temperature is a usual consequence of residence under the tropics, and is not confined to the Negro.[8] The Negro is said to become insane in cold climates; this, however, is not unfrequently the result of his being transported to other countries. Selberg[9] found among the Ashantee Negroes imported into Java, several suffering from insanity. In the New England states of North America, the Negroes, it is said, would become extinct were it

---

[1] Fraissinet, "Nouv. ann. des voy.," ii, p. 293, 1855.
[2] Brehm, i, p. 218.
[3] "Feldz. Nach Taka," p. 67; he contradicts himself p. 168.
[4] M. Park, "Voy. dans l'int. de l'Afr.," viii, pp. 1, 55.
[5] "Trav. in the gr. desert of Sahara," ii, p. 437, 1848.
[6] Bay. Taylor, "R. nach Central Afr.," p. 151, 1855.
[7] Ledyard et Lucas, "Voy. en Afrique pr. Lallemant," p. 116, 1804.
[8] Humboldt, "R. in die Æquinoctial," i, p. 254.
[9] "Reise nach Java," p. 45, 1846.

not for fresh importations. Knox[1] asserts the same thing of the Anglo-Saxon race in America.

The capacity of *blushing* has often been considered as a peculiarity of the white man, and has been denied to other races, and especially to the Negro. Blushing, however, is not merely seen in Mulattoes, and in delicate women of the black race (Lawrence, Lectures, p. 240), but also in Negroes.[2] Monrad[3] asserts that Negresses become darker when influenced by the sense of shame. The Australians also blush.[4] Though the blushings of dark-complexioned peoples must not be taken exactly in the same sense as these phenomena among the whites, still a certain change, a deepening of the colour, in consequence of some emotions, is perceptible in the former. We are, therefore, surprised to find that Roth[5] denies this capacity altogether to the Abyssinians. D'Orbigny observes that the native Americans also blush, though not very perceptibly on account of their complexion. According to Spix and Martius,[6] the change of colour resulting from emotions is confined to educated Indians, who have much intercourse with the whites. The Kalmucks are said not to become red from shame, but pale from fear and terror.[7] The common changes of colour in the face have also been observed in the inhabitants of Tahiti, Marquesas, and New Zealand.[8]

It deserves to be mentioned as a striking peculiarity in the formation of *speech-sounds*,—the cause of which some have sought for in the organs themselves,—that the Negroes have no *r*, the Australians no *s*, and that in Polynesia, the Fiji and Navigation islands excepted, the hissing sounds are wanting. The dialect of Rimatara, Rurutu, Tubuai, and Raivavai seems to have the

---

[1] "The races of man," 1850.

[2] Dupuy, "Journal of a resid. in Ashantee," p. 149, 1824; Golberry, "R. durch d. West Afr.," ii, p. 307, Lpz. 1803.

[3] "Gemälde der. k. v. Guinea," p. 60, 1824.

[4] Barrington, "Hist. of N. S. Wales," p. 10, 1810.

[5] Wagner, "Gesch. der Urwelt," p. 269, 1845.

[6] "Journey," p. 376.

[7] Bergmann, ii, p. 54.

[8] Forster, "Bermerk auf. s. R. um d. Welt," p. 204, 1783; Kotzebue, "Neue R. um die W.," i, p. 73, 1830; Melville, "Vier Monate auf d. Marquesas," i, 166, Lpz. 1847; Mundy, "Our Antipodes, or resid. in the Austr. col.," ii, p. 127, 1852.

least number of consonants of any language, possessing only seven—m, n, ng, p, r, t, v,[1] whilst the languages of the Sahaptin family in North America possess at least nine of them—h, k, l, m, n, p, s, t, w. Hueck[2] says that the Esthonians, like the Hottentots (W. v. Humboldt) are incapable of forming the hissing sounds from the narrowness of the hard palate, which perhaps also exists in other Finnish tribes. The peculiar click of the Hottentots, which led many travellers to consider their language as a mere chirping, deserves also mention. Thunberg[3] and Levaillant[4] have only been able to distinguish three, but Van der Kemp distinguished six of these sounds.[5] But as such clicking sounds have passed from the language of the Hottentots into some words of the Amakosa Kaffirs, and even into the language of the natives of Port Natal,[6] we can scarcely reduce the cause of this phenomenon to a peculiarity in the organs of speech. That this peculiarity is not an innate peculiarity of race, but merely a habit, is proved by the circumstance, that the Hottentot children who have passed their childhood among the white colonists, can on their return home as little acquire these difficult sounds as the missionaries.[7] Information regarding the quality of voice in most peoples, independent of the formation of speech sounds, is almost entirely wanting. It is scarcely doubtful that in this respect similar differences exist, as have been recently observed, among ourselves—namely, that among country people, even among men, the voices are high; but in the cities there are more low voices, and that the former seem gradually to diminish. That the voice of the Negro is rather low and hoarse, and that of Negresses high and shrill, has already been mentioned. The Kaffirs have generally deep bass voices, which are rarely found among the Hottentots.[8]

---

1 Hale, "Ethnogr. and phil. of the U. S. expl. exped.," p. 142, Philad. 1846.
2 "De craniis estonum," p. 9, 1838.
3 "Reise," ii, 61, 1792.
4 "Erste Reise," p. 289, 1790.
5 Lichtenstein, "Reise," ii, p. 605.
6 Thunberg, loc. cit.; Lichtenstein, i, 637; Colenso, "Ten weeks in Natal," p. 60, Cambridge, 1855.
7 "Rheinische missionsberichte," p. 54, 1851.
8 Moodie, "Ten years in S. Afr.," ii, p. 257, 1835.

With regard to the *use of the hands*, it rarely occurs among savage nations that they can use both hands with equal skill, as is said to be the case with the Indians of Yucatan.[1] As far as we know, the right hand is everywhere preferred to the left. In Great Bassam (Guinea coast) the right only is used in feeding, whilst the nails are allowed to grow long on the left hand, which is used for unclean occupations.[2] The word "mara," (left) signifies in the Vei-language also "wrong, unjust."[3] In the Zulu language right and left have a similar signification.[4] The natives of Senegambia, as well as those of the Darien isthmus, use only the right hand for eating.[5] The word "molemmi" (left-handed) occurs as a name among the Beshuanas;[6] it also applies to the ancient Peruvians,[7] whence we may conclude that the right hand is used among them preferentially. This is also the case among the Malays, especially among the higher classes. Ladies of high birth use only the right for eating and saluting (Crawfurd). The Macassars eat with the hand and wash themselves with the left.[8] From the question of the Pelew Islanders, put to Captain Wilson, as to which arm he used, it appears that they have a different use for each arm.[9] Among the North American Indians there are but few left-handed.[10] Hottentots and Bushmen appear only to be able to use one of their hands with skill.[11]

As regards the *perfection of the senses*, civilized man is generally inferior to the savage, with exception, perhaps, of the sense of taste, which is exercised in the variety of aliments, whilst the savage merely satisfies his appetite. As the whole existence of the uncivilized man depends in many cases on the use of his senses, he directs his attention to minute circum-

---

[1] Waldeck, "Voy. pitt. dans la prov. d'Yucatan," p. 66, 1838.
[2] Hecquard, p. 46.
[3] Koelle, "Outline of a grammar of the Vei," p. 199.
[4] Doehne, "Zulu Kaffir Dictionary," p. 228, 1857.
[5] Raffenel, "Nouveau voy.," i, p. 53; Wafer, loc. cit., p. 127.
[6] Burchell, ii, p. 368, 1822.
[7] Ausland, p. 205, 1858.
[8] "Rel. de la capt. du Capit. Woodard dans l'isle de Célébès," p. 150, 1805.
[9] Keate, "Account of the Pelew Isl.," p. 230, 1789.
[10] Say in James, "Account of an exped. from Pittsburgh to the Rocky Mountains," i, p. 284, Philad. 1823.
[11] They are almost *Manchot*. Arbousset et Daumas, "Rel. d'un voy. au N. E. du Cap de B. Esp.," p. 479, 1842.

stances, and combines them with other indications. They possess, observes Leichardt[1] of the Australians, an extraordinary local memory; peculiarly shaped or grouped trees, broken branches, and many other minute marks, seem to be impressed upon them like a photograph, all of which seems to be the result of concentrated attention. Schiel[2] received from a Delaware Indian, descriptions of countries which the latter had not visited for eighteen years, and yet they were found perfectly correct. The European, however, after from three to four years' practice, is also enabled to see twice as far as before, but he rarely acquires the skill in trailing possessed by the natives.[3] Kretzschmar[4] observes, that the Dutch boors at the Cape are almost as skilful as the Hottentots in this respect. Many interesting examples of this kind are related of the Bedouin Arabs, who are able to discern objects at a much greater distance than the Europeans.[5] They pursued without erring the tracks of men and animals among thousands. The Mongrels performed the same feats as the pure races. The Gauchos in South America possess the same skill in tracking as the pure Indians.[6] A Hottentot Mongrel discovered at a distance of more than 1,000 metres the movement of the head of a gazelle concealed in grass.[7] And McCoy[8] says, that the practised white does not show less aptitude in following the trace of animals or of the enemy than the North American Indians. Much of what Daumar[9] states of the high perfection of the senses of the Suafes, the inhabitants of the district Suf, is manifestly exaggerated. It can scarcely be doubtful whether we are in such cases to assume an originally acuter power of perception in uncivilized nations, or an acquired vigour of the senses. Both are perhaps combined,

1 "Tageb. einer Landreise in Austr.," 1851.
2 "R. durch d. Felsengeb.," p. 97, 1859.
3 Hodgson, "Reminisc. of Austr.," p. 249, 1846.
4 "Südafrikanische Skizzen," p. 327, 1853.
5 Ritter, "Erdk.," x, 1099; Riley, "Schiksale u. R. un der Wesk. von Afr.," p. 37, 1818; D'Escayrac, "D. Afr. Wüste u. d. Land d. Schwarzen," p. 287, 1855; Werne, "Feldz. nach Taka," p. 122.
6 Capt. Head, "Rough Notes," 2nd ed., p. 257.
7 Delegorgue, "Voy. dans l'Afr. Aust.," i, p. 135, 1847.
8 "Hist. of Baptist. Ind. missions," p. 344, Washington, 1840.
9 "La Sahara Algérien," p. 193, 1845.

(this is also the view of Rengger,[1] who states that the Indians can distinguish the kind of wild beasts by the noise in the bush, and a mounted horse from an unmounted one by the tramping of the hoof), for it has been observed, that in many animals continued exercise of the senses through several generations, gradually produces a corresponding improvement of the same. An example of this kind is furnished by the Dajakes, among whom such as lead a nomadic life have smell and sight very acute, which is not the case with those who are agriculturists.[2] That the inhabitants of the desert, like their camels and horses, perceive water at a considerable distance, is well known. Even Europeans acquire this power,[3] and it is scarcely surprising that, after a long-continued dryness of the air, a higher degree of moisture should produce a peculiar sensation. In Australia, where Leichardt could observe nothing of this kind in men or animals, Mitchell[4] heard a native use the expression, "the wind smelled of water;" and he found that his dogs discovered water more readily than the natives, and the latter more readily than the Europeans.

Sight and hearing are very acute among the Hottentots and Bushmen (Burchell); the latter see objects with the naked eye for which we require a telescope.[5] This is also the case among the Australians,[6] many Polynesians, New Zealanders, the inhabitants of the Paumotu-Archipelago, who perceive ships at much greater distances than Europeans;[7] and among most hunting tribes of the Mongolian race. The Papuas of New Guinea are also said to possess acute sight and hearing;[8] their sense of taste seems, however, very obtuse, if it be true what Freycinet[9] relates, that one of them swallowed the whole contents of a pepper-box, not only without experiencing any in-

---

1 "Naturgesch. de Säugeth. v. Paraguay," p. 10.
2 Kessel, "Bullet. Soc. Geogr.," ii, p. 514, 1852.
3 Burckhardt, "R. in Nubien," p. 286, 1820; Le Vaillant, Erste R., p. 348.
4 "Journal of an exped. in Tropical Austr.," p. 264, 1848.
5 Lichtenstein, ii, p. 320.
6 Turnbull, R. um d. Velt im Mag. v. Reisebeschr., p. 36, Berlin, 1806; Cunningham, "Two years in New South Wales," ii, p. 13, 1827.
7 Moerenhaut, "Voy.," i, p. 172.
8 Lesson, "Voy. Med.," p. 204, 1829.
9 "Voy. autour du m.," ii, p. 23, 1827.

convenience, but finding the taste excellent. Some sounds which are agreeable to one people produce very unpleasant sensations in others. The inhabitants of Bouka (Solomon's Islands) were enchanted by the sounds of the violin, which caused the inhabitants of Van Diemen's Land to stop their ears.[1] Fiddles and flutes produced no impression whatever upon the Esquimaux.[2] Beshuanas, who for the first time heard a missionary sing, began to shed tears.[3] This applies to other sensations. The Indians of tierra firma, when Columbus came to them, found the odour of brass very pleasant.[4] The Esquimaux in Prince Regent Bay, who eat raw putrid flesh, rejected with disgust, biscuit, salt meat, and spirituous liquors.[5]

The sense of smell is described as well developed among the native Americans. Azara[6] speaks of the great acuteness of sight and hearing among the Charruas, and Dobrizhoffer,[7] tells extraordinary things of the sight of the Abiponians. It deserves to be further investigated as an abnormal fact, that most Indians of the northern parts of the United States seem to be unable to distinguish green from blue, and that the western tribes have only one term for these two colours.[8] Among the languages of Central America, green and blue are also designated in the Quiche, Pocouchi, and Cacchiquel dialects by the same term, namely, "rax."[9] The acuteness of smell in this race is still more remarkable; so that the Caribs and Peruvians can distinguish the white, the Negro, and the American by the smell, and have different names for the various odours,[10] like the Bedouins, who track strayed camels by the smell.[11] The eastern neighbours of the Botocudes, the Machacares, though

1 Labillardière, ii, p. 50.
2 Seeman, "R. um d. Welt," ii, p. 67, 1853.
3 Livingstone, i, p. 192.
4 Herrera, "Hist. gen.," i, pp. 3, 11.
5 J. Ross, "Entdeckungreise um Baffin's Bay ausz.," pp. 46, 52, 54, 1820.
6 "Voy. dans l'Am. merid.," ii, p. 9, 1809.
7 Loc. cit., ii, p. 24.
8 Kohl, "Kitschi-Gami," i, p. 25, 1859.
9 Ximenes, "Hist. del'origen de los indios de Guat.," ed. Scherzer, p. 15, note.
10 Labat, "Nouv. voy. aux Iles de l'Am.," i, p. 157, 1724; Humboldt, "Neu-Spanien," i. p. 245.
11 Burckhardt, p. 300.

no longer savages, but reclaimed Indians (Indios mansos), distinguish by the smell in the abandoned huts the particular tribes of Indians to which they belonged.[1] In North America the Indian prisoners have in former times been employed by the whites to track the enemy, which they did chiefly by the smell. Colonel Church, who distinguished himself by his bravery against the Indians during the first settlement of the Europeans, observes, in his history of the war against the Indian chief Philipp, that the sense of smell of a native is but little inferior to that of a bloodhound.[2] Their sense of smell is said to be so acute, that they cannot bear the strong odour of musk or the like, and they protest that no odour is so agreeable to them as that of the various kinds of food.[3] It seems, therefore, a strange exception, that the Potawatomis are inferior in this respect to the whites.[4] Also among the tribes of Lower Columbia taste and smell are obtuse, but sight and hearing acute.[5] In the Negro,[6] the olfactory, optic and trigeminal nerves are much developed, yet the sense of sight is but moderate; but the hearing is more acute and better developed than in the Egyptian. This should caution us against assuming, as has often been done theoretically, great acuteness from the size of any organ of sense. Thus the considerable development of the ethmoid bone and the organ of smell in the Negro has been considered as an approximation to the brute; opposed to which Jarrold observed, that the Negro did not use his sense of smell to a greater extent than other races, and that, despite the large development of the organ, he effects less by his smell than the native American. Though the approximation, in this respect, to the brute may be admitted on anatomical grounds, it is inadmissible from a physiological point of view. The inhabitants of Kordofan are certainly able, when they pursue fugitive slaves, to trace, like hounds, the tracks of

---

[1] Feldner, "Reisen durch Brasil," ii, p. 146, 1828. Compare, "Memoirs of the Hist. Soc. of Pennsylvania," iii, p. 128.

[2] Drake, "The book of the Indians, biogr. and hist.," Boston, 1845.

[3] Heriot, "Trav. through the Canadas," p. 152, 1807.

[4] Keating, "Narr. of an exped. to the source of St. Peter's R.," i, p. 136, 1825.

[5] Parker, "Journal of an explor. tour beyond the Rocky Mountains," p. 242, 1838.

[6] Pruner, "Ztschrft. der morgenl. Ges.," i, p. 132.

individuals among a thousand.[1] Similar feats are related of the Negroes in the Colonies, especially on the occasions of the wars with the Maroons; yet these performances, in which it is questionable whether sight or smell play the chief part, are, according to what has been stated above, not so extraordinary that they must be attributed to a peculiar gift, nor do they occur in Africa more frequently than elsewhere. B. Edwards[2] asserts, that the smell and taste of the Negro are dull, but sight and hearing acute. Labat[3] says, on the other hand, that Negroes detect snakes by smell. That their other senses are very acute is confirmed by Dallas.[4] The children of the natives of Bonny are said to remain blind for ten days after birth.[5] That the ear is well developed is proved by his love for music, united to a good perception of rhythm and time; his capacity for the perception of melody is said to be less.[6] The music of the Negroes is certainly often not much more than a horrid noise: still a musical ear cannot be denied to them, as the flute and horn music in Ashantee, the music of the Mandingoes, especially in Kuranko, also that in Benin and Dahomey, is described as agreeable and harmonious. In Dahomey they understand how to employ thirds, fifths, and the full chord in music.[7] We must also bear in mind, that a great portion of the popular music in the United States comes from the Negroes,[8] and that slaves hire themselves of their masters to gain money as musicians. Negro melodies are inserted in Bush.[9] If the Maroon Negroes in Jamaica have a particular horn-signal for calling any individual,[10] there is a still more extended use made of musical signals on the Cameroons. Information

---

[1] Russegger, "Reise," ii, pp. 2, 151.

[2] "Proceedings of the Governor of Jamaica in regard to the Maroon Negroes," p. 39, 1796.

[3] "Voy. aux Iles de l'Amérique," ii, p. 35.

[4] "Gesch. der Maronen-Neger auf Jamaica," p. 149, 1805.

[5] Froschel, in "Monatsb. der Ges. f. Erdk. N. Folge," vi, p. 108.

[6] Hamilton Smith, "Nat. hist. of the hum. spec.," 1848.

[7] Bowdich, "Mission nach Aschanti," 1820; Dupuy, "Journal of resid. in Ashantee," p. 106, 1824; Hecquard, "R. an. d. k. v. West. Afr.," p. 121, 1854; Laing, "Voy. dans le Timmani, Kouranko," p. 187, 1826; Bosman, "Viaggio in Guinea," iii, p. 278, Ven. 1752; Dalzel, "Gesch. v. Dahomey," p. 34, 1799.

[8] Pickering, "The races of man," p. 185, 1849.

[9] "Wanderungen zw. Hudson u. Mississ.," i, p. 254.

[10] Dallas, loc. cit.

is communicated by them and a kind of conversation carried on in this manner.[1] This is also done on the Gold coast[2] and in the Bissagos-Archipelago. Royal proclamations are published in this way.[3] Finally, as regards the sense of touch in the Negro, Hamilton Smith describes it as very acute. The Fanti-Negroes discriminate different impressions: they use the middle finger to weigh gold, and prefer this mode to actual weighing.[4]

We believe we are justified in concluding, from the above instances, that the varied powers of the senses do not rest upon a different endowment of individual races, but depend on the different occasions which call them forth, according to the habitual mode of life of the peoples. In endeavouring to give at the end of this section an account of the results obtained by our investigations, we must confess that they are not perfectly satisfactory. The comparison of the Negro with the ape on the one hand, and with the European on the other, has shown that there are certain anatomical differences prevalent among mankind. Though these are neither as numerous and important as has been represented, in order to assign to the Negro an intermediate position between the European and the ape, and though the various peculiarities which distinguish different races cannot be considered as fixed barriers between them, they are still sufficiently great to leave it doubtful whether they lie within or beyond the sphere of changes produced on the physical nature of men in the course of time. In order to decide this question, a further investigation will be necessary, which we reserve for the fourth section. With regard to the physiological comparison between the various races of mankind, we may state that its results are favourable to the theory of the unity of mankind; for everywhere have the various differences which we have mentioned proved to be not fixed, but fluctuating, and dependent on changes of external and internal conditions.

---

[1] Allan and Thomson, ii, p. 307.
[2] Cruikshank, "Achtzehnjähr. Aufenthalt auf d. Goldk.," p. 283.
[3] Durand, "Voy. au Sénégal," an. x, pp. 213.
[4] G. A. Robertson, "Notes on Africa," p. 168, 1819.

APPENDIX TO SECTION II.

ON THE ASSERTED INVIABILITY OF THE AMERICANS, POLYNESIANS, AND AUSTRALIANS.

The facts we have collated appear sufficiently to prove that none of the uncivilized peoples are deficient in viability. There remains, however, one circumstance in favour of an opposite doctrine, which is, the rapid decay of several races and their apparently approaching extinction. We shall, therefore, have to investigate whether the causes of their extinction consist in a defect of their organization, or whether the fact must not be attributed to accidental circumstances. The tribes of which we shall have to speak are the aboriginal Americans, Polynesians, and Australians.

The rapid diminution of the aboriginal population of America is established by the official census, and can thus admit of no doubt. In some regions the diminution may have been only apparent. When we have the statement, that all the peoples which the first immigrants found in Louisiana and Mississippi, have almost entirely disappeared, and even their names forgotten, it may be explained by some misconception. The names of small tribes have frequently, by travellers, been given to represent whole nations, whilst the names are often those of chiefs and their families. The old travellers exaggerated the numbers of the peoples by seeing themselves on their arrival surrounded by a crowd of natives, who had merely collected on the spot from considerable distances either to see or to drive away the wonderful strangers. Hence the old estimates of the native population of America and Polynesia are evidently erroneous. There can, however, be no doubt that the aboriginal population has diminished in a most remarkable degree, which we in the first place attribute to destructive diseases.

The American Indians may, possibly before the arrival of the whites, have been visited by pestilential epidemics, but it is chiefly after the arrival of the whites that epidemics of various kinds, and especially the small-pox, have raged among them. No race seems to have suffered so much from the small-pox as the Americans, whilst the Negroes have at all times been little liable to this epidemic. On the shores of the Gulf of Mexico and upon the Antilles, which were first visited by the whites, the small-pox first appeared, and contributed much, perhaps most, to the depopulation which took place in the large West Indian islands. In the northern parts of the continent they appear to have spread (about 1630) a few years after the arrival of the first settlers, and the natives knew well to whom they were indebted for this fatal gift. In New England the natives thought that the whites carried the small-pox poison in bottles for the destruction of the Indians—a fable which was encouraged by the settlers in order to make themselves feared. Thus Dobrizhoffer quotes the expression of the Indians of South America: "The whites are truly good people; they have given us a rich compensation in the small-pox for the gold and silver they have carried off." The following statements, by no means complete, may give some idea of the devastation caused by small-pox. Of the North Indians nine-tenths perished by it.[1] The Mandans were, with few exceptions, carried off in 1837; the Blackfeet diminished from 30,000 or 40,000 to 1,000. Similar devastations occurred among the Crow Indians, Minatarrees, Camanchees, and Riccarees; among the latter many killed themselves after recovery, from grief at being disfigured.[2] The Omahas lost two-thirds of their tribe.[3] The Indians in California did not fare better (Schoolcraft); in the Missions one-half are said to have perished.[4] In South America the fate of the natives does not seem to have been less hard. Small-pox epidemics raged among the Indians of Paraguay and Gran Chaco,[5] among the Puelches (D'Orbigny), the Corroados, the

[1] Hearne, "R. v. Prinz Wallis-fort bis z. Eismeer," p. 168, 1797.
[2] Schoolcraft, "Hist. of the Ind. tribes."
[3] Washington Irving, "Astoria," p. 119, 1838.
[4] Wilkes, "U. St. Expl. Exped.," v, p. 172, 1845.
[5] Pöppig, "R.," ii, p. 452.

Caribs on the Marañon, and in the whole northern part of Peru.[1] On the Upper Orinoco, small-pox is almost unknown.[2] According to Molina[3] the Indians of Chili had at that period suffered little of small-pox; they must, however, have known its fatal issue, as that author states that they set fire to the huts in which they suspected a patient attacked by the small-pox, so that he might be burned. Falkner,[4] however, states positively that the Araucanians have been visited by this pestilence. In Guiana, the villages Taruma, Atorai, and the Taurai-Indians have disappeared together; and small-pox, measles, and the fear of being bewitched by the Kanaima, have nearly annihilated them. The number of the Macoushis diminishes daily, like that of the Wapisiana and Amaripa, to whom, in regard to language, belong the Atorai.[5] Other diseases besides the small-pox, such as measles, contributed to the decay of the natives. Two-thirds of the aborigines of the Oregon district perished by fevers and the small-pox.[6] Small-pox and measles raged in the Mosquito country.[7] The want of physicians and the perverse modes of treatment to which the patients were subjected, contributed not a little to the fatal issue of these diseases.[8] The so-called upper Chinooks were in the year 1823 reduced by fever from 10,000 to 500, that, as frequently happens among the North American Indians, the living did not suffice to bury the dead.[9]

It deserves mentioning,[10] that the mere contact of different races, though in perfect health at the time of their meeting, frequently produces destructive diseases from which the inferior race, or the aborigines who are visited by the strange race,

---

[1] V. Eschwege, "Journal v. Brasil," i, p. 206, 1818; Labat, "Nouv. voy. aux isles de l'Am.," ii, p. 122, 1724; "Allerhand lehrreiche brief v. d. miss. d. Ges. Jesu.," i, p. 60, Augsburg, 1726; Ulloa, "Voy. hist. de l'Am. merid.," i, p. 349, Amst. 1752.

[2] Humboldt and Bonpland, "Reise," iv, p. 26.

[3] "Essai sur l'hist. nat. du Chili," p. 23, 1789.

[4] "Beschr. v Patagonien," 1775.

[5] Schomburgk, "Jour. R. G. S.," xv, p. 26.

[6] De Smet, "Missions de l'Oregon," p. 19, 1848.

[7] "Bericht über d. Unters. des Mosquito," p. 21, 1845; Young, "Narr. of a resid. on the Mosquito shore," 2nd ed., pp. 24, 73, 1847.

[8] John Dunn, "Hist. of the Oregon territory," p. 115, 1844.

[9] Wilkes, v, 140; Hall, 215.

[10] Darwin, German by Dieffenbach, ii, p. 214.

suffers most. Thus Humboldt[1] observes, that the great epidemics of Panama and Callao occurred after the arrival of European ships in Chili. Fever, cholera, etc., destroyed the natives in the South Sea after the arrival of Europeans. The belief that the whites import all diseases is general in the south, the Gambier islands, Rapa, Raivavai, Tubuai, Rurutu, Rarotonga (Moerenhout), and even among the inhabitants of Pitcairn (Beechey), in Tahiti.[2] In Rarotonga a destructive pestilence broke out immediately after some trading between the natives and the crew of an apparently healthy European ship, (Williams.[3]) This opinion also prevails in Celebes, where Brooke was on that account prevented from landing.[4] The Boers of the Cape, who under Potgieter visited Algoa Bay, are said to have introduced in that part a croup-like disease, with which they were not themselves affected.[5] The belief that the Whites brought with them a virus, which they let loose upon the natives, prevailed all through New England, caused probably by the circumstance that shortly after the stranding of a French ship near Cape Cod, there broke out among the Indians, in 1616, a destructive pestilence, which so depopulated the coast for a distance of several hundred English miles, that the survivors were unable to bury the dead.[6] Assuming the correctness of the above statement, we cannot subscribe the mystical and especially in America, popular theory, that the aboriginal race of the new world would, even without drunkenness, war, or imported diseases, have become extinct by the approach of civilization as "from a poisonous breath, because nature has devoted it to destruction;"[7] that its organization is originally defective, carrying within it the germ of death.[8]

There can be no question that, under favourable circumstances, severely visited peoples may recover their losses, as happened in Europe. Such was the case with the Crees in North

---

1 "Neu Spanien," iv.
2 Turnbull, "R. um d. Welt.," p. 266, 1806.
3 Baseler, "Missions-Blätter," p. 100, 1838.
4 Brooke, "Narr. of events in Borneo and Celebes," 2nd ed., i, p. 48, 1848.
5 Livingstone, ii, p. 307.
6 Drake, "Hist. and antiq. of the city of Boston," p. 30, 1854.
7 Pöppig, Art. "Indier," in Ersch und Gruber.
8 Martius and Dieffenbach, über die Neu-Zealänder.

America;[1] also with the Winnepegs;[2] with Apaches, who recovered again a portion of their country from the Mexicans;[3] and in a still greater degree with the Sauks, who used to adopt their prisoners in their tribes.[4] After the decimation of the population in earlier periods in Greenland by destructive epidemics, it now increases at the rate of one per cent. in North Greenland, and from two to three per cent. in South Greenland.[5] The Winnebagoes, or Winnepegs, have from the year 1812 to 1820 increased from 3,500 to 5,800 souls. As with the Menomonies so with them, the females outnumber the males by one-third, and the number of children is in both tribes proportionately much more considerable than among the Indian tribes who have intermixed with the whites. The Cherokees likewise considerably increased in number before they were compelled to leave the country.[6] According to Olshausen,[7] who opines that the number of Algonquins has rather increased since the arrival of the whites, the number of Cherokees is said to have grown, since 1760, from 12,000 to 30,000, and that of the Choctaws from 16,000 in 1772, to 25,000. However oppressed the natives of Guatemala[8] are by the Spaniards, they increase so rapidly, that the latter begin to fear them. Wells[9] observes, that in recent times the Blacks and Mulattoes in Honduras zealously watch and resist the immigration of white Americans, as they hope shortly to be the sole masters of the country; but Squier[10] says, "All observers agree that the whites decrease in Central America, not merely relatively, but absolutely, whilst the pure Indians increase rapidly, and the cross-breds, the Ladinos, gradually approach the Indian type." Tschudi[11] expressly contradicts the assertion of Weigl and Martius, that the natives began to decay on

---

1 Simpson, "Narr. of a journey round the world," i, p. 87, 1847.
2 Schoolcraft, loc. cit., ii, p. 535.
3 Kendall, "Narr. of an exped. across the prairies," ii, p. 67, 1845.
4 Keating, i, p. 225.
5 V. Etzel, "Groenland," p. 376, 1860.
6 Morse, "Report on Ind. affairs," append., pp. 48, 59, 375, 152.
7 "Dass Mississipi Thal.," i, p. 300, 1853.
8 Gage, "Voy. dans la nouv. Espagne," ii, p. 68, Amst. 1771.
9 "Explor. and adv. in Honduras," p. 197, 1857.
10 "Die staaten von Central Am.," German by Andree, p. 28, 1856.
11 Chap. ii, p. 369.

account of the approach of civilization. The extinction of the Maynas is sufficiently explained by the ravages of disease. Dobrizhoffer[1] shows that the number of the Abiponians had actually increased after infanticide and polygamy had been abolished. In Lima the Indians have, from 1793-1820, increased from 3,600 to 5,000, and a proportionate increase is observed in the whole country; a diminution in taxation, the abolishment of forced labour, and a better treatment in general, afford the only explanation for these phenomena.[2] Moreover, we hear of considerable diminution in the number of other races, without attributing it to an original want of vitality. As well-known instances we may mention the Jakutes and Aleutes, who are greatly oppressed, the Jukagires and Kamschatdales.[3] The Aleutes perish by brandy, famine, excesses, and, it may be added, by a systematic system of extermination on the part of the Russians. Numerous suicides and sexual excesses promote the extinction of the Kamschatdales.

Another principal cause which leads to the extinction of the aborigines of America is their mode of life and their relations to each other. Many of these tribes gather no provision for the winter, but consume their stock, so that they are often exposed to the greatest privations. Whenever an opportunity offers they cause the greatest devastation among the game, and thus deprive themselves of resources for the future. The Indians on Hudson's Bay even believed that the deer increased in proportion as they killed them.[4] As among many Asiatic tribes, so in America, the custom prevails of burying or burning the property of the deceased with him. Among the Sioux the funeral nearly swallows up the property of the deceased, so that the survivors are in distress (Schoolcraft). In the ancient half civilized states of America, as in Mexico and Peru, religious worship included an immense number of human sacrifices, which were also practised by other tribes related to the

[1] Chap. iii, p. 140.
[2] Caldcleugh, "Trav. in South Am.," ii, p. 68, 1825.
[3] Billings, "R. nach d. nördl. Gegenden v. Russ. As. und Am.," p. 121, 1803; Wrangell, "Statist. und Ethnogr. nachr. über d. russ. Bes. in Am.," p. 218, 1839.
[4] Ellis, "R. nach Hudson's-Meerb.," p. 196, Gött., 1750.

Aztecs, and extended to Panama.[1] Without entering into any further details, we may also mention the many internecine wars which the Indians have ever carried on between themselves. From the slightest of all causes, sometimes from mere suspicion of having been bewitched, or from the revenge of an individual who induced his tribe to espouse his cause, wars have ensued, and have become so habitual, that many tribes are incessantly at war. Though these wars have not been generally very bloody, still some were exterminating in their consequences.

Thus the Coppermine Indians were nearly exterminated by the Dog-rib Indians (Hearne); the Moquis by the Navahoes (Schoolcraft); the Osages were, by their numerous enemies, reduced within ten years by one-half.[2] The remainder of the conquered tribe is not unfrequently absorbed by the conquerors, and the name of the former disappears from history. In this manner the Creeks are said to have gradually absorbed the remainders of fifteen other tribes. Thirdly must be mentioned the wars of the Indians with the whites. It will here be sufficient to notice but a few of the principal facts, as we shall have to treat of them in detail in another place. It is well not to lose sight of them in considering the question, whether the European man possesses, in comparison with other races, the character of humanity in a higher degree.

It is an historical fact, that the Natches, the Shawanoes, the Delawares, Potowatomies, Seminoles, Kaskaskias, and several other formerly powerful tribes, have, chiefly by the wars with the whites, been either exterminated, or brought so near to extinction, that they no longer exist as nations. Even at this day the Indians in the gold districts of California are hunted like wild beasts; and recently in Mexico, Indians and white Americans have been hired, and were paid for the scalps of the Apaches. In consequence of some suspicion that other people were killed on account of the prize-money, the practice is now

[1] Ternaux, "Recueil de docum. sur l'hist. des possess. Espagnoles dans l'Am.," p. 115, 1840.

[2] Nuttal, "Journal of trav. into the Arkansa territ.," p. 172, Philad., 1821; Gregg; "Karawanenzüge durch d. West. Praeriesen," ii, p. 189, 1845.

discontinued.[1] Among the so-called heroes of old Kentucky and Virginia there were man-hunters, who, as regards cruelty and barbarity against the aborigines, did not yield to the Dutch Boers on the Cape. Even Schoolcraft, the official historian of the Indians of the United States, feels compelled to admit thus much, though he would willingly ascribe the cruelties of which the aborigines have been the victims to the earlier expeditions of the Europeans to America, when dreams of glory and thirst for gold drove the Christians into distant lands, and when heathens were scarcely considered as men, and were treated like beasts. It is sufficient to mention the incursions of Velasquez, d'Ayllon, Narvaez, De Soto, Menendez, Pizarro, Cortés, to point out the vast misery and the enormous losses which the aborigines suffered from the whites. The history of the conquest of Mexico and Peru, the extermination of the peaceable population of the West India islands, the oppression of the Spanish governors in Yucatan (where the Indians were only employed as beasts of burden), the extermination of the Indians in Popayan Chiquitos by mining labour,[2] have, by the old historians of these countries (among whom we would refer the reader to Ternaux),[3] been preserved by documentary evidence, which fills, unquestionably, one of the darkest pages of human history.

Whilst the hostile collision of the Indians with the Europeans caused their wholesale destruction, peaceful intercourse with the whites was not less injurious to them. Careless of the future, the aborigines of North America readily disposed of large tracts of lands.[4] In most cases they were largely imposed upon, and the consequences were always distressing. To

---

[1] Kendall, ii, p. 62.

[2] The assertion of Azara (ii, p. 240), that the number of Indians in South America had increased where there are no mines, and when only employed in agriculture, is doubtless too general. Seemann ("R. um die Welt," i, p. 211, 1853), is open to the same objection, in maintaining that the number of Indians had everywhere increased where they have kept themselves pure, but had diminished wherever they intermixed with the Whites and Negroes; though it must be admitted that such an intermixture may have contributed to their diminution, as in proportion as intermixture progresses, the number of aborigines of pure descent decreases.

[3] "Voy. Rel. et Mem. originaux," p. 312, etc.; Recueil, p. 46, etc.

[4] Drake, "The book of the Indians," iii, p. 14, etc., 9th edit., 1845.

mention only one instance, the Creeks in less than forty years disposed of a territory of about twenty-eight millions of acres; and though other lands were assigned to them, these belonged to the whites as their creditors. The chiefs only, when they assisted in cheating their own tribes, were on such occasions well cared for.[1] The natives were frequently driven from their fertile districts into marshy, unproductive spots. Since 1840 they were all assigned to the region beyond the Mississippi, on the western boundary of the United States. Many of them perished during these transmigrations, and in their new settlements they either found other tribes already located, or were confined to narrow districts. Want of space brought them into collision with neighbouring tribes, as peoples living by the chase require extensive districts. The whites also introduced the use of brandy, and made them drunkards. Many perished in this way, as they were not, like the Arabs of Algiers, restrained from this vice by love of money.[2] Far from considering intoxication as hurtful or disgraceful, they considered it merely as a means of enjoying a short period of bliss. It was only when the dreadful consequences became generally manifest that some chiefs (of the Kickapoos, Creeks, Cherokees, for instance) tried to stem the current. Whenever the Indians received ready money for lands, it was spent in spirituous liquors. Though at a later period the sale of brandy to the Indians was forbidden, it continued, and it was only since 1848 that a complaint of an Indian chief against a brandy merchant was attended to (Schoolcraft). Even the good intentions of the whites proved injurious to the Indians. The Spanish missions in California had them captured for the purpose of converting them. Many of them died in their new localities. The missions having been abandoned, the Indians returned to their forests. Yet, notwithstanding all these facts, the white American is still surprised that the Redskins do not become civilized, and consoles himself with the thought that Providence has doomed them to destruction; and German scholars have subscribed to that opinion.

---

[1] Featherstonhaugh, "Excursion through the Slave States," ii, p. 306, 1844.
[2] M. Wagner, "Reise," ii, p. 32.

The scanty prolificacy of the native women has also been mentioned as a principal cause of the decay of race, and this phenomenon has been attributed to an original defect of organization. The small fecundity of the native women of North America had already been noticed by Lafitau,[1] and has been confirmed as regards some tribes of the present day. Among the Winnebagoes in 1842, women had on the average but one child; in Oregon, two (Schoolcraft). The causes of these phenomena are not given with the statements; but in other instances the explanation is of a kind as to exclude the idea of an original organic defect of the race. Among the Knisteneux, abortion and infanticide, especially of girls, is frequent (Mackenzie). In South America two children is the average number; and Azara[2] observes, that women get rid of the others by abortive draughts. The Guaycurus and Lenguas, who generally only bring up one child, are, in consequence of this practice, approaching extinction.[3] Among the Botocudes, who are said sometimes to have many children, infanticide and abortion are less frequent. Rengger[4] observed nothing of this kind among the Guaranis, but noticed it among the Payaguas, who by small-pox, drunkenness, and abortion, had been reduced to two hundred souls. Quandt[5] saw in Surinam a native woman with five children. Schomburgk[6] considers it as a rare instance of prolificacy that an Indian possessed nine children by three of his wives. In Brazil an Indian woman has rarely more than four children.[7] Among the Potowatomies, artificial abortion is not often resorted to, but the children are, as among other Indian tribes, suckled for a long period, sometimes to the fourth or fifth year; even one child aged twelve has been seen to suckle. In several parts of Mexico, specially in Panuco, the custom also prevailed of suckling the children up to the twelfth year[8]. In South America this custom prevails among the Guaraunos and other

---

[1] "Mœurs des Sauv. Américains," i, p. 590, 1724.
[2] "Voy. dans l'Am. mérid.," ii, pp. 59, 179, 1809.
[3] Eschwege, "Journal v. Brasil," ii, p. 274, 1818.
[4] "R. nach Paraguay," p. 133, 1835.
[5] "Nachr. v. Surinam," p. 254, 1807.
[6] "R. in Guiana," p. 375, 1841.
[7] Freyreiss, "Beit. z. Kenntniss v. Brasil," p. 118, 1824.
[8] Gomara, loc. cit., pp. 438, 440.

tribes only up to the fourth year of the child, but after this with young animals—a monkey, dog, or opossum.[1] Sterility of the women is frequent.[2] Heckewelder and Lahontan[3] mention that in ancient times the natives did not marry before the thirtieth year, as it weakened the body, rendering it unfit for war. All this is now changed. Too early marriages seem to have contributed to weaken the race and to render the marriages less prolific, a circumstance already known to Aristotle.[4] Schomburgk[5] attributes the decay of the Tarumas in Guiana to the deficiency of women, and to the circumstance that girls marry before the period of puberty. With regard to South America, D'Orbigny observes, that the women, though never sterile, have only from two to three children on the average. Burmeister, however,[6] attributes the diminution of the number of the people to early deaths and feeble productiveness. With regard to the first statement we certainly find that the Cholones, for instance, on the upper Huallaga, scarcely reach the fortieth year, have rarely more than two children, and are frequently childless; but these inhabit an unhealthy region,[7] and this must be considered as an exceptional case.

From the preceding facts it must be inferred, that the sterility of the American race, wherever it occurs, is owing to a variety of causes among the different tribes. The prevalence of artificial abortion renders this sterility more apparent than real. Among some tribes the sexual appetite seems to be proportionably weak in the men;[8] hence the Indian women have intercourse with the Negroes, whilst the men consider it beneath their dignity to cohabit with a Negress,[9] a circumstance which may, perhaps, be connected with the small development of the genitals among the Guaranis, Coroados, etc.[10]

---

1 Schomburgk, in "Monatsb. der Ges. f. Erdk." iii, p. 208.
2 Keating, i, p. 131.
3 Loc. cit., ii, p. 130.
4 Illustrative cases in Lucas, "Traité de l'hérédité," ii, p. 460.
5 "Journal R. Geogr. Soc.," xv, p. 45.
6 "Reise," p. 250.
7 Pöppig, ii, p. 322.
8 Rengger, "Naturgesch. der Säugeth."
9 Spix and Martius, "Reise," pp. 369, 376.
10 Rengger, p. 2; Eschwege, i, pp. 126, 230.

The last circumstance is, however, not general: it is, for instance, not observed in the Puris,[1] nor are there any observations that it influences the productiveness of these peoples. On the other hand, the great abuse of spirituous liquors, and the misery of the natives, the frequent want of means of subsistence, the heavy labour imposed upon them by the whites, may clearly be enumerated as the causes, the combination of which has produced the apparent weakness of the race. How deceitful this appearance is may be proved by the example, that also in South Arabia many marriages are unproductive, although polygamy is not prevalent among the mass of the population. In America, also, there are not wanting instances which contradict the above assertion. The women on the north-west coast are very prolific.[2] Among the North Indians it is considered exceptional if the number of children amounts only to five or six.[3] Among the Chippeways the average number of children is four; sterility is considered a disgrace, being looked upon as the consequence of incontinency.[4] Among the Sioux sterility is rare: from three to eight children is the usual number, and no one remains unmarried.[5] The Mandans have often as many as ten children, but, in consequence of the long period of suckling and the heavy labour of the women, less prolific marriages are frequent.[6] Say[7] found among the Kansas instances of three children born at one birth, and families of thirteen children. An instance of an Indian who had fourteen children by one wife, is also given.[8] Heckewelder[9] knew among the natives a converted Indian family with thirteen, others with six to nine, children; the usual number was from four to five. Among the Omahas, who have mostly from four to six children, and sometimes from ten to twelve,

---

[1] Eschwege, i, p. 163.
[2] Portlock and Dixon, "R. um d. Welt," p. 213, Berl. 1791.
[3] Hearne, "R.," p. 262.
[4] Keating, ii, pp. 152, 165.
[5] Schoolcraft, iii, p. 238.
[6] Prince Max, "R. in N. Am., ii, p. 129; and "Brasilien nachträge und Zusätze," p. 99.
[7] James, "Acc. of an exped. from Pittsburg to the R. mountains," i, p. 124, 1823.
[8] Ausland, p. 997, 1857.
[9] "Nach. v. d. Gesch. der Ind. Völkersch." p. 389, 1821.

sterility is rare, and proceeds, when it occurs, probably from the male, as the women are frequently prolific with other men.[1] Gumilla[2] has made the same observations as regards the South American women. An Osage chief had thirty-seven children by his four wives.[3] A. Vespucci found in 1497 Venezuela thickly populated about the region of Cape Paria; the women were then excellent breeders.[4] Labat[5] also speaks of the great prolificacy of the Caribs. Humboldt and Bonpland[6] mention the great fecundity of the Guaraunos and the Indians in the missions distant from the Orinoco. Of some tribes it has already been observed, that they have not lately decreased, but increased. Finally, it may be mentioned, that Jefferson[7] states, that Indian women who marry European traders, and are relieved of their hard labour, properly settled and well fed, produced as many children as European women: in some cases they have brought up from six to twelve children. Rengger's statements[8] with regard to the Guarani women are to the same effect. West[9] confirms them by observing, that Indian women married to Europeans breed better than with the men of their own stock, though they suffer more during delivery. There can be no doubt that the principal reason of their being more prolific is the improved mode of life. Thus among the Bedouin-Arabs the prolificacy is less than among those who are settled; five children are considered among the Towaras upon the Sinai-peninsula as a very large family;[10] and among the Lapps and Tunguses more than three to four children are rare.[11]

More obscure in many respects than the gradual decay of the native population of America, is an analogous phenomenon in the South Sea and Australia. Here one might feel more inclined to assume a defective vitality of the race, since one of

---

1 Say, in James, p. 237.
2 "Hist. nat. de l'Orenoque," ch. lii, 1758.
3 Ibid., ii, p. 251.
4 "Colleccion de los Viages y descubrimientos," iii, p. 209, 1829.
5 "Nouv. voy. aux Iles de l'Am.," ii, p. 109, 1724.
6 "R. in d. Aequinoctialg.," i, p. 469; and iv, p. 31.
7 "Beschr. v. Virginien," in Sprengel's Beitr. viii, p. 263.
8 "R. nach Paraguay," p. 133, 1835.
9 "Substance of a journal during a residence at the Red R.," p. 54, 1824.
10 Ritter, "Erdkunde," xiv, p. 953.
11 Scheffer, "Lapland," p. 334; Georgi, p. 266.

the chief causes of the depopulation of America is absent in Polynesia, and has not caused very extensive devastations in Australia, namely, the oppression of the whites and the intercourse with them. There is, however, one circumstance which did not so much prevail in America, but seems very effective in Australia, namely, the great mortality among children.

The extinction of a people once healthy and vigorous cannot be explained by a denial of viability, or an original defective organization, or by the assumption of some mysterious cause; we must investigate and search for natural agencies, though we may be obliged to confess that our endeavours to trace them have hitherto not been perfectly successful.

The decrease of the population in Polynesia, concerning which Meinicke[1] has furnished valuable statistical accounts, does not proceed in equal proportions in all the islands. The merry inhabitants of the Tonga and Friendly islands produce many children, and their number is increasing;[2] and in Tikopia every family has three to eight children.[3] On the other hand, the population decreases in the islands of the Samoa Archipelago, on the Gambier islands, in New Zealand, where Crozet[4] found in 1771, in the island bay, twenty villages, each having about four hundred inhabitants. Though these may have withdrawn into the interior,[5] it remains still a vain attempt of Shortland[6] to show that the decrease is merely apparent and not real. If it be true that in the village Te Aro, containing seventy men and forty-two women, there are but twenty-four children,[7] and if similar proportions, as we understand, occur in other places, Fox[8] is perfectly justified in assuming a yearly decrease of at least 4 per cent. Power[9] is of opinion that if the decrease continues *pari passu*, the country will be depopulated about

---

[1] "D. Südseevölker und d. Christenth." p. 111, 1844.

[2] Pickering, p. 83; Quarterly Review, Dec. 1853; Erskine, "Journal of a cruise among the islands of the W. Pacific," p. 161, 1853.

[3] Gaimard, in d'Urville, "Voy. de l'Astrolabe," v, p. 309, 1830.

[4] "N. Reise durch d. Südsee," p. 27, 1783.

[5] Dieffenbach, "Trav. in New Zealand," ii, p. 14, 1843.

[6] "The Southern districts of New Zeal.," p. 40, 1851.

[7] "On the British colonization of New Zeal. by the Committee of the Aborig. Protect. Soc.," p. 52, 1846.

[8] "The six colonies of New Zealand," p. 53, 1851.

[9] "Sketches in N. Z.," p. 119, 1849.

1870. Taylor,[1] an author well acquainted with the country and the people, has recently denied the progressive mortality of the natives, and cites facts against it.[2] Peace, appropriate clothing, diet, and mode of life, may possibly lead to an improvement in this respect.

With regard to Tahiti, where, according to the natives, the diminution of the population had already commenced before the arrival of the whites,[3] Vincendon-Dumoulin and Desgraz[4] have endeavoured to show that the decrease was about one-third from 1770 to 1814, and that from 1814 to 1825 the number of the population remained stationary. In estimating the ancient population, we must not take Forster's account[5] as a basis, when it states that he found in Tahiti a fleet of 159 large double canoes and seventy smaller ones; some of the former with 144 rowers, for it is probable that of this fleet a comparatively small portion only belonged to Tahiti, and the greater part to the large neighbouring islands. The Spanish account of 1778 estimates the population of Tahiti at 15,000 to 16,000.[6] Wilson[7] states that, according to a moderate estimate, the population of Tahiti was in 1797 about 16,000. It is only subsequent to this period that we learn that the population in 1804 amounted only to 5,000.[8] This is probably a great exaggeration, caused perhaps by the circumstance that about that period many young persons were carried off. According to Kotzebue,[9] the population amounted in 1824 to about 8,000, which is about the same number as given by the missionaries in 1813. This agrees with Wilkes's statement,[10] that the population in 1839 was about 9,000; to which he adds, that for thirty years previously the births and deaths had been about equal. Though

---

[1] "New Zealand and its inhabitants," p. 256, 1855.
[2] Compare however, "R. der Novara," iii, p. 128.
[3] King and Fitzroy ("Narr. of the Surv. Voy. of the Adv. and Beagle," ii, p. 520, 1839) are probably in error in stating that destructive diseases only broke out after Cooke's arrival at Tahiti.
[4] "Iles Taiti," p. 288, 1844.
[5] "Sämmtl. d. Rbschr.," xxi, p. 328.
[6] G. Forster's "Sämmtl. Schriften," iv, p. 211.
[7] "Missionsreise in d. stille Meer," Magz. v. R., xxi, p. 333, 1800.
[8] Turnbull, "R. um. d. W.," p. 259, 1806.
[9] "Neue Reise," i, p. 97, 1830.
[10] "U. St. Expl. Exped.," ii, p. 49.

Lesson[1] states that but few old people could be found in Tahiti, and that the number in 1830 amounted only to 500,[2] we cannot but conclude that the decrease of the population commenced about the beginning of the present century, after the Europeans had settled in Tahiti, when within ten years it diminished from 15,000-16,000 to 8,000-9,000, after which time the number appears to have remained stationary. According to the census of the French officials it amounted in 1848 to 8,082; in 1854, to 5,988.[3] Different proportions prevail in other islands of the archipelago. At Borabora, where one birth annually is reported to thirty-two inhabitants, the proportion of births to deaths is 5 : 6.[4] At Raiatea, on the contrary, the population of which, consisting in 1830 of about 1,700, stand morally and physically higher than that of Tahiti, the number has been much increased.[5]

Very decided and well authenticated is the progressive depopulation of the Sandwich islands; regarding which Vancouver[6] stated, that in 1792 a perceptible diminution of the population commenced after Cook's arrival. Exact information dates only from modern times, though all prove that the decrease still progresses.

The annual diminution is calculated to be about 8 per cent.[7] The census for 1832 was 130,313; for 1836, 108,579; for 1850, 84,165. In the year 1848 there were 7,943 deaths and 1,478 births; in 1849, 4,320 deaths and 1,422 births.[8] In 1853 the population amounted only to 71,019; births, 1,513; deaths, 8,026: 5-6,000 of these died of the small-pox;[9] hence it is an erroneous assertion of Bennet,[10] that the Sandwich Islanders are a very healthy people, and free from such fatal diseases as befal the inhabitants of the Friendly Islands. It is remark-

---

1 "Compl. des Œuv. de Buffon," ii, p. 281.
2 "Journal, R. Geogr. Soc.," iii, p. 174.
3 "R. der Novara," iii, p. 197.
4 Steen Bille, "Bericht über d. R. der Galathea," ii, p. 363, 1852.
5 "Journal R. Geo. Soc.," iii, p. 179.
6 "R. nach der Südsee," i, p. 139, Berl., 1799.
7 "Morning Chronicle," May 1, 1850.
8 "Details regarding individual islands," in Virgin., i, p. 267.
9 "Baseler Miss. Mag.," iv, p. 98, 1854.
10 "Narr. of a whaling voy. round the globe," i, p. 242, 1840.

able that this decay of population is so differently distributed in the various islands; nay, that districts in the same island differ in this respect. It is therefore probable, that the chief causes of this progressive decay must be sought for in local conditions, and not in an organic defect of the race. Whilst in Hawaii and Oahu, where in 1840 there were 61 births to 132 deaths, the decrease is certain and large, it seems only apparent in Maui. At Atowai or Kawia, where, among 5,541 adults, there were only 65 women who had more than two children, a missionary found in one district the proportion of deaths to births to be 3 : 1. In other districts, however, the decrease of the population was only about 1 per cent.; in some it was stationary, or slightly increasing; thus at Onihau or Niihau the increase of the population was 4 : 3.

In proceeding to an investigation of the causes of the above phenomena, and bearing in mind the epidemics which apparently break out at the first intercourse of uncivilized peoples with higher developed tribes, we must leave it to the judgment of others whether this would account for the decay of so many South Sea peoples; for it does not apply to all of the Polynesian stock, nor can we assent to the plausible supposition of an original defect of organization.

In ancient times, and before the first arrival of Europeans in the South Sea, the peculiar habits of the Polynesians had already contributed to diminish the population. Drunkenness and gluttony prevailed among the higher, and infanticide among the lower classes of society in many of the Polynesian islands. Only such tribes as the New Zealanders, who seemed ignorant how to prepare intoxicating liquors, did not at first seem to relish the spirituous liquors introduced by the Europeans; the rest were ruined by it, especially after they had learnt from the whites the art of distillation. Infanticide, artificial abortion, and sexual excesses, without the least perception of any moral wrong in this respect, diminished the population, and produced a weakly race. In the Sandwich Islands a family never brought up more than two or three children, the rest were strangled or buried alive.[1] Two-thirds

[1] Ellis, "Polynes. Res.," iv, p. 327, 1832.

of all children born are said to have thus perished.[1] To this must be added internal wars, combined with cannibalism and human sacrifices, for where men eat each other, the gods are generally bloodthirsty, and receive their share. With regard to the devastations caused by wars, we shall mention but one fact, viz., that, at the conquest of the western part of the Paumota Islands, thirty-eight islands were depopulated, and their inhabitants slain or carried into slavery.[2] Moreover, those who possessed the most fertile islands of Polynesia entirely neglected agriculture, and ruined themselves by the greatest prodigality at their feasts, consuming all provisions, so that the lower classes died by famine.

The introduction of christianity in the South Sea islands removed many of these sources of destruction, others were mitigated so that this progressive decay was arrested. The bloody wars, cannibalism, human sacrifices, and infanticide disappeared almost entirely; and it must be denounced as a calumny inspired by party spirit, that French navigators, to serve the interest of their Government and their faith, have endeavoured to spread the opinion, that the depopulation of the Sandwich islands can only be explained by the severe laws and the system of intimidation established and practised by the influence of Protestant missionaries; that the women fled to the forests to kill their illegitimate children in order to escape punishment.[3] We must, on the contrary, acknowledge that the missionaries are entitled to credit for their endeavours to improve the physical and moral condition of the islanders, though their activity cannot be said to have proved beneficial in all respects. Their severity appears to have produced the concealment of many vices and crimes, and the sudden change of the habits of life which were at once and with great strictness forced upon the natives, sometimes may have proved injurious. There can, however, be no doubt that, on the whole, the material condition of the South Sea peoples, which alone concerns us

[1] Stewart, "Journal of a residence in the Sandwich Islands," p. 250, 1828.
[2] Wilkes, i, p. 313; Hale, p. 35.
[3] Laplace, "Campagne de circumnavigation," V, p. 470, 1841; Du Petit-Thouars, "Voy. autour du monde," i, p. 389, 1840; de la Salle, "Voy. autour du monde sur la Bonite," ii, p. 198, 1845.

here, has been improved; and this presents a fresh difficulty in the explanation of a progressive decay.

In order to understand this, we must remember that, at the time of the arrival of the Europeans in the South Sea (as Moerenhout, and especially Meinicke, have proved), there prevailed already an extreme dissolution of social relations, morals, and religion, among the chief nations of Polynesia. This apparent break up of society, the result of long-continued excesses, was much promoted by the arrivals of the Whites. The enervated race of the Tahitians, and the weakened inhabitants of the Sandwich islands, had then much to suffer from the new diseases imported by the Europeans. Next to influenza, great destruction was caused by syphilis constantly imported by 15,000 to 20,000 seamen, chiefly whalers, who landed in Honolulu and Lahaina.[1] Many of these diseases became fatal from the small protection afforded by the scanty dress and defective habitations of the natives. In New Zealand, Dieffenbach considers that the decay is chiefly owing to a change of dress and habits of life, so that scrofula and its allied affections have spread among children.[2] This also applies to the Society islands of Raiatea. The population of Burutu, say Tyermann and Bennet,[3] had, a few years ago, been reduced by fever from 6,000 to 314. The sterility of the women and the mortality among the children, are no doubt closely connected with the decrease of the population. Both phenomena are very common in the Sandwich islands.[4] According to the missionaries only half of the marriages are prolific.[5] The great mortality of the children in the Society Islands, where infanticide has been replaced by artificial abortion, is said to be greatly owing to an improper alimentation. The number of children, which in Tahiti is not large, rarely in the Marquesas exceeds two to one woman.[6] In Samoa, the number of children

[1] Virgin, i, p. 269.
[2] Fox, loc. cit., p. 55.
[3] "Journal of voy. and trav.," i, p. 497, 1831.
[4] Wilkes, iv, pp. 77, 94.
[5] Hines, "Oregon, its history," p. 210, Buffalo, 1851.
[6] Krusenstern, "R. um d. Welt," i, p. 198, 1810; Melville, "Vier Monate auf. d. Marq.," ii, p. 125, 1847. Langsdorff (i, p. 152) asserts that twins are not rare.

is limited by the long continued suckling, sometimes up to the sixth year, or several children are suckled at the same time.[1] In New Zealand, where the proportion of females to males is small, because many girls are killed immediately after birth, a woman has rarely more than two or three children.[2] Perhaps the trade in preserved ornamented heads may have contributed something to the diminution of the population.[3] Psychical causes also appear to have injuriously affected the physical prosperity of the peoples, such as the feeling of powerlessness and certain destruction by the Whites, and the loss of authority of the chiefs among their own people[4]—a circumstance which also contributed to the decay of the Americans, who are absolutely unfit for slavery.

The peoples in the Sandwich islands were in former times much oppressed by their own chiefs. The taxes were enormous, and the labour imposed upon them excessive, so that they were compelled to neglect agriculture to cut sandal-wood and perform other work. Many of them ran away; infanticide and famine raged among them;[5] and even in recent times a progressive poll-tax unfavourably influenced the increase of the population.[6] About a thousand individuals annually leave their native country, proceeding to California, Columbia and other parts of South America.[7] The aborigines of Australia, the inhabitants, at least, of the known parts of that continent, also approach rapid extinction. A tribe of about three hundred souls is said to have diminished within six years to four individuals.[8] The causes of these phenomena are similar to those already stated. The chief of them are diseases communicated to them by European settlers, to which must be added infanticide and great mortality among the children, the small proportion of women, inebriety in the vicinity of the colonies, and sexual excesses.[9]

1 Wilkes, ii, p. 138.
2 Dieffenbach, ii, p. 33; Pickering, p. 82.
3 Quarterly Review, p. 192, June 1854.
4 Fox, p. 56.
5 Jarves, "History of the Sandwich Islands," p. 368, 1843.
6 Walpole, "Four years in the Pacific," ii, p. 245, 2nd edit., 1850.
7 Simpson, "Narr. of a journey round the world," ii, p. 15, 1847.
8 Baseler Miss. Mag., iv, p. 96, 1854.
9 Eyre, "Journals of exped. into central Austr.," ii, p. 320, 1845.

Small-pox carried off in some parts, particularly in New South Wales not long after the year 1788, the sixth to the third part of the natives; though taught by experience they left off the cold water cure, and applied a more appropriate mode of treatment.[1] Small-pox also caused great devastations in the interior,[2] as well as the measles and syphilis.[3] Even the clothing furnished by the colonists often proved injurious to them; from having become accustomed to woollen coverings they felt the want of them when again deprived of these articles.

Infanticide, especially of girls, is frequent: hence the proportionately small number of women.[4] This proceeds partly from superstition, partly from the desire to escape the trouble of rearing them, and sometimes from revenge against the faithless father, especially if he be an European. The great mortality of the children seems also to be caused by the negligence of the parents, and inappropriate diet. Turnbull asserts that three-fourths of the children do not attain the fourth year. Grey[5] does not think that the mortality is great, though much greater than in Europe; he remarks, also, that suckling is continued until the third year. He knew 41 women whose children amounted to 188. The average number of children in a family is, according to Eyre, about five, of which two only are brought up. There are, however, instances of a woman having nine children.[6] This is corroborated in other races. The inhabitants of the North African desert are equally distinguished by their small number of children, about two on the average.[7] It is more rare to find a Hottentot woman with six, than the wife of a colonist with twelve, children.[8] When, however, well-treated and rendered comfortable, the Hottentot women are very prolific, both in their intercourse with the

---

[1] Wilkes, ii, p. 184; Baker, "Sydney and Melbourne," p. 148, 1845; Bennet, "Wanderings in N. S. Wales," i, p. 154, 1834.

[2] Mitchell, "Three exped.," i, p. 216, 1838.

[3] Darwin, "Naturalists' Voyage," ii, p. 213, 1844; Eyre, ii, p. 380.

[4] "Austr. felix," p. 131, Berl., 1849.

[5] "Journals of two exped. in Austr.," ii, p. 251, 1841.

[6] "Austr. felix," p. 130.

[7] Richardson, "Trav. in the Sahara," ii, p. 427, 1848.

[8] Burchell, "R. in d. Innere von Südafrika," ii, p. 175, 1822.

Whites and their own people.[1] The fecundity of the Indian women is equally increased by better nourishment and diminution of labour.[2] A Chippeway woman is mentioned who had fourteen children all grown up. From these instances we are justified in concluding that sterility is not a peculiarity of the race, but is caused by external circumstances.

How much the natives have suffered from the invasion of Europeans is expressed in the following words of a native:—"You Whites," said an Australian, "ought to give us Blacks, cows and sheep, for you have exterminated our opossums and kangaroos; we have nothing to live on, and are hungry."[3] Though in some parts the natives no longer live by hunting kangaroos,[4] it still is in other parts their principal resource for subsistence. They are in the habit of burning down the grass for the growth of a fresh crop for the pasture of these animals, who are driven off by the cattle of the colonists, and the natives disappear from the spot. At present the aborigines possess no right to the country, or rather they never had any; at any rate, England has never acknowledged such a right. The land belongs to the Crown, which practically means that the natives, being English subjects, may be punished for their crimes, whilst the Whites are generally acquitted by their countrymen.[5] This becomes intelligible when we find that the natives can neither be valid witnesses in a court of law, nor are allowed to bear firearms.[6] Latterly, however, they have in New South Wales at least been admitted as witnesses, but in so limited a degree, that their oppression is but little mitigated by the favour accorded.[7]

An attempt has been made to justify the great injustice done to the natives owing to their atrocity, which is greatly exaggerated. According to the "Papers on Aborigines of Australian Colonies,

---

1 Moodie, "Ten years in S. Afr.," ii, p. 350, 1835.
2 Schoolcraft, iv, p. 350.
3 Bennet, i, p. 327.
4 Hodgkinson, "Aust. from P. Macquarie to Moreton Bay," p. 223, 1845.
5 Instances in Eyre, ii, p. 176; and in Du Petit-Thouars, iii, p. 204. There was a criminal process in which the jury for a long time refused to condemn the culprits who were guilty of an unprovoked murder of twenty-eight natives.
6 Howitt, "Impressions of Austr. felix," p. 199, 1845.
7 Eyre, ii, p. 493; "Austr. felix," p. 143.

printed for the House of Commons, August, 1844," p. 318, there were in the district of Port Phillip, since its first occupation, eight Whites killed by the natives and forty-three natives by the Whites.[1] If the natives wish to continue their mode of life, they must quit the region, join other tribes, or become beggars and robbers, which indeed they have become. A general warfare between them and the Whites in Portland Bay and other districts was the consequence.[2] That it is impossible to live with or near them in peace has been often refuted. A settler has frequently succeeded in gaining over the friendship of the natives, so that even in critical times he was not molested by them.[3] This is also proved by the success of the settlement of Moorunde on the Murray in 1841. The natives, who at first were inimical, became, in consequence of the kindly treatment of the colonists, friendly and serviceable.[4] Eyre obtained on this occasion a great authority over them, by which Sturt's expedition into the interior was facilitated. Dawson also knew how to gain them over in Port Stephens, and describes them as peaceable and serviceable. With one man only he was unsuccessful.[5] All others proved docile when well treated, and especially when the principle is adopted of not limiting their freedom more than is absolutely requisite for public safety.[6] Most of the settlers found it more suitable to their dignity to exhibit everywhere their superiority, as the Whites did in America. The natives were shot down whenever they showed themselves; cruelties were committed on women and children.[7] The natives had most to suffer from runaway convicts, and it may be imagined how much a penal colony must have injured the native population,—for New South Wales was one up to 1843, Van Diemen's Land up to 1852, and West Australia has be-

---

[1] Eyre, ii, p. 156.
[2] Baker, p. 154.
[3] Hodgson, "Reminiscences of Australia," p. 81, 1846.
[4] Eyre, ii, p. 461.
[5] Dawson, "The present state of Austr.," p. 265, 1830.
[6] Compare on this subject the extract from the "Australian," Oct. 14, 1836, by Dumont d'Urville, "Voy. de l'Astrolabe," i, p. 489.
[7] Wilkes, ii, pp. 186, 256; Lang, "Account of N. S. Wales," i, p. 37, 3rd edit., 1840; Clutterbuck, "Port Phillip in 1849," p. 62; Byrne, "Twelve years wanderings in the British Colonies," i, p. 368, 1848.

come one recently. The English Government has repeatedly in official documents acknowledged the wrongs done to the natives,[1] and expressed the intention of repairing the injury. If it were true that the colonists have contributed but little to their destruction, and that the main cause, as has been asserted, lies in their own mode of life,[2] then it is inconceivable why they have not long become extinct, since there has not been an essential change in their mode of life. The official protectorate, which, however, seems to have borne but little fruit, was instituted in consequence of the crimes committed against the natives by the Whites. In several parts of Australia a larger number of natives are said to have been poisoned when it became known that they would for the future be protected against oppression.[3] In many parts of New South Wales they made no secret of it, as Byrne[4] states from his own experience, but even boasted that the natives have been got rid of by arsenic.

SECTION III.

THE RESULTS OF INTERMIXTURE OF DIFFERENT TYPES, AND THE PECULIARITIES OF THE MONGRELS.

Before proceeding to the question of the unity of the human species, we have yet to consider a series of phenomena which, though not so decisive as was formerly believed, still possess more than a secondary importance, namely, the results of intermixture and the character of the cross-breeds. These will show that we are not compelled to assume a specific difference between human races. The practical difficulties of fixing the results of intermixture are, no doubt, very great; still they do not much affect the principle laid down.

---

[1] See the document in Tegg's "N. S. Wales' Pocket Almanack" for 1841, p. 147, Sydney.

[2] Schayer in "Monatsb. d. ges. f. Erdk. N. Folge," ii, p. 226.

[3] Eyre, ii, p. 176.

[4] Loc. cit., i, p. 275.

The pains taken to fathom the mode in which the peculiar bodily organization is transmitted from parent to offspring have hitherto been unsuccessful. There has not been wanting a number of theories, but not one has proved itself unexceptional and trustworthy. Thus it frequently happens among animals and human beings that the offspring resembles the male parent in hair, colour, constitution, diseases, malformation and idiosyncracies. As collateral relations (cousins, uncles, and nephews) frequently exhibit the same peculiarities without having received them direct from their parents, we are led to suppose that these phenomena obey a law (the so-called relapse—that is to say, the reproduction of the peculiarities of remote ancestors in the descendants,—has by Girou been considered as a general law, by which he endeavoured to explain all the differences of children from their parents), the comprehension of which would require a profounder knowledge of the dependence of the development of the germ than we at present possess.

Sometimes the father, at other times the mother, has been considered as possessing an exclusive influence on the peculiarities of children. Again it has been asserted that the father influenced the psychical, and the mother the physical, constitution of the offspring; or again, that they influence separate parts of the system. Thus, according to Sturm and Girou, the young in domestic animals resemble the father in the form of the head and the chest, and the mother in the formation of the pelvis and the posterior part, a view which Blumenbach felt inclined to adopt also as regards man. Some were of opinion that, where one child took after one parent, it was both physically and psychically. Others considered the influence of the father paramount, not a few that of the mother, so that the sons resembled the father, and the daughters the mother, a case which, however, is frequently reversed. There was, in fact, no theory which had not its supporters.[1] We quote the following interesting observation of Burmeister,[2] "Generally speaking, the first child exhibits physically the finest organization, and

[1] See Lucas, "Traité de l'hérédité," vol. ii.
[2] Loc. cit., ii, p. 162.

presents intellectually, more than the others, either the peculiarities of the father or of the mother; and it is to be noticed that the first-born son takes more after the mother, and the first-born daughter more after the father. Gradually the children become more robust, physically stronger, frequently plainer and more plump; the qualities of both parents become more mixed, and a decided repetition of the parents or grandparents becomes rarer."

It deserves to be noticed that the cases in which the influence of the father predominates are not so frequent as contrary instances. The influence of the mother on the intellectual nature of the offspring seems so predominating, that Buffon considered it as exclusive: hence the vulgar expression "motherwit," not "fatherwit." The head of the cross-breed, however, takes chiefly after the father.[1] The physical qualities of the father generally predominate among cross-breeds.[2] This is the case among the Mestizoes in the Philippines, whether the father be a European or a Chinese;[3] among the Mulattoes on the Sandwich islands.[4] The Negro produces with a white woman a more Negro-like child than the white man with a Negress.[5] Among the children of Mulattoes—themselves, with few exceptions, descendants of white fathers and Negro mothers,—the white blood predominates,[6] so that the children even of a Mulatto woman and a Negro possess the colour of the mother. Pruner says that the offspring of a Negro and a white woman, though rarely viable, approach the European type sooner than that of a Negress and a white man. Burmeister considers the Negro character as predominating in Mulattoes. The boys have the hair often frizzly, then it becomes perfectly Negro-like; among the girls it is frequently straight. The shape of the head resembles more that of the Negro than that of the European; the forehead is low, the occiput short. The cranium generally is small, the beard stronger than in the

[1] Heusinger, "Vgl. Physiol.," p. 250.
[2] Spix and Martius, "Reise," p. 1183.
[3] Mallat, ii, p. 134.
[4] Bennet, "Narr. of a whaling voyage," i, p. 240, 1840.
[5] Nott and Gliddon, "Types of mankind," p. 373, 1854.
[6] Lyell, "Second voyage."

Negro, the stature on the whole more elegant, especially the hands and feet, which latter are, however, rather flat. It may also be noticed, that among Mulattoes sprung from Negroes and Indian women on the Rio das Pedras (Paranahyba), the Indian character predominates, namely, dark colour, broad chest and shoulders, short neck, large angular head, bushy hair, rather thin lips, well-shaped legs.[1] Pöppig[2] describes the Mestizo—generally the child of an Indian woman and a white man—as resembling more the Indian. The Portuguese Mulattoes also, at Ceylon, who are more numerous than the Dutch, resemble in stature, shape of skull, and features, more the Cingalese than Europeans.[3] Stevenson[4] states, from his own observation, that the father influences the colour of the Mestizo more than the mother. He also observes that the Peruvians call the children of a white woman and a Negro Mulatto, Zambo Mulatto, Quadroon; whilst those of a white man and a Negress, Mulatto woman, or Quadroon, are called Mulatto Quadroon Quintroon, by which he endeavours to prove that the mongrels of a white man approach the European type a generation before those of a white woman. Tschudi,[5] however, considers this an error, and states that the designation is the same whether the mongrels proceed from the father or the mother.

Lucas[6] has by many examples proved that the characters of mongrels are not constant; sometimes those of the mother, at other times those of the father predominate. The Danes produce with Hindoo women, children of European type and vigour; but such is not the case with other European nations (Rush). The mongrels of Europeans and Mongols constantly exhibit the type of the mother (Klaproth); those of Europeans and Hottentots always exhibit the character of the father (Le Vaillant). With regard to the latter, Burchell[7] remarks, that the children

---

[1] A. De St. Hilaire, "Voy. aux sources du R. S. Francisco," ii, p. 253, 1847.
[2] Loc. cit., i, p. 201.
[3] Schmarda, "R. um d. Erde," i, p. 462, 1861.
[4] "Reise in Arauco," i, p. 180.
[5] "Peru," i, p. 161, 1846.
[6] Loc. cit., ii, p. 3.
[7] Loc. cit., ii, p. 185.

of a white woman by a Hottentot are taller, whiter, and of more European features than those of a Hottentot woman and a European. The latter are brown, thick-set men, with hair less crisp than that of the Negro, flat nose, hollow cheeks, no beard, and but few hairs on the upper lip.[1] According to Sparrman,[2] their bones and muscles are more developed than in Hottentots.

Since it results that there is no certain rule with regard to the greater resemblance of mongrels to either of the parents, we must try whether other facts may not throw some light on this question. Some authors have taken as a starting point, the greater or less differences of types. If the difference be important, the mongrel represents the intermediate type;[3] and this intermediate form is, according to I. Geoffrey St. Hilaire, constant. On the other hand, when the parent stocks are less distinct, the mongrel approaches constantly one of the types of either parent. In the intermixture of the Negro and the European, which Geoffroy considers as specifically distinct, intermediate types are constant results. Nott and Gliddon agree in this view, but add that the cross-breeds of different species of men do not, in respect of characters, all obey the same law; for while Europeans and Negroes produce an intermediate type, others (Europeans and Americans) produce types resembling either of the parents.

With regard to animals, for instance, mongrels of wild and tame hogs, dogs, cats, birds, take either after the male or female. We may admit that in man the Mulatto type appears to be constant, but this applies chiefly to the first generation; as by a continued admixture of new elements of the white or black race, a variety of forms is produced, as shown by the following examples. The third child of a three-quarter white woman by a Mulatto (half-breed), had the colour of the father; the other children were lighter in colour than the mother. A Mulatto woman bore to a Negro two children

[1] Arbousset et Daumas, "Rel. d'un voy. au N. E. du Cap de B. Espérance," p. 20, 1842.
[2] "R. nach d. K. d. g. H.," p. 261, 1784.
[3] Edwards, "Des caractères phy. des races humaines," p. 21, 1829.

of her own colour, and eleven others who were even blacker than the father. A Negress bore to a Mulatto, nine or ten black children and two or three of the colour of the father (Nott and Gliddon). In the same family may be seen Mulatto children with crisp, or with light, straight hair (Burmeister). A Negro in Berlin had by a white woman seven Mulatto girls, and four white boys.[1] Lucas[2] relates three similar cases: a white woman had by a Negro a black child, a Mulatto, and a white boy. Campbell[3] mentions a similar case. When d'Abbadie[4] states, that among the red race in Abyssinia, black children are seen, and that among the Negroes of these regions red and black individuals are seen in the same tribe, they are probably mongrels, of which the type is inconstant.

With regard to the mongrels of the American race, we equally observe a great variation in external appearance. The Mestizo-mongrels of white men and American women—recognized in Mexico by their yellowish, weak beard, and somewhat oblique aperture of the eyes[5]—have in Quito small foreheads and coarse hair, small, pointed nose, and good beards; some of them have a fair skin and light hair, others are as dark as the Indians;[6] they are mostly well formed, yet easily recognizable by their low foreheads and great leanness.[7] In the central parts of Peru, on the contrary, of Herculean frame, and a whiter colour, frequently with a yellowish tint.[8] In Chili they are often taller but less compact than the Indians: still they are broad-shouldered, with a short neck, short arms, small hands and feet; and in this as well in hair, cheek-bone, flat nose with large nostrils, resemble the Indians.[9]

In Concepcion they are as white as the Spaniards; some of

---

[1] Siebold, "Journal f. Geburtsh." vii, p. 2.

[2] Loc. cit., i, p. 213.

[3] "R. in Süd.-Afr.," p. 360, 1816.

[4] "Bullet. Soc. Geogr., ii, p. 45, 1855.

[5] Mühlerpfordt, i, p. 261.

[6] Ulloa, "Voyage," i, p. 228.

[7] Stevenson, ii, p. 177.

[8] Unanne, "Observ. sobre el clima de Lima," p. 106, 1815.

[9] Pöppig, i, p. 201.

them are quite fair.[1] The stiff hair which they preserve to the second and third generations is, according to Ovaglie,[2] the only mark which there distinguishes the Mestizoes from the pure Spaniards. Among the Sertanejos of Pernambuco the children of the same parents are rarely all of the same colour, and the difference is in some cases so great, that a doubt might arise as to their legitimacy if the phenomenon were less general.[3] In Paraguay, where the intermixture between Spaniards and Indians has been more general, there are but few indications of Indian blood either in the higher or lower ranks; the features appear here more English than in any other part of Spanish America. In the huts of the poor, children are frequently seen with elongated faces, and light or red hair, as among the Scotch.[4] The North-American Indians, as is often asserted, produce, especially with the Scotch, a powerful race of cross-breeds.[5] The Mestizoes, originating from the peoples at the mouth of the Columbia river, exhibit but few peculiarities of the Indians; they have mostly a light skin, frequently light hair and blue eyes.[6] The mongrels of Europeans and Greenlanders have, as a rule, a European physiognomy, which, however, varies much, the hair being mostly dark, sometimes light; the complexion fair. Psychically they resemble more the Esquimaux, chiefly because they are brought up by Esquimaux mothers, though they are more active, clean, and orderly.[7]

Castelnau[8] makes the following statement concerning the Mulattoes of Minas Geraes:—

1. The child of a white man and an Indian woman resembles the mother: it has stiff hair and oblique eyes.

2. The child of an Indian and Negress, the Cabouret or Zambo, has crisp hair, oblique eyes, and a dark bronzed skin.

3. That of the Indian and the Cabourette has straight

---

[1] Ulloa, ii, p. 34.
[2] "Hist. relatione del regno di Cile, Roma," p. 96, 1646.
[3] Koster, p. 238.
[4] Ausland, p. 977, 1856, according to Mansfield, "Paraguay, Brazil, and the Plate."
[5] Kohl, "Kitschi-Gami," ii, p. 206.
[6] Parker, "Journal," p. 160, 1838.
[7] V. Etzel, "Groenland," p. 339, 1860.
[8] "Exped.," i, p. 205, 1850.

or slightly crisp hair, oblique eyes, and the colour of the Indian.[1]

4. The child of the Indian and the cross-breed of No. 3 resembles entirely the Indian, and is considered equal to him before the law.

5. The child of a white man and a Mestizo is of a light copper colour, has stiff hair and oblique eyes.

6. The offspring of a white man and a cross-breed No. 5 is white, but has frequently black hair and somewhat oblique eyes.

7. The child of a white and mongrel No. 6 entirely resembles the white.

The Zamboes or Cabourets (Mulattoes of Negroes and native American women, called in Peru Chinos) are of a dark bronze colour, and have crisp hair and oblique eyes (Castelnau), whilst in other parts their hair is less crisp than that of the Mulattoes, and they possess the nose and mouth of the Negro, but the forehead, cheeks, and eyes of the Indian.[2] Their physiognomy is much more African than American. The cheek bones are not very prominent, the nose is broad but turned up, the lips thick, but not puffy, the hair half crisp, sometimes merely at the ends, the colour of the skin dark copper or coffee-brown, body slender, but muscular. They are thus described by Schomburgk,[3] in Guiana, where they are only found in small numbers, as (which is also the case elsewhere) Indians do not readily intermix with Negroes, whom they despise. The Zamboes, in the south of the United States, present sometimes crisp hair, with copper-coloured skin, and all other Indian characteristics, and sometimes the coarse hair of the Indian upon the head of a Negro with a black skin. There is here no intermediate type produced by intermixture, but there is produced an irregular agglomeration of the characteristics of the parents.[4] To them belong also the Cafusos, whose enormous wigs have been described by Spix and Martius.[5] The hair rises to 1-1½ feet, and is

---

[1] Compare R. Schomburgh, ii, p. 385.
[2] Tschudi, i, p. 169.
[3] "R. in Brit. Guiana," i, sq. i, pp. 74, 385.
[4] Forey in Schoolcraft, iv, p. 359.
[5] "Reise," p. 215.

curled at the point. The face of the Cafuso resembles more the Negro than the American, but the thick lips are not turned up; the legs are weak, the muscles of the chest and arms are powerfully developed. A similar enormous growth of the hair is also seen among the Cocamas on the lower Huallaga,[1] so that they may be considered as belonging to the Zambo race. It is also observed among the Fiji Islanders, who, on other grounds, are considered as mongrels of Polynesians and Austral Negroes; and it is also probable that the Arab tribe in Taka, among whom Werne[2] observed the same peculiarity, has an admixture of Negro blood.[3]

On reviewing the examples cited, we find the principle confirmed, that the pure races exhibit a more uniform, and the mixed races a variegated, type, and this variation increases as the intermixture progresses.

When, therefore, we hear of a people which, despite a low state of intellectual culture, exhibits a variety in features, nose, lips, as, for instance, among the Tschuvashes,[4] we shall not be wrong in considering it as of mixed origin. With regard, however, to the axiom of Geoffroy, we can only admit that the product of the crossing between the white and the black man is *usually* an intermediate type, whilst variety and inconstancy of physical form is again exhibited in subsequent generations by the intermixture of the mongrels. The principal types of mankind appear to possess different degrees of constancy in their intermixtures. Next to the Negro type, the Mongolian appears to possess considerable constancy.[5] The characteristics of the Hottentots exhibit a similar tenacity. The first alteration in their cross-breeds is that of colour, then of the hair, then follows an alteration of the form of the nose, and, finally, in the shape of the eyes.[6]

---

1 Pöppig, "R.," ii, p. 450.

2 "Feldz. nach Taka," p. 89.

3 In East Africa there are also the Danakil, distinguished by their wig-like hair (Harris, "Highlands of Ethiopia," i, p. 337, 2nd edit., 1844; Pickering, p. 206.)

4 Kornheim, in Erman's "Archiv," iii, p. 74.

5 Ritter, "Erkunde," iii, p. 386.

6 Schmarda, "R. um d. Erde," ii, p. 32, 1861.

The first impregnation seems to exert in cross-breeds, both in animals and in man, an important influence on physical formation. A mare which has first produced a mule produces subsequently indifferent colts; a sow first crossed by a wild boar, a bitch with a dog of a different race, subsequently produce young resembling the first. Thus it has often been observed, that the children of a second marriage resemble those of the first husband.[1] With regard to cross-breeds of various races, instances are recorded of Negresses who, after having first given birth to Mulatto children, had subsequently children by a Negro, which, however, resembled the father of the first.[2] That Negresses, after having had Mulatto children, no longer conceive by a Negro, as has been asserted, is an error. This applies also to Strzelecki's assertion,[3] that the native women of a great part of North America, as well as those of Polynesia, Australia, and Van Diemen's Land, were sterile with men of their own stock after having once been impregnated by Europeans. That he is wrong as regards the Australian women has been shown by Thompson.[4]

In proceeding now to the chief question, namely, the comparison between mongrels and the original types as regards unlimited prolificacy, we may assume as a demonstrated fact, that however many types of mankind we may assume, all of them (as far as our present knowledge extends) are prolific between each other, and produce by intermixture certain intermediate types which exhibit in various degrees the characters of the parents. By crossing, it may be generally asserted, the lower type is improved by a higher type, as, for instance, the Negro into the Mulatto, the American Indian into the Mestizo; and this improvement progresses when the connection of the cross-breeds with individuals of a higher type is continued: thus from Mulattoes spring Tertroon, Quadroon, Quintroon. This improvement of the race corresponds to the deterioration of the

---

[1] Instances of this kind in Lucas, and in Latham, "Man and his migrations," p. 65.

[2] Harvey in Nott and Gliddon, p. 396.

[3] "Descript. of N. S. Wales," p. 347, 1842.

[4] Fechner's "Centralbl.," 1853; Todd, "Cyclop.," p. 1365; and "Munch. Gel. Anz.," p. 197, 1852.

race by pairing the mongrel with an inferior race, for instance, in the Zambo, the offspring of the Negro and Mulatto (this name is sometimes given to the offspring of the Negro and the native Indian). The transition of the mongrels of lower races into higher, and *vice versâ*, succeeds, in a less number of generations, the more they approach the original type. In the Society Islands, where there are but few mongrels, they are said to assume the European type in the second or third generation.[1] The American Indian produces with a Zambo woman (Cabourette), in the second generation, a mongrel resembling the pure Indian; the white with a Mestizo woman, one who assumes the type of a white in the third generation; in four generations Mulattoes may become white, in five generations they may become black.[2] Thus the Quintroon is in law considered as a White in the United States. In Dutch Guiana the Quadroons are in the same conditions.[3] The Mestizo is considered equal to a Negro-tertroon, so that his offsprings are Quadroons. It is scarcely necessary to observe, that these statements refer only to physical conformation, and not to the intellectual capacities of the mongrels, and under the supposition that the mongrel, in order to pass into another race, should uninterruptedly intermix with that race.

On comparing the results of intermixture between various human types with those of the crossing of animals, we obtain analogous results. In some cases three generations have been found sufficient to replace the old race by a new one; and, after the fourth generation, no relapse to the old race is any longer expected. According to Burdach, six uninterrupted impregnations of an inferior race by a higher one are required in sheep and horses; according to others, twelve; and, according to Morel and Vindé, a continuous impregnation is requisite.[4]

---

[1] Bennet, "Narr. of a whaling voy.," i, p. 149, 1840.
[2] Serres' assertion, that in an intermixture of a higher with a lower race, the first parts with at least two-thirds of its character to the mongrel, has not yet been confirmed by facts; and this assertion seems to be a mere sequence of the theory, that the higher races are destined to absorb the lower ones, and to rule them.
[3] Fechner's "Centralbl.," p. 288, 1853, according to Castelnau.
[4] V. Sack, "Beschr. e. R. nach Surinam," i, p. 84, 1821.
[5] Chambon, "Traité de l'éducation des moutons," ii, p. 278.

Elysée Lefèbvre and Girou maintain that crossing with an inferior race should be avoided, for fear of deterioration. This opinion is borne out by the fact, that in the transition of the Negro-mongrel into the white, there remain for a long time some indications of Negro descent. The peculiar odour of the Negro is said to be still perceptible in the Quintroon. The cornea of the Tertroon Mestizo (and, perhaps, in later generations) is somewhat yellowish.[1] The violet colour of the nails near the insertion, and the bluish ring round the eyes, as well as the peculiar shape of the heels and feet, remain for a long time in the Negro mongrels.[2] The darkening of the skin in Hindoo mongrels in advanced age, and the dark colour of the genitals in the former, as well as in the American Mestizo, is a peculiarity which, even after many generations, indicates the source they have sprung from.[3] When, therefore, Nott, as a genuine American, believes he can detect in every case an admixture of Negro blood, even in Quintroons, we may admit all this without adopting his hypothesis, that the Mulattoes become extinct after a few generations, and before they can perfectly assume the type of the white race.

In the United States they are exceedingly acute in the recognition of these minute distinctions, for the fashion, in opposition to the law of the land, proscribes any one in whose veins there is a drop of Negro blood, whilst in Brazil no stigma is attached to mixed descent. Whoever shares the Negro prejudices of the North Americans must certainly feel inclined to assume distinct species among mankind, and consider that a trace of Negro blood, however slight, renders man, morally and intellectually, inferior to the pure white; while, according to Nott and Gliddon, a few drops of European blood produce a decided modification in the moral and physical character of the Negro. There can be no doubt that the Mulatto is more gifted than the Negro, though impartial observers still doubt whether the greater intelligence of the Mulattoes, who are, on this account, preferred for domestic service, is the consequence of an im-

---

[1] Labat, "Nouv. voy. aux Iles de l'Am.," i, pp. 2, 40, 1724.
[2] Day, "Five years resid. in the W. Indies," i, p. 51.
[3] D'Orbigny et Troyer, "Bullet. Soc. Ethnol.," Mai 22, 1846.

provement of the race, or of a superior education, and of more intercourse with the whites.[1] In French West India (Guadeloupe) nearly all the trades are in the hands of Mulattoes, and some of them are rich.[2] They have in 1830 recovered again their civil rights, which the *code noir* of the year 1855 had given them, but later decrees had deprived them of. Their intelligence and activity render them hateful to the Creoles.[3] In Peru many Mulattoes study theology; most physicians in Lima belong to this caste.[4] In the northern parts of Brazil (Bahia, Pernambuco, Maranham), they form a large and active portion of the population.[5] In every rank of society, among lawyers, physicians, statesmen, and scholars in Brazil, there are Mulattoes who distinguish themselves by talent and intelligence; they seem also to possess great capacity for the fine arts, so that men of colour are there received in the best society. Many Mulattoes pass there for whites, and occupy the same position, after their documents have declared them as such.[6] A. de St. Hilaire[7] is of opinion that the Mulattoes in Brazil excel the white in intellect and talent, though they are morally inferior, and share with the Negro the fickleness of character. The Mestizo, who stands nearer to the white by a generation, is inferior to the Mulatto, the latter being more active than the former; thus it is in Brazil, Peru, and Mexico.[8] Koster[9] alone maintains that they possess greater courage and more self-esteem than the Mulattoes, and are, consequently, less subordinate to the white than the latter. The Mestizo is less vigorous, often indolent and undecided; still he is gentle, compassionate, easily excited, but of a changeable disposition, and without valour. The Mexican Mestizoes possess great intellectual endowments; they have a ready wit, are quick of appre-

---

1 Lyell, "Second voyage," p. 266.
2 Granier de Cassagnac, "Voy. aux Antilles," i, p. 255, 1843.
3 Oelsner-montmerqué, d. Creole, e. Vorlesung, p. 23, 1848.
4 Tschudi, i, p. 167.
5 Rendu "Etudes sur le Brésil," p. 30, 1848.
6 De Lisboa, "Bullet. soc. ethnol.," p. 58, Jan. 1847.
7 Loc. cit., ii, p. 52.
8 Spix and Martius, p. 607; Tschudi, i, p. 165; Humboldt, "Neu-Spanien," i, p. 184.
9 "R. in Brasilien," p. 553, 1817.

hension, and possess a lively imagination; those, however, sprung from white mothers are said to be more vicious than the children of the Indian women.[1] They excel the European in agriculture, cattle breeding, and mining labour.[2] The Mestizo in Peru is, according to Pöppig, not so robust as the Mulatto, and often indolent. Tschudi justly draws attention to the fact, that talents among the Indians and mongrels have no field for display, oppressed as they are by the White. According to Pöppig,[3] the mongrel population, with its innate vices, and their hatred against the pure races from which they have sprung, is an everlasting canker of society and political life in South America, as all the shades of the mongrels are hostile to each other and to the pure race. Like the Mulatto, the Mestizo is considered as having inherited all the vices of his parents, without any of their virtues; with the pride of the White, which he carries to excess, he combines the laziness, apathy, thoughtlessness, and inconstancy of the Indian; he is dissipated, ambitious, and cowardly, very tyrannical to the Indian, as the Mulatto is to the Negro; he possesses, however, great imitative talent.[4] The coloured population in British Guiana at present frequently rival the Europeans as mechanics and artists.[5] A very favourable description is given of the capacities and the character of the Mestizoes in Paraguay.[6] The half-breds in Oregon resemble the father in their mental activity, but frequently exhibit something of the wild passionateness of their mother. Quick to learn, well-spoken, and of courteous manners, they are, nevertheless, without any education, and have, moreover, constantly before them the evil example of their parents. They are given to swearing, drinking, and other excesses; excellent hunters, skilful navigators, brave and courageous in battle, open and generous of character, without cunning and hypocrisy; they submit to no

---

1 Muehlenpfordt, i, p. 260.
2 Sartorius, "Mexico," p. 156, 1859.
3 Loc. cit., i, p. 193.
4 Ibid., ii, p. 146.
5 R. Schomburgk, i, p. 47.
6 Gumprecht, "Zeitschr. f. Erdk.," ii, p. 29.

wrong, being themselves careful not to offend others.[1] The Zambo excels the Negro Indian in energy, stature, and vigour;[2] but we rarely meet with such a favourable description of their characters, as that given by A. de St. Hilaire[3] of the Zamboes on the Paranahyba. He describes them as peaceable agriculturists, providing for all their wants; they spin and weave, make their own pottery, are well-dressed, and live in comfortable circumstances. Sarmiento[4] also attributes to the Zamboes of the Argentine republic, talents and progressive civilization. But elsewhere they are in very bad repute, on account of their indifferent character, though we must bear in mind that almost all of them are illegitimate children. The Cocamas are said to be courageous, warlike, and lovers of freedom.[5] The so-called "Black Caribs" of St. Vincent, who once murdered the colonists of that island without any provocation, were Zamboes. In Lima all the great criminals are, according to Tschudi, Zamboes, who are also in Caraccas considered as the worst class of the population. By far the most profligate of all mongrels in Peru are those of Negroes and Mestizoes, or of Negroes and Mulattoes.[6] This applies also to the Zamboes in Nicaragua.[7] Like the cross-breeds of the Dutch and Malay women in Batavia, the Hindoo mongrels of Europeans are weak in body and mind.[8] The mongrels of Europeans and New Zealand women are described as healthy and muscular,[9] but neither bodily nor intellectually do they seem superior to the children of the natives; the latter are open and free with strangers, the former are bashful, and conceal themselves behind their mothers.[10]

Various theories have been founded upon the phenomena resulting from the crossing of different types. Gobineau has en-

---

[1] R. Cox, "The Columbia river," iii, p. 298, 3rd edit., 1832.
[2] Lavayssé, "R. nach Trinidad," p. 357, 1816.
[3] "Voy. aux sources du R. S. Francisco," ii, p. 254, 1847.
[4] "Nouv. Ann. des voy.," p. 302, 1853.
[5] Pöppig, ii, p. 401.
[6] Stevenson, "R.," i, p. 200.
[7] Squier, "Trav. in centr. Am.," ii, p. 153, 1853.
[8] Graf Görtz, "R. um d. Welt," iii, p. 405.
[9] Polack, "New-Zeal.," ii, p. 276, 1838; Schmalda, loc. cit., ii, p. 200.
[10] Savage, "Some account of N. Zeal.," p. 92, 1807.

deavoured to establish the one, that the crossing of different types invariably induces a physical and moral degeneration, and implants the germ of certain decay, whilst Serres considers crossing as an essential means of improving the race, and rendering it vigorous by the infusion of fresh blood from a different stock: he is even inclined to believe that in a perfect intermixture of the chief types is a solution of the problem of the development of humanity. Nott, who thinks to have demonstrated the existence of various human species, endeavours also to prove that mongrels possess little viability, and only a limited prolificacy, and are incapable by themselves of founding a new type, since they have no permanent vitality without re-crossing with one of the parent stocks. It will presently be shown that this theory is as little consonant with the facts as the preceding.

Whatever view we may adopt with regard to the unity of the human species, it would be idle to expect that the mongrels of the various types should be equally viable and vigorous, since there are peoples apparently unmixed who are more or less strong or weak, according to their constitution, mode of life, and climate. Corresponding differences are found in mongrel races. In some cases the mongrels of different stocks are more prolific and vigorous than the stock from which they issued. The Kuruglis (mongrels of Turks and Moors) excel their Turkish fathers in strength and beauty of form.[1] Arabs and Ethiopians (Abyssinians and their allied tribes) produce a fine race, viable in all warm climates.[2] From the intermixture of Europeans with the natives of the Philippines there frequently issue finer children than those produced by the marriages of Europeans between themselves.[3] D'Orbigny is of opinion, that, by the intermixture of various Indian tribes of South America, healthier and more gifted individuals are produced; but he does not think that such is the case when Europeans ally themselves with the natives of those regions. The mixed populations of Paraguay, existing in a similar healthy con-

[1] M. Wagner, "R. in Algier," iii, p. 293, 1841.
[2] Pruner, p. 71.
[3] Mallat, ii, p. 40.

dition,[1] after a few generations, excel the Spaniards of these parts. In the state of Buenos Ayres the coloured race has certainly, since 1778, been reduced from one-third of the whole population to one-fourth. The cause of this seems to be their lesser fecundity and greater mortality in comparison with the Whites. It must not, however, be understood that the coloured population die off in the above proportion, as the diminution is also owing to their fusion with the white population, into which they are gradually absorbed.[2] In Peru, where only the coloured population and the Indians attain a great age,[3] the Cholos (mongrels of Mestizos and Indians) are said to excel all other classes of the population in bodily strength, activity, and talent; yet their education is very indifferent.[4] We may now mention a series of opposite instances. The mongrels of Europeans and natives of Northern Australia about Port Essington do not appear to thrive.[5] Are they, perhaps, like other mongrel children in Australia, killed? In the country of the Fulahs in Africa the Toucouleurs, the descendants of the immigrant Pules (Peuls) and the Negroes, are physically and mentally superior to the latter, but there are found among them, especially in Futa-Torro, many stammerers, blind, hunchbacks, idiots, etc.[6] The children produced by Arabs with the women of Darfur are weakly, and have but little vitality.[7] It has already been stated that the children of a white woman by a Negro are rarely viable; Serres even asserts that they are rarely prolific. The marriages between the French and Indian women of the north of the United States are, on the whole, very productive, and the children, despite the Indian mode of life, take more after the father than the mother, the girls particularly so. If such cross-breeds intermarry, the girls predominate in their offspring; the chil-

[1] Brackenridge, "R. nach Süd.-Am." ii, pp. 74, 152, 1821, according to Azara, Funes, and Passos.
[2] "Zeitschr. f. Allg. Erdk. N. Folge," iv, p. 141.
[3] Pöppig, p. 208.
[4] Brackenridge, "R. nach Süd-Am.," ii, p. 167, 1821.
[5] Macgillivray, "Narr. of the voyage of H.M.S. Rattlesnake," i, p. 151, 1852.
[6] Mollien, "R. in d. Innere v. Africa," p. 174, 1820; Raffenel, "Voy. dans l'Afr. occ.," p. 51, 1846.
[7] Mohammed-el-Tounsy, "Voy. au Darf p. Jomard," p. 277, 1845.

dren are frequently stunted and deficient in vitality—this, at least, is the prevailing belief in that country.[1]

Some of these cases remind us of the axiom of Buffon, that, from the connexion of near relations, morbid affections, idiotcy, blindness, and dumbness arise. It does not yet seem to be ascertained how it stands with regard to domestic animals. In the breeding of blood horses the stallion is made to cover his own descendants. On the other hand, it is asserted that all races of animals are entirely deteriorated in the second and third generation by the coupling of near relations; and such is also the case with man.[2] We know that in many ancient and modern nations, marriages between brothers and sisters, even between parents and their children, frequently took place without a deterioration of the race. Such alliances were made among the Assyrians, Egyptians, Athenians, Persians, some peoples of India (before, and even after, the introduction of Buddhism), the Druses, Mingrelians, the royal family of the Sandwich Islands. This also appears from some legends of American Indians and other nations. Garcilasso[3] narrates that the children of Manco Capac intermarried, and that this was the custom in the royal family of Peru, to keep the race pure. They justified the custom, inasmuch as the moon was both the sister and the wife of the sun. The Inca always married his eldest sister. According to Acosta,[4] only the last Incas did so. Among the Coroados marriages between the nearest blood relations occur frequently.[5] As proofs of the destructiveness of such connexions, the Irish in South Carolina are cited, who for a long time have only intermarried between themselves.[6] The Dutch colonists at the Cape are in the same condition;[7] Lichtenstein[8] had already noticed the frequent presence among them of deaf and dumb, idiots, etc. Davis[9] says also of the so-

---

[1] Kohl in Ausland, p. 57, 1859.
[2] Lucas, ii, p. 904.
[3] "Hist. des Yncas," i, pp. 2, 25.
[4] "Hist. nat. e morale delle Indie," vi, c. 12, Venet., 1596.
[5] Eschwege, "Journal v. Brasil," i, p. 121, 1818.
[6] Nott and Gliddon, p. 408.
[7] Kretschmar, "Süd-Afr. Skizzen," p. 163, 1853.
[8] "Reisen," i, pp. 101, 211, 346.
[9] "El Gringo," p. 146, N. York, 1857.

called Pueblos Indians in New Mexico, that they degenerate because the inhabitants of the same village only intermarry.

We believe we are justified in concluding from the preceding facts, with regard to sexual intercourse and the quality of the offspring, that there exists, both in individuals of the same stock, as well as between different nations, not exactly antipathy, but still incompatibility, which, though not explicable as to its origin, is sufficiently established; and, in spite of this, we are not competent, from the sterility or decay of certain races, to infer a difference of species of mankind as its cause. Such a conclusion is inadmissible, on the ground that there are not a few peoples sprung from the same stock, accounted as deficient in vitality, who perpetuate themselves in full health. For this purpose, we shall examine the contested prolificacy of Mulattoes,[1] as far as it seems founded on facts. It has been asserted that the Mulattoes would become extinct if they could be cut off from any infusion of new blood from the parent stocks.[2] Mulattoes of the same degree are said to be rarely prolific.[3] Nott, especially, has, in his work "On Hybridity," dwelt on the sterility of Mulattoes, which had already been noticed by Etwick and Long,[4] in order to establish their defective vitality. He has, it is true, subsequently abandoned the view, that, of all men, the mean duration of life is least in the Mulatto; and he now only maintains that the Mulattoes in the north of the United States proceeding from Englishmen possessed less vitality than those of the south sprung from dark-complexioned races, such as the Spaniards, Portuguese, etc. Nott's present theory regarding Mulattoes is, that they are less capable of sustaining physical labour than the Europeans and Negroes; that the women are very delicate, have many miscarriages, and are subject to many chronic diseases: that

[1] With regard to the axiom of Geoffroy and Nott, quoted above, as to the sterility of Mulattoes, it is interesting to compare Wiegman's observation, that in plants hybrids are sterile which present an intermediate type between two species; whilst those which partake more of one or the other species, can be propagated by seeds.

[2] Van Amringe, "Investigations of the theories of the nat. hist. of man;" Knox, "The Races of Man," 1850; Ham. Smith, "Natural history of the human species," 1848.

[3] Day, "Five years residence in the West Indies," i, p. 294, 1852.

[4] "History of Jamaica."

they are bad breeders, that the children die young; and, finally, that the Mulattoes, like the Negroes, are little liable to yellow fever. As to the latter point, we have already shown that it chiefly depends upon acclimatization, and not upon peculiarity of race. With respect to the weakness and mortality of the Mulatto children, it is not yet proved whether or not it is to be attributed to the race, and the fact itself is not yet established. Bachman[1] knew Mulatto families in Carolina and New York who, without any infusion of new blood, were prolific through five generations, and are still so. Lewis[2] expressly denies the sterility of the Mulattoes in Jamaica, and says they are as prolific as the black and the white, but they are generally weakly, and their children do not exhibit strong vital powers; hence Mulatto women prefer marrying Whites, so that the Mulattoes are obliged to marry black women. Hombron[3] remarks, on the sterility of various races, that the white and the native American women present the greatest prolificacy; then come the Negro and the Negress, then Negro and the American woman; Mulattoes and white women, as well as Mulattoes between themselves, are also very prolific. Mulattoes moreover form, in the northern provinces of Brazil, such a large portion of the population, that their prolificacy cannot be doubted. The vigorous inhabitants of the Fiji Islands are also, by their language and physical constitution, proved to be a mixed people, sprung from Polynesians and Austral Negroes. The people of the Griquas in South Africa have come from intermixture of Hottentots, Dutch, and Negroes.[4] The Dutch and Hottentots at the Cape intermarry between themselves, and but rarely with either of the parent stock;[5] and yet we hear nothing of their sterility; on the contrary, the offsprings are described as very vigorous. The Rhenish Missionary Journal[6] contains a case of a mongrel who was the father of twenty-four children by one wife.

---

[1] In Smyth, "Unity of the human races," p. 196, 1830.
[2] "Journal of a residence among the Negroes in the W. Indies," p. 55, 1845.
[3] Zoologie in d'Urville, "Voy. au Pole Sud," i, p. 266.
[4] Arbousset et Daumas, in Napier, "Excursions in S. Africa," i, p. 141, 1850.
[5] Barrington, "Account of a voyage to N. S. Wales," p. 189, 2nd edit., 1810.
[6] Page 296, 1850.

It is certainly much more easy to assert the sterility of Mulattoes than to refute it by the few observations we possess on this subject. Wherever sterility occurs it appears rather as an isolated fact, the local nature of which does not admit of its being laid down as a general rule. Thus we must consider it as a local phenomenon that the mongrels of Negroes, Indians, and Whites in Panama are very prolific between each other, but cannot easily rear their children, whilst families of pure blood are less prolific, but bring their children up.[1] The progeny of the Chinese by Malay women in the East Indian Archipelago are said to die early.[2] According to Dr. Yvan, the children of the Dutch and Malay women in Java (Lipplapps) are said to be only productive to the third generation. They are well developed up to the fifteenth year, when they remain stationary; in the third generation chiefly daughters are born, and these remain barren.[3] But all this is an exceptional local phenomenon, for elsewhere these mongrels remain prolific.[4] As a parallel to the sterility of mongrels may be mentioned the assertion, that the children of Europeans in Batavia become frequently sterile in the second generation.[5]

Setting aside the Mulattoes, it has frequently been asserted that mongrels of every kind can only perpetuate themselves by an infusion of fresh blood from the parent stock, not having between themselves an unlimited prolificacy. That children of mongrels are produced in great numbers is already proved by the variety of names given to them in South America:—Choles, children of Zamboes; Kaskes, children of Mulattoes; *Tente en el ayre*, children of mongrels of the same degree,[6] etc. The significance of these terms[7] is given by Blumenbach and by

---

1 Seemann, "R. u. d. Welt," i, p. 314, 1853.
2 "Ztschft. der morgenl. Ges.," vi, p. 573.
3 Graf Görz, Reise, iii, p. 288.
4 Quatrefages, "Révue des deux mondes," Mars, p. 162, 1857.
5 Steen Bille, "Bericht über d. R. de Galathea," i, p. 376, 1852.
6 Ulloa, "Voy.," i, p. 28, 1752.
7 As an illustration of this confusion of terms, the following will serve:—In the West Indies the native Whites are called Creoles; in Brazil, the Blacks who are born there (Steen Bille says, the Blacks only are called so in Brazil). In Peru, the children of Whites and Mestizoes are called Creoles. In Russian America, the Mestizoes are generally designated as Creoles (Erman's "Archiv," ii, p. 461); and in East India, the term is used

Vollgraff.[1] A continued admixture of fresh blood of one element, without a corresponding addition on the other side, would be a sure means of destroying the type, and reducing the people to its original, that is to say, the character of the mongrels could not be preserved under such circumstances. Hence those who consider a fresh infusion as indispensable are obliged to deny the capacity of mixed peoples to perpetuate themselves.

In addition to the preceding instances of mixed populations which subsist independently, we would also mention those of Mexico and the Philippines, possessing partly an undoubted mixed population of Spaniards and natives; of Nicaragua, which, besides 10,000 whites, 15,000 Negroes, and 80,000 Indians, has a Mestizo population of 145,000 souls;[2] the province S. Paulo, with a thoroughly mixed population; and Paraguay, where the Mestizoes (mongrels of Spaniards and Guaranis) intermarry, and the progeny of which forms the great mass of the so-called Spanish population;[3] New Granada, possessing a mixed population sprung from Spaniards, Indians, and Negroes, in which the Spanish blood is greatly predominating, but, in spite of their designation as whites, are not free from Indian and Negro blood;[4] Caraccas, where the mixed population form the majority,[5] and we do not hear anything of defective vitality, diminution, or decay. We learn, on the contrary, that the Mestizoes in New Granada, as well as in the

---

in the same sense (Pfyffer, "Skizzen v. d. Insel. Java," p. 67, 1829). The Mulatto is called Pardo in Brazil; in Buenos Ayres, Mestizo; who again in Brazil is called Mamaluco. The child of a Negro and Mulatto is, in Peru and the West Indies, called Zambo; elsewhere the mongrel of the American and Negro race has the name of Chino; Caboglo in Surinam; Cariboco in Brazil (A. de St. Hilaire, ii, p. 271). Unanne ("Observ. sobre el clima de Lima," p. 105, 1815) enumerates all the crossbreeds found in Peru, with their names. "Quadroon" is the child of a white man and a mulatto woman; "Tertroon" does not seem to be applied in Peru. The child of a Negro and Chino is also called "Zambo," like that of a Negro and Mulatto woman; the child of a Negro and Zambo is called "Zambo prieto." The names applied to crossbreeds in Mexico are given by Muehlenpfordt (i, p. 200) and G. A. Thompson ("Narr. of official visit to Guatemala," p. 523, 1829.)

[1] "Ethnognosie und Ethnologie," i, p. 233.

[2] Scherzer, "Wanderungen durch d. Mittelam. Freist," p. 125, 1857.

[3] Azara, "Voy. dans l'Am. mérid.," ed. Walckenaer, ii, p. 265, 1809; see Demersay, "Bullet. soc. géogr." i, p. 5, 1854.

[4] Mollien, "Voy. dans la Republ. de Colombia," i, p. 150; ii, p. 160, 1824.

[5] Semple, "Sketch of the present state of Caraccas," pp. 53, 105, 1812.

southern part of Chili, greatly increase, and are described by Pöppig as very prolific.

These facts are sufficient to weaken the argument of a specific difference between the two principal races of mankind, as founded upon the pretended sterility of mixed races. They refute, at the same time, the theory that mixed races can only perpetuate themselves by re-crossing with the parent stocks. That mixed tribes, by a continued re-crossing with individuals of a parent stock, revert to it after a few generations, cannot be adduced as a proof of the immutability of an original type, as the few foreign elements disappear. Pöppig, however,[1] says, that it is in the American colonies a well known fact, that mixed tribes, abandoned to themselves, revert again to the original type (to which?). If this be so, it can only be considered as an exceptional case, which certainly cannot serve as a general rule, considering the large number of mixed populations which are self-subsistent. When, further, W. F. Edwards[2] thinks that he can recognize the types of the original races in the mixed population of France, Switzerland, and Italy, supporting M. Serres' assertion of the absolute permanence of original type, we must bear in mind that this is merely a subjective theory without any anatomical proofs, and that we are ignorant as to these original types. Nott and Gliddon go much farther; they are not merely of opinion that all original types are still to be found, but that the type of the skull long outlives the history and civilization of a people, it being incapable of alteration, and is constantly reproduced until again it predominates. We should, therefore, not be surprised were they to assert, with regard to the mixed population of Paraguay which is said so much to resemble the English, that it is not a mixed type, but the genuine old Iberian form of the Spaniards which now reappears in South America. Cautious observers, Schomburgh for instance,[3] confine their remarks to the effect that some peoples, in their intermixtures with others, preserve their peculiarities for a longer, others for a shorter

[1] Art. "Indier," in Ersch und Gruber, p. 359.
[2] "Mém. de la soc. ethnol.," i et ii.
[3] "Bullet. soc. géogr.," ii, p. 63, 1851.

time. Although among some, these peculiarities disappear after a few generations, they are in others preserved after a long series of generations. The latter applies to the so-called "Indians" at Hayti, especially as regards the women. They have symmetrical forms, an olive-coloured delicate skin, large black eyes, and very fine heads of hair. This reminds us of the assertion supported by Geoffroy St. Hilaire, that the characters of an animal race are more constant and permanent in proportion as the race is older, and more changeable the younger the race is.

The intermixture of the various types is one of the chief agents in the changes produced in mankind. Whoever is inclined to consider the principal races as specifically different, doubts the vitality and unlimited prolificacy of mongrels; but still he explains the changes of type from intermixture, because the theory of a specific difference would be untenable if climate, civilization, etc., could by themselves produce that change. With regard to this dilemma, in which the defenders of specific differences find themselves, we would further observe, that it is inconsistent to deduce all changes of types merely from intermixture, as the assertion of the permanence of specific characters would thus partly be refuted. From whatever point of view we may consider the results of the intermixture of different types, we are entitled to maintain that on the whole they are more in favour of the unity of mankind than for the opposite theory.

SECTION IV.

REVIEW OF THE PRINCIPAL THEORIES REGARDING THE UNITY OF MANKIND.

We have hitherto been engaged in enumerating the most important facts bearing upon the question of the unity of mankind, and in investigating their scope. In endeavouring to render an impartial account of the inferences to which these facts lead, we first observed a gradual mutability of the physical type, owing partly to external and partly to internal agents. The degree and extent of this mutability, though by no means slight, is nevertheless, in comparison with the great differences existing between various races, not so strongly marked as to decide the question, whether these differences are to be considered as having specific value. We may, however, say, that the theory which assumes permanent specific differences in mankind, appears to us less probable than the opposite theory; and further, we venture positively to deny the existence of permanency of type in the human form, it being a phenomenon which could only arise from a long continued influence of climate, mode of life, external relations, and defective mental culture, etc.

There seems to exist this essential difference between man and animals,—that the mutability of his physical form has a wider circle than that of the latter. It must not be objected that man being, according to his organization, an animal, such an assumption is gratuitous, inasmuch as the natural laws for the development and changes of the animal economy must be the same for both. It is in the first place undeniable that the same human races can successively live in different climates, and that the whole mode of life and external conditions to which the same race may be subject, may be essentially altered, —not so those of animals; and that the same race of men may pass through various degrees of culture,—which is not the case with animals. If accordingly a wider sphere, with regard to all these circumstances, is granted to man, it is not in contradiction to the laws of nature that the limits of the mutability of his nature are less confined than those of animals. Though we could not entirely assent to the proofs for the unity of the human race adduced by Blumenbach and Prichard derived from analogy, namely, that the differences of human races are less considerable than those found in animals which undoubtedly belong to the same species; still we agree with Prichard when he says, that the external differences of men are not so great as we might expect from the great differences of climate and civilization.

These views have, in modern times, been opposed by theories which are at present very popular, not so much in consequence of their novelty, as of their apparently logical sequence and their connexion with materialistic views. They are based on the view we have just repudiated, that man as a physical being must, with regard to his body and its changes, be in the same condition as animals, and that it is mere fancy to deny his perfect equality as a physical being, and his subjection to the same laws as animals. Man, they maintain, like animals, undergoes but unimportant changes from the influence of climate: like them, man is only changed by intermixture; and as in the animal kingdom new species arise by hybridity (as asserted by some, without the intervention of the Creator), so does it happen by the crossing of various species of men.

Among the men holding these extreme views may be mentioned Hamilton Smith.[1] Lawrence[2] had already maintained that the type of human races is perpetuated in all climates, and only changes by intermixture; to which Smith adds, that each of the chief races is only perpetuated in their original native country, whilst the descendants of other races would there perish without intermixture, but that from such intermixture there issue, as among many animals of various species, intermediate types indefinitely prolific, provided there be a continued infusion of fresh blood from either of the parent stocks. He points out the extinct Paltas[3] on the Titicaca lake, with naturally flattened and receding skulls, the remnants

---

[1] "Natural history of the human species," Edinb., 1848.

[2] "Lectures," p. 448.

[3] The mention of the Paltas, on the Titicaca, by H. Smith, is probably founded in error. Mention is certainly made of a chieftain, in the south, named "Palta," about the time of Valdivias (1550), among the Araucanians (Ovaglie, "Hist. relatione del regno di Cile," p. 187, Roma, 1646); but the people called Paltas existed only in the south of the state of Quito, due north of Loja, near Tumebamba. They are mentioned together with the Cañares and Chaparras, but nothing is said about their cranial shape, or other peculiarities (Cieza de Leon in "Historiad. prim. de Indias," pp. 401 and 409, 1852; Gomara, ibid.; compare, also, Herrera, "Hist. gén.," v, and of later writers; Velasco, "Hist. del reino de Quito," iii, pp. 2, 15.

of very inferior tribes of abnormal form, as the Cagots, Tschuwasches, and some others, the Cumbrie-Negroes on the Niger, reduced to slavery by their neighbours, the extinct Guanches of the Canary Islands and the Ompizes (Vazimbres ?) of Madagascar, in order to support the theory that there are remnants of human races older than the present,—a race which was once surrounded by a different flora and fauna than ours, and which was spread over the globe before the extinction of some species of animals. The Papuas (Austral-Negroes ?) especially, are said to belong to this most ancient population, and date, perhaps, from an earlier period of the history of our planet. This latter point has been descanted upon by Hombron.[1] He assumes, in every part of the globe, several central points of creation, and makes man see the light of the world in three successive periods of creation. In fixing the latter, and the selection of the peoples, he seems very unfortunate. According to him the Samoiedes, Lapps, and all black people, were created first; then came the Mongols, Americans, Egyptians, and Berbers; European humanity was created last. He who feels inclined to assign different periods of creation to the chief types of humanity, will necessarily consider the Negroes as the most imperfect and oldest species, and connect his colour with the greater quantity of carbon contained in the air of primeval times.

On depriving these bold theories of their varnish, we would first draw attention to the fact that it is, under all circumstances, very difficult to ascertain whether human tribes sunk so low are to be considered as originally defectively organized; and that especially in case of their extinction the question cannot be decided one way or another. Where particulars are wanting, both theories are equally tenable. Among the peoples mentioned by Smith, the Cumbries are unquestionably a Negro tribe, universally despised and oppressed, but nothing shows that they specifically differ from other Negroes; by Paltas is probably designated the old Peruvian people with abnormal skulls, the shape of which was by Morton first considered as original, but subse-

[1] D'Urville, "Voy. au Pole Sud. Zoologie," i, p. 184.

quently acknowledged as an artificial deformity. The Guanches, whose skulls resemble those of the ancient Egyptians, belong probably to the so-called Caucasian race; they were a semi-civilized people, in which the nobility were distinguished from the people; even monotheism, and some astronomical knowledge, are ascribed to them by old Spanish authors.[1] As to the rest of the peoples mentioned, exact information is wanting, with exception of the Papuas, and there exists not the slightest ground for considering these older than the rest of mankind.

The assertions maintained at different periods, and lately in America, that human bones have been found in tertiary formations, accompanied by fossil remains, which justified the inference of the existence of man at a period when the surface of the earth had not yet assumed its present contour; they were, until recently, without confirmation, and are still by geologists received with considerable caution. A. Maury,[2] however, and also Nott and Gliddon,[3] endeavour to prove that the finding of fossil human bones and implements is unquestionable; in opposition to which the author of the Essay in the "Deutsche Vierteljahrschrift"[4] only assumes its probability.[5] With regard to the Guadaloupe skeletons, it may be stated that, in consequence of purely local conditions, the process of petrifaction proceeds in that island very rapidly, and therefore these skeletons cannot be adduced as a proof of a remote existence of the human race; nor is the circumstance, that bones of the mammoth are found intermixed with arrowheads, in favour of this theory. Littre[6] merely states that the existence of man in an earlier geological epoch has become less improbable than before by the excavations of Boucher de

---

[1] Humboldt und Bonpland, "R. in die Æquinoctial-Gegenden," i, pp. 153, 283; Golberry, "R. durch d. Westl. Afr.," i, p. 35, 1803; Webb et Berthelot, "Hist. nat. des Iles Canaries; Berthelot, in "Mém. de la soc. Ethnol.," i, et ii; Hodgkin, in "Nouv. ann. des voy.," iii, p. 375.

[2] "Des ossemens humains enfouis dans les roches," 1852; Spring, in "l'Institut," ii, p. 41, 1854.

[3] "Indigenous races of the earth," 1857.

[4] Chap. ii, p. 213, 1838.

[5] Compare Cuvier "Umwälzungen der Erdrinde," German by v. Nöggerrath, i, p. 118, 1830.

[6] "Rév. des deux mondes."

Perthes; and it must certainly be admitted that the probability of this view is annually increasing.

Dr. Lund,[1] who is said to have discovered human fossils in not less than eight different localities (in Minas Geraes), infers that the population of America is more ancient than that of the Old World. Usher relates[2] that, in the excavations for the gas works at New Orleans, a human skeleton had been found at a depth of 16 feet under the cypress forests, the skull of which he considers as belonging to the American race, and the age of which he calculates at 57,000 years. Several of such pretended undoubted cases are quoted. Boucher de Perthes[3] has excavated so-called antediluvian antiquities, stone hatchets, intermixed with fossil bones of extinct animals. Nilssohn,[4] distinguishes three ancient races in Scandinavia, one of which is pre-historic; and Wilde[5] in Ireland, and Wilson[6] in Scotland, described several kinds of pre-Celtic skulls. Although we may pass over and leave to geology the investigation of the theory of the existence of man in an earlier geological epoch, still we may admit a very high antiquity of the human race. We maintain, however, that at present there exists no proof of an earlier race now extinct, nor of the existence of the human race before the present geological epoch. Though it could be proved that Scotland possessed a population before the arrival of the Celts, or that the American race was 57,000 years old, nothing is yet gained for the assertions of H. Smith.

Neither can the remains of old buildings, the object and origin of which is unknown to present generations of the respective countries, be adduced in support of the above theories; for it has repeatedly happened that uncivilized nations have taken possession of a territory, without preserving the history of its former inhabitants any more than their own. And thus the

---

[1] "Nouv. ann. des voy.," i, 363, 1845.
[2] Nott and Gliddon, p. 338.
[3] "Antiq. Celt. et Antédiluv.," Paris, 1849.
[4] "Reports of the British Association," p. 31, 1847.
[5] "Lecture on the Ethnology of the ancient Irish," 1844; Davis, "Crania Britannica."
[6] "Archæol. and pre-historical annals of Scotland," Edinburgh, 1851.

assertion, that before the present human race there existed one resembling the ape, supported by the mystical doctrine of the spontaneous extinction of lower human types, remains without the least scientific proof. Two other assertions of Smith still require investigation, namely, that each of the principal types of mankind (European, Mongol, and Negro), can only perpetuate themselves in their native country, and that each must be considered as a distinct species, from which new types issue by intermixture. We shall best consider these views in connection with those of another naturalist.

Agassiz has given a peculiar support to the theory of the specific differences of the chief types through the influence of climate.[1] His mode of treating this subject is in the main not original, but is similar to that of Swainson[2] who, without himself deciding on the unity of mankind, assumes six zoological provinces, apparently agreeing with the regions occupied by the various races. They are the following: 1. Europe with Asia Minor, and the coasts of the Mediterranean; 2. Asia beyond the Ural; 3. America (all these three with three, the latter with a fourth, problematical subdivision in the extreme south). 4. Africa south of Sahara, the third subdivision of which (South Africa and Madagascar) passes into the 5th. Australia (with New Holland as centre); 6. the north of the old and new world. The corresponding human races would be: the Caucasian, Mongolian, American, the Negro, the Malay, and the so-called Hyperborean. Agassiz has the following observations on this theory.

The boundaries of the zoological and botanical provinces, correspond generally with the distribution of the so-called races of mankind. But the species of animals and plants is originally different in each of these provinces; and even in those where the differences are but slight, no common descent can be assumed if they belong to different provinces, because no species passes across its limits into another province, but (as can be proved by many examples) keeps within its native soil. Hence we must assume, not one but several centres of creation

[1] "Christian Examiner," Boston, July 1850, and in Nott and Gliddon.

[2] "Treatise on the geography and classification of animals," London, 1835.

from which the creatures have spread over the earth,—as many as there are zoological and botanical provinces: and there obtains the same analogy for the human race as for the rest of organized beings.

The chief idea upon which this theory rests has, before Agassiz, been promulgated by Desmoulins,[1] namely, the idea that various centres of creation must be assumed for the animals of different parts of the world, as migrations into regions where they cannot exist are out of the question. Though man undoubtedly possesses a greater capacity for migrations, still his analogy to other organic beings renders it very probable that, like them, he originally proceeded from various centres of creation.

We leave it to zoologists and botanists to say whether this theory of the natural limitation of these provinces can be carried out as strictly as Agassiz imagines; whether it is not rather a scheme which, like many others, does violence to the facts. It is easily perceptible, that if there be no exact limits of the provinces, that is to say, if with regard to some animals it must be admitted that they have migrated from one part into another, the analogy to man, who unquestionably possesses the greatest capacity of locomotion, either does not apply, or at least loses much of its importance. When we learn that some European reptiles are also found in the whole of Asia, even in Japan, whilst all the reptiles of the New World are entirely different from those of the Old World;[2] and further, that the genuine typical forms of the animal world of America differ as much from those of the Old World as the Australian, one might be led from analogy to infer the separate origin of the European, American, and Australian man: but when it is considered that many birds and mammals of the Old World are also found in North America, this probability as regards man again disappears. We shall, however, in order to give to this new theory every chance, not insist upon this, but consider the question from another point of view. We shall examine whether the existing principal types of mankind correspond,

1 "Hist. nat. des races hum.," 1826.

2 Schlegel, "Essai sur la physiog. des serpens," 1837.

with some degree of exactness in the localities which they occupy, with the zoological and botanical provinces assumed by Agassiz.

We meet at the outset with the peculiar difficulty of laying hold of Agassiz's opinions, as he has frequently changed them.[1] Whilst in 1845 he asserts the unity of mankind as a species,[2] we find him in 1850 distribute eleven or twelve, in 1853 (Nott and Gliddon), eight, human species in as many zoological and botanical provinces; and it appears as if he made this last change chiefly to make these provinces better agree with the existing chief types of mankind. The twelve provinces of 1850 are the following:—one arctic; three of the temperate zone in Europe, Asia, and America, the latter in two divisions, the one to the east, the other to the west of the Rocky Mountains; three tropical provinces, the one of the Atlas, exclusive of the Nile valley and the Cape of Good Hope, the second in Asia south of the Himalaya, including the Sunda Islands, the third in America; the eighth province forms New Holland with Van Diemen's Land; then follows, as a province of doubtful independence, Polynesia; the three remaining provinces belong to the temperate zone of South America, the Cape of Good Hope, and the south Polar Circle. But in 1853 he makes the following division:—1. Arctic province; 2. Asia; 3. Europe to the north of the Caspian Sea, in the south to the Indus, inclusive of the northern edge of Africa; 4. America; 5. Africa; 6. India; 7. Australia and New Guinea; 8. Polynesia. We shall chiefly keep in view the first distribution in making some observations from an anthropological standpoint.

---

[1] He endeavours in vain to show, in his essay in the "Christian Examiner," that his opinion as to the unity of species is not in conflict with his theory of difference of origin; for however we may be inclined to agree with him and Meigs (in Nott and Gliddon, p. 350), that the question of unity of species is to be separated from that of unity of origin, still the separation has hitherto been very little attended to by zoologists, who mostly consider that the affirmation of the first question implies that of the second. In Germany, Eberhard ("Die Menschenracen," p. 36, Koburg, 1842) seems to have been the first who considered that the question of unity of origin from one pair, should be entirely separated from that of unity of species. He himself is of opinion that every species has originally appeared in several varieties.

[2] Smith, "Unity of the human races," p. 349, New York, 1850.

The north-polar nations have frequently been considered as a distinct race. This can, however, only be maintained when we simply keep in view their corporeal shape, and the peculiarities of their habits and customs. Forster has already, in his "History of the Voyages to North America,"[1] shown the impropriety of grouping together the Lapp and Samoied, and considering them of the same stock as the Esquimaux. As there is even now a large group of Samoied peoples in the south, extending to the sources of the Jenissei, their undoubted affinity to other Asiatic nations, decidedly indicates their origin from central Asia. Who, moreover, could assume that they sprung up in their cold climate, unless the Creator had gifted them with thick fur, like the ice-bear, that they might not be frozen to death before they had learned to build huts, etc.?

If it be objected that the climate of the polar regions had been warmer in former periods, there must be assumed a gradual acclimatization, which is denied by all those who, like Agassiz, believe that the chief types of mankind are limited to the climatic conditions and zones in which they were born. The polar nations thus manifestly do not originally belong to their present localities.

This may also, on historical and linguistic grounds, be proved with regard to the Indo-Germanic nations of Europe. They have not sprung up in their present localities, but are immigrants from the south-west of Asia. If the Mongols, Tunguses, and their allied tribes, are considered as a family, the original cradle of which was in the temperate region of Asia, their province now extends, in the south, to the sources of the two large Chinese rivers, and in the north, to the Polar Sea. Where, then, is that climatic limitation of individual human species? Where is it in America, the separation of which, in three divisions, according to the zones, is ethnographically perfectly arbitrary? Further, New Holland and Van Diemen's Land are not connected, anthropologically considered, and the province of the south pole is uninhabited. To this must be added, that the Austral-Negroes and Papuas live in

---

[1] Vol. iii, p. 60, Berlin, 1794.

the immediate vicinity of nations which are related to the Malays, whilst the latter extend to Madagascar; and that the tropical province of Asia contains the four most distinct human stocks inhabiting the globe (Caucasian, Mongolian, Malay, and Negro races), with some probability considered as their cradle. There can, therefore, be no question of such a separation of the families of mankind in zoological and botanical provinces, which may, perhaps, more properly apply to Africa, the northern shorelands of which present a flora and fauna distinct from the regions south of the Atlas, whilst similar differences are presented by the Nile valley and the Cape. With these districts correspond, as great ethnographic divisions, the Berbers, who belong to the Caucasian race, the Negroes, the Egyptians, the Abyssinians, and the Hottentots. In all other parts of the globe, it is scarcely necessary to say, there is no correspondence of the numerous subdivisions in special faunas and floras of Agassiz, with the groups of nations inhabiting these parts, and his subdivisions have no anthropological signification.

But what tells against the whole hypothesis of Agassiz, and should at the outset have prevented its adoption, is the circumstance that the cradle of mankind can only be imagined to have been situated in a warm climate; otherwise the first human beings must have perished in a climate where artificial protection and certain kinds of knowledge were requisite to obtain nutriment in sufficient quantity. To this must be added the improbability that, with the great capacity for locomotion possessed by man, and the wants he is subject to in a state of nature, the parent stocks of each human species should have remained in their original country from the period of their first appearance on the globe until the historical period,—an immense space of time. While extensive emigrations contradict such a fixed abode, we find, on the other hand, in many parts of the globe, men of perfectly distinct types living in close vicinity,—facts very unfavourable to the above theory. If it be correct, we need not assume any migrations of peoples; just as Desmoulins considers the Indo-Germans as autochthons in the countries of Scandinavia to the Caspian

Sea and the Indus; the Finns as autochthons on both sides of the Ural; the Turks as autochthons on the Altai and in the north-west of Thibet.

Though the above theories are inadmissible, we must be careful not to fall into the opposite error of deriving all human races from one spot,—the paradise usually placed in south-western Asia,—and attempting to indicate the course of their *original* migrations. We can only speak of the relatively oldest migrations, without asserting whether or not the countries to which they emigrated were already populated before their arrival. Lüken[1] has committed this error; nor has Latham, cautious as he usually is, remained free from it. It is under the influence of such ideas that he makes the Austral-Negroes and the Papuas occupy their present districts in remote times; makes the Australians migrate across Timur from south Asia into New Holland; lets the Polynesians and Micronesians follow them in the South Sea from the present Malay regions, and is much inclined to consider all these different stocks identical in their origin. He deserves consideration, however, when he observes,[2] that primary migrations of peoples are always probable where we—as, for instance, with the Hottentots, Lapps, Celts in Ireland—have extreme localities before us which are very remote from the supposed centre and starting point of the migration.

As it was formerly traditionally assumed that mankind descended from one pair, it was but natural to look for the cradle of humanity, to inquire how the original stocks became divided, and what roads they took when they left their original dwelling place to search for new localities. In modern times many authors have attempted positive counter-proofs. Rudolphi[3] has pointed out the difficulties under which the assumption laboured, that the distribution of mankind over the globe had only proceeded from *one* spot. These difficulties are manifestly nowhere so great as in the South Sea; and yet even there it can be satisfactorily shown that they are not unsurmountable. Not to become tedious, we would here only mention that Japanese

---

[1] "D. Einheit des Menschengeschl.," 1845.
[2] "Man and his migrations," p. 157, 1850.
[3] "Beiträge zur Anthropol.," p. 150, 1812.

are frequently mentioned as having been cast away in the South Sea. Thus they came, by a long involuntary sea-voyage, 1690, to Manilla,[1] in 1832 to Oahu,[2] in 1833 to Point Grenaille, 1½° north of the mouth of the Columbia river;[3] and Humboldt has shown that to proceed from Asia to America, without passing beyond the 55th degree of N. lat., did not require more than a sea-voyage of twenty-four to thirty-six hours.[4] Still more decisive is the agreement of language, tradition, manners, and religion prevailing in Polynesia, from the Sandwich islands to New Zealand; so that the assumption of a different descent of these island populations cannot be admitted. Thus the difficulties of migration cannot be adduced as a proof in favour of the theory that mankind have originated in one particular spot.

On the other hand, the positive proofs in favour of the descent of humanity from a single pair are scanty in the extreme. Without wishing to enter into any discussion with those who have faith in the narration of the Old Testament, the assumption of a single pair appears to us very improbable, as nature would scarcely hang the existence and preservation of any species on so slender a thread as a single pair of human beings. It is true that the ground against descent from a single pair rests only on a teleological, and not on a physical or physiological basis, still it is the principal ground which presents itself. Though the possibility of the descent of mankind from a single pair may be admitted by the analogy of many domestic animals imported into America, which have greatly multiplied from one or a few pairs,[5] there is nothing gained by it for its reality as regards man. Smith and others endeavour to show that the theory of descent from a single pair is preferable to the opposite assumption, inasmuch as we should not, without absolute necessity, multiply causes, and because *one* miracle is more acceptable than many; but it is clear that a mul-

---

[1] G. Careri, "Voy. autour du monde," v. p. 64, 1719.

[2] Bennet, "Narrative of a whaling voyage," i, p. 242; Jarves, "Hist. of the Sandwich islands," p. 27; Wilkes, v, p. 260.

[3] Wilkes, iv, p. 295.

[4] "Neu-Spanien," ii, p. 273; compare also, "Hist. de la géogr. du Nouveau Continent," ii, p. 607, 1836.

[5] Giebel, "Tagesfr. aus d. Natgesch.," 1857.

tiplication of agents is something different from a great complication of acting causes; and that, as regards miraclés, science cannot concern itself about the degree of admissibility, but about a suspension of the natural laws which is in conflict with science; for a miracle, as such, has no degrees. On the other hand, it may be readily admitted that it is but a weak argument when Agassiz, from the analogy of bees and other inferior social animals, endeavours to render the descent of mankind from a single pair highly improbable; for as Smith[1] justly observes, this analogy can neither be extended to all animals, nor is it at all applicable to highly organized beings.

They are completely in error who, adopting the views of Agassiz, assume as many original types of mankind as there are typically different peoples on the globe. It is permissible to assume, that men have appeared in masses in various centres of creation, and that the peoples of the globe have descended from several stocks, whose descendants have intermixed. It might even be difficult, from the known facts, to deny the probability of such a supposition or to refute it: the more is it necessary to be cautious in extending the theory to the solution of the difficult question with regard to the origin of man. By adopting it we escape, no doubt, many difficulties; but none is solved, especially the question, whether the pairs which originated in a centre of creation, simultaneously or successively, were of the same species or not. An indefinite multiplication of human species is inadmissible on account of the resemblances found among many and very remote peoples, to explain which we must either have recourse to paradoxical accidents or to common descent. Common structure of language, and a great number of common radicals, render the unity of the Indo-Germanic peoples unquestionable. It may further be considered as proved that, with the transition of a people from a state of nature into the civilized state, the typical uniformity of the corporeal form is gradually diminished, and gives place to greater variety; there is, therefore, every reason to assume a less number of original types than at present exist.

Finally, it has been clearly ascertained that numerous mi-

[1] Loc. cit., p. 356.

grations of peoples have taken place, consequently they cannot all have originated in the localities they now occupy. But the principle that man can only have originated in a warm climate where all the conditions for his preservation exist, is in conflict with the multiplication of regions considered as the cradle of mankind, at least until it is proved that the age of humanity reaches beyond the present geological epoch.

On recapitulating the results of our investigation, we may admit that though, in some respects, Agassiz's theory cannot be refuted, it is considered, as a whole, too special and speculative to be accepted. The principle which may be assented to in this theory is, that in the hot zone there may have been several spots in which men originated, and from which they spread. In taking into consideration the circumstance that neither the African, nor the Austral-Negroes and New Hollanders, perform sea-voyages, that they possess only miserable boats scarcely fit for river and coast navigation, that there is no indication of their having been navigators or traders at remote periods, we feel little inclined to assume that the black populations of the South Sea are immigrants from Africa. Whoever, on the other hand, assumes only a single region as the cradle of mankind, looks for that region in south Asia, whence the Negro races spread in a north-easterly and north-westerly direction. Again, he who assumes several cradles of humanity, would be obliged, on account of the little capacity for immigration possessed by Negro peoples, to look for them in south Asia, Africa, and New Guinea. The latter theory, namely, the assumption of several cradles of humanity, though incapable of positive proof, is mainly supported by the facts of differentiation between the chief types by climate, and the resemblance of the African and Australian Negro to the ape.

To determine the scope of the first fact, the climatic separation of the chief types, is difficult, as it is not yet sufficiently ascertained; for peoples of essentially different types frequently live in close vicinity (compare the examples quoted in the sequel); and however certain it may be that the Whites cannot perpetuate themselves as a people in all Negro regions, and that acclimatization, in sudden transitions from one climate into another, usually fails, it is still merely a hazardous assertion that Europeans cannot thrive in any country where the Negro prospers. It is equally rash to maintain that a gradual acclimatization of a white people, which from century to century progresses from north to south, into a negro region is impossible. The strictness with which Knox[1] defends the differences of races by climate is inadmissible; he goes so far as to maintain that all immigrants into a foreign climate can only be preserved by a constant infusion of fresh blood from their native country. We hear, however, nothing of a rapid extinction of the Creoles in the tropical colonies, as might be expected if this theory had any foundation. The limitation of animals to certain climates, which was invoked as an analogy, is not so general as to be applied to man, for most domestic animals can thrive in nearly all climates, though they do not attain in them the same size and vigour. The fox lives in the cold north as well as in the hot south; the home of the tiger extends from India to Siberia. Man seems, indeed, in his transitions from one climate to another, to resemble domestic animals, with this difference, that he bears these changes better in proportion as he is civilized. As in foreign climates races of animals degenerate, approaching the type of the native animals, even without intermixture;[2] so does man, unless essential differences in nutriment, mode of life, and cultivation of the immigrants, from that of the natives, prevent it.

As a race of animals cannot long maintain itself in a foreign climate against the native race without constant infusion of fresh blood from the parent stock, but is absorbed by it—because the mass of intermixing elements finally decides the type of the mongrels, and climate gradually produces the resemblance of the foreign tribe to the native,—so a small number of foreign immigrants remains without influence upon the type of the mongrels, whilst a sufficiently large number influences the type of the progeny.

The second point, the resemblance of the Negro to the ape, is a fact which is estimated differently according to the

---

[1] "The races of man."
[2] Lucas, ii, p. 311.

stand-point of the inquirer. It has been connected with the theories on the origin of man, and the ape has been considered as the ancestor of man, which is the doctrine of those who assume a development of animal species: it may be that this transformation was limited to periods of great geological changes, or that it was slowly progressive in the course of time by continuous accommodation to external circumstances.[1]

Although one would not feel inclined to attach much value to this theory in preference to that of the permanence of species, it still appears important, from the analogy in which it stands to a scientific theory of nature and human life. The gradual development of the earth, and of higher forms from lower forms, apparently without any manifestation of new creative power, appears to force upon us that view of the origin of man, whose history seems to show that the higher forms and the development of external and internal life have proceeded from lower forms, and which in course of time they may be destined to supersede. Certain as it is that man has somewhere, and at some period, appeared on this earth, it is equally certain that all scientific analogies tend to show that he originated in a natural way. It must, however, as candidly be admitted, that all analogies indicating the transformation of the ape into a man are as yet wanting to experimental science; nor can we at present scientifically render an account of the natural origin of man, though science is justified in assuming it. But is the investigator bound to establish theories in the absence of facts? Certainly not; the love of truth, on the contrary, forbids it. It is certainly very disagreeable to many to be bound to confess that their wisdom is at an end; but logic, and a real scientific interest, require such a confession where facts are wanting. If a theory can only be supported by a general analogy and not by definite grounds, whilst there is opposed to it a wide field of conflicting possibilities, its foundation is weak indeed, and there remains in its favour but a scanty probability that it may be as we are inclined to expect.

[1] Lamarck and his followers. I. Geoffroy St. Hilaire.

The question as to the affinity between man and the ape, appears as idle at present as that of the original colour of the first pair, whom Lacepède[1] describes, like Hunter and Link, as black, on account of the greater heat of past periods. Buffon and Blumenbach describe them as white, De Salles and others describe them as brownish-red. We would here observe, that the assertion of such relationship (of the ape and man) is, for him who assumes a corresponding progressive improvement of the physical form with the progress of civilization in the human race, an interesting hypothesis; whilst he who decides for the permanence of individual human types and different species of animals, with respect to their external and internal constitution, must ascribe to the effects of external influences an unlimited power for the transformation of the ape into man. De Salles[2] observes therefore very justly, "Affirmer la force créatrice des milieux pour un type primitif, c'est à plus forte raison admettre la modification secondaire de ce type quand l'expatriation a changé les milieux, c'est-à-dire l'air, la lumière, l'humidité ou sècheresse, la nourriture, l'élévation au-dessus du niveau de la mer." But it has not prevented the committal of this gross error:—the so-called races of man are said to represent fixed types, but little changeable by climate, mode of life or mental culture; and yet they are to have originated in consequence of changes of external conditions during the various periods of the history of the globe.[3] Finally, it may be observed, that if man descended from the ape, it is clear that, like the ape, he originally belonged to a tropical climate.

Though fossil apes have been found in regions which now possess a temperate climate, as Gascony, still the contemporaneous existence of man remains as yet to be proved; and if it were proved, it would render the assumption necessary that man existed upon the earth before the present division of the climates. At any rate, it must be conceded that, by the discovery of fossil monkeys, the existence of fossil human bones has been rendered less improbable.

[1] "Ages de la nature," i, p. 255, 1830.
[2] "Hist. générale des races hum.," p. 31, 1849.
[3] Compare, as an example of such false reasoning, the essay on human races in the "Deutsche Vierteljahrschrift," ii, p. 170, 1838.

On the other hand, the fact of the resemblance of the Negro to the ape is made use of to prove that mankind is to be divided into different species. The Negro presents in this case not merely the most striking example of a deviation of form, but also a type apparently constant. Hence many, in investigating the pedigree of man, would have the Negro still more ape-like than he really is: we must therefore be cautious not to exaggerate that resemblance. That the Negro manufactures tools, and learns from experience to subject nature to his wants, that he establishes communities, that he possesses an artificially constructed language, and religious ideas, is undoubted. Still it is undeniable that, if differences of species are to be assumed, the Negro and the White present the most striking examples. Virey considers these two alone as specifically different. It is, therefore, worth while to investigate this question, for which purpose we shall closely examine the Negro type, and the modifications which it presents.

Keeping in view the peoples which inhabit Africa, between the tropics, it has already been observed, that the proper Negro type is only found in the region between Senegal and Niger, and in some parts of Senaar, Kordofan, and Darfur. In the first place, the whole large family of the South African peoples, reaching from the equator to the Hottentots, do not present that type in its purity, though Prichard justly observes, that the gradual transition which we find in bodily form from the proper Kaffirs on the north-east boundary of the Cape Colony, to the natives of Mozambique, and from these again to the natives farther north, compels us to consider these peoples as of the same stock as the Negroes. The proper Kaffirs possess more arched and European-shaped skulls, and less projecting lower jaws than the Negroes; the hair is short, coarse, bushy, less woolly than in the Negro, the cheek-bones are more arched outwards;[1] the lips full, not like the Negroes;[2] the nose but little flattened, sometimes arched; the colour varying from light brown to black; hence Barrow[3] says that,

---

[1] Le Vaillant, "Erste R," p. 356, 1799.
[2] Kay, "Travels in Kaffraria," p. 110, 1833.
[3] Vol. i, p. 203.

but for the colour, the Kaffirs might be taken for Europeans. Throughout Africa, south of the equator, true Negroes are found only in Mozambique, and in Congo in the interior of the country, where the nose is perfectly flattened, and the lips are enormously protruding;[1] whilst towards the mouth of the river the Negro peculiarities appear modified.[2] On ascending the Gaboon, the physical form is found gradually to approach the Caucasian type.[3] From information received by the Portuguese governor, Saldanha, the Muluas inhabiting the interior of the country are said to be handsomer and more civilized than the inhabitants of the coast.[4]

The chief peoples of East Africa to the north of the equator do not represent the peculiar Negro type, from which they deviate still more than the South Africans. Setting aside the Abyssinians and their kindreds, there are the Tibboo, who are described as tall, colour not perfectly black, eyes sparkling, lips full, nose small, but not turned up, short but not frizzly hair.[5] Among those of Kisby, the nose is thick and fleshy, with wide nostrils; in Gunda, on the frontier of Bornou, they have sharp, intelligent features, high forehead, prominent eyes, flat nose, and large mouth.[6] The inhabitants of Haussa have, it is true, woolly hair and a black skin, but their features are regular, with a general resemblance to the European. The Kanori differ from the Haussaua by their broad faces, open nostrils, and thick bones.[7] Among the native peoples of Adamaua, the Battas are the most numorous; their lips are but little protruding, they are well-shaped, and possess regular features.[8] The Bornouese are less black than the inhabitants of Haussa, and have high foreheads, but thick Negro-noses, and round laughing faces with fat cheeks.[9] The Mandaranes have less

---

1 Omboni, "Viaggi nell' Afr. occ.," p. 161, 1845.
2 Owen, "Narr. of voyage to explore the shores of Africa," ii, p. 283, 1833.
3 Hecquard, "R. an. d. K. in d. Innere von West-Afr.," p. 7, 1854.
4 Bowdich, "Account of the discoveries of the Portuguese," p. 17.
5 Hornemann, "Tageb. seiner R.," p. 125, 1802.
6 Denham, Clapperton, and Oudney, "Narrative of travels," i, pp. 25, 52, 2nd edit., 1826.
7 Barth, "Reisen und Entdeck.," ii, p. 183.
8 Ibid., p. 613.
9 Denham, loc. cit., p. 140; Richardson, "Travels in the Great Desert of Sahara," i, p. 264, 1848.

flattened faces than the former, frizzly hair, large sparkling eyes, high but flat foreheads, and somewhat hooked noses.[1] In the district of Marghi, the peculiar Negro type is not met with: the features are fine and regular, lips no more than full, forehead high, colour of a shining black or of a coppery tint.[2] On the other hand, the dirty black and bony Mussgu are, excepting their high foreheads and bushy eyebrows, entirely Negro-like. The inhabitants of Baghirmi are well grown, more muscular than the Bornouese, the nostrils are not widely open, and the women have remarkably regular features. In Wadai, where Mohammed-el-Tounsy[3] mentions a large number of different peoples, without describing them, each of which is said to have its peculiar physiognomy and language, there live, according to Barth, both Negro and Arab tribes. The Nuba, as the inhabitants of Kordofan call themselves, possess woolly hair and very thick lips, not the small flat noses of the inhabitants of the southern mountains of that region, but well proportioned.[4] The mountaineers have less prominent cheek-bones than the Negroes proper, the skin is often of a chestnut colour, and they are generally well made. The old Arab writers (Içthakri, Idrisi) expressly distinguish the Nubians from Negroes (whom later authors confound), and describe them, especially the women, as smooth-haired, with small lips and mouths, which corresponds in the main with the description of modern travellers as regards the Nubians beyond Kordofan. The physical form of the Gallas sometimes approaches the European type, and it is not yet decided to which they properly belong.[5] But in their district, and in that of the Abyssinians, some small tribes of a genuine Negro-type are met with,—the Shangallas,[6] the Doba,[7] and the Doko.[8] The

[1] Denham, Clapperton, and Oudney, p. 201.
[2] Barth, loc. cit., ii, p. 465.
[3] "Voy. au Ouaday," pp. 245, 253, 1851.
[4] Rüppell, "Reise in Nubien," p. 141, 1829.
[5] Rochet d'Hericourt, "Voy. dans le royaume de Choa," p. 269, 1841; Pruner, p. 63; Lefèbvre, Petit et Quartin-Dillon, "Voy. en Abyssinie," iii, p. 289, 1845.
[6] Bruce, "Reise," ii, pp. 433, 537, 1790.
[7] Salt, "Voy. to Abyssinia," p. 275, 1814.
[8] Harris, "The highlands of Æthiopia," iii, p. 63, 2nd edit., 1844; compare Johnston, "Travels in S. Abyssinia," ii, p. 383, 1844, and d'Abbadie in "Nouv. ann. des voy." i, p. 261, 1845.

whole mountain region on the Blue Nile and the Tomat, from Fassokl south to the Gallas, is inhabited by Negroes, who differ, however, from the Shillook and Dinka on the White Nile, being of a finer stock than these.[1] On the White Nile, from 6° to 7° N. lat., the Negro-type disappears gradually towards the south, and among the southern Dinka peoples, so little marked is it "that the greater part of Europeans would resemble them if they were painted black."[2] The Negro-type is accordingly, in East Africa, confined to but few small peoples.

On now turning our attention to the Negro regions proper, between the Senegal and the Niger, we find that there prevails as little, as in other parts of Africa, the same physical type in perfect uniformity, though on the whole, the typical forms of the Negro race are greatly predominating. The Jolofs between the Senegal and the Gambia are of a dark, shining black colour; hair, lips, and nose are Negro-like, but not very decidedly marked;[3] the nose is but moderately flat, the lips not very thick;[4] figure and features frequently noble and regular.[5] The brownish-black Mandingoes have more oval faces than the Negroes proper; the forehead is less prominent, larger, and more receding, especially among the Fulahs; the head is rather pointed towards the crown, the nose is very broad, and the upper lip very large.[6] Some of the Mandingo tribes are not so well made, they have thicker lips and flatter noses than others; this applies to the Susus, as compared with the Bullams and Timanis.[7] The Fulahs, who look down upon the Negroes,[8] and consider themselves as Whites compared with them,[9] do not everywhere exhibit the same colour and type. In the west, they are usually reddish-brown, have flat noses, but not very woolly hair, a broader forehead, and a

1 Russeger, "Reise," ii, pp. 562, 762.
2 Werne, "Exped. zur. Entd. der Q. des Weissen Nil," p. 241. 1848.
3 Golberry, "Reise durch d. Westl. Afr.," i, p. 51, 1808.
4 Park, "Voy. dans l'int. de l'Afr.," an. viii, i, p. 24.
5 Mollien, "Reise in d. Innere von Afr.," p. 41, 1820.
6 Golberry, ii, p. 114; Duncan, "R. in West-Afr.," p. 15, 1848; Raffenel, "Voy. dans l'Afr. occ.," p. 394, 1846.
7 Matthews, "Reise nach S. Leone," p. 94, 1789.
8 M. Park, i, p. 92.
9 Lander, "Reise z. Erforsch. des Niger," ii, p. 278, 1833.

larger facial angle than genuine Negroes, small lips and oval face.[1] Barth[2] describes them as an intermediate race between Negroes, Arabs, and Berbers, and observes, that the men, up to the twentieth year, are often very handsome, but subsequently assume an apish physiognomy, which destroys the Caucasian features. The Jambures, in the country of the Portuguese settlements on the S. Domingo, the Casamanza, and R. Grande, are perfectly black, but have neither flat noses nor thick lips; their features approach those of Europeans.[3] The inhabitants of Cazegut (Bissagos-Archipelago) have agreeable features, and have neither flat noses nor thick lips.[4] The Krus and Grebos have a particularly well-shaped chin; the facial angle is larger, the head more oval, and not so arched as in the Negro.[5] A pleasing roundness of features and an oval face are characteristic of the Odshis; pointed and hooked noses are not common amongst them, but flattened noses and thick protruding lips are rare.[6] This is also the case among the natives of Apollonia.[7] In Aquapim the head is partly globular, the nose broad, lips thick; occasionally it happens that the head is long, the nose pointed, the lips small, nearly European; the last form prevails chiefly among the Ashantees,[8] among the higher ranks of which not only fine women are seen, but regular Grecian faces are frequently met with.[9] These characters are also to be found in the higher classes of Dahomey, where some members of the reigning family "are nearly of Moorish aspect, and not so black as genuine Negroes."[10] The Mahis in the north of Dahomey have long, and high crowned and posteriorly developed heads, so characteristic of the genuine Negro-type, a shorter chin, but less thick lips than the Dahomians, and an almost European nose.[11] The Negroes of Yarriba possess only moderately thick

[1] M. Park, i, pp. 26, 91; Raffenel, p. 263.
[2] "Reise und Entd.," p. 505.
[3] "Bullet. soc. géogr.," i, p. 152, 1846, according to Lopes de Lima.
[4] Durand, "Voy. au Sénégal, an. x," i, p. 185.
[5] Allen and Thomson, "Narr. of the Exped. to the R. Niger," i, p. 124, 1848.
[6] "Baseler Miss.-Mag.," i, p. 53, 1856.
[7] Meredith, "Account of the Gold Coast," p. 61, 1812.
[8] "Baseler Miss.-Mag.," iv, p. 241, 1852.
[9] Bowdich, "Mission nach Ashantee," p. 422, 1820.
[10] Duncan, i, p. 238; Forbes, "Dahomey, and the Dahomians," pp. 17, 50, Paris, 1851.
[11] Duncan, ii, p. 273.

lips, and their nose approaches the aquiline form;[1] those of Iddah, on the Niger, have more rounded features, thinner lips than the Ibus, and large receding foreheads.[2] The natives of Accono-Coono, under 6° 30′, have not such coarse Negro features, and are handsomer, and look more intelligent than the southerns of Omun, resembling in this respect those of Iddah.[3] In the same way, we learn that almost everywhere the decided Negro-type diminishes in these parts from the coast inland. The Edeeyahs (Adiahs) of Fernando Po have longer hair, more silky than woolly, round face, cheek-bones not so high, narrower nostrils, thinner lips, and a finer mouth than their neighbours on the continent; the colour varies from deep black to copper-colour, but the physiognomy is the same in all.[4]

The preceding rather dry enumeration, which might have been rendered more minute, of a great number of variations in shape, was necessary to show how valueless is that asserted fixity of the Negro type. Taken generally, it rests upon fancy, for this type in its purity is limited to comparatively few peoples; and, moreover, there prevails a great number of other types, which may be partly considered as transitions to the European form, and partly as deviations and modifications of Negro peculiarities, without any approach to other races. That such transitions, between the Caucasian and Negro-type, are not wanting, has been shown in the quoted examples, and has been pointed out by various travellers. The traveller from Cairo up the Nile to Nubia and Senaar, finds himself, on account of the small gradations by which the Egyptian passes in the Negro, embarrassed to decide where the white race ceases and the black race commences.[5] The transitions are imperceptible; it is only near Assuan that there is a sudden change from the Egyptian to the Nubian type.[6] On progressing from Tunis towards the south, there is

[1] Clapperton, "Tageb. der zweiten R.," p. 382, 1830.
[2] Allen and Thomson, i, p. 325.
[3] Becroft, in "Journal Roy. Geo. Soc.," xiv, p. 272.
[4] Allen and Thomson, ii, p. 194; "Nouv. ann. d. voy.," ii, p. 281, 1845; Boteler, "Narrative of a voyage to Africa and Arabia," ii, p. 423, 1835.
[5] "D'Escayrac d. Afr. Wüste und d. Land der Schwarzen," p. 184, 1855.
[6] Dandolo, "Viaggio in Egitto," p. 182, 1854.

also a regular and gradual transition of features and colour into the Negro-type perceptible, especially in Tozar; "and if it were possible to bring from these countries an ethnological collection to Europe, the greatest sceptic would feel convinced that time and locality alone are the causes of these fluctuating differences."[1] We attach, however, but little weight to this gradual fusion of both types which presents itself to the traveller, since it can scarcely be doubted that North and Central Africa contains a great number of mixed populations. It is, however, more important to observe that the whole South African family, where we have no reason to suppose a sufficient admixture of northern elements, form, with regard to their cranial development, a well-defined intermediate link between the black and the white races.

Whilst admitting that a considerable number of African peoples, even the inhabitants between the Senegal and the Niger, owe their deviations from the pure Negro type to an admixture of elements from a higher race; still it remains clear, that on the one hand these mongrels do not become extinct, as is usually the case in the hybrids of some species of animals, nor lose the acquired type by reversion, but preserve it: and that on the other hand, the attempt to explain all considerable deviations from the pure Negro type, which occur generally among African peoples by intermixture, may be supported by preconceived theories, but not by actual facts. It would not be difficult to indicate as great a number of different types in other parts of the globe. We shall, however, confine ourselves to a few examples, which plainly show that these types are nowhere so perfectly distinct as to be considered as specifically different. Races decidedly different, dwell, no doubt, in many places near each other in the same climate; for instance, on the Senegal, Moors and Negroes; in many of the Polynesian islands and in the South Sea, Malays and Polynesians, beside Negro-like populations; in Europe, Lapps and Scandinavians, etc. This shows that climate alone can hardly change in a very great degree the type of a people, that it may be one of the agents,

---

[1] Davis, "Evenings in my tent," ii, p. 3, 1854.

but standing alone it has not a decidedly marked influence. But in spite of that striking difference in form which we meet with in several regions of the earth, each of the chief forms which comes in contact with another becomes mingled with it by a series of gradations, each bearing a peculiar local stamp, just as we might expect from the peculiar external and internal conditions in which these individual tribes live. The Finnish peoples are, as regards the corporeal form, such an intermediate link between the Mongolian and Caucasian races, just as the Hindoos have been considered as intermediate between the former and the Malay race. The Tchuktchi and Korjäks, the Esquimaux and some West American nations, whose cranial form approaches the Mongolian, stand between Asiatics and Americans, and the Esquimaux themselves (who, on the Atlantic are easily distinguished from the American Indians), are gradually mingled with them on the coast of the Pacific. Botocudes felt so surprised at the sight of the Chinese that, from their resemblance to them, they called them their uncles.[1] From the Mongols and the Tunguses to the Samoiedes[2] there is a natural transition in respect to language and physical and geographical relation; and this is also the case from the Samoiedes to the Ainos, and from these to the Esquimaux.

That a definite limitation of some chief forms cannot be maintained, is moreover shown by the fact that some peoples, though very remote from each other and manifestly unconnected, present great resemblances. The Californians greatly resemble the Negroes of Guinea, New Guinea, and the New Hebrides, in shape of head and face,—their hair, however, is not woolly. All travellers are struck with the slight external differences existing between Europeans and the Marquesas islanders. The head of the Tahitian might be taken for European were it not for the wide nostrils and large lips.[3] Some New Zealanders have perfectly European skulls, whilst the features approach those of the North American Indians (Dieffenbach). The Hottentots, on account of their colour, shape of

---

1 Hollard, p. 197, after St. Hilaire.
2 Neumann in A. Wagner, "Gesch. d. Urwelt," p. 311, 1845.
3 Lesson, in "Complément des œuv. de Buffon," ii, p. 206.

skull and face, have by many been included in the Mongolian race, though they are separated from it by their woolly hair growing in single small bunches. The Georgians and Tscherkesses possess perfect Grecian skulls; yet their language forbids the idea of their consanguinity to the Indo-Germanic nations. According to Tschudi,[1] the cranium of the Aymaras approaches nearly that of the Guanches.

A further objection, of considerable weight, against a fixed separation of the chief types, and consequently against the assumption of specific differences, is afforded by the fact that individuals who, in their external character, deviate considerably from the parent stock, exhibiting that of a foreign tribe, occur in all parts of the globe. It has already been mentioned, that laterally compressed skulls and oblique incisors, are frequently found in Europeans. Oblique eyes, projecting lower jaw, small square foreheads, crania elongated upwards or backwards, prominent cheek-bones, appear in families the Germanic origin of which is undoubted. Lucae[2] has given a sketch of such a skull[3] which much resembles the macrocephalous Asiatic of Blumenbach.[4] There is, further,[5] the skull of a Hessian criminal, of the Marburg collection, which in form entirely agrees with that of the Peruvian skulls, as regards the flattened forehead, strongly developed occiput, and flattened coronal region; and finally,[6] there is a skull which in many respects reminds us of the Mongolian formation. Pure Arabs are sometimes, in their native country, perfectly black. The prognathous form of the face, with a light complexion, is seen in many Egyptians. Thick lips and flat noses are met with in European nations; for instance, among the Slavonians. Even woolly hair is seen in some instances in northern nations; but a single character, observes Pruner, establishes no decided mark of distinction, they must all be combined. However much we might agree with him in this respect, we find in it a confession that race-characters do not constitute specifically fixed differences: hence it seems to us illogical, when he says,

[1] Müller's, "Archiv," p. 98, 1844.
[2] Schädel, abnormer form.
[3] Table iii.
[4] Decas, i, tab. 3.
[5] Table vi.
[6] Table xvii.

"that it is impossible that one race-character should pass into another without intermixture." Another explanation in favour of the specific difference of races has been attempted by Giebel.[1] He asserts that Negro resemblances, or other deviations from the Caucasian form which now and then present themselves in Europeans, are so superficial that they do not much affect the Caucasian type. He, however, refutes himself[2] by declaring in another passage, that such analogies of form, wherever they do occur, affect all the proportions of the body.

Other individual deviations from the original type have been mentioned by Lüken[3] and Weerth[4]. They refer to the inhabitants of Carinthia and Styria; the Chinese and South Sea islanders, who in many instances approach the European forms, whilst Chinese physiognomies are said to be frequently met with in Poland (Schadow, Polyklet); the Tartars, who by their projecting lower jaws, pointed chin, and long teeth, differ considerably from the Mongol type, which is also the case with Kalmucks. Among the latter, Pallas observed fine figures, and individuals with fair hair. Even among the Tunguses, who represent so decidedly the Mongol type, there are found some individuals with a European physiognomy, light blue eyes, straight or curved nose, brown hair, and strong beard.[5] Seemann[6] met with an Esquimaux, of the tribe of Hotham Bay, remarkably Negro-like, and another who had a strikingly hooked Jewish nose. The Slavonians present a very remarkable example of great differences among allied nations. They are dark in the south-east of their districts; the Poles present a different aspect; the Russian peasants have often light brown or red hair; so that these peoples differ externally from each other more than from some other Indo-Germanic nations.

Deviations in colour, eyes, hair, are particularly numerous. Some of these deviations have been considered as the result of disease. Not wishing to repeat the facts already mentioned,

---

[1] "Tagesfr. a. d. natgesch.," p. 55, 1857.
[2] Page 105.
[3] "D. Einheit des Menschengeschl.," p. 15, 1845.
[4] "D. Entw. der Menschenrassen," p. 17, 1842.
[5] Prichard, iv, p. 410.
[6] "Reise um d. Welt," ii, p. 53, 1853.

we would only add the following.—Red hair is frequently noticed among Negroes and Mulattoes;[1] also among the Papuas[2] in the South Sea, where Quiros was struck by it;[3] in Tahiti, New Zealand, and elsewhere;[4] in Timor,[5] among the Esquimaux,[6] among the Esthonians and Wotjakes,[7] among the Hindoos and the Arabs of Yembo, more rarely in Ceylon, Cochin-China and Tonkin.[8] Especially remarkable are the great differences exhibited by the peoples of the table-land above Dilli (Timor). Some of the natives have a dark yellow colour; the parts exposed to the sun are covered with light-brown patches; the hair is straight and thin, its natural colour reddish, or of a dark chestnut-brown. There are also found in Timor all intermediate shades of the skin, from dark yellow to black or chocolate-brown; and the hair from red and straight to the short and woolly hair of the Papuas.[9] Red hair and variously coloured eyes are also met with among the Congo-Negroes and the Bushmen.[10] Brown eyes are very common in Bonny.[11] Among the Akoos (Yarriba), the iris is light-brown or dark chestnut, sometimes dark sea-green.[12] Even at Madagascar there are blue-eyed women.[13] Scarlett[14] saw in Peru a perfectly black Negro-boy with light blue eyes, whose mother had one eye black and the other blue. Kabyles with red hair and blue eyes are mentioned by Bruce[15] and others, and Blumenbach quotes similar instances. Barbot states that the wives of the Galibis (Caribs) in Guiana have mostly blue eyes; and Wallis found in Tahiti people with brown, red, and

---

1 Marcgrav, Lopez, Winterbottom, etc.

2 Sonnerat.

3 1605, according to Torquemada, "Monarquia Indiana," v, c. 66, 1723.

4 Forster, Wallis, Marion, and Duclesmeur.

5 Van Hogendorp.

6 Charlevoix.

7 Gmelin.

8 Blumenbach, "De gen. hum. v. n.," pp. 165, 169; De Salles, "Hist. gén. des races hum.," p. 246, 1849, according to Desmoulins.

9 W. Earl, "The native races of the Indian Archipelago," p. 179, 1853.

10 Lopez, "Warh. Beschr. des K. Congo," p. 5, ed. de Bry., 1597; Burchell, ii, p. 225.

11 Köler, p. 89.

12 R. Clarke, "Sierra Leone," p. 149, 1846.

13 Rochon, "Reise nach Madag. in Mazin v. Reisebeschr.," viii, p. 24.

14 "South America and the Pacific," ii, p. 166, 1838.

15 Vol. i, p. 27.

flaxen hair. In Nutka, there are men with brown and light hair.[1] Among the Cayawas or Cayowas, near the sources of the Rio Branco, a tributary of the Paraguay, there are fair-complexioned individuals with light hair, who seem to be of pure blood;[2] and Velasco[3] says of the Gaes people on the Marañon, that their hair is as fine as that of Europeans. Pickering[4] is therefore wrong in maintaining that, excluding Albinoes, flaxen hair, red hair, and blue eyes, are only met with in the white race. With regard to the colour of the skin, there are also among the Pehuenches strikingly white Indians who have the colour of a German peasant.[5] Thus the Spaniards found in Macapana when they conquered the country, young Indian girls who had been brought up in seclusion, white as Europeans, which was also the case in Santa Fé.[6] Among the Aguanos and Barbudes, on the Huallaga river, the males were sunburnt, but the women were as white as the Spanish females, some of them even had red hair (according to the reports of the Jesuits in the seventeenth century).[7] To the Araucanians belong the much whiter Boroanos, living between the rivers Imperial and Tolten, 38½°-39° S. lat.;[8] they are considered, by Molina,[9] perfectly to resemble northern Europeans in figure and colour. However much he may elsewhere[10] insist upon it that they are neither Albinoes nor cross-breeds, still, as we shall show in the sequel, the view that they are Mestizoes (an opinion recently adopted also by Smith[11]), is much more probable. Ancient historical documents, referring to that country, leave no doubt on the subject.

After these examples, we may expect that a closer examination of individual peoples will make us acquainted with still greater deviations from their original type, than those who as-

---

1 Roquefeuil, "Journal d'un voy. aut. du monde," ii, p. 189, 1823.
2 Castelnau, ii, p. 395.
3 In Ternaux, "Recueil de documents," p. 288.
4 "The races of man," 1849.
5 Pöppig, "Reise," i, p. 463.
6 P. Simon, "Noticias de las conq. de Tierra Firme," i, pp. 2, 4, 1627.
7 Rodriquez, "El Maranon y Amazonas," iii, c. 3, Madrid, 1684.
8 Pöppig, "Reise," vol. i.
9 "Essai sur l'hist. nat. du Chili," p. 313, 1789.
10 See his "Saggio sulle storia civile de Chile," p. 10, Bologna, 1787.
11 "The Araucanians," p. 293, New York, 1855.

sume a fixed specific form are inclined to admit. In the face of the above facts, the only alternative for such as contend for a plurality of human species, is to multiply them still more. We have already indicated the difficulties of such an alternative, for such it is; we would therefore only add, that the same reasons may be urged against the assumption of a hundred or more species, as against the assumption of only two species. In members of the same family, diversities are as frequently observed as in individuals of a foreign stock; and in individuals of the same stock, without intermixture, differences such as are exhibited by distinct races. However few may be the tribes included within one species, there will always be found diversities amongst them, among their families and individuals, as great as the differences exhibited by the assumed number of species; on which account they cannot be considered as specific distinctions.

He who assumes only as many species of mankind as there are principal forms of cranial and bodily shape, at most from five to seven, will in the end find himself obliged to abandon his theory. He obtains specific characters fluctuating as much between extreme limits as the individual who assumes but one species of man, and he is therefore obliged to admit, like the latter, the great influence of external agents. At any rate, it is perfectly arbitrary to consider certain principal forms as specifically different which are partly extreme forms (as the Negro-type), partly intermediate (the American type), and subordinate types. "The break up of one principal form into physically and morally distinct families of man, is not much more explicable than the races themselves."[1] If it be contended, with regard to the first, that they have become developed in the course of time by the agency of external and internal forces, there is no reason to deny it as regards the latter. If minor differences of each species could arise in this manner, it only requires sufficiently long periods and appropriate conditions to produce greater differences. There is not even any necessity to adduce a frequently expressed assump-

[1] "Deutsche Vierteljahrschrift," ii, p. 247, 1838.

tion, that at a remote time the human organism was more plastic under external agencies, just as every individual and every people has a juvenile period before their transition from the natural to the civilized state, in which they are more plastic than at any later period.

We conclude, therefore, that there are no fixed and definitely limited forms which can be considered as specific differences; but that if the human species is zoologically to be brought under some chief divisions, it is a mere classification furnished to us by striking analogies. Lesson[1] observes very justly, "*On ne devrait en effet adopter les distinctions de races ou d'espèces*[2] *que comme des moyens artificiels destinés à préciser nos idées dans l'étude de l'homme, et à le rendre plus facile.*" J. Müller[3] expresses himself in a similar sense when he says, "that a rigid division of mankind is impossible. The given forms differ in typical peculiarities; but there is no certain scientific principle for fixing the limits specifically. It might be more proper to distinguish all peoples as *constant* and *extreme* forms of variations, than to distribute them into races. This seems impossible, nor does science require such a division; to attempt it leads unavoidably to an arbitrary assumption." Tartars and Finns will always occupy an unknown position between the Mongolian and Caucasian race; Papuas and Alfurus between Malays and Negroes, etc. The impossibility of a rigid separation is confirmed by an experimental study of race-characters, and also by the fact that only small collections of skulls exhibit decidedly different forms; whilst large collections fill up the gaps between them, showing continued transitions from one form into every other.

If, in order to oppose the argument founded upon the above facts, many originally different human species are assumed in that part of Africa situated between the tropics, all difficulties are removed, inasmuch as such assumptions

---

1 "Voyage médical autour du monde," p. 156, 1829.

2 As regards species, this is an error, though it is true with respect to races. The question in relation to the first has been awkwardly treated, for they have disputed whether species were created or were only by us introduced in nature. Species are, no doubt, objective realities, not merely thoughts or models according to which nature acts.

3 "Handbuch der Physiol.," ii, 114.

cannot be refuted until it is definitely stated which tribes constitute these different species. The American school, following Morton, which assumes that men have been created in masses of peoples, entertains this opinion, and would rather not admit any influence of external conditions upon the physical peculiarities of mankind; there are, it asserts, no races, but only an indefinitely large number of species of man. Vogt, who has propagated this doctrine in Germany, is even of opinion that individual nations are not to be considered of mixed origin, because the known mongrel types of the Mulattoes, Mestizoes, etc., are not exactly found in them, and that consequently, hundreds of originally different stocks must be assumed; all which only acquires its validity by the erroneous supposition, that types are perfectly unalterable by external influences. Let us, therefore, subject that assertion of an absolute immutability of race-types to a closer investigation.

The chief, if not the only, proofs are derived from the old Egyptian monuments and the Jews. Blumenbach[1] recognized upon the first, three different human types: that of the Negro'; a second, which he calls the Indian type; and a third, which is said to be produced by the influence of the Egyptian climate, a relaxed flabby form, short chin and prominent eyes. At a later period, Morton[2] distinguished Pelasgic, Semitic, and Negro skulls among those of the old Egyptians. B. Taylor[3] still more decidedly points out upon the old Egyptian monuments, the distinguishable forms of Negroes, Persians and Jews. Others, especially Mariotte, believe they can recognize in pictures, above 5,000 years old, the type of the Fellahs of the present day.[4]

Nott and Gliddon[5] have in this manner endeavoured to prove the immutability of some chief types and consequently the permanency of all: they assert that, as far as history reaches,

[1] "De gen. hum. var. nat.," p. 188.
[2] "Crania Ægyptiaca."
[3] "Reise nach central Afrika," pp. 97, 447, 1853.
[4] The various results of the anthropological relations of ancient Egypt have been collated by Courtet de Lisle in "Nouv. ann. des voy.," ii, p. 299, 1847.
[5] "Types of mankind," 1854.

these forms have always existed; whilst de Salles, following Lepsius, maintains that skulls of an earlier period than the fifth and sixth centuries B.C. no longer exist in Egypt, and well observes that the present Fellahs ought not to present the old Egyptian type, if types be permanent, as in Egypt so many intermixtures had taken place: the former[1] endeavouring to prove, that the Nubians had already inhabited their present localities 3,500 years ago, as shown by pictures representing the outlines of the face, and beards. Cranial measurements are not mentioned, but every one knows what a difference in external aspect is produced by a different head-dress in the same individuals, as may be seen in the pictures of the inhabitants of Tierra del Fuego in the work of King and Fitzroy.[2]

All that can legitimately be inferred from the old Egyptian monuments, amounts to this—that the most striking race-characters have essentially, and for a long period, persisted as we see them at present, and that under the same conditions they remain unaltered. Even the believer in the agency of external influences, would be surprised, if in Africa where Negroes existed in remote times, there were no skulls found resembling the skulls of living Negroes; and there is hardly a thinking man who would assert that 3-4000 years ago the civilized nations of antiquity and the Negroes who were always treated by them as slaves, did not then possess the cranial type which they now exhibit.

In order to prove the permanence of type, and the importance of climate, the Jews have been instanced, whose national physiognomy is depicted upon the ancient monuments of Egypt. Even in Malabar, where it was formerly believed that in the course of time they had assumed the type of the Hindoos, they have, according to Buchanan and other travellers, remained essentially unchanged, for only the so-called white Jews in that region are of pure blood, whilst the black Jews are Hindoos or Hindoo-mongrels.[3] In order properly to appreciate this fact we must bear in mind that by this people religion and habits have

---

[1] "L'Institut.," ii, p. 40, 1846.
[2] "Narrative of the voyage of the Adventure and Beagle."
[3] Nott and Gliddon, p. 118.

in every region of the world been preserved with unexampled tenacity, that their whole domestic economy and degree of civilization have remained everywhere the same, that they have in every region lived in a state of oppression which forced them to a closer connexion between themselves, and to preserve their peculiarities. Wherever they existed, be it in Europe among Christians, or in Africa among the Moors, their fate was the same; they lived as an excluded caste, whose only resource was to obtain wealth in order to secure a certain degree of power and position. No wonder if their cranial type as well as their character remained on the whole unchanged. The uniformity of their skulls is, however, not yet exactly ascertained. Sandifort[1] gives the following proportions of length, height, and breadth of two Jewish crania $= 190 : 226 : 148$ and $= 190 : 190 : 130$, indicating considerable variations in that people which is generally quoted as an instance of constancy and uniformity of the cranial development.

There is no want of instances which plainly show that the sphere of variation in individual peoples or races; when closely examined, is as great as that of the whole human race; and these proofs have been chiefly furnished by those whose studies have been directed to the cranial structure of various races. M. I. Weber[2] has distinguished four principal types of crania, with which the shape of the pelvis corresponds. The oval skull of the European, the round one of the American, the cuneiform of the Negro, the square-shaped of the Mongol. Among the examples for the second form, he gives that of an European, a Jew, and a Kalmuck; among the third form, an European and a Bugis; the last form he found also in Europeans and Kaffirs. There occur, therefore, in every race, cranial shapes foreign to it, and consequently there are no perfectly fixed marks of race. This also applies to the shape of the pelvis. Even all the Kalmuck skulls which Weber examined did not possess the square Mongol, but rather a globular form. Blumenbach[3] also men-

---

[1] "Tabulæ craniorum."

[2] "Die Lehre von den Ur-und Racenformen der Schädel und Becken des Menschen," 1830.

[3] "Decas craniorum," iii, p. 6.

tions the skull of a Lithuanian which perfectly resembled that of a Congo-Negro, and Godron[1] mentions a Negro skull of a perfectly European shape. That Retzius[2] found the old Swedish skull corresponding with the present shape proves but little for the constancy of forms, when it is considered that great variations in this respect prevail among the same people. "I have," says Prince Max,[3] "compared a whole series of genuine Mandan skulls, and found great differences as regards the receding forehead and the flattening of the skull." Some have perpendicular, others receding foreheads.[4] Engel,[5] who assumes twelve chief types, seems by his measurements to confirm the observations of Weber. He includes in his third form, besides Germans and Tschechs, also Magyars, a Javanese, a Guanche, and a Bedouin. In his sixth form there are, besides Tschechs and Germans, the skulls of several Negroes, a Hottentot, a Malabar, a Bengalese, a New Zealander. In his tenth chief form the skull of a Negro child, an American Indian, etc. If Engel[6] is further of opinion that there are race-types, and even caste-types of crania, which, however, are not inherited, but chiefly depend on the nature of aliment, and the thickness of bone, that is to say, on the addition of osseous matter received by the skull, we might expect that the thickness of the cranial bones should be unexceptionally analogous to the cranial forms, which, however, is not confirmed by the facts.

The attempts of a natural division of mankind rest principally upon the supposition that the chief types possess a high degree of constancy, and this enables us to ascertain the affinity of varieties which constitute the great divisions of mankind.[7] The weakness of the basis upon which these attempts

---

[1] "De l'espèce et des races," p. 106, Nancy, 1848.
[2] Müller's "Archiv," p. 94, 1845.
[3] "Reise in N. Am.," i, 235.
[4] Ibid., ii, 106.
[5] Unters. über Schädelformen," 1851.
[6] Page 120.
[7] In a more rational way than we are accustomed to find in the American school, Meigs (in Nott and Gliddon, "Indigenous races," etc., pp. 223, 349) observes, that not only is every cranial type subject to change by climate, but similarity of its type proves as little a common origin as variation proves a different origin. We are, then, entitled to ask with some surprise, what this school contends for, if it admits that the skull is no certain mark of descent?

are founded, becomes apparent at once on comparing them with each other, when we find as many different classifications as there are authors; so that we cannot help agreeing with Hollard[1] when he says, that zoologists generally agree as to animal species and their characters, but are always at loggerheads with regard to the number and types of human races, which they sometimes wish to establish as distinct species. That, with respect to affinities of peoples, the external habitus alone is not sufficient to enable us to classify them, is proved by the gross errors committed by authors who have trusted to its constancy. Thus, for instance, we find in Desmoulins that the first human species consists of Indo-Germans, Finns, and Turks; the sixteenth are the Semitics, the first branch of which is made to consist of the Arabs, Persians, Kurds, Jews, Moors, and Abyssinians; whilst the Etrusco-Pelasgi constitute the second, and the Celts the third branch of the Semitics. In America, two species are said to exist,—the Caribs forming one, and the Guaranis the other. Broc, who also classifies according to physical characters, places the Hindoos among the Mongols and Malays. Bory[2], following the same principles, includes in his first species, the Georgians in the Caucasus, the Pelasgi, Celts, Germans, Slaves; with regard to the Aztecs, he seems doubtful whether they belong to the hyperborean or Mongolian species; the Gypsies in Spain he considers as Malays. He further distinguishes three species of Americans; the first of which reaching from the land of the Esquimaux to Guiana, whilst the third only embraces the Patagonians. Such absurdities show indirectly, and better than anything else, how we should appreciate this pretended constancy of physical type as a criterion of affinity of race.

We may, perhaps, be reproached for having selected the least reliable authorities in order to arrive at a certain result from the perversity of their assertions. We shall therefore exclude them, as well as the eccentric views of H. Smith and others, and only refer to such as are known as careful observers and cautious investigators, but who, trusting to the

[1] "De l'homme et des races hum.," p. 263, 1853.
[2] "L'Homme," 2nd ed., 1827.

perfect constancy of the cranial form, felt justified in inferring from it affinities of races. Lesson[1] declares not only the Malays as a mixed people of Hindoos and Mongols, the Micronesians as Mongols, who had arrived later in the South Sea than the Polynesians; but the latter as manifestly the descendants of Hindoos, and the Austral-Negroes and Papuas, as the progeny of African Negroes. Junghuhn[2] considers, judging from the skull, the Balinese as genuine Battas, with which the Alfurus of the East Indian Archipelago as well as the Bugis and Macassars are allied, whilst he believes that the Malays are not related to them, but form a separate race. Pickering[3] groups together the Malays, Siamese, Burmese, Cochin Chinese, and Japanese, and does not hesitate to include also in that group Californians, Mexicans, Creeks, and Cherokees. Retzius[4] believes, on account of the resemblance of the cranial formation, in the affinity of Turanian, Scythian, and Sarmatian families with the Pelasgi; whilst, on the same ground, he is inclined to consider the Finnish-speaking Kareles, as allied to the Arabs. Though Hartmann[5] has endeavoured to render it probable that the Kareles are not Finns, but a foreign people who had formerly lived on the Ladoga lake, it is quite certain they are not Arabs. D'Omalius d'Halloy[6] groups the Lapps with the Samoiedes on account of their cranial shape. W. F. Edwards[7] declares the Magyars to be partly Slavonians and partly Huns. Nothing can more plainly prove that the corporeal and cranial type may be the same in peoples of different stocks, and may differ so much in peoples of the same stock, than the fact, that a skilful observer is unable to recognize to which the individuals belong. Certainly, those who believe in the absolute permanence of types judge differently. They consequently exhibit a singular acuteness in the detection of mixed types. Thus

---

1 "Voy. Med.," pp. 157, 163, 185.
2 "Die Battaländer," p. 282, 1847.
3 Pages 105, 134.
4 Müller, "Archiv," p. 392, 1848.
5 "Abh. der K. G. der Wiss. v. Stockholm," 1847.
6 "L'Institut.," ii, p. 5, 1840.
7 "Des caract. phys. des races hum., 1829," in "Mém. de la Soc. Ethnol.," i, p. 71.

Bory[1] recognizes in Mexico, in spite of the number of preceding intermixtures, still the type of the Americans, and the diversities of the inhabitants of the west coast from the other native Americans; and Nott and Gliddon[2] recognize, upon some of the oldest monuments of Egypt, already a very mixed people. We are almost tempted to ask them, How they know that God has not originally created some mixed types?

The proper definition of physical characters of races and peoples is as yet deficient in scientific precision. The practised eye generally decides on resemblance and dissimilarity. Hence there has slipped in a sort of mysterious augur-wisdom in our science,—a knowledge resting more upon feeling and a kind of artistic intuition than upon fixed rules,—upon an indefinite something which was only manifested to the connoisseur. Thus the door was opened to quackery which does not fail to make itself felt. An investigation of the facts leads us to the inference, that as it certainly cannot occur to any ethnographer to separate in the lands of the Moors, the Berber, Gothic, Phœnician, Roman, Greek elements, etc., according to cranial shape, or to distinguish in Greece the Slavonian and Hellenic elements, it is certain that the absolute permanence of the physical type is nothing but a prejudice, possessing no scientific title whatever to serve as a basis for the assumption of a plurality of human species.

Whatever number of principal types of mankind may be assumed, if they are considered as specifically different, it becomes always requisite with regard to the peoples belonging to these original types to admit either a relatively considerable mutability of the type by external and internal influences,—as every people has its own peculiarities,—or else to admit an intermixture of species. In the first case, the power of these influences is strictly limited by the assumption of species,—limits, the fixing of which is purely arbitrary: in the second case, in which all changes are reduced to intermixture alone, we add to the great improbability contained in the assertion, that nearly

[1] Vol. i, p. 274. [2] Page 233.

all the peoples of the earth were true mongrels, a second one: that all these mixed types possess a persistent vitality without any infusion of fresh blood from the stock they have sprung from; and further, that their own types are preserved without any reversion to that of the parent stock, by which the assumed specific differences are neutralized and rendered illusory.

It is unquestionable that, among the causes which induce permanent changes of type, intermixture is the most potent, and that in comparison with this agent other influences seem less important. Though this circumstance renders the supposition of several originally different races in some degree probable, it still remains, in by far the greater number of cases, impossible to determine whether an intermixture of different elements has taken place at all, and how far it has progressed. Intermixture, moreover, as we have seen, is not the sole agent. We can, therefore, scarcely go further than this,—that everywhere, and especially when in an uncivilized state, a number of human beings, possessing the same habits and modes of life, will, by continued intermixture of the individuals between themselves through a series of generations, if they live in a state of seclusion, acquire in the course of time a nearly uniform external type, *whatever may have been the original elements.*

The whole result of the preceding investigation may therefore be summed up to this effect:—that the known facts not only permit the assumption of the unity of the human species, but that this view presents less difficulties than the opposite theory of specific differences; because any number of species assumed, appears equally arbitrary. But as the principal arguments in favour of unity of species rest upon the mutability of the human organism by internal and external influences, the limits of which are unknown to us; and as in the absence of any exact information as to the length of time they were in action, we cannot decide whether the power of these influences was sufficient to produce the existing differences, the question of unity of species remains an open one. Even if it were satisfactorily proved that the magnitude of the changes which a human family may in course of time undergo, equalled the differences between the Negro and the European, it would still remain uncertain whether, in fact, the one descended from the other. The question as regards unity of species might then be considered as answered; but not unity of descent. We possess scarcely any facts which may serve as a basis for the solution of the latter question; and in whatever way it may be decided, the solution can only claim some degree of probability.

SECTION V.

ON THE CLASSIFICATION OF MANKIND.

It needs no justification if, in passing from the physical to the psychological investigations concerning the unity of the human species, we offer some few remarks on the starting points from which the classification of mankind has been attempted. Though we do not pretend to settle the dispute between naturalists and linguists, in regard to the value which they attach to their respective arguments, still the following remarks may, perhaps, assist in removing several prejudices which, founded upon a one-sided conception, have obstructed a proper estimation of some important points.

In the various attempts which have been made towards a classification of the human species, the main object which has been kept in view was not merely a general grouping of the races according to their resemblance, but a division of the peoples according to their descent. This object was the more naturally followed, inasmuch as the possibility of a common descent was, in all classifications of mankind, either tacitly or expressly assumed. Such a division of mankind, resting upon community of descent, may be formed from three different points of view, which we may term—the physical, the linguistic, and the historical stand-points. The results obtained by no means agree. The physical and linguistic grounds for a certain classification are frequently in conflict; and so it often happens that one of these arguments is considered as of inferior importance,—a partiality which is frequently exhibited by naturalists who were, and still are, the principal expounders of the theories of human races.

A classification of mankind according to affinity, may be said to rest on a sure basis, if inferences from authenticated historical data warrant it; but these do not reach so far back in time as the inferences which may be drawn from linguistic and anatomical data, and moreover, the former extend only to a small portion of the globe. The historical stand-point, therefore, occupies the background; though it acquires a secondary value where we find a conformity in manners, traditions, architecture, works of art, etc., which conformity could not easily have been accidental.

The study of languages may afford more certain indications. If the grammatical structure, the speech-sounds, and a large number of radicals, agree in the languages of two or several peoples, their relationship may be considered as proved. There only remains against this assumption, the possible and somewhat rare circumstance of a people losing their own language and changing it for another,—a case which must not be assumed without positive proofs. Though a difference in language does not necessarily lead to the inference of a distinct origin of the respective peoples, still their assumed affinity is thereby reduced to an incalculably remote period.

Although the anatomical arguments may without difficulty be applied to the classification of the whole human species, they can scarcely claim more than a general grouping according to external resemblance. The proofs, as regards affinities of human races on anatomical grounds are, as we have shown, uncertain, partly because the methods of cranial measurement have not yet reached the desirable degree of perfection, and chiefly because it is as yet very doubtful whether there are constant anatomical differences, not merely between the large groups of peoples, but also within individual nations.

We shall now enter upon the special consideration of the above mentioned three principal points of view.

The old attempts, with regard to the natural division of the human race, were chiefly founded on the visible differences exhibited by human beings, such as the colour of the skin and the quality of the hair.[1] It was, however, soon found that these presented too many deviations to allow great importance to be attached to them. Thus the colour of the skin is not sufficiently constant in the same people; and the changes it presents from one family of peoples into another, are uncertain. Generally speaking, dark colour of the skin is found in combination with black hair, and a black or brown iris; on the other hand, fair complexion is combined with light or red hair, and a light brown, blue, or greenish iris. The second combination is generally, though not exclusively, peculiar to the northern or white race. If to this be added, that the hair of the Negro frizzles in consequence of the elliptical form of its diameter, we obtain a division of mankind into tribes of light complexion and straight hair, into tribes of dark complexion and straight hair, and, finally, into families of dark complexion and frizzly hair.

This basis of a division according to colour and hair, has recently been abandoned. Only D'Omalius d'Halloy[2] still considers colour and hair as decided distinctions of race. He includes the Finns and Turks in the white race; and in the brown (Malay), the Hindoos, as a mixed people of white Arians and black aborigines, the Abyssinians, and the Fellahs. Though he may be wrong in attributing greater constancy to the colour of the skin than to the peculiarities of the skeleton, it must be admitted that with many individuals of mankind it would remain doubtful as to which family they belong, if the colour and the hair did not furnish us with certain indications. A greater degree of constancy is now generally attributed to the shape of the skull. It is agreed, that it presents a basis for a natural division; and this mark of distinction becomes the more important as it gives some indications with respect to past generations.

With regard to the principal cranial types, from which the rest may be considered as deviations, we find that Blumenbach,

---

[1] See Blumenbach, "De gen. hum. var. nat.," p. 296, 3rd edit.
[2] "L'Institut.," ii, p. 86, 1844.

the founder of this theory, designates the Ethiopian[1] and Mongolian forms as the extremes between which the Caucasian occupies the centre, the American being placed between the latter and the Mongolian, and the Malay between the Ethiopian and the Caucasian. The various races, distinguished by Blumenbach, are placed in the following order:—Negro, Malay, Caucasian, American, Mongolian; so that the White, assuming the unity of the human race, appears as the medium or normal type of humanity. On taking, however, into consideration not merely the shape of the skull, but other anatomical differences, there can be no doubt that the White and the Negro form the extremes; the latter, on account of his resemblance to the ape, which nearly disappears in the white man.

Blumenbach's division into five races is either too large or too small, manifestly corresponding with the geographical scheme of five parts of the globe. Lacépède and Duméril added a sixth variety,—the so-called Hyperborean race of the polar regions; whilst Virey[2] considers the Hottentots and Papuas as the sixth chief variety, and the Negro and the White as distinct species. The facts, however, would lead either to the adoption of the three principal types, according to Cuvier, namely, the Mongol, the Negro, and the Caucasian, named by some writers after Shem, Ham, and Japhet, or to assume a considerably larger number. Prichard, Smith, and Latham, are inclined to adopt the former division; Pickering assumes eleven, Bory fifteen, Desmoulins sixteen, and Agassiz and Nott an indefinite number, of species. Hombron[3] assumes, even in Australia, the population of which was hitherto considered by all ethnographers as belonging to one family, a number of distinct species, and declares the inhabitants of Van Diemen's land to be also of a distinct species.

[1] It is scarcely necessary to mention that the term "Ethiopian" is as improper as the term Caucasian, which Blumenbach used simply because the skull of a Georgian woman seemed to him as the best representative of this type, without any intention on his part to express thereby an opinion as to the cradle of these peoples. We shall, however, abide by these designations, as they are generally adopted.

[2] "Hist. nat. du genre hum.," i, p. 318, 1834.

[3] "Zoologie," i, p. 312, etc., in Urville, "Voy. au Pole Sud."

If the Malay and American be added to the three chief forms adopted by Cuvier, we can scarcely avoid adding the Australians, Austral Negroes (Negrillos), the Papuas, and the Hottentots. Nor will this be sufficient. All the intermediate tribes between the Negro and the white, namely, the Kaffirs, Nubians, Gallas, Abyssinians, and Berbers, have an equal claim to consideration. This applies also to the Battas, the cranial form of whom is intermediate between that of Europeans and Malays.[1] With the Mongolian type there is further associated the so-called Hyperborean type, though the assumption of a separate polar race presents many difficulties, as already shown by Vater,[2] and indicates a considerable deviation. But least of all can the aboriginal Americans be comprehended in the division; for, whatever Morton and his school may assert as to the similarity of the cranial type in all the varieties of South and North America, it is shown by their own researches that differences of shape are as considerable there as in those parts in which they are considered as fundamentally different. Some are long-headed, some short-headed,[3] others, again, are round-headed; the present Peruvians have small square skulls, with a compressed occiput.[4] Tschudi[5] has pointed out three essentially distinct cranial forms of the original inhabitants of Peru. It could be easily shown, that, having proceeded thus far in the division of mankind, there can be no halting place; but we must go further, and adopt an unlimited number of types. It would be necessary to assume fixed differences between nations to whom, on historical and linguistic grounds, we cannot ascribe a separate descent. We thus become convinced, that, from a mere anatomical point of view, nothing certain can be inferred as to the consanguinity of races; and that it is therefore, in every respect, advisable to adopt the above three chief types, which, moreover, as we have already shown in their intermixture with others, exhibit the greatest persistence.

---

1 "Junghuhn d. Battaländer," ii, p. 6.
2 Mithridates, iii, p. 317.
3 Retzius, Müller's "Archiv," p. 503, 1855.
4 Morton, "Cran. Am.," pp. 65, 115.
5 Müller's "Archiv," p. 98, 1844.

To Retzius belongs the chief merit of having laid the foundation of an ethnographic craniology. Proceeding from the principle, that the psychical individuality of a people is expressed by the development of the brain as indicated by the skull, he distinguishes first *dolichocephalic* and *brachycephalic* crania, the former shape depending on a considerable development of the posterior lobes of the brain, and the latter on their comparative shortness, which causes them in some instances to be more developed in breadth. The functions of the posterior lobes are considered by Retzius as very important. To this general division Retzius adds a secondary classification, according to the form of the face, as follows:—

1. Gentes dolichocephalæ orthognathæ,
2. Gentes brachycephalæ orthognathæ,
3. Gentes dolichocephalæ prognathæ,
4. Gentes brachycephalæ prognathæ.

The two first are only found in Europe. In Asia all the four shapes are met with in almost equal proportions. The third and the fourth are the predominating types in the South Sea. In Africa the third type predominates, though the first form also occurs in that part, as well as the second type in the South Sea. In America the third and fourth forms alternate, including, to a less extent, the second type, so that the greatest variety and intermingling of types is to be found.

From the details given by Retzius,[1] it clearly results that no consanguinity can be established between the peoples exhibiting the same cranial types. Thus in Europe there belong to the *brachycephalæ orthognathæ* the Turks, Lapps, Slaves, Basques; in Asia the Samoiedes, Burates, Affghans, Persians. To the *brachycephalæ prognathæ* in the East Indies and the South Sea belong the Tahitians, Malays, Papuas; to the *dolichocephalæ prognathæ* in Africa, Negroes, Hottentots, and Kopts, etc.

Zeune[2] distinguishes three extreme cranial types: high skulls

[1] Müller's "Archiv," p. 271, 1848.
[2] "Ueber Schädelbildung," 1846.

(Europeans and Asiatics in the west and south of these parts, as far as India); broad skulls (Mongols and many Malay peoples); long skulls (Negroes). These three chief types are also found in the New World: the first among the Natchez and Choctaws; the second among the Caribs and Macusis; the third in Peru, among the Huancas and Incas; so that we have, on the whole, six chief divisions. Between the above extreme types there are intermediate forms, probably the result of intermixture. Thus the Turks, Slaves, Magyars, Finns, Lapps, and many Malay peoples, are intermediate between the Mongol and Caucasian; the Papuas, Alfurus, and Hottentots, between the Mongol and Negro-type; the latter originating, perhaps, from intermixture between Negroes and Malays.

The preceding synopsis of the chief attempts of classifications shows one fact very clearly, namely, the disagreement of all authors who have treated of this subject, both in principle and execution, whenever they pass beyond the three chief types which distinguish the Negro, the Mongol, and the European. This disagreement either proves that the subject is indefinite, or that science is as yet not sufficiently advanced to give a decisive answer.

It cannot be our intention to depreciate the meritorious efforts as regards the investigation of the cranial race-theory. It is highly probable that there exists in every people a national form of skull, to establish which would be of great ethnographic interest. There is, however, no question that the inferences of identity of tribe from an identity of skull, or of consanguinity from a similar cranial shape, are as doubtful as the conclusions to a different stock from a deviating cranial form; for similar types are presented by peoples living at the most remote distances from each other, who cannot, without a far-fetched hypothesis, be presumed to be allied; whilst, on the other hand, great varieties of cranial forms are found among peoples whose consanguinity is undeniable. Finally, the variation of shape in individual national types is as yet too little known to determine which form is within or without the sphere of that particular type.

How cautious we should be in concluding from cranial measurements to consanguinity of tribe, is shown by Hueck,[1] who found the measurement of Esthon skulls mostly agreeing with that of two Tartar skulls, although they are generally different in form. Zeune observes, that, according to Retzius, the Scandinavians have long-heads, the Slaves short-heads; yet he found the skull of a Swede to be shorter than those of two Russian female skulls. The Avar skull found near Grafenegg in Austria has, by Tschudi,[2] been considered as of Peruvian origin, on account of its similarity to those of the Huancas; whilst Meyer[3] asserts, that the skulls of the latter are perfectly identical with the microcephalæ found in the Crimea. No further commentary is necessary to show what confusion would result if the cranial shape were assumed to be an absolute mark of race.

The question may here be asked, why the skull has been preferentially selected to determine the race—do the other parts of the skeleton exhibit a less degree of constancy? Hardly; but the skull was not only the most accessible, but the most characteristic part, from its supposed relation to the psychical qualities of man, however obscure this relation may yet be, for, as to the fables of phrenology, these have been rejected by German science. There can be no doubt that the skull has been too exclusively considered as a permanent mark of race, and it has become necessary no longer to neglect other physical characters, for it is only in their entirety that they can afford any satisfactory clue as to the peculiarities of each race. Which of these peculiarities is the more or less important will only be determined after a long series of investigations. A fair beginning has been made by Quetelet, whose measurements have extended to the proportions of individual parts composing the body. He has arrived at the result,[4] that in the European race the proportions of the body are constant, and that the measurement of but few individuals is necessary to find the normal proportions; he considers it, moreover, as probable that the human body is, in its forms and proportions, more definite than any

[1] "De craniis Esthonum," p. 9.
[2] Müller's "Archiv," p. 277, 1845.
[3] Ibid., p. 510, 1850.
[4] "Bullet. de l'Acad. des Sc. de Belg.," xv, P. i, p. 580; P. ii, p. 16; xvi, P. ii, pp. 11, 17; xvii, P. i, p. 344; P. ii, pp. 38, 95.

other production of nature. Among the American race, putting aside the greater breadth of the chest and the smaller feet, there is a great resemblance of proportions with those of the finest European forms. Among the Chinese the deviations are not very considerable, excepting with regard to hand, foot, and length of arm, which are generally smaller in them than in the European; the female hand is, however, distinguished by a greater size. Schultz,[1] on the other hand, asserts, that he found considerable differences in the proportions of parts among Russians, Letts, Tscherkesses, Tschuwashes, Negroes, and Jews.

We subjoin a short table of measurements possessing an anthropological interest:—

1.—*Cranial Measurements.* Retzius, in Müller's "Archiv," p. 84, 1845. (Swedes, Slaves, Finns, Lapps), ibid., p. 498, 1855. (Pampas Indians), in "Nouv. Ann. des voy.," iii, p. 119, 1847. (Abyssinians, Basuto-Kaffirs), Van der Höven, in Müller's "Archiv," p. 433, 1844. (Slavonians), Philipps, in Schoolcraft, "Hist. of the Ind. Trib.," ii, p. 385. (North Am. Indians), Robt. Clarke, "Sierra Leone," p. 48, 1846. (Various Negro peoples), Hushcke, Schädel, Hirn, and Seele.

2.—*Measurements of Cranium and the most important parts of the Body.* Freycinet, "Voy. aut. d. m.," 1827 (Papuas, Sandwich Islanders, Australians, etc.). Sandifort, "Tab. Cran.," 1838 (Greenlanders, Romans, Amboineese, Kaffirs, Hottentots, Bushmen, North Americans, Singalese, Chinese, Japanese, Papuas, Australians, Koluschee, Guanches, Turks, Negroes, Javanese, Jews). Hueck, "De Cran. Esth.," 1838 (Esthonians, Lapps, Tschuktshes, Kalmucks, Tartars, Letts). Lesson, "Voy. aut. du m.," 1829 (Mozambique Negroes, Papuas, Alfurus, Polynesians). Schultz et Quêtelet, loc. cit. (Ojibbeways, Neapolitan giant, American Hercules, Chinese, Kaffirs, Negroes, European soldiers). Duttenhofer, "Ueber die Emancip. der Neger," p. 77, 1855 (Negroes), Burmeister, "Geol. Bilder," ii, Negroes; Thomson, in "Brit. & For. Med. Chir. Review," p. 489, 1854; and Fechner's "Central-Blatt," p. 417, 1854, New Zealanders. Wilkes, "United States Exploring Expedition," v, p. 539, 1845 (Polynesians). Flinders, "Voy. to Terra Australis," i, p. 68, 1814 (Australians).

More important and certain results have been obtained from philological investigations.

It probably would never have occurred to a zoologist to group the Indo-Germanic, Semitic, and other tribes in the same family. The anthropologist could only wait for and appro-

[1] Froriep's "Neue Notizen," xxxv, p. 164.

priate the results obtained in this way. When, therefore, the naturalist, in opposition to the linguist (as is frequently done) speaks of the absolute constancy of cranial types, and significantly points to those cases in which whole nations have changed their language, it looks not merely like ingratitude, but like envy.

The natural forms of intellectual life seem to be subject to as many changes as the mental peculiarities of individuals; hence it was believed that a greater constancy of type is to be found within the sphere of physical organization. The appearance may possibly be deceitful, and more extensive investigations may exhibit an equal uniformity in the mental as in the physical organization. Philology gives a certain probability to this idea, for not only may we from the language of a people draw some correct inferences as to its intellectual state, as Crawfurd[1] has done with regard to the original state of civilization of the Malays, but, generally speaking, the linguistic peculiarities are the most important of those of intellectual life; because, on the one hand, they are in their origin as independent of conscious reflection as of the influence of external circumstances; and because, on the other hand, they are transmitted and appropriated by later generations, and thus exhibit, in all essential points, a high degree of constancy. Whatever is created by the conscious will is subject to multifarious changes by further reflection, but not that which, like the form and structure of language, is transmitted by unconscious imitation, which is thus withdrawn from reflection.

These general psychological considerations show the great importance of linguistic researches in relation to the consanguinity of peoples. We shall, therefore, endeavour to specify the claims of philology to be heard on this question.

The two chief points which are to be considered in comparative philology are the grammatical structure of a language, including the articulated sounds, and its vocabulary. According to the present state of science, both of them must correspond to infer a genealogical relationship of languages. Comparisons

---

[1] "History of the Indian Archipelago," 1820.

of vocabularies, formerly so much in vogue, are now deemed insufficient, as these comparisons were without method, proceeded from no fixed principle, and the estimation of the prevailing differences of words was quite arbitrary. Even in languages where the resemblances of many words are unmistakeable, it cannot be decided from them alone, whether they have been transmitted or merely borrowed, whether they are the consequence of a genealogical relationship, or of an exchange or communication from one language to another originally distinct, but which subsequently came in contact. Many of these vocabulary resemblances may also be accidental, and produced by identical original invention. The extent and degree of the resemblance of individual words must also be taken into consideration, as well as their signification, especially such as designate common things indispensable to peoples even in a low state of cultivation; for these are not so much altered in an exchange of languages as those belonging to things found only among peoples more civilized. But all this does not invalidate the general principle, that word comparisons alone are insufficient to decide upon the affinity of languages.

It seems, then, that, in judging of the affinity of languages, greater importance is attached to grammatical structure than even to the resemblance of the roots of a language. Equality of original invention with regard to the structure of language among perfectly distinct races is, on account of the great complications and great variety of grammatical proportions so improbable that it nearly amounts to an impossibility. It appears, therefore, requisite that two languages should, on comparison, agree to some extent in both the chief elements before we can decide on their affinity. We shall endeavour to point out the reasons which justify us in inferring the consanguinity of peoples from the quality of the grammatical structure of their languages.

When a language is transmitted from one generation to another, not merely the words, but their mode of connexion, as sentences, is also transmitted and appropriated by unconscious imitation, and thus becomes fixed. The latter point is not sufficiently appreciated, though it is quite clear that we do not think in words, but in whole sentences; hence, we may assert, that a living language consists of sentences, not of words. But a sentence is formed not of single independent words, but of words which refer to each other in a particular manner, like the corresponding thought, which does not consist of single independent ideas, but of such as, connected, form a whole, and which determine each other mutually; hence the great importance of the relations of words which are afforded by grammatical structure. We shall illustrate this by some examples.

In the sentence, "He will to-day in the night watch his enemy in order to kill him," the chief idea, to which all others are added, is the action of watching. The sensible image of this action can be immediately conceived and reproduced by us. The action of watching is first defined, as in this case, a future action, and this future is defined as occurring to-day. The external circumstances are further to be defined (in the night), the subject and the object of the action (he—enemy), and the relation of the subject to the object (*his* enemy); then the object of the action, which is expressed in the form of a second action (kill), the object of this second action, and the relation of the same to the object of the first action, a relation of identity (him—his enemy). Consequently, the above sentence—on leaving out all indications of the relations of the individual ideas which connected them, and instead of the pronoun "he" place the name of a person—would be expressed thus,—

"Watch (future—to-day)—night—Cajus—enemy—kill—enemy."

Such a sentence, consisting of unconnected words, which would compel the listener to seek for himself all the relations of these ideas, would certainly be better than no speech at all, as it might be understood in spite of its obscurity. The apparent imperfection would also be greatly lessened if there were some fixed rules by which the relation of the words might be recognized; such as that the governing always precedes the governed, the chief idea always the subordinate idea, and so forth. In such a state are the asynthetic, monosyllabic languages, which, like the Chinese, in the absence of all separation of the parts of speech, express the relations by the position of the words. To these languages belongs, probably, the idiom of the Yebus in the west of Benin (d'Avezac); whether, also, that of the Othomi in Central America is as yet doubtful.[1]

A language is, undoubtedly, more perfect in proportion as all the relations of the individual ideas occurring in a sentence may be easily recognized. The means of effecting this are innumerable; such as the formation of the particular word-forms added to substantive words designating a certain modification of the sense of the latter: for instance, the future, the past, the negation, the possibility of an action; the variation in the sounds occurring in the words modifying their sense and relation to others; the combination of several words in one word, etc.

The American languages, which are called polysynthetic, are so characterized that they usually consist of an agglomeration of independent words: thus, in the Sahaptin, *hi-tau-tuala-wihnan-kau-na,* means, he travels past in a rainy night; *hi,* he; *tau,* refers to something in the night; *tuala,* to something that is done in rain; *wihnan,* from *wihnasa,* to travel on foot; *kau,* from *kokauna,* to pass by; *na* designates the aorist and the direction (Hale). In the Dakota, *ba,* as a prefix of the verb or adjective, designates that the action has been effected by cutting; *bo,* by shooting or blowing; *ka,* by striking; *na,* by pressure or by the foot; *pa,* by pushing; *ya,* by the mouth (Riggs). In a similar manner do the so-called agglutinated languages, to which the Tartar, Turkish, and Finnish idioms belong, express the relations of the chief idea to the subordinate ones, by adding relatively substantive words to the unchanged root of the word which designates the chief idea in a sentence; so that compound words are formed, in which the relations of the chief idea are amalgamated. The Magyar language has thus, for instance, twenty post-positions which can be combined with the substantive noun. From *sevmek* (Turkish), "to love," may be formed *sev-dir-ish-e-me-mek,* to love mutually,

[1] Pott, p. 256.

cannot be forced; *dir* gives to the word a transitive, *ish*, a reciprocal, *me*, a negative, signification; *e*, indicates impossibility. Nevertheless, according to the opinion of linguists, the polysynthetic languages of America must not be placed in the same class with the agglutinated languages of Asia, as their chief characters greatly differ (Pott). The peculiarity of each of those last mentioned languages, depends on what and how many secondary ideas are incorporated with the chief word, and by what means this is effected (prefixes, infixes, suffixes, changes of sound); and finally, what secondary ideas and relations remain unexpressed.

The ideas of action rarely arise in our minds without some definite relations to persons, things, time, place, etc. If these relations are designated by changes in the word itself, by sounds which *per se* have no definite sense, the language is said to be an inflected language: *amabis*, loving, with relation to the second person as the subject of action, and the future. This principle of expressing the relations of the chief idea to secondary ideas by changes in the chief word may, in every individual language, be more or less completely carried out, by which a great variety of languages becomes possible, occupyingacertain intermediate position between the inflected, agglutinated, and polysynthetic (incorporating) languages. Thus many American languages, which Gallatin[1] considered as inflected languages (which is denied by Pott), have a great number of tense and modes. The Selish has two futures, (I shall, I will), an optative (I should), a reflective, reciprocal modus, a modus of object (I go in order to), etc. The Cherokee has still more.[2] In the Sahaptin languages, nearly every part of speech may be conjugated,—"Man," I am a man, thou art a man, etc.; "over," I am over it, thou art over it, etc.

We do not pretend to have given a characteristic of the chief types of language; we merely endeavoured to show, by some striking examples, the great influence of the type of a

[1] "Transactions of the American Ethnological Society," ii, p. 23.

[2] Worcester, in Schoolcraft, "" History of the Indian tribes," ii, p. 446.

language upon the ideal world; for it is clear, that regulation of the latter greatly depends upon the former. Entirely asynthetic, monosyllabic languages, allow our individual ideas, which correspond to individual words, to stand in independent juxtaposition, merely indicating some rude distinctions between chief and secondary ideas. In contrast with them, polysynthetic languages force us to grasp the whole idea, and intimately to connect the secondary ideas with the chief idea, to take in at one glance the whole situation, not piecemeal and successively. That they prevent the dismemberment of ideas in a greater degree than the former, is proved by many substantive nouns in these languages, like "hand," "father," "son," occurring, not separately, but always in connexion with a possessive pronoun. It is of the greatest importance, for the regulation of the mass of our ideas, how many and what secondary ideas our language induces us to connect as integral parts with the chief idea to which they refer, or what may be added as relatively independent parts. It is not less important whether, as in inflected languages, the relations are expressed by particles which, separated from the chief word, have no distinct signification. These grammatical forms of the mother language become habitual to us before we arrive at reflection; for what language presents combined in one sound, we conceive together, and what it presents in a separate form, we conceive as relatively separate.

These elementary habits in connecting individual ideas, belong to the most important special laws to which the conception of man is subject; and on account of the power which they exert in the elementary construction of our ideas, an essential change of the structure of a language in a people, which continues as a people, is highly improbable. There is no doubt that a gradual change in the grammatical structure of a language is possible; and if it be probable that all merely grammatical words (forms) were originally words of independent signification, and that even the syllables of inflection sprung from originally independent words, which were merely added to the chief word,—then there exists between the types of language as little an absolute constant difference as between the chief types of the corporeal form; but such a possibility of an original unity of languages is, as Pott[1] observes, far indeed from being proved.

The idea of an original language of the whole human race, so much discussed in the last century, is by science now considered as a chimera.[2] Neither would it amount to a proof of the unity of mankind, if among languages of different grammatical structure, such as the Chinese and Sanscrit, there were found a number of similar roots.[3] W. von Humboldt has remarked, that though the three chief types of the known languages may be considered as an ascending scale of the development of language, it can neither be proved, nor is it probable, that they have originated among themselves. Nevertheless, Max Müller has recently advanced the latter theory. According to him, the first stage of the development of language is a juxtaposition of independent words (family stage); the second is characterized by an incorporation of relations in the governing word (nomadic stage—agglutination); the third changes the governing word to designate the relations (political stage—amalgamation). This interesting scheme has not met with approval among philologists, and has been especially opposed by Pott, who assumes a plurality of originally distinct languages. Though philology may not be absolutely opposed to the origin of the human race from one pair,[4] there is at present no prospect of supporting it by proofs, as Bunsen and Müller have attempted.

One might be inclined to adopt this view on considering, that the light which philology has hitherto thrown on the affinity of peoples extends to but a small portion of the earth, and in casting a glance at the summary of Balbi[5] of the languages of the globe. He assumes 860 languages, which he thus classifies:—

1. Asia, with 153 languages in seventeen families: Indo-Germans, Tamules, Semitics, Georgians, Caucasians, Tunguses

---

[1] "Zeitschrift d. Deutsch. Morgenl. Ges.," p. 405, 1855.
[2] Martin, "Essai sur l'origine du Lang.," p. 32, Paris, 1835.
[3] Schleicher, "D. Sprachen Europas," p. 29, 1850.
[4] "Die Ungleichheit menschl. Rassen," pp. 202, 242, 272.
[5] "Atlas Ethnographique," Paris, 1826.

(with Mongols, Turks, Samoiedes, and Finns), Zenniseis, Kuriles or Ainos, Jukagires, Korjäkes, Kamschatdales, Polar-Americans in Asia, Japanese, Koreans, Tibetians, Chinese, Indo-Chinese. The latter and the Caucasians are probably to be subdivided in several families (Pott).

II. Europe, with 53 languages in seven families: Iberian, Basque, Rhætian-Etruscan, Illyrian-Albanese, Indo-Germanic (Greeks and Latins, Celts, Germans, Lithuanians and Slavonians, Gypsies), Finns (Lapps, Esthonians, Magyars), Semitics, Turks.

III. Africa, with 114 (according to Kölle, with 150-200) languages, among which the Berber and the Kongo family (the South African language) are the most extended.

IV. Oceania, with 117, in three families: Malays and Polynesians, Melanesians (black nations), and Australians.

V. America, with 423 languages, which, excluding California, separate in North America in thirty-two different stocks. In South America, Rivero and Tschudi have estimated the number of languages from 280-340, of which four-fifths are radically different.

It is scarcely necessary to caution the reader against the authenticity of the above data, when we consider that the definition of what must be considered as a distinct language is rather arbitrary. The numbers are, however, hardly too high. When we take into consideration the many languages spoken in a comparatively small space, owing to the want of intercourse or complete isolation of small tribes, in various regions of the globe, we would rather be inclined to assume a higher number of radically different languages on the globe than Balbi did. The maximum of different languages appears to prevail in Central America, and thence northwards on the western coasts from California to the land of the Esquimaux,[1] in Asia, in the Caucasus, in Africa, in the south of Abyssinia, in Wadai (where there are twenty), in Bornou (where there are thirty), and in Andamana, where Barth[2] has distinguished some thirty distinct languages. The island Timor possesses, accord-

[1] Hale, p. 197.
[2] "Zeitsch. d. Deutsch. Morgenl. Ges.," vi, p. 412.

ing to Crawfurd, no less than forty different languages; the number is also said to be very considerable in Ende and Flores, as well as in the interior of Borneo; and even upon the small islands of the South Sea, inhabited by blacks, four or five different languages are not unfrequent. In every part of the world there is a large number of different languages met with, in regions which may be supposed to have been the passage-roads during the migrations of peoples. Either upon these roads, or at a moderate distance from them, smaller or larger masses seem to have halted, and permanently settled.

It yet remains for us to say a few words with regard to the relation of the physical and the linguistic proofs of division in Anthropology. Where both agree as to the affinity of races, there can be no difficulty; this, however, is not often the case. If the points of view are different, two cases may occur: either anatomy or philology is in favour of affinity. The first case can scarcely surprise us, when within each of the great natural divisions of mankind, we find languages of a radically different type (for instance, among the Chinese and Mongols, Germans and Basques); for we must bear in mind that the above division includes nations, the physical differences of which are still sufficiently great to render the assumption of their having originally sprung from the same stock not absolutely demonstrable; whilst, on the other hand, though originally from the same stock, an early and complete separation is the only assumable ground for a radical difference of language. If this conflict between anatomy and philology is, in such a case, merely apparent, it becomes real and unsolvable, when languages, clearly ascertained to be related, are found among peoples whose physical characters are widely distinct, unless such phenomena can be explained by intermixture, or an exchange of language, or both together.

Cases of the latter kind cannot be decided by general rules; and for such, a careful investigation of the particular conditions is requisite. It may, however, be assumed, that language generally affords a safer guide than the physical character of a people, for the following reasons. In the first place, the typical peculiarities of languages appear to be proportionally less changeable, whilst we have shown that the physical peculiarities are more so; thus, originally different stocks acquire a resemblance to each other in the course of time, whilst originally similar stocks become dissimilar. Again, where peoples within historical times have met and influenced each other, words have gradually passed from one language into another, just as they may, without foreign influence, undergo a change or disappear altogether; but never has the grammatical structure of a language accommodated itself to a new one, but rather the whole language has disappeared, and has been supplanted by the new one; for such a change of the structure of a language would presuppose a transformation of ideas and the mode of connecting the elements of thought, which we deem next to impossible. This is confirmed by thieves' and vagabond dialects, which always borrow their grammatical structure from a language ready made, whilst the words are newly-formed and mutilated. Thus, the jargon spoken in Oregon, in the region of Fort Vancouver, consists of words belonging to the English, French, Nootka, Chinook, and other languages.

Another ground for the principle laid down is, that the scientific method at present applied in comparative philology possesses a higher degree of authenticity, and offers better guarantees for its results than the methods of physical anthropology and craniology. As a proof of this may be mentioned, the greater unanimity of linguists with regard to the results of their science in comparison with the disputes among naturalists as to the theory of races.

Moreover, the positive principles on affinity of nations laid down by philology, claim greater reliance than the negative ones supported by naturalists. We have seen that even great resemblance of the physical characters of two peoples affords no positive proof for their real affinity; whilst philology may, in many instances, adduce an undoubted proof to that effect.

We are therefore bound to declare against all those authors, who, like Nott and Gliddon,[1] assert, in relation to the Berber

---

[1] "Types of Mankind," p. 205.

tribes, that affinity of language proves nothing in favour of unity of origin, since, as is the case with the Jews, a frequent exchange of language takes place. There are certainly examples of this kind, but they present the important peculiarity that, without exception, the people which loses its language and exchanges it for another, has ceased to live as a people, has been absorbed by the other, whether conqueror or conquered, and forms with it an amalgam, from which the adherents to the doctrine of the permanence of physical types are less able to extract the composing elements, if the linguists fail to do so. We are ready to admit that though the proportion of an intermixture of different nations may be manifested to the linguist by the comparative number of foreign elements introduced in a language, as for instance, the Malay, which possesses 5 per cent. Arab and 16 per cent. Sanscrit words; still the quantity of linguistic elements does not always correspond to the quantity of foreign blood, so that philology cannot give a decided opinion as to the genealogy of peoples strongly intermixed, any more than natural history is able to do.

When small remnants of a scattered people lose their language among nations of different stocks, such instances cannot be adduced as a proof that exchanges of languages are of frequent occurrence, and that language offers no certain indication as to the affinity of nations. Thus, the few hundred Bosnian soldiers who, in 1420, were sent by Sultan Selim into lower Nubia, where they settled, have not preserved their language. The scattered Hottentots in the Cape Colony, which are of mixed blood, speak only Dutch.[1] Many Chinese born in Manilla speak only Tagal;[2] the Chinese in Banjermassing, and many other parts of Borneo, speak only Malay.[3] The small tribe of the Brothertons (Algonquin-Indians) have adopted the English as their language,[4] which may be explained by the circumstance that they are composed of the

---

1 Napier, "Excursions in South Africa," i, p. 181, 1850.
2 Virgin, "Erdumsegl. der F. Eugenie übers. v. Etzel," ii, p. 195, 1856.
3 "Rheinische Missionsber.," p. 67, 1853.
4 Schoolcraft, "Algic Researches, New York," i, p. 27, 1839.

remnants of several tribes, Mohicans, Narragansetts, Pequos, Nanticockes, etc., who had no language in common;[1] many Germans in the United States have done the same. The Spaniards in the mining districts of Peru exchange their native language for the Quichua,[2] especially in Cuenca, and other parts of Ecuador.[3] Among the inhabitants of Zamboanga, in Mindano, the number of which does not exceed 7,000, a corrupt Spanish has established itself, consisting of Spanish and native words mixed up in various combinations by different individuals.[4] Nor can such instances be adduced against language as indicative of race, in which a population, consisting of heterogeneous elements, finally adopt the language of the dominating caste, as happened with the Negroes at Haiti, who adopted the French. Negroes of various African nationalities, brought as slaves into America, everywhere speak the languages of their masters, though in a mutilated manner. In Brazil they speak Portuguese;[5] in the Mauritius (Ile de France), French.[6] In the English West Indies they speak the well-known Negro-English; there is also found the Negro-Portuguese, or so-called Jew-language, in Surinam.[7] In the Danish colonies, a language prevails consisting of words chiefly Low-German, with the omission of all inflexions.[8] In a similar condition, as regards language, is the present population of the Marian islands, or rather of Guaham, for the other islands are now deserted. It consists of a mixture of the original natives (who, under the oppression of Quiroga, are said to have diminished to 2,000), some immigrants from the Carolines, imported natives from the Philippines, and also Mexicans.[9] According to

---

[1] Schoolcraft, "History of the Indian tribes," v, p. 506, note 2.
[2] Pickering, "The Races of Man," p. 277, 1849.
[3] Seeman, i, p. 209.
[4] Trad. Lay in "The Claims of Japan and Malaisia upon Christendom," ii, p. 113, New York, 1839.
[5] Koster, Reise in Brasil," p. 574, 1817.
[6] Example of a narration in one of the dialects of Negro-French may be found in Freycinet, "Voyage autour du monde," i, p. 407, 1827.
[7] "Zeitschrift d. Deutsch. Morgenl. Ges.," xi, p. 324.
[8] Oldendorp, "Gesch. d. Miss. auf St. Thomas, St. Croix, and St. Jan., p. 424, 1777; and Wullschlägel, "Gramm. und Wörterb. des Neger-Englischen."
[9] Chamisso, Bemerk. in "Ansichten auf einer Entdeckungsreise," p. 78, 1821; Kotzebue, "Entdeckungsreise," ii, p. 129, 1821; De Pagès, "Reise um d. Welt," p. 143, 1786.

Mallat[1] they speak Spanish, and have adopted many Spanish customs; but according to D'Urville,[2] the imported population do not speak Spanish, but the language of the natives,—the Chamorro. In America, also, the Spanish has frequently replaced the languages of the natives, especially in S. Salvador, Nicaragua, and Costa Rica, the original languages of which are unknown. These phenomena do not, however, appear to be so general as Latham asserts;[3] but are limited in Nicaragua to certain districts, are more frequent in S. Salvador, and occur also in some villages in Honduras.[4]

As in these cases the exchange of language may be explained from extensive intermixture of the natives with the Spaniards, so also among the Guayqueriers, a branch of the Guaraunos on the coast of S. Margaretha, who now all speak Spanish, and differ much in external appearance from individuals of their own stock.[5] This likewise applies to the populations of Baradéro, Quilmos, Calchaguy, and S. Domingo Soriano, on the river Negro, who not having been by the Jesuits united in communities, have preserved their liberty, and pass now as Spaniards, whose language and customs they have adopted in consequence of intermixture;[6] also to the inhabitants of Chiloe, whose original language is almost entirely forgotten and replaced by the Spanish.[7] With regard to the Changos, who reach from Huasco to Cobija, the accounts are contradictory. According to some they are Indians, according to others they are the descendants of Spaniards, who in the olden time had settled there; their language seems to be a corrupt Spanish; they dress like the lower classes of Chili, and have had, as is asserted, little intercourse with the Spaniards.[8] The Indians of the environs of Rio Janeiro have also almost entirely lost their

---

[1] "Les Philippines," i, p. 342, 1846.
[2] "Voyage de l'Astrolabe," v, p. 277.
[3] "Journal of the Royal Geographical Society," xx, p. 189.
[4] Scherzer, "Wanderungen durch d. mittel am Freistaaten," pp. 165, 402, 348; 1857.
[5] Humboldt und Bonpland, i, p. 467.
[6] Azara, "Voy. dans l'Am. mérid.," ii, p. 217, 1809.
[7] King and Fitzroy, i, p. 278.
[8] De la Salle, "Voyage autour du monde sur la Bonite," ii, p. 13, 1845; St. Cricq, "Bullet. Soc. Geog.," ii, p. 304, 1853; Philippi, in Petermann's "Geogr. Mittheil.," p. 56, 1856.

language, and speak Portuguese.[1] It is, undoubtedly, an exaggeration that one million of the aborigines of America have exchanged their native for an European, language.[2] The natives of unmixed blood have scarcely done so in a single instance; only mixed populations, in a state of slavery, have allowed the language of the rulers to be forced on them.

Thus we often see small tribes absorbed by stronger ones; by ceasing to exist as a people, they adopt the language of the more powerful tribe. Ancient Rome, which had absorbed so many foreign elements, presents a striking example. It has already been mentioned, that many American Indian nations have absorbed a number of minor tribes. It occurs, however, occasionally that a people absorbed by another may still preserve its language, like the Yuchi, incorporated by the Creeks; perhaps the circumstance that the women of the Caribs possess a different language than the men, may result from a similar event. In such cases, much depends on the will of the conqueror, and the tenacity with which the conquered keep to the peculiarities of their race,—a quality which different tribes possess in a different degree. The caste of the serfs among the Bracknas, in the north of Senegal, are the Zenaghas,—a Berber tribe which, by its masters the Assani, had the Arabian language forced upon them,[3] like several Kabyle tribes of the province Constantine, who have adopted this language.[4] Thus, many scattered Vindjha peoples in the East Indies have exchanged their language for a filial language of the Sanscrit. On the other hand, that the conquerors lose sometimes their language to the conquered, is instanced by the Normans in the tenth century, and the Longobards.

In all these cases, in which a people has lost its language, it has by intermixture ceased to exist as a people; and neither the consideration of physical types, nor philology, can give any clear indication of its existence, unless supported by special historical documents. It must be an extremely rare case in which,

---

[1] Von Eschwege, "Journal v. Brasil," ii, p. 16.
[2] Humboldt und Bonpland, v, p. 774.
[3] Leo Africanus, "Bossi e Negri delle Nigrizia occ. Torino," i, p. 112, 1838.
[4] M. Wagner, "Reise in Algier," ii, p. 11, 1841.

according to Pott's assumption,[1] the Parthian, *i. e.* the Scythian conquerors of Iran, found themselves, by losing the grammatical structure of their own language, which was replaced by a very simple one,—that of the Pehlwi, which belongs to the Iranian languages. Thus, in Sicily, the nön-Greek peoples forgot their own language in consequence of intermixture of the natives with the Sikeliotes, and the forced transportation of whole communities; the whole island became a Greek territory, and remained so to the middle ages.[2] Where, however, such a case is not proved by history, we are not justified in adducing such rare exceptions in support of assumed theories. Such an error is committed by Berthelot,[3] in asserting that the present inhabitants of the Canary islands are still, physically and morally, the ancient Guanches, having only lost their language; though he confines himself merely to some similarity of both in customs and mode of life, and describes two different types of Guanche mummies, without even maintaining that they are the types of the present natives. Retzius commits a similar error,[4] in stating that the Kareles have lost their own language and appropriated the Finnish, because they possess oval heads, while the Savolax is globular-headed, and the Tavastlander square-headed. Such assumptions, without historical evidence, are inadmissible. Pott says justly,[5] "If colonies are to be able to suppress languages, or essentially to alter them, they must possess a lasting power which must be concentrated in important cities, otherwise they will, with their own language, perish in the mass of the subjected peoples."

In contrast to the phenomenon of the loss of a language of a people, or rather, as is most generally the case, of the extinction of the same as a people, together with its language, stands the not less frequent phenomenon of individual languages which sustain their independence. The Spanish language in Manilla has, in spite of the secured possession of the Spaniards, made in that part as little progress as the English language in the

---

[1] Art. "Indogerm. Sprachstamm," Ersch. u. G., p. 52.
[2] Niebuhr, "Röm. Gesch.," i, 174.
[3] "Mém. de la Soc. Ethnol.," i, p. 146.
[4] Müller's "Archiv," p. 395, 1848.
[5] Loc. cit., p. 81.

East Indies. The Malay in Singapore, and the Sowaheili on the east coast of Africa, have remained the dominant languages, notwithstanding the long rule of the Arabs over that region. The Arab language, though in a corrupt state, has maintained itself in Malta; and notwithstanding their dispersion, the Gypsies, and in many places the Jews, have preserved their languages.

The historical point of view which may serve as a guide in the division of mankind and their affinity, can hardly be separated from linguistic considerations, since the peculiarities of language present the chief evidence which throws light on the history of a people; and the knowledge of historical development remains imperfect and fragmentary in proportion as the linguistic data are defective. We have, nevertheless, ventured upon the separation of the linguistic and historical stand-points, partly because it was our endeavour to explain the relation in which the first stands to the physical theory of the division of mankind, with which it is frequently in conflict, and partly because, with regard to the great majority of peoples, there exists no history; so that, in the absence of all historical documents, we are limited to their language and the reports of travellers, which, though frequently very meagre, are still important as the only sources we possess.

The historical consideration, in as far as it differs from the linguistic consideration, is, in most cases, compelled to remain satisfied with the comparison of the traditions of peoples, their religious ideas, their festivals, funeral ceremonies; then their chronology, architectural remains, tools, clothing, ornaments, and arms; and their social and family life.

From these ethnographic data, conclusions of comprehensive scope have been hazarded; migrations and affinities, and even the descent of mankind from a single pair, or at any rate, an original cradle of the human race, has been inferred from the tradition of the flood,[1] prevalent among so many distant nations.

[1] According to the views of Cuvier and Buckland, the universality of the traditions of the Flood may be explained by a corresponding universal revolution in the crust of the earth 5-6,000 years ago. Other geologists flatly deny the universality of such a revolution (see Jameson. zu Cuvier's "Umwälzungen der Erdrinde, deutsch von Nöggerath," ii, p. 191, 1830). The flood tra-

We must here observe, that analogies in either of these points, taken individually, afford no proof whatever in favour of affinity, and even similarities in several points possess only a secondary importance; for partly may they, under similar conditions, spontaneously arise in peoples who had always lived in a state of separation; and partly may they have been the result of a short intercourse between two different peoples. How cautious we ought to be, and how just the principle is, that all such analogies can only be considered as secondary arguments in favour of affinity, will be seen by the following examples:—

The analogies existing between Asiatic and American peoples have been collated by Delafield.[1] Most of these peculiarities prove nothing, as they concern things which are frequently met with among uncivilized nations of the most remote regions. Whilst the Mongolian type nearly approaches the American (Bradford), the structure of their respective languages differs essentially.[2] The chief points of resemblance are the following. The Schamanism of the Mongol tribes, based on fire-worship,[3] finds its counterpart in the religious ideas and ceremonies of most of the Indian tribes of North America. A. von Humboldt has noticed striking similarities of the old buildings, and the religion of the Aztecs to that of the Tartars and Tibetians. Squier[4] has pointed out the resemblance of the old temples of Yucatan to those of Buddha in India.

The doctrine of a periodical destruction of the world and of its reconstruction, prevails in Tibet and India, as well as in old Mexico; the first destruction was effected by earthquake, the second by fire, the third by a storm, the last by water. The

---

ditions among some peoples, may be explained from the fact of shells being found inland in great numbers, whence they concluded that inundations had taken place at some period. Among other nations, that which appears as an ancient tradition is manifestly of modern Christian origin, by its similarity to the Mosaic records, and other accidental circumstances. The first was the case among the Greenlanders (Cranz, "Historie v. Groenland," i, p. 262, 2 Aufl., 1770); the second was found among the Namaquas (Moffat, "Mission Labours in South Africa," p. 126, 1842).

[1] "Inquiry into the origin of the Antiquities of America," Cincinnati, 1836; Bradford, "American Antiquities," New York, 1841.

[2] Pott, "D. Ungl. menschl. Rassen," p. 257.

[3] Erman's "Archiv f. wissl. Kunde v. Russland," viii, p. 213.

[4] "The Serpent Symbol," New York, 1851.

parallels of Humboldt refer to the chronology of the ancient Mexicans and some Indian peoples. The zodiacal signs of the Mongols are arbitrarily selected names of animals, the same as serve for designating the years: mouse, ox, leopard, hare, crocodile, serpent, horse, sheep, ape, fowl, dog, swine. The Mandshus, Japanese, and Tibetians have, instead of the leopard, crocodile, and sheep, the signs tiger, dragon, and goat. The days of the months of the Mexicans have partly the same names,—hare, serpent, ape, dog; instead of the leopard, crocodile, and fowl, they have the signs of the ocelot, lizard, and eagle; the other five animals of the first series were unknown to them. Of the moon-calendar of the Hindoos, seven signs are met with in Mexico,—serpent, tube, razor, sun-orbit, dog-tail, house. What may be inferred from these facts is simply this, that an Asiatic origin of many elements of civilization in Mexico, is not less probable than numerous immigrations into North-western America from Asia, as we shall prove in the sequel. On such grounds, no proof of the descent of Americans from Asia can be inferred. But what under other circumstances might be considered as trivial, namely, that Coxcox, of the Mexican legend, corresponds to Noah and his ark, and that even the green twig in the beak of the bird is not wanting, acquires in this case some importance, combined as it is found there with the analogy of baptism with water. Still these coincidences do not necessarily lead us to a definite conclusion, though they afford indications which deserve to be further investigated.

When we merely find conformity of customs like the following,—genealogy by the female line; burying the arms, and other valuable property, with the deceased; cutting off the flesh from the bones of corpses, and worship of the dead; referring all diseases to evil spirits; treatment by magic, peculiarities which the Madagascans possess in common with many American tribes,—there is no necessity for inferring either affinity or intercommunication. But when we find in Madagascar a peculiar construction of bellows in use, formed like a double pump, it may serve as a subsidiary argument that the population of Madagascar is descended from the Malays, for the very same kind of bellows is in use in Sumatra,[1] in the Lutu islands (Wilkes), in Borneo, among the Dajaks,[2] in Mindanao,[3] in Timor,[4] and in Dory in New Guinea.[5] How little resemblances of domestic arrangements signify by themselves, is shown by King,[6] who during his survey of York Sound on the Roe river in Australia, did not find two huts built perfectly alike; and Simpson,[7] who saw in a camp of Flat-heads in North America, tents of every possible construction. The same mode of procuring fire, by whirling a thin piece of wood in the hole of a larger piece, prevails in Australia, North and South America, among the Kaffirs and Bushmen,[8] also in the Carolines and Aleutes; whilst in Radak, and in the Sandwich Islands, a small piece of wood is placed in the groove of a larger piece, at an angle of 30°, and rubbed against it.[9] The Algonquins, in North America, strike fire by means of two stones.[10] The remarkable custom which Xenophon ascribes to the Tibarenes in Asia Minor, that at the birth of a child the father goes to bed and is attended to, is of such a kind that, if it be found among different nations, one would, on account of its singularity, feel inclined to assume that an intercommunication must have taken place. This, however, becomes impossible, when we learn that the custom prevails, not merely in West Yünnan (M. Polo), in Bouro,[11] but also in Africa, in Cassange,[12] among the Basques in Biscaya,[13] and most frequently in South America,[14]

---

[1] Marsden, "Sumatra," p. 347, Berlin, 1788.
[2] Brook, in Keppel, "Expedition to Borneo," p. 75, 1846.
[3] Dampier, "Nouv. voy. autour du monde," ii, p. 9, Amsterdam, 1701.
[4] Péron, "Voyage de découv. aux ter. Aust.," 2nd edit., atlas, pl. 46, 1824.
[5] W. Earl, "Native races of the Indian Archipelago," p. 76, 1853.
[6] "Narrative of a survey of the coasts of Austr.," i, p. 431, 1827.
[7] "Narrative of a journey round the world," i, p. 143, 1847.
[8] Alberti, "Desc. phys. et hist. des Caffres," p. 36, Amst., 1811; Campbell, "Reise in Süd-Afr.," p. 37, Weimar, 1823; Barrow, "Reise durch d. inneren G. des Südl. Afr.," i, p. 281, 1801.
[9] Chamisso, "Entdeckungsreise," p. 154.
[10] Lafitau, "Mœurs des Sauvages Americains," ii, p. 242, 1724.
[11] Ausland, p. 1046, 1855.
[12] Zuchelli, "Miss. u. Reisebesch. nach Congo," p. 166, 1715.
[13] Rougemont, "Le peuple primitif," ii, p. 420, 1855.
[14] The unanimity of travellers forbids our considering this custom as a fiction. The cause seems to be a peculiar superstition. Among the Caribs it is said to rest upon this,—that the husband is not allowed, at the birth of a child, to kill any large but only small game, as birds, etc.,—perhaps, in order that the wife might not be obliged to overtask her powers in the

namely, among the Caribs,[1] in the Pearl Island, near Carthagena,[2] on the Ucayale,[3] on the Solimoes, among the Juris,[4] on the Tapajoz, among the Mundrucus,[5] and among the Abiponians.[6]

These examples prove how cautious we should be in arriving at conclusions when we find merely conformities in such and similar things, as they offer no secure basis by themselves for inferring the affinity of peoples.

---

preparation of larger animals, hence the husband passes the greater part of the day in his hammock (Quandt, "Nachr. v. Surinam," p. 252, 1807). Among many peoples we hear of a continuous fasting of the husband on such occasions, among the Conibos on the left bank of the Ucayale, among the Indians on the Orinoco (St. Cricq, "Bul. Soc. Geogr.," p. 289, 1853; Gilii, p. 274). According to Labat ("Nouv. voy. aux îles de l'Am.," ii, p. 123, 1724), this fasting lasts, among the Caribs, thirty to forty days, but only takes place at the birth of the first son, and is thus a religious custom.

[1] Fermin, "Descr. de la col. de Surinam," i, p. 81, Amst., 1769; Lavayssé, "Reise nach Trinidad," 1816, denies it.

[2] Allerhand, "Lehrreiche Briefe, v. d. Miss. der Ges. Jesu," i, p. 56, 1726.

[3] Tschudi, "Peru," p. 235, 1846.

[4] Spix and Martius, p. 1186.

[5] Ibid., p. 1339.

[6] Dobrizhoffer, "Gesch. d. Abiponer," ii, p. 273, 1783.

PART II.

PSYCHOLOGICAL INVESTIGATION.

If the examination of the physical peculiarities of the races of mankind had irresistibly led to the result, that the question as regards the unity of mankind must be answered in the negative, we might have been relieved of the necessity of inquiring into the psychical endowments of the various races; or we might have simply endeavoured to ascertain whether the specific physical diversities corresponded to the differences in psychical manifestations. But the psychological investigation becomes highly important, if not indispensable, for the solution of the chief question when we find that, though anatomy and physiology furnish us with stronger grounds in favour of the unity of mankind, as a species, than the arguments adduced for the opposite theory, they are of such a nature that they cannot be considered as decisive. Again, however conclusive the physical arguments in favour of unity might be, they would lose their validity if it could be established, that there existed permanent psychical differences, presenting impassable barriers to the development of individual races.

The psychological aspect of the question has not, it is true, been entirely overlooked; but its importance has either not been sufficiently estimated, or it has been treated with a superficiality that would surprise us, if "the reason why" were not so clear. If it be somewhat difficult to arrive at a just estimation of the mental capacity of individuals known to us, it is still more difficult to estimate the psychical capacity of whole nations or races: the judgment is, in such cases, generally subjective. Individual nations occupy at different periods, different scales of development; and though from the actual performances we may arrive at an estimation of the faculties which produced them, they would seem to vary at times. In addition to these difficulties, there is the circumstance, that the external and internal causes, which in one people effect the transition from a primitive to a civilized state, are as much hidden from us as the causes which prevented the development of another people and apparently fixed it in the position which it once occupied. All this produces an inclination to cut the matter short, by assuming a different endowment for individual races,—an assumption rendered probable by the description of the chief features of the thoughtless Negro, the restless nomadic American, the cannibal south-islander. The primitive man stands in such striking contrast to the civilized man, that the latter in his vanity considers the former as specifically different; that he himself once occupied a similar position, he does not seem to take into any serious consideratien.

The reports we possess of the mental condition of uncultured nations are numerous enough, but far from sufficient to enable us to form a correct estimate of their inner life. Fragmentary as those reports are, we derive from them no information as to the mode of thinking and feeling peculiar to these nations, nor as to the intellect manifested in many ways which, superficially considered, appear frivolous or atrocious. Hence, religion, customs, and legends of such peoples, have hitherto been treated as mere curiosities; but no pains have been taken to understand them so as to deduce from them proper inferences with regard to psychical peculiarities, or a proper characteristic of the uncivilized man.

There is another circumstance which deserves notice, namely, that hitherto the problem of unity of species has been almost exclusively treated by naturalists, who considered the psychological side of the question either as foreign to the main subject, or as of secondary consideration. If the question was mooted at all, it was under the assumption that the psychical peculiarities of nations corresponded with their physical characters, especially with the structure of the skull; in short, these things were treated with a levity not unusual among physiologists when speaking of psychology. From the external resemblance of the Negro to the ape, the internal resemblance was deduced without much ado. The cranial capacity was, however, chiefly relied upon to measure the mental capacity.

Morton, especially, has endeavoured to establish that the mental capacity of nations or races is always proportional to the volume of the head; and though, as we shall show, the contrary results from what he endeavours to prove, his assertions have been generally assented to.[1] In Germany, the same views were previously held. Recently, however, Engel[2] observed that there were considerable doubts whether the mass of the brain differed in crania of different types; or whether the contraction of the skull in one direction was not compensated by an expansion in another; and whether the various cranial shapes had any influence on cerebral activity. Though we may fully acknowledge the importance of the fact that the Indo-Germanic and Semitic nations, which have ever been, and still are, the representatives of civilization (from the Semitic races the three chief theistical religions have emanated), either excel, or at any rate do not yield, in cerebral development to any other race; and assuming even as probable the assertion of Lawrence,[3] that the great diversities in the mental development of nations can only be explained from innate differences of cerebral structure; still the axiom, that the shape and capacity of the skull indicates the proportion of mental capacity, remains unproved. "Why," asks Prichard, pointedly, "have the Georgians, despite their Greek crania, never been mentally distinguished? Why has Greek and Roman civilization yielded before the Germanic? Why, we may ask, has it at all declined, since the cranial shape and the cerebral struc-

[1] See Hamilton Smith, p. 159; P. de Remusat, "Révue des deux Mondes," 4me livre, 1854.

[2] "Untersuchungen über Schädelformen," p. 124.

[3] "Lectures," p. 416, 3rd edit., 1823.

ture have remained unaltered?" On consulting history, we may easily find other examples showing the overthrow of nations who were once highly civilized, possessed of beautifully formed crania, by peoples of inferior mental capacity, and less developed skulls. Notwithstanding the incontestable superiority of the white man above the other races, the Turks and the Magyars have entered Europe, obtained great conquests, and become permanently settled. The larger cranial capacity of the white race could not prevent it.

Turning to Parchappe's measurements,[1] we find the races stand in the following order, according to the volume of the head:— Caucasians, Negroes, Mongols, Americans, and Malays. The first is distinguished by the greatest length of the head, and the greatest development of the forehead and occiput; in the Negro, the length is the same; it is less in the Mongol and the American, and considerably less in the Malay. Lawrence, on the other hand, places the Malay, with regard to cranial capacity, between the European and the Negro, and the American between the European and the Mongol.

In the tables of Tiedemann,[2] the mean capacity of the skull is:—

	Cases.		Ounces.
For the European - - - - - -	135	-	$40\frac{8}{9}$
„ American - - - - - -	31	-	$40\frac{1}{8}$
„ Mongol - - - - - -	43	-	$39\frac{2}{5}$
„ Malay - - - - - - -	77	-	$38\frac{1}{6}$
„ Adult Negro - - - - - -	48	-	$37\frac{11}{12}$
„ Asiatics and Africans of the white race	39	-	$37\frac{2}{5}$

It is singular enough that these mean values, derived from Tiedemann's data, are opposed to the axiom which he has deduced from them, namely, that the brain of the Negro is not smaller than that of the European; just as Morton's measurements are in opposition to the results which he infers from them. Morton says,[3] that the mean cranial capacity in the European amounted to 87 cubic inches;

[1] "Recherches sur l'encephale."
[2] "D. Hirn des Negers," 1837.
[3] "Crania Americana," p. 260.

in the Mongol, 83; Malay, 81; American, 80; Negro, 78; but at a later period,[1] after further measurements, Morton changed the order,[2] so that the Malay comes immediately after the Caucasian, with 85, the Negro with 83, the Mongol with 82, and the American with 79, cubic inches of brain; and accordingly the American race (which is confirmed by Meigs, in Nott and Gliddon[3]), is, in this respect, the least favoured. He is thus frequently in conflict with his own assertions, that cranial capacity corresponds with mental endowment. The old Peruvians and Mexicans, the only American nations which had arrived at a high degree of cultivation, possessed a cranial capacity of 76 and 79 cubic inches.[4] Nott and Gliddon[5] give to this so-called "Toltecan family,"[6] on the average only 76·8 cubic inches. An old, half-civilized people in Peru had only 73, and the higher ranks of the old Peruvians 75, cub. in.;[7] that is to say, as much as the Hottentots and the Alfurus,—the result of 155 measurements,—whilst Morton gives to the barbarous nomadic nations of America, as the mean results of 161 measurements, 84 cub. in.;[8] to the Creeks, Iroquois, and Esquimaux, 87 and 88 cub. in.; *i. e.*, as much as to Europeans, but much less to the more gifted Cherokees; to the Hindoo 75, and to the Negro 78 cub. in.[9] In order to sustain his axiom, he adds, as a good phrenologist, that the barbarous Indian tribes, by defending their liberty, have proved themselves to be better endowed than the slavish Peruvians and Mexicans; and Philipps,[10] as well as Nott and Gliddon, skilfully evade the question by the assertion, that in barbarous nations the lower

---

1 Silliman's "Am. Journ. of Science," 2nd series, ix, p. 247.
2 Nott and Gliddon, "Types of Mankind," p. 450.
3 "Indigenous races of the Earth," 1857.
4 "Crania Americana," p. 261.
5 "Types of mankind," p. 446.
6 Morton frequently speaks of Toltecan skulls he had before him. It must be mentioned that he designates by "Toltecans," very inappropriately, we think, all the ancient South and North American cultivated nations indiscriminately.
7 Schoolcraft, "History of the Indian Tribes," iii, p. 239.
8 Nott and Gliddon, 82·4 cub. in. In opposition to Morton, Warren maintains that, from the measurements of the crania in his collection, the old civilized nations of America were distinguished from the barbarous by larger foreheads and superior cranial shape (Prescott, "History of the Conquest of Mexico," 2nd edit., 1844.)
9 "Crania Americana," pp. 173, 195, 247.
10 In Schoolcraft, iii, p. 331.

faculties of the occipital region are predominating; whilst the anterior part of the brain—the intellectual portion—is not so much developed as in the Peruvians and Mexicans. However, it unfortunately happens that the latter, in spite of their cultivation, had low receding foreheads; and that, as regards the savage tribes of America, a flattened, small developed occiput, has, by Morton himself, been considered as typical. As another contradiction, may be mentioned, that the old Egyptians had only 80 cubic inches,[1] and must accordingly, like the Hindoos, old Peruvians, and Mexicans, have possessed less brains than the barbarous nations which lived in their vicinity. By the way, we may mention, that according to Tiedemann's and Morton's tables,[2] the difference between the mean cranial capacity of the Englishman and Irishman amounts to 9 cubic inches, and that between the Irishman and the Negro only to 4 cubic inches.

Huschke[3] has recently made numerous measurements, and found that, though in all races relatively large and small skulls occur, the size of the cranium increases from the lower to higher races, among whom the largest crania are met with. But even his special data do not support his general propositions. They are as follows:—

MEAN RESULTS OF CRANIAL CAPACITY.

	Ounces.	Cases.
Male Europeans	40·88	441
„ Americans	39·13	31
„ Mongols	38·39	46
„ Negroes	37·57	54
„ Malays	36·41	98

It may be immediately seen that this series does not agree with any of those quoted, but that it proves as little the proposition, that cranial capacity and mental qualifications are corresponding; for the gifted Malay has, according to the above

[1] Mean results of 55 cases, Silliman, loc. cit.; Nott and Gliddon, "Types," pp. 280, 432, 450.

[2] Quoted by Bachmann, in Smyth, "The unity of the human races," p. 262, 1850.

[3] Schädel, Hirn, und Seele, 1854.

[3] "Crania Americana," p. 260.

table, the least quantity of brain, and the Mongol less than the American. One might feel inclined to set aside the first objection, as Huschke has done,[1] namely, that the cranial capacity of the Hindoo, which according to him only contains 27 ounces of brain, is to that of the European only = 2 : 3. This he explains from the circumstance that the Hindoo, on the average, is only 4 feet high, whilst the European is 6 feet, and that therefore the brain is proportional to the size of the body. This explanation is unsatisfactory, for the Hindoo is, on the average, 5 feet 2 inches high;[2] nor is it all applicable to the Malay, who is not on the average smaller than the Mongol. Another difficulty is, that the old Egyptians possessed, next to the Hindoos, the smallest skulls of all Caucasian races (Huschke). That some American nations have uncommonly large heads, was proved by the fact, that the hats fabricated in Paris for the natives of Canada and New Orleans during the war of liberation, were all too small for them. The inhabitants of Tierra del Fuego, the Esquimaux, and the natives of Van Diemen's Land, have all, with a compact structure, uncommonly large heads, which seems to be the case with all inhabitants of cold regions, Caucasians included, in comparison with the inhabitants of warmer climates.[3] Virey[4] observes, that the Russian possesses a more capacious skull than the Swede; the Kalmuck and Tartar; a larger cranium than the civilized European; but the Laplander is particularly distinguished by a greatly developed cranial structure. Desmoulins has also pointed out the disproportion existing in the Mongol, and especially in the so-called Hyperborean race, between the size of the head and mental qualification. Finally, instances are not wanting which prove that the same or similar intellectual and moral dispositions coexist with different cranial formations; and *vice versâ*, different dispositions with the same or similar cranial shape and capacity. We see one and the same people, in the course of its history, proceed from barbarism to civiliza-

---

[1] Page 49.
[2] Lassen, "Ind. Alterthumskunde," i, p. 402.
[3] Parchappe, loc cit., p. 51.
[4] "Hist. nat. du genre humain," i, p. 66, 1834.

tion, and again relapse from its high state, and its capacities decline; but as the cranial shape (as is usually assumed), remains the same, the assertion that the intellectual faculties are dependent on it, is not even consonant with the doctrine of the immutability of race-crania. We are thus compelled to renounce the doctrine that the capacity of the cranium indicates the amount of mental endowment.

Having disposed of this preliminary question, and shown that the size of the skull presents us with no criterion for the peculiarities of intellectual life, we must endeavour to indicate the path we ought to pursue in these investigations.

As, in physical respects, all men may be considered as belonging to the same species, if it can be proved that the greatest physical differences occurring among them, are not more considerable than such as may have arisen in the same people in the course of time; so may we, in psychical respects, count all as belonging to the same species, if it can be shown that the greatest differences of their mental development and their intellectual and moral culture, are not greater than the differences of the degrees of civilization which the same people passes through in its history. Here the question is not either to prove or to refute that *at present, e. g.* an individual Negro, or the Negro race generally, is capable of the same intellectual performances as an European civilized people; for nations are as much dependent on the historical basis of their vital development as individuals, and it is impossible that peoples passing through different stages of development should be capable of the same intellectual performances. But if by the term capacity be designated—what alone should be designated by it—not the possible performances at any given time, but such as are possible to the living generation under the most favourable circumstances; then it becomes clear, not only that the capacities of a people may change in the course of time, but that the judgment, as regards the unity of mankind, depends on the solution of the question, whether, under favourable circumstances, in the course of time, all nations and tribes are capable, or not, of reaching the same degree of mental development.

Though we may all agree that the capacity of the Negroes is at present far inferior to that of the White race,—and who would not admit this?—nothing can be deduced from this admission in favour of the assumption, that there exist specific psychical differences among the races of man.

Like our preceding physical investigation, the results of the present inquiry will depend on the solution of the question relating to the greatest differences existing in the various races as regards mental development, and the greatest changes which in this respect take place among the same people.

If we find in the same stock, or in different peoples at different periods, or at the same period in different nations, psychical diversities which equal or approach the generally existing differences, the latter cannot be considered as specific. This also holds good when the differences of individuals, apart of course from morbid phenomena (idiocy, etc.), approach that maximum. The intellectual development of individuals is doubly important for our investigation; partly because the most and the least gifted of every people gauge the limits of its intellectual capacity, and thus furnish us with an indication whether or not we have to do with specific differences; and partly in as far as the most gifted may, under favourable circumstances elevate the people to which they belong, to a higher degree of civilization, and (what is inseparable from it) to a higher degree of mental capacity.

It is easy to see, that for the solution of this question a perfect and special description of the intellectual life, and all its peculiarities of barbarous nations, is requisite, as its affirmation or negation can only be obtained by contrasting their chief features with the most striking performances of civilized nations in their historical development. Reserving the details for the sequel, we will consider here the psychological problem generally.

We may start from the assumption that, as in the life of individuals, so also in that of nations, all cultivation is something secondary, resting upon a gradual progress to a better state than was the primitive or natural state of mankind. This natural state, marked by the absence of all cultivation, we must imagine to have been the original condition of every race; and though we would not designate it as an utterly barbarous and degraded state, we must consider it as a mode of human existence in which all intellectual and moral forces were yet undeveloped. But though we are compelled to proceed from the assumption, that all peoples have passed through a period so absolutely uncultured, that originally they were psychically equal, there yet remains a possible supposition that some—owing to superior predispositions, perhaps in consequence of an innate specific impulse—have more easily, and from slighter external influences, worked their way out of that original state, than other peoples who not only were unable to effect this, but who were also unable to appropriate the elements of foreign civilization.

Keeping the latter point in view, our first task must be to find out the specific characters of man generally, *i.e.*, those which distinguish him from the brute, in order to learn whether or not these characters pertain to all races and individuals. The second question, then, will be, whether within these characters, which constitute the psychical essence of man, there exist permanent differences which compel us to view the races of mankind, not as varieties of one species, but as species of a genus. In attempting a solution of this question, we shall—availing ourselves of existing materials—have to sketch a picture of the natural state of man, which, free from philosophical theories, must be founded on our actual knowledge of mankind. In order finally to arrive at a correct estimation of the differences between the various stocks in mental development, we shall have to take into consideration the circumstances which induce man to leave the natural state; whereby we may learn whether the existing differences in development are the result of specific differences in mental endowment, or the consequence of different surrounding media, mode of life, contact with other nations; in short, of differences of their historical events, or possibly of the combination of both.

SECTION I.

THE SPECIFIC CHARACTERS OF MAN.

We deemed it superfluous, in treating of the physical characters of man, to enter into any details as regards the differences which distinguish man from the brute, as they are too well known. With regard, however, to his psychical life, the differences are not so patent; for even now we meet with authors who, perhaps judging from their own experience, consider that the mental life of the lower races is not superior to that of the ape. The witty saying of Beaumarchais, "*Boire sans soif et faire l'amour en tout temps, c'est ce qui distingue l'homme de la bête,*" has been defended in all seriousness, even by those who, unprejudiced, have merely judged from the impressions produced upon the European by a perfectly uncultivated people. From the various judgments passed on so-called savages, it is no idle question to inquire into the essential differences which separate man from the brute, as these marks of distinction form the common basis for the mental life both of the savage and the civilized man.

It is not sufficient for this object to find a term by which this specific difference can be designated so as to be generally acceptable. Various formulæ of the kind have been given, and we may assent to some without preferring any in particular. When we attribute to man, exclusively, reason or perfectibility, and deny them to animals, the question must be, in what sense we take these significant terms. Moreover, this perfectibility, which is so often described as a general criterion of humanity, is, by some authors, denied to the inferior races; whether rightly or wrongly will be shown by the historical consideration of individual tribes and their mental characteristics. We are thus induced to lay aside general notions, and to keep to particulars. Moreover, it is difficult to doubt that some animals, though they have no history in our sense, possess a certain perfectibility, such as the dog and the horse. There is no doubt that it is not by the spontaneous impulse of these animals, but by the influence of man, that they leave the natural state and reach a higher degree of mental culture. To convince ourselves that these animals are really capable of such a mental improvement, we need only compare the Arabian horse with its wild parent stock. Constantly in intercourse with its master and his family, it is cared for like a member of the family, and, like a near relation, the animal takes an interest in all that concerns the family: it learns to understand human actions and occurrences; and that it sometimes acts spontaneously and seemingly sympathizes with the misfortunes and joys of the family, has been supported by many examples. Can we, then, deny perfectibility to these animals, or doubt that their sphere of thought is capable of enlargement beyond what appears its natural limits?

We must, then, search for more decided differences between man and the brute than such as are designated by the term "perfectibility," and we must look for them in the performances peculiar to mankind. This investigation will, at the same time, teach us the circumstances and relations upon which the character of perfectibility, exclusively attributed to man, rests.

That man learns from experience, is one of the most important but not a specific peculiarity. Common observation of our domestic animals sufficiently shows that they also profit by experience, frequently in a very short time, and the lesson thus acquired lasts for life. Elephants, who have once and decisively experienced the superiority of man, are usually docile afterwards. Wild horses, caught with the lasso, use every effort to set themselves free, but once tamed they prove docile for ever. Monkeys who have once burned their lips in swallowing hot liquids, afterwards wait with patience until they are cooled;[1] but this profiting of former experiences does not seemingly pass beyond a certain point. Thus monkeys are frequently caught by means of pots placed into the earth, filled with maize, through the narrow neck of which they are able to introduce the empty hand, but unable to withdraw it

---

[1] Bennet, "Wanderings in New South Wales," ii, p. 158, 1834.

when filled. Now, though we would not deny that the uncivilized man, overcome in a similar manner by sensual desire, does not reap all the fruit of his experience; still, it would be difficult to catch men in so simple a manner as are the monkeys.

We must not, however, estimate too lightly what animals really learn from experience. The mysterious word "instinct" conceals, in the psychical life of animals, more intellectuality and less mechanism than is usually assumed. We would adduce as a proof the important fact, that the known phenomena which we are accustomed to ascribe to an instinctive fear of man, are probably the result of experience,—be it from a tradition unknown to us,—from a kind of instruction given by the parents to the young, or that later generations have by nature become more cautious and shy, whilst their progenitors became so by experience. We are led to this view by the conduct of animals in countries which were never inhabited by man. All kinds of birds, says, Darwin,[1] not excluding birds of prey, are, on the Galapagos islands, perfectly tame,—all may be approached so near as to be struck or caught. According to Cowley and Dampier (1684), they seem formerly to have been still more confiding. Even on the Falkland islands, where there are falcons and foxes, the same observation has been made. It is, however, different as regards birds of passage, who have acquired experience in other countries. On Possession Island (Victoria Land), the penguins appeared inclined to obstruct the progress of the crew of Capt. Ross.[2] In Kordofan, the birds are less shy if the sportsman appears in a dress different from that worn in the country.[3]

On comparing man with the brute in this respect, the teachings which he derives from experience, are not only more comprehensive, but they exercise a deeper influence on the whole formation of his external and inner life, and enable him to occupy a dominating position even in the lowest state of civilization. Just as the civilized man conquers the savage,

---

[1] "Naturalists' Voyage," chap. xvii.

[2] "Voyage in the Southern and Antarctic regions," i, p. 189, 1847.

[3] Pallme, "Beschr. v. Kordofan," p. 153, 1843.

so does the latter overpower the brute, not so much by physical as by mental force. He uses their instincts in a variety of modes to deceive them, imitates their sounds, catches them by baits, and hunts each species according to its peculiar habits.

As this accommodation to circumstances and their skilful use shows, even in the most savage nations, a decided superiority above the brute creation, so it is not less exhibited in the subjection of nature to human objects. Protection against the influences of the climate by dress and habitation, manufacture of tools, and instruments for fishing, hunting, etc., the preparation of food, are found among every people on the globe; in all which we find a far greater use of experience than is found in the most gifted animal. What has formerly been related of the natives of the Marian Islands, namely, that they were unable to light a fire, has been proved to be fabulous. At Fakaafo only (Union Islands, north of the Samoa Archipelago), where the inhabitants live entirely on cocoa-nuts and pandanus, no trace of cooking or firing has been found,[1] but they seem scarcely to have any use for it.

Next to the teachings of experience, must be mentioned the important privilege of the designating or representing faculty by which man gives fixity to and regulates his thoughts, and exchanges them with others. Whilst animals possess but imperfect means of communication, and consequently every individual leads, if not externally yet internally, an isolated life, we see man in every stage of his development constantly endeavouring to give expression to his emotions by sensible images and sounds. In this kind of activity, as Schleiermacher observed, is manifested an essentially human peculiarity. Originally he finds a certain relief by giving audible and visible expression to his feelings. This is not the place to enter into any particulars as regards the origin of language; all that we here require is, to point out the possession of language, and its use as a specific human peculiarity.

It is now generally admitted, that even the most barbarous

[1] Wilkes's "Narrative of United States' Expedition," v, p. 18, 1845.

nations possess a language with a more or less regular grammatical structure. Though it be more than probable that animals possess some means of intercommunication, their performances in this respect have only a very distant resemblance to language. Nature has limited most of them to the production of but few sounds and gestures.

Deficient in ideas, animals can only give expression as regards their concrete condition. Human language presupposes not merely definite individual conceptions of separate qualities, but of their relations to each other, so to say, an articulation of ideas by which alone a designation by grammatical forms becomes possible. However low a language may be in its development, it could neither express thoughts nor render them intelligible, if in the ideal world of the speaker, as well as in that of the listener, such a regulation of thought did not exist; and this is one of the proofs that the psychical condition of man, however uncultivated he may be, is specifically different from that of the brute. But inasmuch as the possession of a language of regular grammatical structure forms a fixed barrier between man and the brute, it establishes at the same time a near relationship between all peoples in psychical respects, agreeing as they do in the most essential peculiarity of intellectual life, namely, in the power of arranging the relations of substantive separate ideas so as to give them a definite oral expression. In the presence of this common feature of the human mind, all other differences lose their importance, and make us more inclined to consider them as merely differences in degree; the more so as there are peoples who, despite their mental degradation, possess a language by no means undeveloped as regards grammatical structure. We agree, therefore, with Pott,[1] "If theology feared that an original difference of language, which linguists assume, would involve the original unity of the human species (which by no means follows), the science of language restores to theology the psychical unity of mankind, compared with which the physical unity must yield in importance."

---

[1] "Von der Ungleichh. menschl. Rassen," p. 243.

This is amply proved by the reports on the mental qualities of uncivilized nations, furnished by a great variety of travellers. Everywhere we find essentially the same type of intellectual activity: the same motives for action, the same mental emotions, the same passions, the same mode of irritation, association, etc., are observed in the savage as in the civilized European, without any distinction of race; and as soon as we can appreciate the motive for action, we find, even in the most ape-like Negro, a homogeneous human nature.

There is much in the inner life of animals which will, perhaps, ever remain unintelligible to us. What may be their motives for action, what determines their conceptions and associations of ideas, especially their mechanical instinct, is scarcely known to us, for it is very doubtful whether the instinct which impels them rests upon some obscure conceptions or upon something specific. But in the presence of human beings we are never in the same dilemma. However great the difference between their mental culture and ours, we may, if time and opportunity are favourable, learn to understand all their actions, and we are thus justified in assuming in the human species, only differences in culture.

Next to speech must be mentioned some other specific differences which distinguish man from the brute, namely, the use of a number of external signs expressive of the relations in which persons permanently or temporarily stand to each other; salutation; the signs of veneration or contempt, of peace and friendship, or the reverse; of agreement or disagreement, etc. Further, the distinctive marks of rank in clothing, head-dress, ornament, and other marks on the body. Thus, a shorn head frequently marks the slave in Africa; an artificially compressed head, in America, distinguishes the free man; scars of certain forms, and in certain spots, generally distinguish the tribes among Negro peoples. The tattooed figures in the South Sea seem originally to have had the same object in view.

Another comprehensive class of marks deserves mentioning, such as ornamentation of external life, having little reference to the material well-being. This is found even among the rudest nations, and is really specifically human. However poor and miserable, man finds a pleasure in adorning himself. He adorns his person, his instruments, etc., with the greatest industry, and even supports, as in tattooing, great physical pain for this object. What impels him is simply the pleasure to be beautiful in his own eyes and to be admired by others, and so he bepaints and bedecks himself, and all that belongs to him. Variegated colours and their grotesque combination, musical sounds and their variations, are agreeable to him; he finds a certain satisfaction in depicting by lines and colours what has interested him; he constructs musical instruments, and thus he beautifies his life, the mere attempt of which raises him, on account of the intellectual basis upon which it rests, far above the scale occupied by the most gifted animals.

A third chief peculiarity of man must be mentioned,—his social character, with which his capacity of speaking stands in intimate relation. Aristotle called him, on account of this character, not a gregarious, but a political being. Men associate together, not merely under the guidance of an individual, as is the case with many animals, but their association in tribes and families is more consistent. The individuals are not so isolated as animals belonging to the same flock; but the exchange of thought by language leads them to more intimate relations between each other,—to greater sympathy. True, not everywhere do human beings, living together, form a state, the nature of the country and the dispersion of the population frequently prevent this, as in Australia; but nowhere are peculiar social customs absent, whilst the habits of gregarious animals seem to be everywhere the same: everywhere we find practical ideas of property and right. The small value attached to property by savage nations, must not induce us to think that they know nothing of property. Common property of a tribe or family is acknowledged everywhere, where peoples come in contact: property in the soil, which a stranger must not enter without the permission of the proprietor, seems to be sometimes more fixed among savage nations than we are inclined to believe. Private property is nowhere wanting when individuals may have to dispute the possession of any goods; but such disputes exist everywhere.

The ethical importance of private property is founded upon this, that it enlarges the sphere of activity in the individual, and secures his future. This enlargement of his sphere only becomes important to man, because he looks into the future, and wishes to protect himself against possible future evils. Property can thus only belong to those who do not, like animals, live merely in the present, but who look forward into the future. In order that property should be respected, it must be distinguishable. Again, in order that it should fulfil its object, property must be transferable, which is only possible if the will to transfer and that of accepting it can be communicated by intelligible signs. But all these presuppositions, which constitute the essence of property, prove again the unsurmountable barrier which separates the rudest nation from animals.

Though all peoples do not possess a regular commonwealth, they nevertheless form a society in which there are certain gradations, which ultimately develop themselves into a distinction of ranks. Human society everywhere has some common interest in opposition to the private interests of the individuals composing it. A common external enemy, or a common misfortune by natural agencies, would suffice to call forth such a common interest. One or more individuals acquire authority, and are either feared or respected. Such relations are wanting in no human society, and have but a distant resemblance to the rivalry shown among some animals, and to the influence which leaders of the gregarious animals acquire.

Among the social peculiarities, there is also to be mentioned a specific feature, the attachment to his country, family, and people, owing partly to the personal relations of individuals. This attachment does not exist in animals, deficient as they are in individualization: an animal can easily be separated from one flock and attached to another; whilst for man, however uncivilized he may be, such a separation from a locality,—where by language, personal intercourse, and a thousand habits his being has taken root,—is always painful, making him feel that for his happiness he requires not merely human society in general, but some definite individuals by whom he is understood. It is the great misery to which the Negro is exposed which renders it possible that he nearly forgets this human desire, rejoicing merely in a sensual existence, and finding his happiness in eating and drinking, idling and sleeping. But such facts as these, which can only be explained by an entire perversion of the natural human relations, by no means prove that the character of humanity is absent in the Negro. It is chiefly language which separates and unites mankind, by impressing the national character upon the individual, and the peculiar mode of thinking and feeling belonging to his stock, drawing thus closer the bonds which unite the individuals as a whole. The power of public opinion, to which also the uncivilized man is subject, shows how sensible he is to the applause or censure of his fellow-men.

We have now considered the specific psychical activity of man in three directions:—in availing himself of surrounding natural phenomena for his own objects, profiting largely by experience; in giving outward expression to his internal feelings either by language or other visible signs; in his social relations with their concomitant rights and property, leading to certain gradations in society, and to a closer attachment to his own people. Though we find here the elements from which science, art, and morality gradually arise; there is yet another principle, leading to a higher spiritual development, namely, the religious element. This is nowhere entirely wanting; and though it may manifest itself in the crudest form, its influence can be traced in the history of every people.

It has been asserted, that there are peoples among whom there is not a vestige of religion; and, on the other hand, that all known peoples have their gods. A strict investigation has established that the first assertion is false, and the second not true. All depends on what is meant by religion and religious worship, otherwise the contest about the universality of this principle is merely a play upon words. Though it may be admitted, as indeed it is the truth, that there are some savages among whom hitherto religious ideas—taken in a restricted sense, a belief in divine beings—have not been found, it must be noticed, that they are generally those peoples of whom our knowledge is very scanty, and that on becoming better acquainted with them, religious sentiments have been detected, as is sufficiently indicated by certain superstitious ceremonies. We would here only mention a few such instances. It has been asserted, that the inhabitants of the Arru Islands neither believed in God nor a future life;[1] yet they possess carved images of men and beasts, who protect their habitations from evil spirits.[2] The Dajaks, on the Lundu river, in the north-east of Borneo, have neither priests, nor temples, nor images; still, they have omens and augurs,[3] and traces of old Hindoo worship have also been found among them. Neither images nor any religious worship have been met with in New Caledonia;[4] still, the natives have their tabus, magic, and magicians. Thus, Anderssen[5] could find nothing approaching religious worship among the Ovambos; yet, he observes, very justly, that on nearer acquaintance we shall find that they, too, have some idea, though a very crude one, of an invisible power.

It is certain that all peoples do not believe in a God who directs everything in the world; but if by religious belief be understood the conviction of the existence of invisible mysterious powers which, in various modes, influence the phenomena of nature, so that man and his fate is dependent on their favour, we may safely assert, that every people possesess a kind of religion. No doubt, in peoples standing in the lowest scale of civilization, this religion is merely a belief in spectres, still, the religious element is recognizable. Moral ideas appear not originally allied with these religious views. Thus, we find that the Kamtschadales consider only the transgression of their superstitious customs as sin; to pierce coal with a knife, to scrape off the snow from the shoes, etc., they consider as

---

[1] Cooke Taylor, "Natural History of Soc.," i, p. 167, 1840.

[2] Kolff, "Voyage of the Brig Dourga," translated by W. Earl, p. 159, 1840.

[3] Brooke, "Narrative of events in Borneo and Celebes," i, p. 23, 2nd ed., 1848; Journ. R. G. S., xxiii, p. 78.

[4] Lascazas, in "Nouv. ann. des Voy.," i, p. 332, 1855.

[5] "Reisen in Südwest Afrika, Deutch," von Lotze, i, p. 214, 1858.

very wrong, and attribute to it diseases, whilst the coarsest vices appear to them venial. Moral ideas flow from an essentially different source than religion, but both are associated when man reaches a higher degree of civilization. We must also consider as erroneous, the opinion that morality and religion have grown out from a common root, namely, conscience.

Though man may be considered as the lord of the creation, his dominion is by no means a secure one; the less so the lower he stands in psychical development: his wishes and aims are not fulfilled, his plans are frustrated, misery and want overtake him. Whose fault is this? who effects it? These are the questions which occur both to the savage and the civilized man. The first answer which man returns to his own questions is generally to the following effect:—There is an inimical power which *wills* my misfortune,—a wicked being which, with invisible power, leads me to destruction. The belief in spirits is extended to all nature, the course of which, though apparently uniform and regular, still appears to the uncivilized man as incalculable. Man sees in the natural sensible phenomena something more than material forces; he sees in them supernatural powers and a supernatural connexion,—he spiritualizes nature. We find all uncultured peoples in this condition; and though they may be deficient in definite ideas of a God and fixed forms of worship, the religious element, so far from being absent, influences their whole conception of nature.

Temples are not everywhere erected to higher powers, nor images nor sacrifices made; but, in great need, invocations of such powers, and attempts to appease their wrath or malice are nowhere wanting. Their habitations are usually imagined to be on high mountains, or in inaccessible places. Dreams, uncommon occurrences, disease, and even natural death, are ascribed to the influence of spirits. The fear of the dead, and the honour shown to them, among all uncultured nations, are partly connected with the belief that the departed souls return to the earth, and like other spirits, reappear in an animal form to plague the living. This is essentially the essence of the religious ideas which we found developed with remarkable uniformity among savage peoples.

In recapitulating the sum of specific human peculiarities, we find that the general question, as regards the psychological basis upon which the differences between man and the animal rest, consists of a series of special questions, as follows: How does it come to pass, that man gains so much more from experience than the brute? that he is capable of giving expression to his ideas? that he has the sense of beauty? that he looks into and cares for the future? and that, finally, he believes that there is a spiritual world beneath the material world?

The last of these questions is the most easily answered. As man has wishes, pursues certain objects, and recognizes that he has a will which regulates his actions, he attributes all this to external nature, whenever he is hindered by it in the attainment of his objects. He can only conceive the course of nature from the analogy to his own actions; so that all natural phenomena whose powers he experiences, are considered by him as acting and willing beings. With regard to the specific peculiarity, that man looks into and cares for the future, it may be observed, that the faculty is altogether empirical, for all expectation of what is to come depends on the recollection in what order and sequence events occurred in the past.

To what extent an individual is capable of profiting by experience, chiefly depends on the correctness with which he has conceived past phenomena, and the mode in which he compares them with present circumstances. Particular circumstances may contribute to present the past to us in a more or less vivid light, but the essential conditions always remain,—the mode and the strength of the original conception. We must therefore assume that there is an original difference between man and the brutes in the mode of conception, and consequent recollection of external phenomena.

We must here point out that the natural requirements of man for the preservation of his life and protection against the elements, are more various and more difficult to be procured, and require greater mental efforts than those of animals, and that consequently he is driven to thousands of expedients by which he is both taught and psychically developed. By his upright walk, nature seems to have destined him to take a comprehensive view of surrounding objects; whilst the possession of "the instrument of instruments," as Aristotle calls the human hand, equally indicates his capacity for a higher mental development.[1] All these are, no doubt, important attendant circumstances, contributing in a high degree to the preservation of man's capacity to learn from experience, as compared with that of brutes; but these are merely subordinate, not fundamental conditions. Little would it avail man that his wants are more multifarious than those of brutes, that nature grants him less, that he must use his own exertions, and that his necessities stimulate him to use his senses and his natural instruments, if he were not enabled to do so by his greater powers of perception and recollection of individual phenomena and their relations.

That there exists in this respect a very great difference between man and the brute, is established by many facts. When in a state of liberty, animals appropriate only clear conceptions of the few things relating to their food and mode of life. Everything else passes by them unnoticed, though they possess equally acute, and in some respects stronger, senses. But all their senses are not developed in an equal degree; thus the sense of smell is more developed, the selection of their food being chiefly dependent on its exercise. Man, on the other hand, requires all his senses for the satisfying of his wants; hence, not one of them acquires such a predominance as we see in most animals. If to this development of all the senses be added, a better memory for received impressions, a larger basis for a higher psychical development becomes manifest. Having thus disposed of one great distinctive feature between man and the brute, as regards his capacity to profit by experience, we shall now investigate two other specific characters,—individualization, and the power of speech.

---

[1] Buffon maintains, that the greater intellect of some men, in comparison with others, may be explained from the more extended use of the hands made by the former in early childhood.

With regard to the power of speech, we have already indicated that its essential psychological condition—of which alone we treat in this place[1]—consists in the possession of an articulated ideal world, of such a nature, that single conceptions corresponding with relatively substantive objects, are kept separate, whilst their constantly changing relations to each other are clearly distinguished by us. But the fulfilment of this condition depends again on the original mode of conception of things, and on the degree of distinctness with which what has been conceived is again reproduced. If the perception is imperfect and one-sided, the conceptions, which can only reproduce the perceptions, are equally so; and this is the reason why animals are incapable of speech. They are not deficient in the conception of individual things relating to their vital necessities, but these are comparatively few in number; all other impressions of the senses produce only a confused aggregate, and the distinction of the relation of individual impressions cannot be accomplished. In man, all senses are equally called upon to receive impressions from the external world; he thus acquires separate conceptions of separate objects, and their relations to each other, by which speech becomes possible.

On the same conditions, but more intimately, depends the more distinctive individuality by which man is separated from the brute. Speech, and the personal relations induced by it, influence the individualization of characters. It is by means of language that individuals enter into various and more intimate relations to each other; the experiences which they gather in their intercourse give a particular impress to each individual, varying according to the variety of his connexion with other individuals who have contributed to its development. We have already had occasion to observe, that the language of a people testifies to the degree of civilization, and that its grammatical structure decisively influences the psychical peculiarity; it separates the national characters of peoples, and frequently acts upon the development of individuals.

[1] It is scarcely necessary to observe, that we do not explain here the origin of language, but merely the psychological condition for its possibility.

This enlarged individualization within the human species, rests upon a richer vital development, founded upon a peculiar conception of the results of experience.

There is only one specific peculiarity mentioned by us which cannot apparently be traced to the same foundation; namely, the sense of the beautiful, so that man does not remain satisfied with merely providing for his physical wants, but ornaments his body, and what belongs to him in various ways. It may be that such attempts are not made where an individual lives in perfect isolation, that they are founded on vanity and desire of distinction above others; still, the problem is not solved by it. The impression produced on the mind by music belongs to this, like other sensual perceptions which do not merely supply vital necessaries. The agreeable sensations and pleasurable feelings of which animals are capable, seem to be much less various, and almost exclusively confined to the gratification of the lower senses (smell and taste). We are not far wrong, if we consider this limitation to the gratification of the lower senses as one of the chief causes of the psychical inferiority of animals.

When we consider how decisive, for the mode of our conceptions of things and their remembrance, is the interest we take in a particular object, and how this interest determines the degree of intensity and direction of our attention, we must feel inclined to trace back the differences existing between man and animals, in their original modes of conception and the strength of memory, to an original difference in the interest taken by different creatures. The interest in an object is proportional to the pleasurable feeling experienced or expected from it. In man, there are many perceptions of the higher senses allied to such pleasurable feelings, which induce him to pay greater attention to their development and impressions; whilst the pleasurable feelings of animals, being chiefly limited to the gratification of the lower senses, induces a defective appreciation of things, and prevents a higher intellectual development. We shall not attempt here to decide the difficult fundamental psychological question, whether the original mode of conception decides the form of psychological life; as the differences between man and brute only concern us in this place, it may be sufficient to have shown that essential differences do exist, which influence the progressive elevation of the former, and the stationary condition of the latter.

SECTION II.

PRIMITIVE STATE OF MAN (NATURAL STATE).

We have examined the specific characters of humanity, and traced them to their psychological basis. But though it has been shown that its essential characters belong, without exception, to all races, it has been left undecided whether there may not be special peculiarities which must be regarded as specific differences between various subdivisions of mankind.

This question has been but superficially considered by opposing parties. On one side we hear the uncivilized nations of Africa, America, Australia, etc., designated by the stereotyped expression, "irreclaimable savages"; and on the other hand, the unity of mankind and the origin from a single pair, is deduced from the fact, that all nations possess languages of a certain grammatical structure, that all possess similar notions of supersensual things, and religious sentiments. There is no doubt that these great psychological facts deserve the utmost consideration, and are undervalued by the opponents of the theory of the unity of mankind. We agree, therefore, with Smyth in maintaining[1] that these psychological facts are as much opposed to the assumption of specific differences, as the physical phenomena which are adduced are in favour of that assumption. But in all this the doubt yet remains, whether, within the chief characters, there may not be permanent differences which may compel us to divide mankind into various species.

To solve this question, we shall pursue the same path we have hitherto followed: we shall examine the greatest differences in

---

[1] "The Unity of the Human Races," p. 249, 1850.

the psychical phenomena of mankind. To attain this object, we must first of all direct our attention to the primitive or natural state of man from two points of view: first, whether we find man, at least approximately, in a natural condition, and in what condition we find him.

As all civilization is something secondary, and is only developed in course of time, it is clear that the natural (uncivilized) man must, wherever we find him and whatever may be his qualifications, appear so dissimilar to us as regards his psychical life, as to lead us to assume between him and ourselves specific differences which do not exist. Again, we find so great a difference in mental development between the civilized Europeans and the so-called savages of other parts, that we are inclined to attribute it to a radical natural difference. The question is, whether we are justified in coming to that conclusion, or whether the greatest actual differences in the development of psychical life are only the result of a *fluctuating* difference in culture.

The period when man first appeared on this globe, and was in his actual primitive or natural state, cannot be determined. For many reasons it is highly probable that a very long period of time must have elapsed before the commencement of the historical epoch. Some chronological calculations have been deduced from geological data. The period which has elapsed between the present time and that of the coal formation, has, from the progressive cooling of the mean temperature of the earth, been calculated from 5-9,000,000 of years. From the recession of the falls of Niagara (annually from one to two feet), Lyell concludes that the formation of the valley of that river, which is more recent than the diluvial formation, reaches at least 35,000 years back. Though it cannot be proved that the age of man extends beyond the diluvial formation, there is still less reason to consider him younger, as at the diluvial period all essential conditions for the existence of man were present, and since that period no considerable changes have occurred on the surface of the globe. It seems, therefore, that we may imagine the age of mankind to reach somewhere between the rather remote limits of 35,000 and 9,000,000 of years.

There is another circumstance, namely, that man has nowhere been found in an actual primitive state. Everywhere we find him in possession of some artificial instruments, generally of war, a minimum of clothing, etc. But in all these things, as well as in their mode of life, savage tribes have been found so stationary, that they have been considered incapable of progress, and yet the progress they have actually made from a primitive state is already considerable; for it is just these primary inventions, seemingly nowhere absent, which are the most difficult, and require a long time before they are accomplished. To those especially, who assume that mankind spread gradually from a certain spot over the whole globe, the period requisite for such a purpose must appear a very long one indeed; for we never see nations voluntarily leave their dwelling places, unless pressed upon by natural phenomena or enemies. Almost all migrations proceed very slowly; and hence in all parts of the earth, the peoples who had occupied the land from time immemorial, looked upon themselves as natives of the soil they inhabit. Among the oldest civilized nations known to us, the Egyptians for instance, their inventions date from a period for which history furnishes us with no chronological standard. More than inventions and migrations, languages, and the physical peculiarities of the various races, indicate the great antiquity of mankind. It is exceedingly improbable that a language of a complicated structure should have issued from the mouth of man when he first appeared; it approaches to a psychological impossibility. The slowness with which a child learns to speak is a proof of it, and yet the child has nothing to invent, but only to appropriate. Children learn the grammatical forms very gradually; these forms cannot have been produced at once, for that which is expressed by them, the relations of individual conceptions, cannot have at once been present to man. From the unconscious or involuntary basis upon which language no doubt rests, we must conclude that it was not constructed in a short time or sprung into life at once. We should further take into consideration the great lapse of time which the branching off and substantive development of individual languages derived from the same stock, must have required. The break up of an original into several filial languages may in some cases have proceeded more or less rapidly; but from the circumstance that the mass of radically different languages is so large compared with the probable original cradles and stocks of mankind, we are justified in assuming the age of mankind upon the globe to reach back for a long series of thousands of years, especially when we consider that language is only propagated by tradition from generation to generation, and that it is seldom that great changes in a language are produced within a short lapse of time. What has just been stated in regard to language applies also to physical types, which everywhere exhibit a high degree of fixity, and are at any rate only changeable within long periods. Whether we derive the intermediate gradations between the extreme types from long continued climatic or other influences, or from intermixture of originally and essentially different types, everything points to a past period which cannot be measured by our historical standard.

There is, then, no hope of finding man anywhere in an actual primitive or natural state. Whence, then, are we to derive our notions of such a state? To this question three answers may be given, which we shall have to examine separately. What man is by nature must be exhibited by the human child, which proceeds immediately from nature; we must, then, empirically study the so-called savages, whose state, though not absolutely primitive, more or less approaches it.

There is much to be said against judging of the primitive condition of man from the condition of infancy. Infancy is a rapidly passing stage of development of the individual, with which we may, perhaps, compare the youthful state of mankind, but cannot exactly parallelize it. Deficiency of experience and of mental development are common to both, but in this there prevail so many differences, that for our object very little can be inferred. We need only be reminded that the primitive man neither possesses the undeveloped physical organization of the child, which renders the latter so helpless, nor is he, like the child, led to a higher development by example and imitation. Moreover, the child is already born with the peculiarities belonging to his stock, and possesses, as we have already seen, at the beginning of his life, certain physical and psychical characters hereditarily acquired, which prevent us from considering him as the representative of a primitive state. From this it would appear, that not only cannot we take infancy as the standard of the primitive condition of mankind, but that the latter can nowhere be found; and it is folly to search for its characters, partly because man at all times must have learned from tradition through his parents, without which supposition we cannot think of him, and also because he must everywhere have exhibited the typical character of his stock, and not merely the general peculiarities of humanity.

The discussion of this point becomes difficult as we find ourselves on the limits of our experimental knowledge. Since we cannot obtain from science any clue as to the origin of man, it must remain undecided whether there ever have been men who have grown up without any traditional instruction from others, and whether they have not at all times possessed, besides the general characters of humanity, also certain separate peculiarities of stock. But all these doubts are, for our question, only of subordinate interest. We might even admit that the "natural man" is a mere fiction, and has never anywhere existed in reality, like a circle or an ellipse in a geometrical sense, and which, like all abstract notions, possess an individual existence, without at all impairing their value in a scientific investigation. We wish here to obtain a clear idea how we must think of man as he was before, and independent of, all cultivation, and it is for this object quite indifferent whether there have ever been individuals perfectly corresponding to that state which we term the natural state. That man at his first appearance upon the earth, and immediately after it, must have approximated to that state seems pretty evident from the absence of cultivation, which we were obliged to assume.

From what has been stated, it is clear that this primitive state is neither represented in children, nor in those individuals who, born of civilized parents, have grown up in an isolated state in forests, and have been found again in an adult age. Such persons have formerly been described as real natural men, though there is no doubt that they were only degenerated.

What man is when divested of all cultivation, is a question which has been frequently asked and differently answered. It is difficult to realize this abstraction, but much easier to convince ourselves that it does not lead to an idea of a paradisiacal state of innocence and bliss, the result of uncorrupted human nature founded upon a happy harmony of slender knowledge, few desires, and the absence of all passions. There is no doubt the natural man does not possess the refined concealed vices of a corrupt society, from the sight of which Rousseau's sickly imagination shrunk, and caused him to indulge in a dream of the original goodness and purity of mankind; but what he certainly does possess are the ugly features of external and internal crudity, the necessary attendants on an entire absence of intellectual and moral culture.

On imagining man deprived of everything which is the effect of cultivation, he represents merely the product of the power which called him into life, resembling an individual of perfectly neglected education, upon whom experience, instruction, or example have exercised no influence, and who consequently is inclined neither to good nor evil, having not yet learned to distinguish between them. The first thing which would strike us as characteristic, would be his perfect dependence on surrounding media, his whole inner life would be their product. The primitive man first becomes that which the circumstances in which he is placed make of him. The aliment afforded him by nature, the mode by which he can obtain it, the protection he requires against external agents, the inventions requisite to supply his wants,—all are taught by nature which surrounds him, and which thus determines his mode of life. The instruments he makes, the skill he acquires, the magnitude of the efforts requisite to attain his objects, and the degree of development of his psychical activity, will at the outset mainly depend on the external media in which he is placed. No sooner, however, has he supplied his pressing necessities, than his physical and mental efforts cease.

This latter circumstance is a highly important point, exhibiting a chief feature in the character of the uncultured man —his remarkable indolence. The cause is not exactly that, in the natural state, man is forced to make great efforts to support himself, so that rest affords great enjoyment. The true cause we apprehend to be that man by nature shuns every kind of labour; that he undertakes none which is not absolutely requisite for his well being. Though his indolence may have brought him to want, notwithstanding his experience may have enabled him to foresee his fate, he concerns himself little about the future, but he hopes for the best. Indolence and thoughtlessness, in an incredible degree, are characteristic of perfectly uneducated human beings, and it requires but little knowledge of the lower classes, even in Europe, to perceive that indolence is enjoyment to man in the natural state, and not merely in consequence of moral degeneracy. If we could for a short time remove the motives of vanity and ambition from the civilized world, even he who has the most lofty ideas of human nature, would soon find that indolence is the ideal of most people.

It is nothing but poetical fancy which endows the primitive man with a desire for intellectual progress; the habit of indolence induces him to remain in his actual condition. He never from internal impulse and without any external agency, desires to become civilized, just as the lower classes in Europe abandoned to themselves desire nothing of the kind so long as their material interests are not suffering; and yet they have before their eyes the results of a higher civilization: hence the comparatively slow progress of humanity. "The world would look quite different," observed Hume, "if man possessed by nature a little more love for useful activity; for his indolence seems to keep him fixed for a long time at every stage of his development."

Peyroux de la Coudrenière[1] appears to have been the first to promulgate the theory that the white race alone is psychically active, and possesses by nature that peculiar desire of knowledge which Aristotle ascribed to man generally, and that consequently all higher culture of other races can

[1] "Mém. sur les sept espèces d'Hommes," Paris, 1814.

only be explained by its being communicated to them by the white race. He found many disciples, among whom, in Germany, we would mention Klemm[1] and Wuttke,[2] who assume permanent differences between active and passive human races.[3] A closer examination of the peculiarities of mankind renders such a division very doubtful.

However much we may be inclined, at the first glance, to lament that man in a state of nature exhibits at every stage such inertness and disinclination for progress, our judgment undergoes a material change on a closer investigation. It is just in proportion as the higher desires are absent, that the gratification of the lower propensities becomes possible, and the simplicity and small extent of the conditions upon which the contentment of man in a primitive state depends, render his life enjoyable. His inner life, it is true, moves in a very limited circle; but it is undisturbed by that feverish desire for an improvement of his condition which torments the more developed man. The inner contest in man arises chiefly from his desire after a higher development; it only becomes possible with the growth of higher desires which are not easily satisfied. Thus far it is true to designate the progress to civilization as the source of mental distress; but we must not conclude from it that the natural state of man is the ideal of Paradise, the loss of which we have to lament; for it is only in proportion as man is removed from the primitive state that his physical, intellectual, and moral development is accomplished.

Besides these two chief characters of the primitive man,—his perfect dependence on external media, and his indolence,—there is another feature, the licentiousness of his egotistical desires, and the absence of steadiness and plan in all his actions. Restraint and self-control are nowhere engrafted upon man by nature; they must be learned, and are but slowly acquired. This is shown in the intercourse with others, even as we see it in children and persons brought up

---

1 "Allge. Culturgesch."

2 "Gesch. des Heidenthums."

3 In a similar sense, Carus distinguishes night, day, and dawn men (Negroes, Europeans, Mongols, and Americans).

without any control. Endeavouring to subject others whenever they come in conflict with his own interest, every individual leads originally an isolated life. However repulsive these characteristic features of the primitive man may be, they are not manifestations of malignity, but as in the child and the perfectly uneducated the result of capricious desires. The absence of steadiness in the pursuit of a certain object, the action from sudden impulses, render the uncultivated savage unintelligible to the civilized man, so that he judges him in a variety of ways.

If the correctness of the preceding characteristic of the primitive man be admitted, then we are justified in designating the majority of the uncultivated nations of the globe as primitive peoples (*Naturvölker*—peoples in a state of nature), because though not exactly in a primitive or natural state, they still occupy a scale of development which pretty nearly approaches it; for all the peculiarities which we attributed to the primitive man are found among them, and all agree in this respect. To consider, on the other hand, all uncultivated nations as degenerate, as fallen from a previous elevation, would be to assume that culture was the primitive, and barbarism the secondary state of man.

We shall now compare the more prominent empirical information we possess of uncultivated nations, in order to see whether our characteristics of the natural state of man be correct.

The inhabitant of the north does not emigrate to the south to improve his condition, nor does the inhabitant of the south desire to exchange his climate for a more favourable one. In spite of the many diseases to which, for instance, the inhabitants of Darfur are subject, they love their country, have no wish to emigrate, but desire to return when they have left it.[1] It is reasonable to suppose that this attachment to their native country, even among nomadic nations, may partly arise from their ignorance that there are finer climates, more abounding in natural products. This is not always the case. With

---

[1] Mohammed-el-Tounsy, "Voy. au Darfour," p. 296, Paris, 1845.

all the misery a people may endure, it generally considers its own country as the best in the world, and its manners and customs as the most preferable. Cavazzi[1] gives a graphic description of the Congo-negroes, who, after having emigrated, return like the Kru-negroes to their native country, there to enjoy what they may have acquired. This sentiment seems general among negro nations; and especially in such parts of America as are visited by Europeans, the natives have the firm belief that the Whites have only left their homes in search for happier climates. We are, indeed, told of an Abiponian who worked hard for his passage to Buenos Ayres in order to gratify his desire of seeing the world.[2] Du Pratz[3] also speaks of a native whom a similar desire drove into the world; but such cases form rare exceptions. From the inhabitant of Tierra del Fuego to the Hottentot, man in the natural state remains content with his lot though living in the greatest misery, while it is difficult to find among the civilized nations of Europe one people which is similarly contented. Hence the following expression of an experienced man becomes intelligible: "There are positions in which a thinking man feels himself inferior to a child of nature, in which he begins to doubt whether his firm convictions are little better than high sounding prejudices."[4] This at any rate is certain, that every race, as Strzelecki observes,[5] has its own ideas of happiness: the restless striving of the civilized man appears to the uncultivated man as childish, whilst the enjoyment of an apathetic rest—the ideal of the latter—would be extremely irksome to the former.

The principal motives for action among uncultivated nations may be reduced to three: physical well-being, chiefly directed to the gratification of the appetites, sexual enjoyment, and indolence, in consequence of a reluctance to every kind of labour; social enjoyment, effected partly by subjecting the members of family to the will of one man, and partly by obtaining greater power over others; and, thirdly, habit, the power of which

[1] "Beschr. v. Congo, Matamba, und Angola," p. 76, 1694.
[2] J. P. and W. P. Robertson, "Letters on South America," iii, p. 186, 1843.
[3] "Hist. de la Louisiane," 1758.
[4] Cowper Rose, "Four Years in Southern Africa," p. 173, 1829.
[5] "Description of New South Wales," p. 343.

influences all actions, and to a great extent perpetuates physical and moral misery. Some are inclined to add a fourth motive which actuates the uncultivated man—the superstition peculiar to an eudæmonistic religion; but this group of efficient motives belongs to the first class; for it is clear that his physical well-being alone influences his religious ideas, and secures their power over him.

The external life of uncultivated nations does not admit of a description common to all, being different according to the different circumstances producing it. Some of them are hunters, others fishers, root diggers, berry collectors, or they carry on these occupations alternately according to the seasons. Dress, habitation, domestic furniture, arms, and the arts which they exercise, all depend on their modes of life; but with regard to their inner life, we find among them everywhere a remarkable uniformity. There have been frequently assumed, says Hugh Murray,[1] far greater diversities in the degrees of cultivation among uncivilized nations than really exist; permanent differences have been described which are unimportant, or do not exist at all.

The individual character among uncivilized nations is not so decided as among the cultivated. Want of self-control, improvidence, intemperance, indolence combined with perseverance in the pursuit after actual necessaries, and ornamentation of the person, are general characters.

Gluttony, drunkenness, and sexual excesses, are the most generally spread vices. Next to licentious festivities, savage passion is displayed in the chase. When there is abundance of game, the hunter exhibits, like a soldier in battle, the greatest rage; he finds delight in killing and destroying the game indiscriminately and uselessly. Hence hunting tribes require a great space, and are frequently in want, as they do not economize their provisions. The hundredth part of the game killed by the Zulus, observes Delegorgue,[2] would have been more than sufficient for him and all his companions. There are peoples who suffer annu-

1 "Enquiries respecting the Characters of Nations," Edinb., 1808.
2 Vol. i, p. 430.

ally from famine, and nevertheless neglect to lay in provisions or to cultivate the soil for their support. A characteristic trait proving utter carelessness for the future is mentioned by Labat,[1] namely, that the Caribs sell their hammocks cheaper in the morning than in the evening. The great indolence and thoughtlessness which renders uncivilized nations so disinclined to improve their miserable condition, has led to the conclusion, that they are utterly incapable of effecting anything which requires industry and perseverance. That such a conclusion is unwarrantable is proved by the surprising patience which they evince in manufacturing their furniture and dress with the simplest tools. As instances, may be mentioned that the Indians of Peru sometimes spend two years in weaving a blanket,[2] and devote five to six hours to paint their bodies. The Bosjesmen are especially distinguished by their perseverance, when once they are roused from their lethargy. "Nothing can induce them to leave the track of game, nor will any difficulty deter them from an enterprise once resolved upon."[3] Such firmness of purpose is, however, rare among uncultivated nations, as they are commonly very changeable in disposition. Without being absolutely malignant and treacherous, uncultured peoples soon become faithless, crafty, and deceitful, especially when they feel themselves secure; and this not so much from self-interest, as from a momentary impulse, which irresistibly leads them to gratify their desires. That this is taking a just view is proved by many examples in which robberies and assassination by savages have been prevented by changing their current of thought in drawing attention to some artificial trick, or by some other entertainment. If Dentrecasteaux (1792), and other writers of that period, describe uncultivated nations, *e. g.*, the inhabitants of Van Diemen's land, as peaceable children of nature, it is partly owing to the then prevailing opinion that all corruption belongs to the civilized state, partly, it may be owing to the circumstance that some navigators treated the aborigines kindly,

[1] "Nouv. Voy. aux Isles de l'Am.," i, pp. 2, 18, 1724.
[2] Ulloa, "Voy. historique," p. 336, Amst., 1752.
[3] Lichtenstein, "Reise im Südl. Afr.," ii, p. 319, 1811.

made them many gifts, and met with kindness in return.[1] In modern times, however, the above view as regards uncivilized nations has undergone a great change, many writers now considering man in a state of nature little better than the ape; and it would be difficult to decide which of these views is the most erroneous.

Taking into consideration the characteristic qualities of uncivilized nations, we must be prepared to find great abnormities in moral respects, not merely in individual actions but in the fixed habits of life. There is no doubt that cannibalism, infanticide, and similar deeds, have been and are still practised without any consciousness of their criminality. Though it may originally have been either revenge or misery which led to cannibalism,—as related of the Zulu people of Immithlanga (Intlangwein), that famine first drove them to eat their own children, since which time they commenced regularly to devour their prisoners of war,[2]—anthropophagy in time became a habit.

In like manner may be explained the many instances of moral degradation exhibited by uncivilized peoples. The principle of revenge seems to be universal among them. Blood for blood is a strict duty, and a ransom paid by the murderer to the nearest kinsman is only accepted where property has acquired a higher value, and where wealth gives power. "The most sacred duty of the Australian is to avenge the death of his nearest relation; until he has accomplished this he is mocked by the old women—his wives, if he be married, would soon leave him. If unmarried, no girl speaks to him; his own mother would constantly cry and lament at having given birth to so degenerate a son; his father would treat him with contempt."[3] It is well known that similar views exist among the natives of North America. "There seems to be a complete absence of moral sentiment among the

---

[1] Latterly this view has been abandoned, and only a faint echo of it appears in Schomburgk's statement ("Reise in British Guiana," ii, p. 240, 1847), that the feelings for morality and virtue are nicer among Indians than among ourselves.

[2] Gardiner, "Narrative of a journey to the Zulu country," p. 185, 1836.

[3] Grey, "Journals of two Expeditions in Australia," ii, p. 240, 1840.

Negroes of East Sudan, who not merely excuse theft, murder, and treachery, but consider these actions as praiseworthy in man. They first learned under the Turkish rule to distinguish murder from justifiable homicide in war. Lying and deceitfulness are considered as marks of mental superiority, and those who suffer death on the gallows are buried with the same honours as the rich merchant or the Sheik."[1] It is, however, a remarkable fact, showing that there is a natural moral feeling among even the rudest nations, that, *e. g.*, the Australians in the region of Port Essington, when they are detected as thieves, offer no resistance;[2] and that in the Sandwich Islands the discovered thief returns the stolen property without reluctance.[3]

We must now turn to the social relations of uncultivated peoples. In marriage and family life we find two characteristic features—the enslaved state of woman as the weaker being, and polygamy. The male is independent, as he has to defend and support his family. The female is despised and considered as merchandise. How little chastity is esteemed is evinced by the language of the Bosjesmen not distinguishing girl from wife.[4] In the north of Peru a girl is more courted if she has had many lovers before marriage,[5] which is also the case in Wydah.[6] Sexual excesses committed by girls before marriage are of little importance; continence is only required of married women. It has even been asserted that chastity among Negroes only means that pregnant and menstruating women should abstain from illicit intercourse.[7] Of the absence of romantic love there can under such circumstances be no question, although it may not be entirely wanting among some uncultivated nations. Generally speaking there prevails, in consequence of early gratification of the sexual passion, an unaffected and passionless relation between the sexes, which must not, as Delegorgue has suggested, be attributed to a greater natural gentleness of un-

1 Brehm, "Reise-skizzen aus Nordöst-Afrika," i, 162, 175, 1855.
2 Jukes, "Narrative of the surveying voy., of H.M.S. Fly," i, p. 354, 1847.
3 Wilson, "Missionsreise in das stille Meer," Mag. v. Reiseb., xxi, p. 291.
4 Lichtenstein, i, p. 192.
5 Ulloa, "Voy. de l'Am. mérid.," i, pp. 343, 1752.
6 Des Marchais, "Voyage en Guinée," Amsterdam, 1731.
7 Smith, "Trade and Travels in the Gulph of Guinea," p. 249, 1851.

cultured nations in comparison with that of the civilized European.

The woman belongs to the man who has purchased her from her parents; he can therefore discard, lend, exchange, or sell her. The power of the husband over his wife seems to be greatest on the Fiji Islands, where the women among the common people are not merely articles of commerce, but are frequently killed and eaten by their husbands without their being punished for it.[1] The wives of the father sometimes pass to the son as an inheritance. The wife only, not the husband, can commit adultery. Polyandry, though, as Wuttke observes,[2] opposed to the notions of uncultured peoples about marriage, is not only cogitable as a matter of necessity, but is also practised from political or religious motives.[3] Polygamy, on the other hand, proceeds from the estimation of the female sex among uncultured peoples, and can scarcely have been the consequence of the overplus of females caused by war; though it may be admitted that a greater mortality of the males, as for instance, is caused in Greenland by a dangerous and noxious mode of life,[5] may have contributed to establish the custom. It is chiefly the result of woman being considered as property and a beast of burden capable of being applied to useful labour. Another circumstance which leads to polygamy is the early fading of woman (in the East Indies girls marry at the age of twelve, and are old between twenty-five and thirty), whether it be in consequence of the climate, or of being overworked. Among some African nations women are considered unclean during the whole period of lactation, during which all intercourse with the other sex is strictly forbidden. It has been asserted that

[1] Wilkes, iii, p. 192.

[2] "Geschichte der Heidenthums," i, p. 184.

[3] Dessalles' description ("Hist. gén des Antilles," i, p. 197, 1847) of polygamy and polyandry among the Caribs in the West India Islands, is unreliable. Polyandry, however, is found as a permanent custom among the Avanoes and Maypures in South America (Humboldt and Bonpland, "Reise," iv, p. 477); also in Ladakh, in the highland of Thibet, in the alpine state of Sirmore, although the inhabitants of the latter region seem to be Hindoos (Ritter, "Erdk.," iii, pp. 623, 752, 880). The arrangement is, that several brothers have but one wife between them. In Ladakh, the eldest brother must support the children. One ground of the custom may be, that the support of a wife is expensive.

[4] Cranz, i, p. 218.

where polygamy exists conjugal fidelity is very lax. This is only true so far, that it chiefly exists among uncultivated or half-civilized nations; but it can scarcely be said that polygamy, as such, favours licentiousness. That polygamy frequently causes dissensions among the women and disturbs domestic peace may be true, but is far from being so general as asserted. Among the Zulu and other Kaffir tribes (by no means the only examples) there prevails no jealousy among the women: the first wife tries to gain so much as to enable her husband to purchase a second and a younger wife. Her authority is then increased and her labour lightened. The women, in fact, prefer polygamy to monogamy, as the love for their husbands is, from being purchased, rarely a personal affection.[1]

It seems, thus, that polygamy is not so generally injurious to family peace as is frequently assumed. Its social danger lies in this, that, supposing the sexes equal in number, there must be left a great many men unmarried, which may give rise to other vicious habits.

It can scarcely have been a feeling of shame which originally induced man to cover his nakedness. The New Zealander covers his body merely to protect himself from the cold, and by no means to conceal his person.[2] Just as the half-civilized Guanches were quite naked, not on all, but on some of the Canary Islands, so the Puris are to this day, men and women; also the Patachos, Botocudes, etc.[3] This is also found to be the case upon a small island near Apollonia; only when they go on a journey they cover themselves, and then scantily.[4] Especially where business requires it, there is not the least reluctance to expose the person. Caillié[5] saw in Bambarra, laundresses walk about quite naked before strangers. It is therefore surprising that the laws of the Susus (Mandingo people) condemn him to slavery who looks at women bathing,[6] whilst in Yucatan both

---

[1] Steedman, "Wanderings and Adventures in South Africa," i, p. 240, 1835; Delegorgue, i, p. 154; ii, p. 231.
[2] Crozet, "Reise durch d. Südsee," p. 70, Leipz., 1783.
[3] Prinz Max, zu "Wied R. nach Brasil," i, pp. 136, 286, 333, 1820.
[4] Boudyk, "Voyage à la côte de Guinée," p. 158, 1853.
[5] "Voyage à Temboctu," ii, p. 115, 1833.
[6] R. Clarke, "Sierra Leone," p. 33, 1846.

sexes bathe together.[1] Some Indians on the Orinoco, where both sexes go about naked, were at first ashamed to wear clothes,[2] as it seemed to them indecent to appear before strangers unpainted.[3]

The original motives, however, of painting and tattooing the body could hardly have been to cover nakedness from a feeling of shame; the former was resorted to for ornamentation, the latter to mark the tribe or the family. The disinclination to wear clothes is pretty general among uncivilized nations. The feeling of shame, if it exist, extends only to the presence of strangers, particularly Europeans; it is only before them that the women of Timor veil the bosom, and the Indian women of Brazil wear a cest.[4] This applies also to the Australian.[5] If dress were the result of a feeling of shame, we should expect it to be more indispensable to woman than to man, which is not the case. Among many African tribes the males only cover the body.[6] Among some of these tribes married women go about naked, but not unmarried girls.[7] In Australia, also, girls before marriage wear an apron, which is laid aside afterwards.[8] Among the Guanches the reverse takes place.[9] The latter custom arises generally from a better moral tone, the dress of girls being used as a mere stimulant. In Akra the girls, as distinguished from married women, go about perfectly naked; and among some Sererer tribes the want of clothing is a mark of virginity.[10] There remains, however, an unfavourable explanation, namely, that a girl is permitted to exhibit her charms, but the wife is the property of the husband, at whose command she must dress. To appear naked before another

[1] Heller, "Reise in Mexico," p. 217, 1853.
[2] Gumilla, "Hist. de l'Orenoque," chap. vii, 1788.
[3] Gilii, "Nachr. v. Guiana," p. 253, 1785.
[4] Spix und Martius, "Reise," p. 370; Péron, "Voyage de Découv.," 2nd edit.; Freycinet, iv, p. 18, 1824.
[5] Barrington, "History of N. S. Wales," p. 37, 1810; Eyre, "Journals of Expeditions into Central Australia," ii, p. 216, 1845; Hind, in "Journal of Roy. Geogr. Soc.," i, p. 40.
[6] Barth, "Reisen u. Entdeck.," ii, p. 473.
[7] Ibid, p. 467.
[8] Barrington, loc. cit., p. 23.
[9] Webb et Berthelot, "Histoire nat. des Iles Canaries."
[10] Zimmermann, "Vocabulary of the Akra language," pp. 190, 253; Boilat, "Esquisses Sénégalaises," p. 104, 1853.

person passes here and there, as a mark of submission. In the kingdom of Melly all the slaves were formerly obliged to be quite naked, and all the women had thus to appear before the Sultan.[1] There are peoples among whom the males only are dressed;[2] but even where the women go about quite naked, as among the Chevas and Tumbucas on the Zambesi, it does not affect their chastity.[3] On the Orinoco, where the missionaries on exhibiting marima shirts say, that clothes grow upon the trees, the males are seemingly more ashamed of their nakedness than the females.[4]

The influence of habit and custom is very great in these matters. The following examples are not uninteresting. On the Marquesas they are not at all ashamed to go about naked, but it is considered indecent not to bind up the prepuce.[5] In New Zealand and many islands of the South Sea the males are ashamed to lay aside the suspensory.[6] The Fellah women (which also happens in other Mahommedan countries) have no hesitation in exposing every part of the body except the face. The Tubori women in Central Africa go about quite naked, wearing only a narrow strap, to which is attached a twig hanging down behind; they feel greatly ashamed if by chance the twig falls off.[7]

In passing from sexual and family relations to the social condition of uncivilized nations, but little can be said that is generally characteristic. Families generally live near each other independently under their own chief, gradually forming little societies, without any form of government, until internal dissensions or external attacks compel them to unite and submit to the sway of one or more individuals who have proved their prowess or their wisdom. Such peoples may, however, remain for a long time without any organization, oscillating be-

---

[1] Ibu Batuta, "Journal Asiatique," i, p. 221, 4me série.
[2] Koelle, "Polyglotta Afr.," p. 13.
[3] "Ausland," p. 262, 1858, according to Monteiro.
[4] Humboldt, "Reise in die Æquinoctialg.," iv, p. 101: iii, p. 95, ed. Hauff.
[5] Langsdorff, "Bemerk. auf. e. "Reise um. die Welt," p. 137, 1812; Lisiansky, "Voyage round the World," p. 85, 1814; Roquefeuil, "Journal d'un Voyage autour du monde," i, p. 303, 1823.
[6] D'Urville "Voyage de l'Astrolabe," ii, p. 482.
[7] Vogel, in Petermann's "Mittheilungen," p. 138, 1857.

tween a state of perfect independence and one of despotism. It is an erroneous view to consider this oscillation among rude nations as degrees of social development, instead of attributing it to its natural cause.

The disputes occurring between indviduals are either adjusted by a third party who interposes his authority or who is chosen to act as arbiter, or what is more usual among primitive nations, the interested party is left to find his own remedy. Among many such peoples, ordeals are instituted to decide the matter. The disputes among individuals frequently involve whole families and tribes in feuds; but it is chiefly superstition or hunger and misery which lead to wars.

The religious ideas of primitive peoples have already been touched upon in a general sense. They are based upon a personification of striking natural forces on which man believes his fate depends, ascribing any misfortune to the action of independent spirits. Ungrateful as man generally is when in luck, he sees, even when in a primitive state, nothing in the success of his plans but the usual course of nature or the result of his sagacity. Thus originally his view of nature which coincides with his religious ideas is about this—that among the spirits which direct nature and the fates of man, the evil spirits are either exclusively active, as is asserted of the Indians of Caraccas, who only believe in a wicked original being,[1] or so far predominant that the good spirits are made subordinate. Though the existence of the latter is not altogether denied, they are but little attended to either in thought or prayers, worship or sacrifice, since they are already by their nature friendly to man. All these spirits, are of course, conceived as analogous to the nature of man.

The religion of the primitive man is thus throughout—a crude polytheism[2] without poetry, even without mythology, or

---

[1] Depons, in "Magaz. v. Merkw. Reisenbeschrift," xxix, p. 143.

[2] Rougement, however ("Le People Primitif," 1855), considers monotheism as the original religion imparted to man by an original revelation, and that pantheism formed the transition to polytheism. He endeavours to trace this primitive monotheism in the confused legends of uncultured peoples, by ascribing a cosmogonic meaning to these myths. It is unquestionable that some of the most remote peoples frequently agree in this respect. Thus, the flood legends are almost universally found in America,

rather a gloomy unconnected belief in spectres and spirits, destroying all faith in the natural course of phenomena. Even these religions have been considered as stages of development, which is, however, not confirmed by experience. Wuttke[1] designates the deification of natural objects as the first stage of natural religion, manifesting itself in the worship of the elements, plants, animals; the second stage is Fetishism; the third demon-worship, Schamanism. All this is much too artificial, an idle logical scheme with which the facts do not correspond. The belief in spirits among the Negroes, which is usually designated Fetishism, though in many respects differing from that of the Australian and American, is not essentially distinct. The principle, the whole conception of nature, the relation of man to the spiritual world, is pretty much the same; and we are astonished at this uniformity among nations so distant—an uniformity tending to show that in this respect in what constitutes the kernel of mental life they all belong to the same species.

In order to complete this general description of the psychical life of primitive nations, we must consider their sense of the beautiful. The great difference in taste is so universally acknowledged, that we may expect but little that is generally applicable, since individuality, mode of life, surrounding nature,

which does not necessarily prove that the traditions relate only to one great flood. There is certainly a charm in giving a symbolical signification to the traditions of uncultured peoples, and thus rendering them rational and interesting; but it is, in most cases, a futile undertaking, for the following reasons:—1. We know but a few fragments of these traditions. 2. The legends are so variable among uncultured peoples, that scarcely two individuals relate them alike. Some of these are evidently invented by individuals whose object, perhaps, is to acquire some influence. 3. A close examination of the religious opinions of uncultured peoples forbids us, in most cases, to ascribe a cosmogonic meaning to their insipid traditions. 4. It is as psychologically impossible that there should exist a tradition of the primitive history of mankind, as that an individual should recollect his own birth, or the first events of his life. 5. As regards the agreement of certain legends, they may possibly point to some early connexion of the respective peoples, but nothing as to common descent (we may, for instance, ask whether immigrants, say Buddhists, had once come from Asia to Mexico? but not whether the old Mexicans originated in East India or China?). Many of the traditions have only an apparent resemblance; and others may be explained from the circumstance that mankind were, in many regions, as regards the natural forces, placed in the same conditions, and led to the invention of similar traditions.

[1] "Gesch. des Heidenthums," i, p. 50.

the historical fate of a people, are more influential in this respect than upon moral development. Even the symbolism of colour differs among individual peoples, though here and there we meet with an interesting conformity. The colour of mourning at the death of near relations is yellow in some Asiatic regions, and among the Quiches in Guatemala;[1] brown among the Persians; blue among the Turks; white among the Chinese, Anamese, and Siamese;[2] the colour is dark blue in Elmina;[3] dark blue and black among the Quichuas.[4] The Australian when in mourning paints his body white, or draws merely a white line across his forehead, nose, or cheeks.[5] The Omahas also use white paint when in mourning;[6] whilst among the natives of North America black is generally the colour of mourning, and red the colour of war. Among the Mandingoes in the region of Sierra Leone white is the symbol of peace.[7] Among the Ashantees and other negro peoples white is the colour of joy, and they paint themselves white on their birthdays.[8] Priests, ambassadors, and warriors are dressed in white among the Yebus.[9] Persons who have gained a suit, or been acquitted of some crime, dress in white in some parts of Africa. The natives of Elmina, in opposition to the belief of other negro tribes, imagine the good god to be of white, and the bad god to be of a black colour.[10] Among the inhabitants of Tierra del Fuego white is the colour of war, red that of peace and friendship.[11] Yellow, the favourite colour of the Malays and the lowest Hindoo castes,[12] is at the same time the colour of priestly clothing among the Birmese.

---

1 Ximenes, "Hist. del. Orig. de los Indios," p. 214, ed. Scherzer.
2 Virey, "Hist. nat. du genre humain," iii, p. 86.
3 Boudyck, p. 180.
4 Tschudi, "Peru," i, p. 353, 1846.
5 Baker, "Sydney and Melbourne," p. 150, 1843.
6 James, "An Account of an Expedition to the Rocky Mountains," i, p. 282, 1823.
7 Matthews, "Reise nach Sierra Leone," p. 89, 1789.
8 Halleur, "D. Leben der Neger West-Afrikas," p. 31, 1850.
9 D'Avezac, "Notice sur le pays et le peuple des Yebus," in Mém. de la Soc. Ethnol., ii, p. 70.
10 Boudyck, "Voyage à la côte de Guinée," p. 179, 1853.
11 King and Fitzroy, "Narrative of the Surveying Voyage of the Adventure and Beagle," ii, p. 177, 1839.
12 Crawfurd.

Even in the estimate of human beauty there is the same disagreement. Crawfurd[1] maintains that the views of the Malays correspond in this respect with our own; and it has otherwise been assumed that the ideal of beauty is the same among all peoples. This, however, is quite erroneous. Desmoulins[2] is no doubt too rash in his conclusions from the deviations which the sculptured portraits of the Chinese and old Mexicans exhibit from the Greek ideal; for although right in the main, it is questionable whether these portraits were intended to represent the beautiful. We are assured that the Negroes, who generally imagine the Devil to be white, consider a black shiny skin, thick lips, and flattened noses as the type of beauty;[3] and that the Tahitians, among whom "long-nose" is considered as a word of insult, for the sake of beauty compress the forehead and the nose of the children.[4] The artificial deformation of the head among so many American nations also indicates a difference in the ideas of personal beauty. An Australian woman had a child by a white man: she smoked it and rubbed it with oil to give it a darker colour.[5] A yellow, not a white girl is considered a beauty in Java.[6] To have white teeth, "like dogs," instead of black coloured teeth is considered ugly and disgraceful, just as the natives of North America consider vegetable food as beastly aliment. A servant of the king of Cochin China spoke with contempt of the wife of the English ambassador (1821) that she had white teeth like a dog and a rosy colour like that of potato flowers.[7] And even a recent European traveller[8] assures us that whoever is once accustomed to the grotesque painted visages of the Indians, considers unpainted countenances unmeaning and ugly.

Ideas of courtesy and manner differ still more than those of beauty and ugliness. Among peoples who live chiefly in a

---

[1] "History of the Indian Archipelago," i, p. 22, 1820.
[2] "Histoire naturelle des races humaines," p. 229, 1826.
[3] Moore, "Travels into the inland parts of Africa," p. 93, London, 1730.
[4] King and Fitzroy, ii, p. 527.
[5] Barrington, loc. cit., p. 32.
[6] Pfeyffer, "Skizzen von der Insel Java," p. 41, 1829; Selberg, "Reise nach Java," p. 182, 1846.
[7] Laplace, "Voyage autour du monde," ii, p. 463, 1833.
[8] Kohl, "Kitchi-Gami," i, p. 29.

state of war, the forms of salutation are merely the result of distrust of strangers, as among the American Indians, Australians, the Danakils in Africa.[1] As curiosities may here be mentioned that among the Malays civility requires the head to be covered, the back turned, and the eyes cast down.[2] In Sumatra, it is uncivil to mention one's own name. In Java and the Eastern Carolines, one must not stand upright nor sit down in the presence of high personages. It is rather peculiar that the Arowakes in conversing do not look at each other, as they say dogs do so.[3]

We must finally mention as characteristic, the general absence of all cleanliness among uncultured nations,—one of the first conditions of beauty in the eyes of the civilized man. This is not always owing to mere neglect, for dirt is sometimes a protection against cold. It is rare that this uncleanliness proceeds from principle, as in Hamaruwa on the Benuwe (Tchadda), where the wives of the Fulahs are cleaner than the men who, as warriors or conquerors, despise cleanliness and ornaments.[4] How much all judgment on these matters depends on habit and custom is proved by the Sandwich islanders, who collect and eat their own lice, but feel disgust at eating from a plate in which a fly has been drowned.[5]

We have endeavoured to illustrate the natural state of man from two different points of view—first, by inquiring how we may imagine him independent of all experience and of all cultivation; secondly, what experience teaches us of the psychical life of such peoples as approach nearer the primitive, than the civilized state. The answers to these two questions bear such a great similarity that we may, on the whole, designate the uncivilized nations—namely, those of whom it cannot be proved that at any time they occupied a higher stage of development,—as primitive peoples (Naturvölker). We are the more justified in doing so, as the traces of that condition which we have assumed to have been the original state are still to

[1] Johnston, "Travels in South Abyssinia," i, p. 154, 1844.
[2] Crawfurd, i, p. 98.
[3] "Quandt. nachr. v. Surinam," p. 267, 1807.
[4] Crowther, in Petermann's, "Mittheilungen," p. 225, 1855.
[5] Stewart, "Journal of a residence in the Sandwich Islands," p. 156, 1828.

be found among civilized nations, for by cultivation the nature of man may indeed be improved, but can never be changed.

The facts we have to adduce in support of the correctness of our estimate of the natural state, admit yet of another point of view of still greater importance. They prove incontestably that the greatest differences in the development of intellectual life, have no specific importance, but are fluctuating, forming nowhere fixed limits between the degrees of civilization, that they run into each other in the most complicated way, so that on psychological grounds we cannot divide mankind in various species.

The civilized European is accustomed to look so much down upon the so-called savage, that he deems it an insult to be compared with him; and yet, even in the midst of civilization we find the traces of customs, manners, and modes of thinking, which, like the relapse of civilized men into a savage state, prove their intimate connection.

The assumption of Prichard that the oldest inhabitants of civilized Europe were in no way superior to the present inhabitants of Africa can neither be proved nor refuted in our ignorance of pre-historical times; the decision must depend on our conception of the primitive state of man. This theory acquires probability from the circumstance, that even now, as we are assured, there are communities in Ireland, and even in the heart of France, the civilization of which is scarcely higher than that of many Negro tribes, and that a comparison of the free Negro population in the larger cities of the United States, especially of New York and Philadelphia, with that of the above-mentioned Irish districts, turns to the advantage of the free Negroes.[1] Stephens[2] has observed, that the sight of the Russian peasants and a comparison of them with the Negroes in the Greek and Turkish army, has compelled him to abandon the theory of the superiority of the white race—and Stephens is an American! What in such cases has been effected by social oppression has in other cases been the result of isolation, and the want of intercourse with the civilized world, combined with

[1] "Quarterly Review," p. 29, December, 1849.

[2] "Incidents of Travels in Greece, Turkey, and Russia."

the influence of surrounding nature. What would have become of the transmarine colonies of the tough and almost indestructible English without a constant reinforcement of civilized men from the mother country? In spite of all progressive tendency ascribed to the white race, we answer unhesitatingly, it would either have perished or returned to barbarism. These results are everywhere constant, where intercourse or the influx of fresh forces is for a sufficient length of time interrupted.

In the plains of Cordova and San-Luis (Argentine Republic) the pure Spanish race predominates, the young females are frequently of a white rosy colour and delicate structure, yet living in a state of isolation the Spaniards have not exhibited greater activity and a stronger tendency to civilization than the aborigines of that country. The German and Scottish colony south of Buenos Ayres, with their flourishing and neat villages, form a decided contrast to the former.[1] The white settlers south of Buenos Ayres are scarcely less rude and barbarous than the Indians. Criminals and the scum of all nations who take refuge among them instruct them in all that is wicked. Many cruelties and devastations are committed by these lawless men over whom the Indian chiefs have no authority.[2] The Creoles of the La Plata States are almost as godless and dirty as the Indians. To construct wind-mills is beyond their mechanical talent, and notwithstanding the great fertility of the soil, there is no garden to be seen on the high road from Buenos Ayres to Barranquitos. Except in the villages there is no cultivation of the soil. To catch lice is the chief amusement of the women, who offer them to strangers as dainties;[3] they are dirty beyond measure; they are even deficient in curiosity.

A similar description is given of the inhabitants of Tucuman.[4] The Indians of Rioja are simple-minded sober men, whose disputes never lead to bloodshed; they are more industrious and per-

---

[1] Sarmiento, loc. cit.

[2] Garcia, in De Angelis, p. 12; "Colleccion de obras y documentos," iii, 1836.

[3] Dobrizhoffer, "Gesch. der Abiponer," ii, p. 445, 1783; Renger, "Reise nach Paraguay," p. 393, 1835.

[4] Miers, "Travels in Chile and La Plata," i, pp. 28, 30, 314, 1826; Andrews, "Journey from Buenos Ayres through Cordova," etc., i, p. 187, 1827.

severing than the Spanish Creoles, and their festivals never exhibit the same coarseness which distinguishes those of the Creoles.[1] Many of the common utensils and tools of the Chilise, carts, looms, ploughs, are extremely clumsy, scarcely better than those of the Indians; the axe[2] is chiefly used, the saw but little. They are outdone by the superior agriculture of the Araucanians.[3] They are very cleanly in their persons;[4] they bathe several times daily, and by their cleanliness in the villages, the Indians of the tropics in America contrast with the immigrant South-Europeans.[5] In the vicinity of Talcahuano (Chili) D'Urville[6] found such miserable dirty huts, that they could scarcely stand comparison with the habitations of the Polynesians. Helms, after describing the indolent habits of the Creoles of South America,[7] adds: "The Indians are the only industrious class in this country." The colonists in the Llanos of Caraccas are too lazy to dig a well, though they know that they could find the finest springs at a depth of ten feet. Even at this day, there may be found in New Spain, flourishing Indian villages and a well cultivated soil near miserable villages of white Creoles.[8] Ploughs are there in use, made of wood without any iron, and are always drawn by oxen, never by horses;[9] and the Spanish Californians, whom Simpson[10] has described as lazy and degraded, still avail themselves of a miserable plough and the canoe of the Indians. In Brazil the structure of bridges is neglected even on the high road from Rio Janeiro to Villa-Ricca, and agriculture is carried on according to the model of the Indians. The forest is burnt down; they sow, reap, and abandon the land after a few harvests.[11] The Brazilian peasant, especially in the central and northern

---

1 French, "Journal, Royal Geogr. Society," ix, p. 398.
2 Gardiner, "Visit to the Ind. on the frontier of Chili," pp. 155, 163, 1841.
3 Genoux, in "Bullet. Soc. Geogr.," i, p. 150, 1852.
4 Stevenson, "Reise in Arauco," i, p. 5, 1826.
5 Pöppig, "Reise in Chile and Peru," ii, pp. 352, 354, 1835.
6 "Voyage au Pole Sud," iii, p. 47.
7 "Travels from Buenos Ayres, by Potosi, to Lima," pp. 15, 36, 2nd edit., 1807.
8 W. Thompson, "Recollections of Mexico," p. 1, 1846.
9 Duflot de Mofras, "Exploration de l'Oregon des Calif," p. 17, 1844.
10 "Narrative of a Journey round the World," 1847.
11 A. de St. Hilaire, "Voyage dans l'intérieur du Brésil," i, p. 191, 1830.

provinces of the empire, is both lazy and proud; he despises labour as dishonourable; he cares little for habitation and dress, suffering rather from wet and cold;[1] his religious ideas, his belief in wood-spirits and other spectres, is as absurd as that of the Botocudes.[2] The children of the Portuguese settled in the Sertajo grow up indolent and become prodigal; their farms fall into decay. Ignorance and superstition, belief in witchcraft, spectres, and amulets, are universal; they have lost all the dignity of human nature, and only pass from their apathy to the grossest sensuality. Though pacific and hospitable, they are devoid of any intellectual or moral activity. Women and gambling form the sole objects of interest; and there are here some few Portuguese refugees who have forgotten religion, the knowledge of the use of money, and even of salt.[3]

In Goyaz it is not much better; the colonists are enervated by early excesses; concubinage is so common among them that a married man is an object of mockery. Poverty is prevalent; their indolence is remarkable; fraud, especially falsification of the gold, is general. Something similar may be found in other mining, and gold districts.[4] The thirst for gold and labour is succeeded by wealth and prodigality; then succeed enervation, misery, poverty, and all vices. There has for a long time existed in the islands Fernando Noronha, a Portuguese criminal colony. No trace of agriculture is visible there, nor is any amelioration of their miserable condition thought of. The people smoke, gamble, or lie in their hammocks; they have but a miserable ferry boat, so that Webster[5] exclaims in astonishment: "is it possible that these people are the progeny of the seafaring Portuguese, who were so eminent as navigators?" In Africa, the condition of the Portuguese is equally miserable. On the west coast, where they settled in the sixteenth century and have intermixed with

[1] Rendu, "Etudes top. méd. et agron. sur le Brésil," p. 24, 1848.
[2] Prinz Max, "Reise nach Brasil," ii, p. 59, 1820.
[3] A. de St. Hilaire, loc. cit., ii, p. 304.
[4] A. de St. Hilaire, "Voyage aux sources de la rivière San Francisco," i, pp. 127, 173, 218, 316, 373; ii, pp. 75, 243, 1847.
[5] "Narrative of a voyage to the South Atlantic Ocean," ii, p. 23, 1834.

the Negroes, and are pretty numerous, they live in forests; and it is their influence which obstructs the progress of the Liberia Republic among the Negroes.[1] The indolence of the Portuguese on the east coast of Africa nearly equals that of the Negroes; their chief object is an existence which may be attained by the least possible effort.[2] The horrors of their dominion and their own degeneration are described by Omboni.[3] In Angola, they have introduced no other agricultural implement but the hoe; and maniok, which affords but small nutriment, is still the chief vegetable aliment.[4] The condition of the Europeans in the Banda Islands is but little better.[5] Nearly all the Spanish and Portuguese colonies rival each other in proving how little these nations are able to spread civilization in other regions, since separated from their native country they are not even capable of preserving the culture they have brought with them. The English and the French have in this respect proved more successful; but this superiority can only partly be ascribed to the superiority of the original stock, and to the care of the government of their mother-countries to keep up the intercourse of the colonies with the civilized world. Nevertheless, we learn that in the Mauritius, for instance, the population of which is chiefly French, the condition of agriculture before the advent of the English (1810), was as bad as in the Spanish colonies: ploughs were scarce, and the fields were not manured.[6]

It may be objected that several of the instances cited referred to mixed populations and not to pure Europeans. Still, it must be admitted that even in these cases the European blood, despite the improvement of the race which is usually ascribed to its infusion, has not proved its efficiency in raising the breed one step above the condition of the aborigines; and that even in such cases where there was no intermixture, or a

---

[1] Foote, "Africa, and the American flag," p. 72, New York, 1854.

[2] Owen, "Narr. of a voyage to explore the shores of Africa," ii, p. 13, 1833.

[3] "Viaggi nell. Afr. occ.," p. 100, Milano, 1845.

[4] Livingstone, ii, p. 72.

[5] Kögel in Ausland, p. 1066, 1857.

[6] D'Unienville, "Statistique de l'Ile Maurice," i, p. 305, 1838.

very slight one, the degeneracy of the population was nearly the same. The assertion that the European alone is capable of taking the initiative in civilization, and that the impulse thereunto is a peculiarity of the race, must, after the quoted facts, be considerably modified, for they prove at least that the white man is not much less dependent on external circumstances in his progress towards civilization than the black man. This is plainly shown when we consider man in his individual capacity.

The savage, though he may have lived for some time in civilized society, is generally but superficially changed. Young Australians brought up by Europeans have escaped to the woods when grown up;[1] and similar instances are related of North American Indians. In order not to draw erroneous conclusions from such cases, we must consider that these individuals could not fail to observe that they played but a sorry part among the Whites; perhaps, also, an instinctive impulse drove them again to seek their freedom. Civilization is a state which the uncultivated man, be he European or African, resists with all his power, according to the law of inertia; but it does not irresistibly lead to the conclusion that savage peoples are irreclaimable. If, on the one hand, the savage does not take freely to civilization, though surrounded by it, we find, on the other hand, that the civilized man, living among savages, relapses after a short time into a state of barbarism, which, on that account, we must consider as the primitive state of man. In New Zealand, there are many such degenerate Europeans, whose character and mode of life resemble those of the natives.[2] Numbers of such instances are to be met with in Australia and North America; nor was it in many cases necessity, but a predilection for a roaming life; it was free choice which made these men return to barbarism. Towards the end of the last century it very often happened that some Whites were

[1] Braim, "History of New South Wales," ii, p. 240, 1846.
[2] Mundy, "Our Antipodes," ii, p. 124, 1852; Polack, "New Zealand: being a Narrative," i, p. 52, 1838; "Die Neuseeländer nach d. Engl.," p. 258, 1833. Kay, in "Caffraria," p. 400, 1833.

adopted by Indian tribes.[1] Froebel[2] says that in Mexico, where the natives frequently kidnap individuals, there are many instances of their perfect naturalization among the savages. There are said to live in the valley Simbura, at some distance from Carimango in the province Loxa in Ecuador, Spaniards of pure blood sunk into a complete state of barbarism, possessing a degenerate language, without a trace of historical tradition.[3] Europeans perfectly degenerate, in fact cannibals, like the natives, have been found by Lery[4] among the Tupinambas, and latterly they have been met with on the Fiji islands,[5] as a parallel to which may be mentioned that the habit of eating human flesh spread in the thirteenth century, first in consequence of a famine, among all classes of the Egyptian population.[6] How much civilization and degeneracy depend on external circumstances has been repeatedly proved. Before the breaking out of the war with the Iroquois (1685), says Charleroix,[7] the French were entirely unprotected, and constantly surrounded by pressing dangers; nevertheless they lived like savages, in perfect carelessness, nor made they any attempt to discipline and combine their forces. Careless and improvident, says Irving,[8] of a hunting expedition through the prairies, as hunters generally are, they feasted continually, without any thought of laying in a provision for the following day. Does the savage act otherwise? As regards moral dispositions, it can still less be maintained that the white race possesses any great advantage above other races. The atrocities we see committed by savages (and sometimes by ourselves) in cold blood, without the least scruple, and their insensibility to all moral relations, has something so repulsive for the civilized man, that he feels inclined to assume that they

---

1 Baily, "Journal of a Tour in 1796," p. 770, Ausland, 1856; Wilkes, "United States Exploring Expedition," iv, pp. 357, 360; v, p. 148.

2 "Reise durch den Wester der V. St."

3 Tschudi, "D. Kechua-Sprache," i, p. 8. According to Velasco, "Hist. del reino de Quito," iii, pp. 2, 15, 17, who, perhaps, followed Alcedo.

4 "Reise in Brasil übers," p. 258, 1794.

5 "Ausland," p. 936, 1857.

6 Abd Allatif, bei Humboldt und Bonpland, "Reise," iv, p. 373.

7 "Ges. v. Neu-Frankreich," p. 286, in Allg., "Hist. der Reisen."

8 Ausflug auf die Prairien.

are specifically different beings. We, however, soon learn that such a theory is not tenable on these grounds.

We need not refer to the atrocities of the miserable Arnauts in the war of Mohammed Ali,[1] nor to the Turko-Russian war, and the late rebellion of the Hindoos against the English, for, independently of the low degree of civilization of these nations, the exasperation of the struggle may, to some extent, excuse them. Let us grasp the life of the European apart from such extraordinary impulses, and in a state where he is not kept in bounds by the law. How the Russo-American Company behaved to the Aleutes, and even their own people, may be learned from Langsdorff;[2] the former were treated much worse than slaves. Though sick, they were worked to death; the moribund were put into damp huts, and provided neither with firewood nor proper victuals. The Europeans living in Khartoum, on the Nile, belong to a variety of nations, and are described as civilized; but Russeger, Brehm, and all other travellers, unanimously describe them as the most worthless and unscrupulous men in the world, living as slave dealers, without any law, and given to all possible vices.

The worst in such cases is, that with the decline of morality the moral sense itself gradually degenerates. The frontier peasants at the Cape find nothing morally wrong in the razzias which, without any provocation, they undertake against the Bosjesmans, though they would consider it a heinous sin thus to treat Christians.[3] This reminds us of the Bosjesman who knew nothing of the difference between good and bad actions, adding, after some hesitation, that it was right in him to steal the wives of other men, but wrong in others to steal his own wife. The oft-praised pioneers of the West of North America acted in a similar manner towards the Indians, and their moral judgment in this respect was the same as that of the Dutch peasants. The backwoodsmen of Old Kentucky are brought up in the hatred of the natives, and shoot them down

---

[1] Werne, "Feldzug Von Sennaar nach Taka," p. 116, 1851.
[2] Vol. ii, pp. 63, 80.
[3] Thompson's "Travels and Adventures in South Africa," i, p. 396, 2nd edit., 1827.

without the least scruple, though they are generally humane towards the White. No doubt some of them have grievously suffered from the massacre of their families by the Indians. They accordingly look upon the Indians as wild beasts, and treat them as such.[1] Thus we perceive that the European acts in such cases entirely on the principle prevalent among savages, namely, that vengeance, if it cannot reach the guilty, may be taken on the tribe to which he belongs; for instance, the Bedouin Arab makes the Turk responsible for the Turk, the Frank for the Frank, the black for the black.[2] We need scarcely refer to the morality of the slaveholders in the United States. The Catholic missionaries in Congo looked with horror upon the slave trade carried on by Protestants, but had no objection that Congo negroes should be kidnapped by Catholics and carried into Catholic countries.[3] In our own time even we find the moral judgment very elastic, and just adapted to the prevailing practice; habit makes us so familiar with this, that only striking deviations become perceptible. Thus we read that in Java the seducer of another man's wife is judged very indulgently, the husband only being ridiculed; whilst the seduction of another man's housekeeper is considered a very reprehensible act, for which the offender is excluded from all society.[4] Some hundred years back there prevailed in Europe quite a different morality. Slave trade, cruelties of every kind against non-Christians, were considered as perfectly justifiable. We may mention, by the way, that Edward III. of England forbade his "right noble lords and right honourable ladies" to carry on piracy and highway robbery, not on the grounds of justice and morality, but simply because these acts injured the revenues of the crown, and deterred foreign merchants from visiting the country.

The natives of America have often been reproached with an incorrigible vice of drunkenness peculiar to the red race, and which leads them to certain destruction. This may also be as-

---

[1] Hoffman, "A Winter in the Far West," ii, p. 30, 1835.
[2] D'Escayrac, "Die Afrika Wüste und d. Land der Schwarzen," p. 170, 1855.
[3] Zuchelli, "Merkw. Miss. u. Reisebeschr. nach Congo," p. 226, 1715.
[4] Selberg, loc. cit., p. 168.

serted as regards many other uncivilized nations. We see nothing in this but the irresistible power which sensual gratification exercises on man in a state of nature, careless of the future and unconscious of the degrading consequences of the vice. Without laying much stress on the efforts made by some Indian chiefs to stem the progress of this vice, we would mention that Europeans also perished in masses in consequence of their drunken habits. Among the lowest class of the Cape colonists there are but few who are not drunkards.[1] The greater number of the first white settlers on the Derwent river in Van Diemen's Land were prematurely cut off in consequence of this vice, and Ross[2] asserts that half of the deaths were directly or indirectly the result of drunkenness.[3] Braim[4] denies that drunkenness is at present prevalent in New South Wales, but Byrne[5] asserts the contrary. In Sydney, says Majoribanks,[6] there are from two hundred to three hundred wine vaults, and there are consumed ten times as much spirituous liquors as in other places; for every adult spends on the average about £20 per annum on this article. As regards the natives of America, the Araucanians are considered the most decided drunkards, but D'Urville[7] observes that the Chilise differ very little from them in this respect. The old Germans are somewhat differently judged, at least in Germany! At their drinking-bouts, when individuals frequently gambled away their personal liberty, there still reigned "a youthful dignity and force," and "this still life differs infinitely from the brutish stupor in which other savages indulge when they are satiated with fighting and plundering."[8] Butcheries, cruelties, treachery, cunning, breaches of faith, were frequent among them, from the exasperation caused by the Roman wars, and yet they are represented to us as men in whom even at that

[1] Moodie, ""Ten Years in South Africa," i, p. 53, 1835.
[2] "Hobart Town Almanac," 1831.
[3] Laplace, "Voyage autour du monde," iii, p. 478, 1833.
[4] "History of New South Wales," ii, p. 317, 1846.
[5] "Twelve Years Wanderings in the British Colonies," i, p. 136, 1848.
[6] "Travels in New South Wales," p. 31, 1847.
[7] "Voyage au Pole Sud," iii, p. 55.
[8] Rückert, "Culturgesch. des Deutschen Volkes," i, p. 77.

time ideal motives, public spirit, and love of liberty greatly predominated!

The degraded position of women among uncivilized peoples has been made too much of, as it is not a permanent but a fluctuating feature. We would not discuss here the delicate question whether the demoralization in these things among ourselves is not concealed beneath more refined forms, whilst it is seen in its nakedness among savages. Though wives are not sold in the market, marriages in the higher ranks are conducted pretty much like mercantile transactions.

Although among the ancient Germans, woman was purchased, she was not considered as mentally inferior to man, but only as physically weaker, and requiring protection. But such a noble conception of woman is rare. In Greece and Rome females occupied a subordinate position. In Sparta, where marriage (as in Plato's republic) was considered a purely political institution, as a means of producing stout citizens, a third party might be the representative of the husband if the marriage proved unprolific. In Athens, where rape was only considered as an offence against the husband or father, and was merely punished by a fine, the hetæræ only were well-educated women. A parallel to this state exists at present in Java, where the Ronggeng, though a hetæra, enjoys a certain honourable position, for even princes dance (dandak) with her, and when she marries, all immoralities of her former life are forgotten.[1] Old Christian authorities looked at marriage only from a sensual point of view, and have seriously doubted whether women had souls. We must, therefore, not feel surprised that Chinese, Hindoos, and Mohammedans positively deny that they have any soul. If a Chinaman is asked how many children he has, he only mentions the boys; if he has only girls, he answers he has no children.[2] Accordingly woman is by these peoples treated as merchandize. Among some tribes of the Moors it is considered an act of politeness and hospitality to offer a woman to the stranger.[3]

---

[1] Epp, "Schilderungen aus Holländisch Indien," p. 401, 1852.
[2] Duhaut-Cilly, "Voyage autour du monde," ii, p. 369, 1834.
[3] Chénier, "Recherches hist. sur les Maures," iii, p. 125, 1787.

It is not so much owing to the estimation of woman as regard for the rights of the husband, that in Java it is considered a great insult to place the hand on the head of the wife ;[1] and the inviolability of women in the whole of the East may also be ascribed to the gravity and self-esteem of the males. A Turkish Bey of Assuan, who was insulted by a Fellah woman on account of some sentence he passed on her husband, left the divan in a rage, exclaiming at the same time, "If thou wert a man, by the beard of my father thou shouldst be flogged to death."[2]

We believe we may be justified in concluding that the moral endowment of the white-race differs in nothing from that of other races, for it is clearly shown that the rude primitive nature breaks out in the civilized man whenever wholesome restraints are removed. Crude habits and manners among savages must not be considered as specific peculiarities of race, though we might strongly be so inclined on witnessing a scene like that described by Parkman,[3] of North American Indians, like wild beasts, devouring a buffalo they had just killed, their faces and hands all besmeared with blood. It even produces upon the European a disagreeable impression to see Turks eat, digging about in the dish with their fingers, and to hear their constant eructations.[4] The American habit mentioned above is also found among the Danakils in Africa, who are usually included in the Caucasian race.[5] In order not to lay too much weight on such external habits, we should remember that a long series of parallels may be drawn between the customs of so-called savages and many cultivated nations of antiquity, such as tattooing, scalping, preserving the heads of enemies as trophies, etc. Not to become tedious, we refer to the collation of such analogies to the authorities below.[6] With re-

---

1 Pfyffer, "Skizzen v. d. Insel Java," p. 25, 1829.

2 Brehm, loc. cit., ii, p. 62.

3 "The California and Oregon Trail," New York, 1849.

4 Werne, loc. cit., p. 107.

5 Johnston, i, p. 160.

6 Lafitau, "Mœurs des Sauvages Américains," ii, p. 257, 1724; Carli, "Briefe über America," deutsch, von Hennig. 1785; Martius, von d. Rechtsztde (1832), "Die Neuseeländer nach d. Engl.," Leipz., 1833.

gard to what is considered proper or disgusting in food, we would only mention that the worms found in the bamboo cane are as eagerly eaten by the Brazilians as those of the palm in Guiana are relished by the Whites.[1] Many Europeans relish some species of lizards and large bats, and the beautiful Creole women in Mauritius roast the nests and larvæ of yellow wasps, and also the grubs found in certain old trees, and consume them as dainties.[2]

If, finally, in order to prove that there are specific differences in the psychical life of nations, we refer to the great and apparently constant differences in intellectual development, we shall meet with similar objections. De Salles[3] observes with regard to our modern European civilization that it was, in regard to its intellectuality, nothing else but a *rayonnement de la science de la minorité sur l'ignorance des masses*, and Hunter[4] adduced as a proof that there were no specific differences among mankind, a comparison of Newton with the rest of his countrymen in regard to mental development. The same disparity in mental endowment and development exists among all peoples, as amongst us. Artistic and scientific genius exists among Negroes and Americans, as well as amongst us; and if pre-eminent men of one people lead it from a state of barbarism to civilization under favourable conditions, the stability of the black races has not for its chief cause, deficiency of mental qualification so much as other circumstances. When Foissac[5] points out that all great men excepting Mahomet, belonged to the temperate zone, and ascribes this phenomenon to the effect of the European climate, we reply, that great talents can acquire only a transitory influence over uncivilized peoples which have no history, there being no proper field where their efforts may produce fruit. Moreover, every thing shows that the most civilized peoples of modern times have only gradually emerged from their original

---

[1] A. de St. Hilaire, "Voyage au Brésil," i, p. 433; Bancroft, "Naturgesch. v. Guiana a. d. Engl.," p. 148, 1769; Schomburgk, "Reise in Guiana," p. 429, 1841.

[2] D'Unienville, "Statistique de l'Ile Maurice," i, p. 259, 1838.

[3] "Hist gen. des races humaines," 1849.

[4] "Disp. inaugur. de hominum varietatibus," p. 42, Edinburgh, 1775.

[5] Loc. cit., p. 246.

barbarism in which we still find many nations sunk, whilst primitive crudeness now and then breaks forth even among the most civilized. Where is the warranty that we may not relapse into such a primitive state? Who can calculate the time during which the present cultivated nations remained stationary? Where are the proofs that the so-called lower races are condemned to remain in their present state? The few thousand years we are in advance of them in civilization, are, considering the great antiquity of the earth, too short a period for us to form a decisive judgment of the capacity of all mankind.

Though it can be shown that in North America and in the South Sea, a wide-spread civilization formerly existed, which had already greatly declined at the arrival of the Europeans, nothing of the kind has been found in Africa; for what Smyth[1] and others have asserted of the ancient civilization of Negroes, seems fabulous and only based upon the hypothesis that Negro nations were formerly in possession of the South of Asia, and had also contributed much to old Egyptian civilization, apparently proved by the Negro-skulls found in old Egypt. Still less probable is Dunmore Lange's assertion, that the black race of the South Sea had formerly occupied a much higher position than at present.[2] Though such unfounded assertions cannot induce us to estimate the capacities of the so-called lower races more favourably than is usually done, we must, on the other hand, be on our guard against the unfavourable influences drawn from the gross superstition so prevalent amongst them. We need only refer to the old Germans, who burned horses and weapons with their dead, and on important occasions sacrificed human beings.[3] Moreover, the belief in witchcraft, spectres, etc., is not yet extinct amongst us. In the last century, when princes were lying in state, a well-furnished table was provided for the dead in the chapel, and faithful catholics still entertain the most extravagant expectations from the purchase

---

[1] The unity of the human races," N. York, 1850.

[2] "Cooksland, in North-east Australia," p. 362, 1847.

[3] We must not omit mentioning that the custom, to sacrifice human beings, among Persians, Greeks, Romans, Egyptians, Celts, Franks, Goths, may safely be traced to cannibalism as its source (J. G. Müller, "Gesch. d. Am. Urrelig.," p. 629, 1855).

of popish bulls, quite analogous to the amulets of the Negroes and other savages.[1] A parallel to it exists at this day in Dauphiné, where every passer-by throws into certain chasms a little stone, as an offering to the mountain spirit; where at new year's and St. John's Eve a meal of cheese, bread, and wine, is served up in every house for the wandering Fadets and Blanquettes; where soothsayers (devins) are consulted against fever and pestilence; and where sick men and beasts are cured by pronouncing some unintelligible gibberish.[2]

The above facts, selected from among the more important, appear to us sufficient proof for our argument as regards the mental relationship of the civilized European with primitive nations. They have at the same time confirmed our view that the natural state of man is not a state of original purity and perfection, but just the reverse.

But though we may, after what has been stated, feel inclined to answer the question, whether there be specific differences among mankind, in the negative, we cannot consider it as solved so long as there remain so many objections to such a view. It is said that the Negro, the American Indian, the Australian, and many others, show themselves everywhere incapable of taking the initiative in civilization; what prevents them doing so, if it be not their inferior mental endowment? Their resistance against cultivation is such that the teaching and the example of the White have no power over them. They remain just what they are and ever were. The European alone progresses, there is within him a mental impulse in which the other races are deficient; if such be not the case, what are the causes of the progress of the former and the retrogression of the latter?

Before discussing this subject, which we reserve for the next section, it may be necessary to offer some considerations calculated to support the theory of the psychical unity of the human species.

Even in recent times, the proposition has been often de-

[1] Marchand, "Neueste Reise um die Welt," i, p. 50, Leipz.; Lavayssé, "Reise n. Trinidad, Tabago, und Venez.," p. 423, 1816.

[2] Von Glümer in Ausland, No. 15, 1855.

fended, that there were no differences whatever in the mental endowment of races;[1] that mental dispositions are not transmitted, but are alike in all races; that their development depended entirely on surrounding nature, and on education, the former determining the wants of man, and thus compelling him to greater or less efforts in order to supply them. It cannot be denied that a great part of the most striking differences which human beings exhibit may be ascribed to the above conditions, but the failure of the attempts to educate the little children of some savages prove, at any rate, that there is no absolute equality of mental disposition either among peoples generally, nor among individuals of the same people. If, by original disposition, be meant that mental capacity which a people possessed before any cultivation, it cannot be proved that it was specifically different in individual races, since in all probability they must for a long time have remained without cultivation, and have only developed themselves from the primitive state which must have been the same in all. If, on the other hand, we speak of the mental endowment of a people at a certain period of its history relating to a stage of its development, we must keep in view that it continually changes, and that this endowment cannot be considered as something permanent. It is only the continuity of the vital development of a people, or of an individual, which suggests to us that this development, even before its accomplishment, was a pre-formed capacity. Now, it is by the other side readily admitted, that the mental performances of an individual, or a people, do not depend on mental endowment so much as on external circumstances, education, etc.: it is also admitted that the same individual if at the beginning acted upon by different external circumstances, would either have been better or worse developed, would have evinced higher or lower mental and moral qualities, and would have acted quite differently than he does at present.

We can only avoid this dilemma by its being understood that when we speak of mental capacity and mental endowment,

---

[1] Frankenheim, Völkerkunde, p. 134, 1852.

we mean that which is peculiar to a people or an individual at a given time, or, in other words, that we must not speak of mental capacity or endowment as universally applicable, but only in relation to a certain period and condition in the life of the subject. Hence it is clear that mental endowment is not immutable, being constantly changed in the course of life; and that though the fixed character of brutes, which psychically remain the same, must be sought for in their mental capacities, the differences of mankind cannot be traced to the same cause, unless the absolute incapacity of mental improvement in some races be demonstrated, namely, that they must remain stationary under all circumstances, and are confined to some definite limits which are passed by other. Instead of positive demonstration, we have only vague assertions on the improvability of the so-called savages and the excellence of European civilization.

If, according to the usual view, the civilization of a people is the simple product of its mental capacity, then the powerful influences of surrounding nature, historical events, and education, are underrated; and we commit, moreover, the error of ascribing to the people as a whole a mental capacity which is only possessed by individuals. These differ greatly in mental capacity; and for the development of a people it is of considerable importance in what relations these individuals stand to each other and to that people, for upon these relations depends their influence on society at large. What, therefore, appears as the endowment of a people, is mainly determined by the effects produced on the mass by individuals, each of whom with his special gifts becomes a factor at a certain period in the social machinery; and as the performance of a machine depends on the combination of its parts, so does the development of a people depend on the mode of combination of differently gifted individuals at definite periods and under particular conditions. From this point of view, the notion of people is not collective, but that of a constantly fluctuating yet specially definite combination and collocation of individualities, on which depends the degree of development that is generally attributed to the people as a whole. To consider the mental endowment of a people as something constant and given once for all, is inadmissible, based as it is upon an empty, scientifically useless abstraction. There is no agent, real and substantive, which can be considered as the spirit of a people or of humanity; individuals alone are real. But as there exist highly gifted individuals and geniuses among all races, and as happy occasions for their activity may occur among all races, we dare not deny to any race the capacity for progress and a higher cultivation.

Our investigations of the physical changes of man have rendered it probable that the race-type may, by the influence of climate, aliment, mode of life, and social condition, be slowly, and to some extent only, altered. Parallel with this physical transformation, we may also assume a change in mental capacity, which, from its very nature, never exhibits itself in peoples as something fixed and unalterable, but as fluctuating, which is proved by the rise and decline of civilization among the same people. Materialists, as well as their opponents, admit that physical changes influence the development of mental capacities.[1] We assert, moreover, in opposition to the usual theory, that the degree of civilization of a people, or of an individual, is exclusively the product of his mental capacity; that his capacities, which designate merely the magnitude of his performances, depend on the degree of cultivation which he has already reached. The capacities of a people do not alter merely in the course of time, but according to its historical fate. An old civilization which has continued for centuries (shown also in the differences exhibited by the children of the same people in different ranks of society) produces, in combination with an altered mode of life, social relations, etc., gradually a race of men altered, both externally and psychically.

If, then, we are agreed that an absolute judgment regarding the mental capacity of a people or race is impossible, it must also be admitted that it would be extremely difficult to base upon it specific differences of mankind. Two groups of facts

[1] Remarks on the subject will be found in my "Allg. Pädagogik," p. 42.

are opposed to it. The one group teaches us that the peoples which occupy the lowest place in humanity, and approach the primitive state, do not all belong to the same, but to different races; the other shows that within every race there are peoples of different degrees of development, and that peoples of the same stock may live near each other, the one progressing, the other remaining in a stationary condition.

The inhabitants of Tierra del Fuego, the Australians, the Bushmen, and the Hottentots (included by some in the Mongol race) and African peoples, occupy the lowest stage in mental and moral development. To these may be added certain tribes of the aborigines of the Deccan and some other partly straight or frizzly-haired natives of the East Indian and South Sea islands, who are not sufficiently known to us to allow of a decided judgment. Some of the latter, on nearer acquaintance, have not proved so crude and savage as they were described. Of all these peoples it can be shown that external nature and their social condition rendered progress next to impossible, living as they did in a sterile stony country, which, on account of surrounding enemies, they were unable to quit.

It is true enough that none of the above peoples belonged to the so-called Caucasian race, but, as will be shown, there exist also among the latter remarkable contrasts. Leaving out of view the peoples of the north-east of Africa, of whom it is yet doubtful whether they belong to the white race, we might still mention the Berbers, the Guanches, and Abyssinians, among whom a higher civilization has never taken root. Abyssinia is a Christian country, but its Christianity consists merely of external ceremonies, in a blue string of silk, which as a mark of faith, is worn round the neck in crosses and rosaries. The Christians are there far beneath the Moslems in industry and honesty.[1] Marriage is rarely solemnized in the church, as it is then indissoluble. Polygamy, though not authorized, is tolerated (Rüppell); there is but a small fine attached to adultery; nor is there any difference made between legitimate and natural

[1] Rüppell, "Reise in Abyss.," i, pp. 327, 366, 1840; V. Katte, "Reise in Abyss.," pp. 37, 97, 1838.

children (Bruce). Cruel punishments by mutilation are common, the mode of warfare is barbarous, and the victor cuts off the genitals from the conquered, without killing him, to carry them off as trophies.[1] Diseases are ascribed to witchcraft and possession, and are healed by exorcism.[2] The Guanches, though a half-civilized people, made human sacrifices in the sixteenth century. In some of their islands (Lancerote and Fortaventura) there existed a kind of polyandry, which permitted a woman to have three husbands, whilst monogamy prevailed in the other islands. They seem not less distinguished by their indolence, for, though islanders, they have never built ships or boats.[3] The inhabitants of the island Sokotra, now Mohammedans, formerly Jacobite Christians, belong to the Arabian stock. They possess scarcely a boat fit for the coasting trade, denoting, as Guillain justly observes,[4] a mental obtuseness and apathy not met with in the most isolated islands of Polynesia; and yet this condition has continued for centuries. De Barras[5] says of them, that they live in caves and ravines, and, like most of the Abyssinians, with whom he classifies them, are clothed in undressed skins. The Arabs in Nubia never think of bodily efforts so long as they have anything to subsist upon, and prefer to live in misery than labour to improve their condition.[6] Thieving and ingratitude form the chief features in the character of the Arabs of the north-east coast of Africa.[7] The Egyptians are equally deficient in the power to execute a work by themselves; yet they are fit for all kinds of work, but they must be driven to it by the stick; they can do everything under the superintendence of those they fear. If, then, in the presence of these facts, we hear the indolence of the Negroes spoken of as a peculiarity of the race, which can only be overcome by the whip, we oppose to it the instance

---

[1] Bruce, "Reise zum Entd. d. Quellen des Nil," iii, 284, 1790; Rochet d'Hericourt, "Seconde Voyage," p. 187, 1846; Brehm, iii, p. 234.

[2] Johnston, loc. cit., ii, p. 328; Salt, "Voyage to Abyssinia," p. 422, 1814; Harris, "Highlands of Ethiopia," ii, pp. 157, 190, 2nd edit., 1844.

[3] Berthelot, in "Mém. de la Soc. Ethnol.," i, pp. 121, 155, 185, 210.

[4] "Documents sur l'hist. la géog. et le comm. de l'Afr. or.," ii, pp. 1, 360, 1856.

[5] "Geschichte der Entdeck. der Portugiesen," ii, p. 12; iii, p. 112, 1821.

[6] Hoskins, "Travels in Ethiopia," p. 259, 1835.

[7] Werne, "Feldzug v. Sennaar nach Taka," pp. 121, 126, 1851.

of the Arabs, who once ruled the finest parts of Europe, and both in science and art, excelled most nations of that period.

In order to prove the natural superiority of the white race over all others, particular stress has been laid on the circumstance that wheresoever they came in contact with the latter, they invariably became their masters. But this superiority, as can be easily shown, is not owing to the race as such, but to their civilization. Gunpowder, brandy, faithlessness, and cruelty, were pretty much the chief means by which the aborigines of their respective countries were subjected. The old world furnishes two remarkable exceptions to the above assumption. In Hungary and Turkey, peoples of a foreign stock have permanently fixed themselves and subjected the white race; and in Africa, the Turks subjected the Arabs and the Berbers. How long in the West Indies, the dominion of the Whites, constituting only 5 per cent. of the population, may last after the emancipation of the Negroes, is very doubtful, unless there be a constant reinforcement from the mother-country.[1]

On casting a retrospective glance at the numerous facts, and the various points of view from which we have endeavoured to elucidate the main question, we are irresistibly led to the conclusion that there are no specific differences among mankind with regard to their psychical life. The great difference in civilization amongst peoples of the same stock, testifies that the degree of civilization does not chiefly depend on organization or mental endowment.

Those modern authors who recognize only a specific psychical difference between the white and the black races, proceed in the manner of those who assume specific physical differences between them—namely, they view only the extremes; and their task would be easy enough were it not for the intermediate transitions. Nevertheless, there is also in this respect a remarkable parallelism between the mental and physical provinces, inasmuch as the differences of mental endowment and development in individuals of the same race, and in the same people at different periods, are not less considerable

---

[1] Dowding, "Religious Partizanship," p. 55, 1854.

than those which are described as specific in the chief races. Hence it is inadmissible to assume with Klemm and Wuttke, active and passive races; to consider like Eichthal, the white man as the representative of the male, and the Negro as the representative of the female element in the "organism" of humanity, and to consider both as necessary, but essentially differently endowed members of it. It is further unreasonable to ascribe, like Nott and Gliddon, to the lower races merely animal instincts, but to the white races a higher instinct for mental progress which impels them to their historical development. All those schematizing theories, however plausible they may be, are irreconcilable with a close investigation of the facts, and we hope in the sequel to prove their groundlessness by more special proofs than we have hitherto been able to adduce.

SECTION III.

ON THE VARIOUS DEGREES OF CIVILIZATION, AND THE CHIEF CONDITIONS OF ITS DEVELOPMENT.

The investigation of the greatest differences existing in the psychical life of mankind, has proved unfavourable to the assumption of specific differences, which we felt warranted in considering as merely fluctuating, and traceable to the opposition of nature and cultivation. The correctness of this view cannot, however, be considered as established, until the degrees intermediate between the natural and the civilized state have been exposed, so as to show that the progressive mental development of some peoples, and the remarkable stability of others, essentially depend upon other causes than on the differences of their original mental endowment.

That the so-called lower races do not emerge from the barbarous state in which they have apparently been from time immemorial, that they exhibit no desire to leave it, that in spite of example and teaching they seem to remain what they ever were, can no doubt very easily be explained by the assumption of specific differences. Such an explanation, however, loses its probability when we can show that external conditions and historical events possess a more decided influence on the degree of the development of mankind. In order to arrive at a true estimate of human nature itself, and the various states of civilization in which we find man, we must first examine what it is that induces him to leave the natural state, what leads him from one step of development to a higher one, and what delays and prevents his mental elevation or renders it stationary.

These questions are as comprehensive as they are difficult, so that a satisfactory answer can scarcely be hoped for. This consideration does not restrain us from making the attempt, though we are conscious that the results can be but incomplete. Besides, such an investigation however imperfect it may be, deserves some acknowledgment in opposition to the simple declaration that the various degrees of civilization resulted from specific psychical differences, inasmuch as it traces the differences of culture back to certain causes and motives, whilst the assumption of specific psychical differences cuts the matter short *ab initio*, thus leaving the various phenomena of progressive civilization unexplained.

The paramount influence which surrounding nature has on the development of the human being, is generally admitted. It is usually the more powerful the nearer a people is to the natural state, and diminishes in influence in proportion as human art and science gain power over it, though even in civilized communities, agriculture, industry, or trade, remain permanently under the influence of the nature of the country. It is evident that the manner in which the above pursuits are followed is one of the most important agents, and gives a national stamp to the mental individuality of a people.

The first and most important influence which man experiences from surrounding nature is that of its climatic condition. It is not easy correctly to estimate its influence upon mental development; for we meet here with the same difficulty, as when we treated of its influence in physical development, inasmuch as it acts in combination with other agents, and we are unable positively to state what belongs to it exclusively. Thus much may, however, be asserted—that a hot climate renders physical, and still more, mental labour difficult, induces man to consider every kind of effort as a greater evil, and indolence as a greater enjoyment than is the case in temperate or cold regions. The European experiences such sensations when he settles in a tropical climate, and it can scarcely be supposed that they are essentially different in the natives of hot climates, because their organism is not only habituated to them, but also conforms like that of the European to his own climate. Although we may admit that the influence of climate acts more intensely on strangers than on the natives, it can scarcely be denied that the latter, whose organism is in harmony with the climatic condition of their country, possess by nature such qualities of temperament as are only gradually developed in the immigrant. The intense reluctance against labour of any kind, especially mental, among the Europeans in Africa, the white Creoles in West India and other tropics, is generally known. It must further be taken into consideration, that the European is, in his own country, brought up to labour and self-control, which the natives of the above countries are not. We can thus hardly make the mental capacity responsible for their want of energy. When we hear of the "unconquerable disinclination" for mental efforts which distinguishes the Whites in hot climates,[1] it must, at least, appear very doubtful whether they would by themselves have there acquired that high degree of mental development from which they now look down with contempt upon the Negro. Foissac[2] has pointed out that in many tropical countries where the mortality is great (in Batavia, 1 : 28; in Guadeloupe, 1 : 27; Bombay, 1 : 20; Guanaxato, in Mexico, 1 : 19), there was also a proportionately great prolificacy. We cannot agree with him in considering this circumstance as the cause of these peoples constantly remaining in a certain state of childhood. Thus much, however, must be admitted, that the

[1] Europeans at Java complain that the climate admits of no mental effort. Their children show a decided reluctance to engage in serious occupations; drawing, music, etc., they learn easily (Selberg, "R. nach Java," p. 189, 1846).

[2] Loc. cit., p. 164.

physical precocity which is the effect of climate shortens the period of infancy (the long duration of which has been considered as a distinguishing feature of man above brutes), so that shortly after puberty both sexes enter into new relations, in which they are burdened with cares for others which leave them neither the inclination nor the leisure for their own further development.

If, moreover, as is frequently the case in the torrid zone, nature yields her gifts freely in supporting man, labour and mental activity naturally languish, and the mind is rendered passive. Again, if nature, as in very cold climates, bestows her gifts too sparingly, the great effort to obtain the actual necessaries of life consumes all powers; and there results, in this case also, though from opposite causes, a proportionate desire of rest and a mental obtuseness, which prevent any attempt at a higher civilization. The Pisang or Banana tree, which is for the inhabitant of the torrid zone what the cereals are for West Asia and Europe, produces in the same space twenty times as much aliment as the latter. "We often hear in the Spanish colonies the assertion, that the inhabitants of the *Tierra caliente* cannot raise themselves from the state of apathy in which they have been sunk for centuries, until a royal decree orders the destruction of the Banana plantations."[1] As, moreover, lakes and rivers contain innumerable birds, it is conceivable that the want of domestic animals cannot be much felt. In Nicaragua, and also in Costa Rica, a small family may, for six cents, buy as much food (chiefly beans) as they require for a week.[2] Hence, there is no inducement to labour in these parts. Guyot[3] observes, that, with regard to the effect of surrounding nature on man, the native of the tropics may be compared with the son of a princely house, and he of the north with the son of a beggar, he of the temperate zone as belonging to the middle classes, which state alone experiences all the impulses for labour and civilization. History confirms it, that all cultured nations, and especially such as have taken the initia-

[1] Humboldt und Bonpland, "Reise," ii, p. 12; Humboldt, "Neu-Spanien," iii, pp. 12, 23, 142.

[2] Squier, "Travels in Central America," i, p. 274, 1853; Wagner and Scherzer, "Costa Rica," p. 147, 1856.

[3] "Grundz. der vgl. Erdkunde," p. 227, 1851.

tive in development, belong to the temperate zone, though a certain grandeur in material civilization cannot be denied to some peoples of hot countries. These phenomena are probably connected with another influence of climate upon the mental peculiarity of man, namely, its influence upon the imagination. A hot climate has, in every respect, a relaxing influence; with the reluctance to bodily effort, there is a corresponding inertness of thought and deficient energy of the will. But this laxity is associated with a greater intensity and restlessness of movements, a greater amount of physical and psychical irritation whenever the state of rest is abandoned. The incredible efforts and lasting power which the Negro exhibits in the dance, the explosions of the passions, the licentious excesses, prove the remarkable ability of the southern character to move within much greater extremes than the inhabitants of temperate climates. It is not that the native of the tropics is more easily aroused; only, when aroused, the energy is far more intense: we need only refer to the running "Amock" among the Malays. We find among the natives of a hot climate a comparatively low psychical culture, which has never properly penetrated the mass, a cultivation the remarkable material performances of which could only be effected by the most unlimited despotism. The grotesque ornamentation of their images, the grandeur of their buildings, the fantastic representations of their deities, all which transcends the imagination of the northern nations, give abundant testimony of the eccentric "glowing" fancy of the inhabitant of the tropics, as well as that displayed in all Oriental tales. The peoples of the south have a particular predilection for glitter and splendour, and for riotous pleasures, whilst their sense for the really beautiful, for calm contemplation of the beauties of nature, is very defective; even the South European, like the Mexican, is enthusiastically fond of pyrotechnic displays. The Brazilians also celebrate their festivals with the greatest possible noise; artillery discharges and fireworks are indispensable adjuncts.[1] The Oriental, observes Ritter,[2] and especially the Arab, is deficient in the perception

[1] W. H. Edwards, "Voyage up the river Amazon," chap. xix, 1847.
[2] "Erdkunde," viii, p. 42.

of the beauties of nature, which distinguishes the European. It is a rare exception that the inhabitants of Ualan (Carolina) cultivate flower gardens,[1] and that some Polynesian tribes use flowers as ornaments.

It has often been observed that Southrons differ in many characteristic features from the Northern inhabitants though belonging to the same people, a difference not so much, perhaps, the result of the climate itself as of the different mode of life. Lyell,[2] speaking of the hospitality to strangers in the slave states, observes, "There is a warm and noble candour in the character of the Southerners, which mere wealth cannot impart, and there is in their bearing a dignity, without stiffness, which is very pleasing." The descent of these Southrons is essentially the same as of the inhabitants of the Northern states, but they are not, like the former, engaged in a constant rivalry with each other: they live as planters, in the consciousness of possessing unlimited power over their slaves upon their own property. All this produces a certain feeling of security, which induces them neither modestly to conceal their virtues nor to be ashamed of their vices. In like manner we find in Europe, among the Southern nations, a richer imagination, a greater vividness, combined with less perseverance, whilst the Northerners are more serious and reserved, less noisy in their pleasures, and more phlegmatic. Here, also, we find that education and social habits, which impose a greater degree of self-restraint, are more potent than the climate. Still there must be a definite influence of climate in this respect when we hear, that in all parts of Spanish America there exists as great a contrast between the inhabitants of the hot plains and those in the Cordilleras, as between the Northern and Southern nations of Europe; the former appear to the latter cold and lifeless, whilst the Southrons are accused of levity and inconstancy.[3]

Wherever climate, the nature of the country, and social relations are decidedly unfavourable, man's progress to civilization is seriously obstructed. An unhealthy climate enfeebles

---

[1] Lesson, "Voyage méd. autour du monde," p. 128, 1829.
[2] "Second Voyage."
[3] Humboldt, "Neu-Spanien," iv, p. 319.

body and mind, so that man's efforts scarcely suffice to provide for his physical existence. If nature yields quantitatively but a scanty subsistence, man is frequently exposed to want, and physical and mental debility must be the result. If, in addition, his nation is surrounded by inimical tribes, so that it must live in a state of isolation, every progress is clearly obstructed whatever may be the original mental endowment. But in such a condition are most of the peoples who occupy the lowest scale in civilization: the Bosjesmans, the natives of Tierra del Fuego, a considerable number of the Australians; also the black aborigines of many East India islands, who live, as it were, imprisoned by the Malays of the coast, and the savage tribes of the Vindjha mountains, of the Deccan, and other parts of India, etc.

The results will be more favourable, where a people living in a healthy climate is master of the soil and its products. In such a condition are the greater portion of the natives of America and Africa, and they stand somewhat higher in civilization than the above-mentioned nations. It is surrounding nature which first determines the direction of their activity, for on it depends what means, instruments, and skill are requisite to satisfy their daily wants, and what difficulties they have to contend with. It is easily seen how great must be the difference it makes in the character of a people, whether the chase, fishing, gathering of fruits, or the breeding of cattle and agriculture constitute the essential subsistence of a people.

Where vegetable food is not abundant, there will originally arise a tendency to a hunting life—first, because, if successful, it yields in a short time a large amount of aliment; and secondly, because the excitement which attends it is more adapted to the feeling of strength and the natural inclination than the tame collecting of fruit. However, the first important result of a hunting life is, the scattering of the population in small masses which require a large area, which by itself renders any advance in civilization impossible, a relatively dense population with its multifarious reciprocal relations being an indispensable condition of civilization. The hunters, moreover, must follow the game; they form no permanent settlements; their migrations entangle them in various wars for the possession of fresh lands—all which obstruct civilization. Sometimes it is but one beast upon which the existence of such hunting tribes depends. Thus, in the immense prairies between the Rocky Mountains and the Mississippi, it is the buffalo. It provides the Sioux with aliment, clothing, sinews for their bows, thread, strings, harness and saddles, water-vessels, boats, glue, and skins, etc.,[1] just as in many tropical countries the palm tree provides most of the necessities of the natives. Wherever the game is not fit to supply these wants, the animal and the mineral kingdom must yield their quota. Wood, stones, and bones are used as weapons until some happy accident leads to the use of metals—a decided step towards a superior material culture when it rests upon invention, but much less so when the introduction of the metals depends on a stranger, because of their fabrication being unknown to the natives.

The chief characteristics of the hunter result from his mode of life; he becomes familiar with danger; accustomed to hardships, he grows bold and energetic. A feeling of independence is developed, in the wars with his neighbours he is never entirely subjected and reduced to slavery, as his steeled elastic organism still retains something of the original impulse for liberty. As a warrior, hatred and revenge stimulate him to bold deeds; but there is also cunning, treachery, and cruelty in his character, for a certain savageness is the almost unavoidable concomitant of the habit of killing and the excitement attendant on hunting; the cunning it requires, the mode of slaying the game, lead to a corresponding treatment of human beings who meet him as enemies. Wild animals are the benefactors of the huntsman, as his subsistence depends on them, but often his life is endangered by them; hence his religious ideas are shaped accordingly, the animal world is for him a spiritual world, a realm of mythological beings.[2]

---

[1] Perrin du Lac, "Reise in d. beiden Louisianen," ii, p. 27, Leipz., 1807.

[2] It is a mistaken idea of Muller's ("Gesch. der Am. Urrelig," p. 60, 1855), that the primitive man beholds in the animal a manifestation of the general power of nature, and not a being with individual consciousness. On the contrary, the primitive man looks upon all phenomena as individual phenomena; the idea of a universal power of nature is beyond his conception.

Simpson[1] observes justly, that the character of peoples living together in masses differs greatly from those who wander about scattered in the woods, or live by fishing. This is especially shown on comparing fishing with hunting peoples.

The fisher requires instruments differing much from those of the hunter. They are generally less varied in shape, nor does the fisher require such an acute perception of the phenomena of nature; his experience is less, and hence his mental horizon is more limited. His mode of life is not apt to call forth that energy of character which distinguishes the hunter; he is not a warrior, has no ambition, no confidence in his own strength, no love for liberty. The greater security for subsistence without much effort makes him indolent, and he is generally very deficient in cleanliness. Fishing peoples, however, occupy a higher state when they live on the coast, carrying on a coasting trade, and in the struggle with the elements they have to display more invention and courage than the river fishers. The intercourse with strangers also contributes to stimulate their activity, especially if fishing does not form their sole means of subsistence. The gathering of wild growing fruits is but little calculated to promote intellectual development; it becomes nevertheless important as leading to the cultivation of the soil, the thought of which must naturally arise when the fruit does not grow in sufficient abundance. It is the cultivation of the soil which may be considered as the first and necessary stage from which civilization proceeds.

Agriculture may, however, be carried on in a way that proves but a weak lever of civilization. Numerous instances in all parts of the world may be cited to that effect. In the north-west of the great prairies of North America rice grows wild in large quantities, extending from 31-50° N. lat., and

---

When water, a tiger, a serpent, do any mischief, it is an individual evil spirit which has incited them to do so. It is not the genus or the species which inspires the primitive man with awe, and which he worships. Even where all the animals of a certain species are worshipped, it is only the particular individual which is honoured as the incarnation of an individual spirit. The travestying of natural forces into mythological persons, does not correspond with the intuition of the primitive man; but he beholds in what *we* call nature a number of mysterious, arbitrarily acting, individual beings.

[1] "Narrative of a Journey round the world," i, p. 251, 1847.

from the Atlantic to St. Peter's River,[1] and next to fish is the chief nutriment of the Chippeways and other tribes. It is not sown, whilst many other North American peoples, besides being hunters, also sow some cereals, chiefly maize. Among these agriculture is only a temporary expedient; they carry it on irregularly, reap what they have sown, and move further on, thus remaining nomadic despite their agricultural pursuits, which, moreover, only occupy them in summer, whilst the chase is followed in winter. Under such circumstances, it is evidently, as regards the civilization of a people, of little importance whether they cultivate the soil, or merely gather the wild growing fruit, for they do not become attached to the soil; and in such cases agriculture contributes but little to change the character of the people.

Neither do we find in most Negro countries any progressive civilization, though agriculture exists to a considerable extent, the mode of life not being nomadic, and the social relations being more developed than among the natives of America. But the comparatively low degree of civilization among the Negroes may be chiefly explained by the relaxing effects of the climate, the geographical position of these regions, the few requirements as regards dress, food, and habitation, all which nature yields in abundance, and are obtainable by the simplest efforts. The quantity and productiveness of vegetables, the possession of domestic and gregarious animals, combined with the industry of the women, who mostly cultivate the soil, are more than sufficient to provide the Negro with all the comforts which check the impulse to a higher civilization.

We perceive hence that even the breeding of domestic animals and cattle by itself is not sufficient to lead to progressive civilization. A nomadic pastoral life cannot be considered as an advance compared with a fishing or hunting life. The Hottentots were in possession of numerous flocks and herds when the Europeans first visited their country; and the Kaffirs are a pastoral people to this day. Cattle breeding does not necessarily lead to a settled life, though it is compatible with

[1] Keating, "Narrative of an Expedition to the source of St. Peter's River," ii, pp. 107, 146, 1825.

it, and renders it more secure if combined with agriculture. It is on this combination that progressive civilization depends; separately they effect but little. Here it may be right to mention, that in the whole of America, Peru alone, at an early period, had domesticated animals, namely, the llama and alpaca, whilst of edible plants, it possessed the potato and the quinoa. With the exception of Peru, pastoral life could not prevail in the New World, the want of which, as Humboldt[1] has shown, exercised a decisive influence on the civilization of the inhabitants. The dog was much used as a beast of burden, and its influence on the mode of life of the natives was unimportant. Even the horse, which the Europeans introduced into the Northern and Southern continent, has proved ineffectual in America as a means of civilization, showing plainly that the effect produced by the most important domestic animals depends on the mode of life and the degree of cultivation which the people had then already acquired. The buffalo chase, without the horse, must be more difficult and less productive, as the buffaloes are gregarious, and swiftness is more requisite than craft. Little apt for breeding in general, the American has not used the horse for such a purpose: he catches it according to his requirements, so that this animal merely contributed in inducing him to continue a hunting life. On the other hand, the camel, which was but introduced into Africa from the East in the third century,[2] is, in the deserts of North Africa and Arabia, often the sole means of subsistence; its milk, its endurance and usefulness as a beast of burden, have rendered these parts accessible, and almost everywhere has this animal exercised an important influence on the mode of life. This applies also to the horse in relation to the equestrian nations of the interior of Asia and the greater portion of Arabia.

The climatic conditions which so much influence the temperament and character, and the natural products which determine the modes of life, are not the sole agents in the develop-

---

[1] "Reise in die Æquinoctialg." ii, p. 382, ed. Hauff.
[2] "L'Institut.," p. 136, 1857.

ment of civilization. The geographical position of the country, the quality of the surface are no mean elements.

Unquestionably important as all these elements are, we must be cautious not to exaggerate them. Montesquieu has evidently over-estimated the influence of climate by propounding the theory that republics can only thrive in cold, despotism only in hot countries, and constitutional monarchies in temperate climates. Latterly, it has even been promulgated that moral purity and courage are incompatible with tropical heat, and a love of liberty has been ascribed to mountaineers, etc. Granted that some of these relations actually exist, they must be limited thus far, that dissipation and excesses are more peculiar to the southern temperament, and moderation to the nothern temperament. A deduction of the national character and the civilization of nations. solely from the nature of the climate and the soil, as Weerth[1] has made, is easily refuted. With regard to the above-mentioned characteristics we are reminded that the morals of the Kamtschatdales, Aleutes, and some other northern nations are as corrupt as possible; that the bravery of the Arabs, of some Malays and Negro-tribes is exemplary; that carnage and cruelty reach a very high degree among many hunting nations of North America; whilst on the other hand, many inhabitants of the tropics in America, as well as in Africa, are distinguished by their peaceable character, and that mountaineers can more easily escape subjection than the inhabitants of valleys. An innate love of liberty moreover distinguishes the tribes occupying the plains of North America. It is equally inadmissible to transfer the poetical impressions which the civilized man receives from what is grand in nature to the primitive man, as all æsthetical conceptions of nature are partly the reflex of a rich cultivated imagination, which the primitive man does not possess. The religious ideas and legends of primitive peoples prove this sufficiently. Plants, useful or dangerous animals play in them a sensible part, but of the conception of the grand and beautiful in nature there is no trace, nature being exclusively looked at in rela-

[1] "D. Entw. der Menschenrassen," 1842.

tion to its use or its danger, and the fear with which it inspires man.

No less caution is required in estimating the influence of geographical condition on human civilization. Guyot deduces from geographical conditions alone, the axiom, that the peoples of the three large northern continents of the globe have the mission to undertake the psychical development of humanity, whilst those of the southern parts have only to follow them, and that some have no substantive power whatever to become civilized by their own efforts.

If the question were merely to decide which countries are, in consequence of their geographical condition, most capable of promoting civilization, Europe would certainly bear away the palm. C. Ritter[1] has shown that Europe possesses proportionately the greatest coast-line, that the positions of its islands and peninsulas are excellent, whilst other quarters of the world are much less favoured by nature. Thus the interior of Africa is almost shut out of this advantage; the interior of Asia seems destined for ever to remain the home of nomadic life; whilst the forelands and peninsulas of this part are by nature rendered accessible to civilization. Ritter also points out with regard to Egypt,[2] that the seclusion of that country by the desert, the regular rise of the Nile,—the condition of all fertility,—the absence of tide, and some other circumstances, have naturally led to that concentration of activity and seclusion which distinguished old Egyptian civilization. Whilst the peoples beyond the valley of the Nile remained nomadic, those within the valley passed easily from a pastoral to an agricultural life, and the river stimulated their scientific efforts in the development of navigation, water-works, and indirectly, geometry, astronomy, and chronology. That the stationary character of civilization in some peoples is frequently owing to the disadvantages of surrounding nature has been exemplified in the Bretons.[3] A nomadic life was impossible in

---

[1] Ueber räuml. Anordnungen auf d. Aussenseite des Erdballs in d. Abh. d. Berl. Akad., 1849.

[2] "Erdkunde," i, p. 875.

[3] Courson, "Hist. des peuples Brétons," i, p. 186, 1846.

their country. Isolated by mountains and surrounded by enemies, it was too confined to furnish them a subsistence without agriculture; its steep coasts exposed to the westerly winds did not admit of fishing during a portion of the year, nor was the nature of the country favourable to the chase or a nomadic pastoral life. The more difficult culture is, the slower is its progress, and every industry requires, as Chaptal expresses it, like every plant, its own peculiar soil.

The importance of the above conditions for the development of the life of peoples is manifest. There can be no doubt whatever that the variety of surface, combined with a temperate climate, have been essential elements in the production of that high degree of civilization which Europe has reached. This, however, does not justify us in attributing the civilization of the European, nor the barbarism prevailing in Africa and Australia, to geographical conditions alone. Thus we find that the difference existing in Africa between the Negroes of the coast and the interior is just the reverse of what we might expect according to the above theory, for the latter stand, in spirit and character, much higher than the former. Whilst elsewhere the proximity of the sea promotes civilization, it isolates, as Hollard observes, in Africa, whilst the interior is more favourable to the intercourse of peoples.

Two points must never be lost sight of in estimating the influence of geographical conditions in promoting or obstructing civilization. The first is the relative value of these conditions, which partly depends on the degree of civilization already obtained by a people, and thus differs in its effects; and secondly, the important distinction of positive impulses to culture from merely occasional opportunities, which may remain unused, if the former be wanting. These two points are intimately connected. The example of Europe shows that what we have termed occasional causes of civilization are the more made use of, the higher the degree of civilization which has already been attained by a people. A favourable geographical position, the nature of the coasts, the richness of the soil, either on or below the surface, become important means of progressive development. It is for this reason that Europe must present the greatest development; but that the transition from a primitive state to a higher degree of civilization was rendered more easy in Europe than elsewhere is very doubtful, since geographical conditions alone do not constitute positive impulses to civilization.

The relative influence of geographical conditions on culture is shown in many instances. The influence of the sea on the progress of nations depends partly on the nature of the coasts. Good harbours promote trade, colonization, etc.; a deficiency in this respect obstructs them. All this, however, depends on the development of the art of navigation; where this is wanting the sea obstructs trade and civilization. Latham observes justly,[1] that for the Turk on the Hellespont a small stream presented an obstruction, owing to the absence of means for water carriage. Hence it is unscientific to generalize *à priori* in respect to the influence of land and water as means of natural intercourse or the spreading of nations. The desert, the prairie, or the ocean are limits which confine the spreading of tribes or peoples, or ways which favour it, accordingly as the camel, horse, or ship are available for service. The degree of civilization of the people itself alone proves decisive. The inhabitants of the oases in the African deserts are under the influence of the caravan trade, which impresses the character of a considerable portion of the North Africans with a strikingly uniform stamp; they are necessarily traders, but neither the geographical conditions, nor even the possession of the camel, would have made them so if, ignorant of cattle breeding, they had abandoned this animal to itself, as the native Americans did with the horse.

Streams, bays, the vicinity of the sea, all invite emigration, but they do not impel to it, least of all do they influence the savage, who has no desire to see the world, but gladly remains where he finds support unless driven away by want or enemies. It seems, therefore, more correct to attribute the stability of Chinese and Indian civilization to the relative isolation of the

---

[1] "Natural history of the varieties of man," p. 129, 1850.

interior of these countries by natural conditions, than to deduce the origin of their civilization from the advantages offered by their geographical position, for, in this respect, that portion of India which is still more favoured has never attained a substantive civilization. The peoples of the Deccan, notwithstanding the favours of nature and their intercourse with the Hindoos, are but little civilized. The Celts, also, have remained more stationary than the Teutons, and, though they have often been displaced, and suffered great deprivations, still they were, like the latter, favoured by their geographical position.

Although, generally speaking, it is quite true that the presence or absence of certain animals, plants, or minerals, in combination with the geographical conditions, partly determine the degree of civilization which may be attained by a people through its own efforts, it is on the other hand also demonstrated, that a great portion of the natural advantages remain neglected, that animals fit for breeding are abandoned to themselves, that cereals are not cultivated, minerals remain hidden in the earth, and all this either because necessity or the requisite knowledge was absent, and thus the natives, notwithstanding the wealth of surrounding nature, never emerged from the state of barbarism. The influence of natural conditions is best exhibited in peoples whose perfect seclusion guarantees to them the possession of their country. The best known instances of that kind are furnished by some islands of the South Sea and the Indian Archipelago. In the latter there are tribes of the Malay race, who not unfrequently, both as regards physical and social development, stand lower than the Papuas of the coasts, and even the Australians of Port Essington.[1] W. Earl[2] also observes, that in the Indian Archipelago the state of cultivation of the natives seemingly depends not so much on race as on surrounding nature. Near the sea and on the rivers they usually become navigators, in the table lands agriculturists, for which reason he abandoned his former theory of an immigation of Polynesians to North Australia. In the majority of the Polynesian islands we see in earlier periods a harmless, thoughtless

[1] Logan, in "Journal of the Indian Archipelago," vol. i.

[2] "The native races of the Indian Archipelago," p. 235, 1853.

population, without any distinctive character, surrounded by a nature so rich and varied, as scarcely to call forth any bodily labour. Devoid of all moral ideas, they consider physical enjoyment as the chief object of life. The tyranny of the nobility, intercourse with the neighbouring islands, and, in some parts, wars between the tribes, influence civilization, and exercise a sort of antagonism against the influences of the agencies of the natural conditions. The inhabitants of the high islands of volcanic origin in Polynesia, generally occupy a higher scale than those of the Coral islands, who, kept down by the paucity of nature, are more savage and dirty in their habits, and less accessible to strangers.[1]

If it be our chief object to ascertain the acting impulses which induce man to leave the primitive state, we must turn to the consideration of social and historical conditions; for, however important natural and geographical advantages may be as occasional causes, they only produce a positive effect by the mode of life which is adopted by their agency and by the abundance or deficiency of the necessaries of life which they afford—but even these influences become either a propelling or repelling force by the social consequences which they produce.

This is first shown by the migrations of peoples which are usually caused by natural conditions, and by the wars in which they become in most cases entangled.

These two constitute, unquestionably, the most potent levers acting on civilization. Deficiency of means of subsistence or a powerful enemy, may force a people to leave their native country. Even in present times, the Indians separate in tribes if the chase prove unproductive. Exploring parties having been first sent out, the separation is peaceably effected, and friendly relations are established between the separated parties. The separation may also have been caused by internal discord, or they may have been dispersed by external wars.[2] These migrations, frequently extending over vast tracts of land, and through different climates, proceeding very gradually, become very pregnant in their results in bringing the

[1] Latham, loc. cit., Pickering, p. 68.
[2] Hunter, "Memoirs of a Captivity among the Indians," p. 180, 1824.

peoples in contact with other branches of mankind either friendly or inimical to them.

The influence which these migrations produce upon the civilization of the respective nations may be beneficial or not, though in the majority of cases the good effects are predominating. These migrations in the first place prevent a firm foundation of social order and the habit of regular labour, engendering a desire for constant changes. The Hottentot, though he may be in a good place and has no complaint against his master, leaves him suddenly, as he cannot long bear the uniformity of his life, but returns as suddenly to his former service.[1] The Gauchos frequently leave their masters for no other reason "than that they have served them long enough."[2] Whoever has been brought up in the Pampas of Buenos Ayres is unfit for any work which is not in some way connected with cattle-breeding. To live in a city, or as agriculturists, would be intolerable to those people. Most of them have never seen a town, and know not how old they are. Their only ambition is to be good horsemen, their favourite occupation cattle-breeding; trade and every kind of industry are despised, neglected, and abandoned to the stranger.[3] We are, therefore, not surprised to read in Darwin that the number of horses, and the abundance of provisions in Montevideo checked all industry.

Another unfavourable consequence of migrations is this, that the transition from a rich to a poor country exposes the respective peoples to want and a loss of the civilization they had previously attained, whilst the sudden transition from want to abundance may induce a degeneracy not less inimical to progress. Whether and how far these evils may be avoided, depends not so much on the new natural conditions as on the skill and character of the immigrants, and on the useful animals and plants they may introduce into their new country.

---

[1] Moodie, "Ten Years in South Africa," i, p. 215, 1835.

[2] Ausland, p. 28, 1858.

[3] MacCann, "Two thousand miles ride through the Argentine Provinces," i, p. 57, 155, 1853; and the description of the Gauchos by Azara, "Voyage dans l'Amérique mérid.," ii, p. 292, 1809; Head, "Rough notes taken during Journeys across the Pampas," p. 258, 1826.

The happiest combination in this respect is generally when the art and skill already acquired are not forgotten, but may be further developed. Nearly all migrations lead to an accommodation to new circumstances. Fresh difficulties prepared by enemies or the elements, require new efforts and inventions, just as any new animal and every particular species of the chase requires a peculiar skill, knowledge, and experience. Different means of subsistence must be adopted, and the habits of life become essentially altered—all of which stimulate psychical activity. The expansion of the mental horizon becomes greater when greater skill is required to satisfy such wants as called forth but little exertion in the abandoned territory. It is thus clear that in such cases every thing depends upon what relation the condition of the new country stands to the civilization, requirements, and habits of the immigrant people. If the nature of the country and the condition of the people are favourable to progress, a vagabond people may become agricultural and settled; if unfavourable, it will sink again into nomadic life.

Migrations become very important in their effects through the reciprocal influences of the various nations who come in contact, which is rarely of a peaceable nature at first. Friendly intercourse among peoples, as among individuals, is something secondary. Distrust and jealousy, the desire of exclusive possession of the goods of life, are but natural, especially in a poor country, and when the first contact of peoples is usually hostile. The incessant wars in which we see uncivilized nations constantly engaged, partly prevent their progress; but, on the other hand, it is war which rouses them from their psychical indolence, and prevents them sinking into a state of lethargy. War, no doubt, rouses all the passions, but, at the same time, it calls for great efforts, and stimulates invention. But this is not all. Wars require, above all, a union of force, which is not easily effected without it. Whether this union be loose or only temporary, whether its duration depend on the individualities of the leading persons, and then on the spirit of submission or independence of the people in general, still an important step has been gained. Individuals who formerly lived in a state of isolation are now animated by a common interest, and united in common action, so important for the social development of a people. One of the most important effects of war is this, that the commanding and obeying elements temporarily subsisting in war become permanent after its termination; for though the wars of savages do not immediately lead to the establishment of despotism, still the relations between master and servant, between conqueror and conquered, are established, relations which, in various forms and degrees, are found in all the higher stages of civilization, and seem, in fact, indispensable to its development.

The notions of right are developed by wars, for it is only after the peoples have measured their strength that they commence making mutual concessions, and especially so with reference to defining the boundaries of their possessions. The first consequence of war is, that fixed relations are established between peoples, which render friendly intercourse possible, an intercourse which becomes more important from the interchange of knowledge and experience than from the mere interchange of commodities. The reception of the conquered among the victors leads frequently to the same result, the latter appropriating, not only the labour, but the arts of the conquered. It is chiefly the collision of a civilized with a barbarous people which, directly or indirectly, influences the latter, as exemplified in the collisions of the Romans and Germans. There must, however, be rather a fusion than an enslavement. Individuals, however highly civilized when settling among savages, can never effect a transformation of the latter; they will rather sink down to their level, and degenerate or remain isolated amongst them, and, if they produce any effect, it will be merely transitory.

As regards the effects produced by intermixture of peoples and tribes on mental endowment, and the mode in which it modifies temperament and mental peculiarities, all that is known is, that a remarkable transformation actually takes place. As we have already stated, there are two opposite theories, both of which are equally extreme and erroneous. Gobineau is of opinion, that intermixture between different races contains the germ of the necessary decay and final extinction of all civilization; whilst Serres and others maintain that intermixture is the essential lever of all progress. Though we cannot entirely assent to the latter theory, it is unquestionably more acceptable than the first: for whenever we see a people, of whatever degree of civilization, not living in contact and reciprocal action with others, we shall generally find a certain stagnation, a mental inertness, and a want of activity, which render any change of social and political condition next to impossible. These are, in times of peace, transmitted like an everlasting disease, and war appears then, in spite of what the apostles of peace may say, as a saving angel, who rouses the national spirit, and renders all forces more elastic.

It certainly must remain undecided how far these wholesome results are to be attributed to mental intercourse or to physical intermixture: that, however, the latter is justly considered as a lever of historical development results from the fact, that it has never been absent in a civilized country the ethnographical condition of which is known to us. The old Roman civilization has, besides the non-Indo-Germanic element of the Etruscans, also absorbed other non-Latin tribes, and as regards Greece, modern scholars (Kortüm) consider the Pelasgi as an entirely or partially Semitic-Phœnician—at any rate, as an Eastern people, which was essentially different from the rest of the population. That non-Greek tribes (Carians, Leleges, Tyrrheni) lived in Greece before the immigration of the Hellenes, and have gradually become assimilated to the latter, has been rendered certain by historical investigation.

There is found, however, in South and North America, a numerous mixed population who are considered incapable of a high degree of civilization. Semple[1] and Mollien[2] describe the intermixture of races in Caraccas and New Grenada as the source of corruption. In the cities and villages the greatest dissipation prevails; to lie in the hammock, to smoke, gamble, to see bull fights, are the greatest enjoyments. Religion has no influence: sins are confessed and forgiven; indolence and apathy characterize the population. The complaint is so far

[1] "Sketch of the present state of Caraccas," 1812.
[2] "Voyage dans la République de Colombia," 1824.

unjust in applying the standard of European culture to these mixed races. There are neither in the North nor in the South of America instances wanting of these mixed people having taken the initiative in the civilization of the natives; at any rate, they confirm the theory that the mental capacity of mongrels is generally greater than that of the lower of the two races from which they sprung. There are even cases which render it probable that two peoples of an equally low degree, by intermixture produce mongrels of greater capacity; just as is asserted that by the engrafting of a wild sapling upon a wild fruit tree, the fruit is improved.

Density of population, so essential an element of progress, is determined by surrounding nature, for everywhere we find them combined, so that the former has been considered both the result and the cause of civilization.

It has often been suggested, that the cradle of mankind must have been in a hot country, because there only prevailed the conditions necessary for man's existence in a primitive state; and that the East Indies, which possess all animals fit to become domesticated, were probably the home of these animals, as of all our cultivated plants. We have also seen that nature, however rich, gives originally no positive impulse to civilization.

Secondarily, but not primarily, does it favour civilization, *i. e.*, not its first origin, but its progress only; and only in this respect is it true that the great table-lands alone, like Thibet and Abyssinia in the Old, Mexico and Peru in the New World, were the natural cradles of civilization.[1] Rich table-lands only indirectly promote civilization, by inducing a rapid increase of the population, which compels the people to spread, to leave their original habitations, to take the most useful plants and animals with them and import them into poorer regions.

Gützlaff has observed, that in China the great mass of the population has too much bodily labour to obtain the necessaries of life, to evince any mental activity. This shows that too

---

[1] Pickering, "The Races of man," p. 300, 1849.

dense a population may obstruct civilization. Though necessity may indirectly be a means of civilization, it is not so under all circumstances. There are not a few barbarous nations who suffer annually from want of provisions, and though in possession of useful plants, never attempt to cultivate the soil. Distress, no doubt, impels them to greater physical and mental efforts, but these cease with the distress.

If the population be thin and the country productive, there is but little or no inducement to labour, as everyone can easily obtain the necessaries of life for himself and his family. Individuals remain in such cases independent of each other, excepting on particular occasions; there is no community of interest,—no union of forces. The social relations beyond the family extend chiefly to patriarchal hospitality, which diminishes and disappears with the progress of civilization. The original motive for hospitality is the desire for society, curiosity, and the sympathy for the helpless, derived from bitter experience. These relations assume a different aspect with the increase of the population. The intercourse between individuals, the interchange of thought and of goods, are increased by living in close vicinity and immediate contact; comparisons as regards their position and performances are made,—they become rivals, and disputes arise. The rivalry extends to labour, which, besides present necessaries, is also to provide for the future. There arise contrasts between wealth and poverty. The possession of goods is more estimated, as it can only be obtained by labour, and private property must be protected. The increase of the population renders agriculture a necessity; and from the already existing inequality, relations are developed between master and dependent, which is already a step towards the foundation of despotism, as opposed to that original liberty and perfect independence of individuals. We have now arrived at a stage from which the development of society may, under favourable circumstances, be more or less rapid.

Before proceeding further, it may be as well to cast a retrospective glance at the question, whether our investigations justify us in attributing the stability of most peoples in a low scale of civilization, as essentially due to the natural conditions and mode of life under the influence of which they stand; or whether we must assume a specific difference of mental endowment, since the above physical and social forces appear insufficient to explain the phenomenon.

According to the teaching of the American school,[1] the higher races are destined to displace the lower. This extinction of the lower races is predestined by nature, and it would thus appear that we must not merely acknowledge the right of the white American to destroy the red man, but perhaps praise him that he has constituted himself the instrument of Providence in carrying out and promoting this law of destruction. The pious manslayer thus enjoys the consolation that he acts according to the laws of nature which govern the rise and extinction of races. Such a theory has many advantages: it reconciles us both with Providence and the evil dispositions of man; it flatters our self-esteem by the specific excellence of our moral and intellectual endowment, and saves us the trouble of inquiring for the causes of the differences existing in civilization. This theory has thus obtained many adherents; whilst there are some who consider this one of the reasons which render the assumption of a specifically higher mental endowment of the white race, improbable.

In opposition to this American doctrine, we maintain that the psychical endowment of the various races was most probably originally the same, or nearly so; that the earlier or later emergence of individual peoples from the primitive state essentially depended on the natural and social conditions in which they were placed; and that by these external circumstances in their manifold concatenations, the extent and rapidity of their development was mainly determined. We must not omit referring here to a principle already touched upon—namely, that the development of mankind in the course of time produces a favourable predisposing influence on the psychical endowment of the progeny, which increases with the progress of civilization, which predisposition must be less the nearer a people is to the

---

[1] Agassiz, Morton, etc., etc.

primitive state. This partly explains why we see so many peoples apparently stationary, whilst others proceed rapidly from a certain point.

The solution of the question is rendered difficult at the outset if we do not abandon the false theory, arising from the exclusive view of our European civilization, that there is anything in the nature of man generally, or of some tribes particularly, impelling them to civilization; whilst, on the contrary, the uncivilized state is, originally, natural to all. When Humboldt,[1] in declaring for the unity of mankind, and against any difference between higher and lower races, adds, "There are more plastic, but not more noble races; all are equally destined for liberty," the apparent contradiction can only be explained in this way; that the greater natural inclination and capacity for civilization manifested by some peoples, is nothing original, but something acquired in the course of their development, which, under favourable circumstances, might have been equally acquired by peoples who appear at present less capable of civilization.

The investigation of the question is not less impeded by referring, like Stanhope Smyth, De Salles, and others, the beginning of all civilization not to the nature and activity of man, but to the immediate influence of God. This view has been supported by the circumstance, that the first elements of civilization, as far as history reaches, always appear as communicated from one people to another, and that of no people can it be proved how, where, and when they have become civilized by their own inherent power. However true this may be, it is easily explained, since history neither reaches nor can ever reach back to the primitive condition of man. All this manifestly does not justify us in assuming a direct communication of the necessary arts and knowledge, or of language, by God to man. Moreover as, strictly speaking, there is no commencement of civilization in an absolute sense, but merely a gradual passing from one state of culture to another, it remains as difficult to explain how a people already emerged from a primi-

---

[1] "Cosmos," i, p. 385.

tive state can, without direct interference of God, make any progress in civilization, as how it was possible for them to take the earliest steps which served as a basis for their further development.

The impediments which obstruct the progress of primitive peoples and keep them in a state of barbarism, are multifarious. A nomadic life and constant warfare, have become a second nature to them; they have but few wants, and these are more easily satisfied than those of the civilized man; they are content with their position, feel themselves comparatively happy, and desire no change; their reluctance to labour, and their carelessness for the future, induce them to neglect what appears to them useful and necessary. The apathy with which they look at everything not immediately bearing on their necessities, scarcely exciting a passing curiosity, prevents their learning from experience. These impediments to progress are pretty much the same among all uncivilized peoples, and it requires no great acuteness to perceive that the assumption of a specifically different endowment of races is at least unnecessary to explain the differences in their civilization.

Among the elements of civilization, agriculture unquestionably occupies the first place: it is the chief basis of it, nor can true civilization grow out of any other soil. This applies to agriculture, only so far as it constitutes the essential means of subsistence, especially in connection with cattle-breeding, which renders hunting superfluous.

It is the unproductiveness of the chase, of the fisheries, of fruit and root gathering, which leads to and gradually developes the cultivation of the soil. Without being impelled to it by want, no primitive people will spontaneously turn to agriculture. To pursue agriculture successfully, requires perseverance and patience, which primitive nations do not possess. Simpson[1] observes very justly, that one of the main difficulties of the transition to agriculture consists in the circumstance that they are accustomed immediately to expect and to enjoy the fruit of their labour. Hence it appears, that where there does not

1 "Narrative of a journey round the world," i, p. 251, 1847.

exist a slow and steady transformation of the mode of life from an irregular and changeable activity to more uniform industry, agriculture requires a special condition if it is to reach that extent and regularity, by which alone it becomes the basis of civilization.

Social conditions favour agriculture by establishing the relations of master and servant, and so does slavery, which is a usual consequence of war. Peoples who have no agriculture, or consider it only as a secondary affair, generally kill their prisoners of war, or more rarely adopt them in their own tribes; such, however, as cultivate the soil make their prisoners work. Slavery thus spreads with agriculture, whether it has originated from war or not, and agriculture gains in extent and regularity, so that it becomes in time the chief means of subsistence for the people. Since all the work is performed by others, it gives to the free people that leisure which is requisite to secure for them a comfortable existence.

This latter circumstance is, in some respect, rather an impediment than a help to civilization, for, however true it is that leisure is requisite for intellectual development, still in that leisure itself there is for the primitive man no impulse to serious mental activity. The promotion of civilization by agriculture lies rather in the circumstance that it accustoms to regular labour, renders the people less inclined to war, produces an attachment to a fixed habitation, and a settled mental disposition differing from indolence.

The important influence which agriculture, however imperfect, exercises upon the national character, is shown in many instances. The Indians of the Cordilleras in South America, who like agriculture, are peaceable and timid; those of the plains bold and enterprising, finding pleasure in the dangers of hunting the jaguar and the wild bull, or taming the horse.[1] The greater capacity for progress in the agriculturist is shown by comparing him with the hunter: the former sees his inferiority to the white man, and is more easily induced to improve his condition; whilst the latter despises the arts of the European, and,

---

[1] Mollien, loc. cit., ii, p. 168.

in the feeling of his independence, deems himself the superior. A great portion of the Negro and South Sea peoples, who possess very indifferent agricultural implements, acknowledge the superiority of the Europeans in this respect, and endeavour to imitate them; whilst the American hunting tribes merely stare at the civilization which constantly meets their eye, and turn their backs upon it, showing but little inclination to live among Europeans.

The agriculturist leads a more secure life, less exposed to accidents than the hunter; his labour is less exciting and less dangerous, nor is he agitated by the same expectations and fears. Agriculture and a fixed habitation increase the means of subsistence, diminish toil, especially of the females, rendering them more prolific, and thus contribute to the increase of the population. Regular labour induces sobriety; manners and customs are established among settled inhabitants, which are incompatible with a licentious wandering life; internal and external peace becomes a necessity, for man wishes to enjoy the fruit of his labour. He does not attack from a desire to conquer; he merely defends what he possesses; he feels the necessity of a regulated social life, for he has built better houses, rendered them more comfortable, and his enjoyments have gradually multiplied. Already among pastoral tribes, observes Falconer,[1] there obtains, in comparison with hunting and fishing nations, a considerable extension of private property, and an increase in its value; and crimes against property are often very severely punished. Though originally the strong has subjected the weak, and the latter has submitted both from fear of punishment and an instinctive admiration of manly power, the times are now changing: a government founded upon mere individual authority is no longer deemed sufficient, and a desire arises for fixed social relations. The settled agriculturist now obtains his subsistence by moderate labour, and the population increases in proportion. Migrations no longer occur unless forced upon the people by external or internal wars, a wandering life is now opposed to newly acquired habits, and to attachment to the native soil.

[1] "Remarks on the influence of Climate," p. 328, 1781.

It results from the preceding observations, that agriculture contains many of the essential germs of civilization, though they are rarely fully developed. We may at the same time remark, that peoples which have never been under the necessity of abandoning a nomadic life, who possess no beasts of burden, should not be reproached with an incapacity for civilization, as the assumption of an innate impulse for culture and labour, without being driven to it by necessity, is a mere fiction. If such peoples should become civilized by their own native force, we should consider them as more highly gifted than the Europeans.

It is true that we do not everywhere, even when agriculture constitutes the chief means of subsistence, observe such rapid progressive development as we might be led to expect. A variety of causes may prevent such progress. If nature is too generous, and very little labour is required for raising the necessaries of life, physical indolence must be the result. This disadvantage, under which many Negro countries labour, only disappears if the superfluities of the native soil find an outlet by trade, and the people require articles of necessity or luxury peculiar to foreign countries. It has already been observed, that agriculture loses the greater part of its beneficial influence if exclusively carried on by slaves. Agriculture produces in time an inequality in the possession of goods. Individuals grow in wealth, whilst others who do not reap the fruit of their labour become dependent. The consequence is, that there is no love of labour, for "people who live by the work of their hands are only industrious when they enjoy the fruit of their handiwork, or have been trained to constant activity."[1] The spirit of oppression and of self-interest which prevails in society undermines or destroys all moral feelings, as may be seen in many peoples of Africa and the South Sea.

We are thus introduced to another essential agent of civilization, namely, the development of public law and government. Their influence is very great, but it is difficult to arrive at its true value. By some it is considered as all powerful.

---

[1] Wrangell, "Statist. in Ethnog. nachr. über d. russ. Besitz. in Am." p. 217, 1839.

Barthes[1] says, that political conditions chiefly determine the manners and the national character; the climatic conditions determine the physical peculiarities; and, if both co-exist unchanged for several centuries, a race is produced which, if it remains unmixed, may perpetuate itself in other climates, and under different political relations. Passy, on the other hand, has endeavoured to prove,[2] that though the power of political and social institutions may promote or retard national progress, it is not determined by them, inasmuch as the same institutions constantly change among the same people. At any rate, we cannot but recognise in climate, mode of life, density of population and its intermixture with foreign elements, and the development of mental activity, powers which are but remotely governed by laws, whilst they undoubtedly influence the formation and efficacy of the latter.

The security of private property is the most important of all legal institutions, and the very basis of civilization. Its origin among primitive peoples and its development depend chiefly on the relations between the mode of life and the necessities of the population, and the area and natural conditions in which they live. Among the Indians of Magna the aggregation of a number of people in the same spot was the main cause of the establishment of landed property.[3] Among the Indians on the Orinoco, fisheries, hunting districts, &c., are common property of the tribe, but the land becomes private property as soon, and so long, as it is cultivated.[4] As the Northern Nicobares are more densely populated than the Southern, private property is better defined in the former, where boundary stones are placed, which is not the case in the latter.[5] Considering the deficiency of water in Australia, it is not surprising that the natives lay claim to the water of the rivers, near which they live.[6] Next to occupation and long exclusive possession, it is the labour expended which gives origin to private pro-

[1] "Nouv. élémens de la sc. de l'homme," ii, p. 274, 1806.
[2] "L'Instit.," ii, p. 19, 1845.
[3] Pöppig, "Reise in Chile, Peru, und auf d. Amazonenstr.," ii, p. 374, 1835.
[4] Gilii, "Nachr. v. Lande Guiana," p. 327, 1785.
[5] Steen Bille, "Bericht über d. Reise der Galathea," i, p. 288, 1852.
[6] Mitchell, "Three Exped. into the Interior of E. Australia," p. 304, 1838.

perty, and makes it respected by others. This respect, which among primitive peoples is generally enforced by the proprietor himself as the chief (who does not willingly interfere in the disputes of individuals, nor is he generally looked upon as a natural judge), has an important moral effect, since it leads to self-control, and places limits to general covetousness. In order to rouse and sustain the exertion of regulated efforts, security of property and its enjoyment are essential.

These happy results are destroyed by oppression and arbitrary power. Wherever these exist accompanied by extortion, the very appearance of wealth is carefully avoided. Thus the natives of Loango breed but few domestic cattle, and prefer hunting, as the officials of the rulers rob them of the former.[1] In Tahiti the cultivation of the soil was neglected, because the Arreois on festival occasions either destroyed or took possession of the crops.[2] Dampier[3] attributes the indolence of the inhabitants of Mindanao, formerly an active people, to the prevailing despotism. This must not, however, prevent us from acknowledging the latter as a primary necessary element in the development of society, nor from under-estimating the beneficial effects which may frequently result therefrom.

Where the people can support themselves without much effort, owing to the productiveness of the country, where the population much increases, and inequalities of property or social position arise, the masses must be kept in order by force. Under such circumstances, it is of small importance for society whether that superior power is subject to fixed laws, or whether it is equitably exercised; what is really essential is, that some authority should be established, for in such cases any government is preferable to a state of anarchy. Pure despotism has at least the advantage, that labour is enforced and order maintained. If the despotism lasts, it imparts to the masses the habit of labour, and the original unbridled savageness gives place to a sedate submissiveness not unfrequently allied with hypocrisy and a cringing disposition. In this sense must be under-

---

1 Proyart, "Hist. de Loango, Kakongo, et autres roy.," p. 32, 1776.
2 Wilson, "Miss. Reise in d. still Meer," p. 314, 1800.
3 "Nouv. voy. autour du monde," ii, p. 3, Amst., 1701.

stood the observation of Brooke,[1] as regards the Chinese, that they exhibit in their character all the signs of having lived in a despotic and densely populated country, whilst it may be easily detected in the character of the Malay, that they belonged to a favoured climate which neither forced them to labour nor to control their passions. The latter observation cannot, however, be applied to all Malays, for many of the Malay tribes live under despotic governments. These occupy a higher position in civilization,[2] and also exhibit the effects of despotism upon the national character, as may be seen in the Javanese.

We thus find that the first steps towards civilization can neither be taken nor maintained by primitive nations without the intervention of an energetic despotism; for all liberty which is to benefit social development must be directly proportional to the moral restraint which society imposes upon itself, be it by the power of public opinion, a feeling of honour, education, or religious conceptions. But such a moral restraint diminishes in proportion as a people approaches the primitive state. Under such circumstances, despotism acts beneficially, though it may rest only on conquest or the assumption of power to which the people submit either from fear or in expectation of greater security for life and property. It is in rich countries especially where despotism is first developed and long maintained : great fertility of the soil, also produces an indolent people little inclined to make great efforts for their political liberty. Crawfurd[3] well observes that the uniformity of the seasons and of the natural products, contribute much, in combination with the social condition in tropical regions, and especially in the East Indian Archipelago, to produce mental indolence—all which explains the remarkable fact that there is no instance of a free constitution in the torrid zone among peoples which possess any civilization. Closely connected with the above facts, is the circumstance that the inhabitants of rich countries are rarely courageous and brave; they are effeminated partly by their mode of life, and partly by the influence of despotism.[4]

---

1 "Narrative of events in Borneo and Celebes," i, p. 11, 2nd edit., 1848.
2 Crawfurd, "History of the Indian Archipelago," iii, p. 4, 1820.
3 Loc. cit., ii, p. 37.
4 Falconer, p. 186.

It may be that the muses only flourish among free rude nations, as indeed it has been attempted to prove from history; it may be true that despotism, in many cases, impedes the progress to a higher civilization, still such is not the necessary result, though it must be admitted that the favourable or unfavourable effect which it produces depends upon the accidental disposition of the ruler. In despotically governed countries there is no public opinion and no moral force among the peoples; what passes as such is merely the reflex of the views of the despot. In all the Mohammedan states in Africa, the man whom the sovereign degrades is despised and maltreated. Everything that is ordered is considered right and proper; everything that is forbidden is looked upon as bad and disgraceful. This slavery of conviction is still greater among some peoples. The Matebeles (Zulus) believe in the greatest absurdities, and among others that their chief Moselkatse can look forward into the future, and if any one were to doubt that he can produce rain by ascending to the sky, he would be treated as a traitor. One of the Zulus being told that these are mere delusions, replied, "one must be very cautious in expressing any doubts on the subject."[1] On the other hand, we find in Java, where all jurisdiction proceeds from the king or his lieutenant, that there are cases in which despotism is the most essential means of developing the moral sense of the nation. In the legal language of Java, theft is called "a crime against the king's property," unlawful wounding is called "wounding the king," "regicide."

As it is our chief object to investigate the main forces which influence the development of human society, we shall only mention the sum of the effects on civilization by living in communities. These are—the discipline of the masses, they being gradually habituated to obedience and self-control; greater protection for life and property, which enables the people to devote their activity to other purposes; the establishment of a community of interest and action against external powers, etc.

---

[1] "Baseler Miss. Mag.," iii, p. 141, 1856.

It would be difficult or impossible to give a sketch of the progressive development of society in various directions, influenced as it is by so many and various causes. We must, therefore, confine ourselves to pointing out some other social elements of considerable importance in the development of civilization.

We have already had occasion to observe, that, by the inequalities in the distribution of property, there arises a rivalry which, in one respect, stimulates activity, but also gives cause for disputes, and irritates the passions. This rivalry, accompanied by its beneficial and detrimental consequences, produces a permanent antagonism in society. If to the distinction between the rich and the poor there be added that between the governing and the governed elements, a series of contrasts is established, and the rivalry for the possession of property is now directed to the possession of power and honour.

The development of such antagonistic forces becomes very important, both directly and indirectly, for the progress of culture. It leads, in the first place, to a community of such elements in society whose interest is opposed to that of others. The first step is, that the members of a family originally united by the autocratic will of a man unite with their relations. These family bonds, no doubt, form the essential basis of all civilization.

It is not necessary to descant upon the mode by which the gradations in society lead to the more extensive union of men. Common interest, as opposed to other motives, also leads here to common efforts and greater performances: in order to effect the latter, division of labour presents itself as an effective means.

On comparing the various classes of society, we find as striking differences in their inner as in their external life. The feeling of security, the consciousness of a prominent position, the servility of others, the command over the enjoyments of life, give to the character of the higher ranks a direction and a development as essentially distinct from that of the lower classes, as they differ in nutriment, dress, habitation, and consequent protection from the effects of climate. It has already been pointed out how great is this influence upon the physical peculiarities of mankind, and it needs no proof that they are equally potent as regards psychical life. We can hardly err in considering the development of the above social contrasts as the chief cause of the known phenomenon that, with the progress of civilization, the differences of individual capacities, physically and intellectually, become more striking in society. Among rude nations, the contrasts between master and servant, rich and poor, high and low, are usually connected with birth, and are commonly maintained with such strictness that the transition from one caste to another is forbidden. It is rare, however, that this exclusiveness is maintained in its original rigour. External and internal commotions produce a greater variety in the condition of individuals, the distinctions become gradually obliterated, and in course of time the various classes become intermixed.

It has been said that, "the more nature, the greater the peculiarity of character; the more art and culture, the greater the resemblance of character."[1] This, however, applies only to the civilized world, and even here only under certain limitations; with regard to the comparison of primitive with civilized nations, it is entirely erroneous. Hale[2] also maintains that it is a mistake to attribute to savage nations a certain uniformity of character, of feelings, and passions, but that it was civilization which produced that uniformity; and he adduces as a proof, that the yellow and the black races of the Pacific, who live close to each other, differ more from each other than any two European nations. Though this may be admitted as regards peoples, it does not apply to the characters of individuals; the latter invariably more resemble each other among savage than among the cultivated nations, as the comparison of the native Americans with the more advanced Polynesians plainly shows. But this increasing individual dissimilarity, which seems to extend amongst civilized nations, which is a natural consequence of the differences of social condition and

---

[1] "Schmid. Einl. z. de la Chambre's Anleitung z. Menschenk." p. 62, 1794.
[2] Ethnogr. and Philol. of the U. S. Expl. Exp.," p. 13, Philad., 1846.

increasing intermixture of the various classes, becomes again a powerful lever for progressive development, by producing a corresponding difference in the pursuits and inclinations of individuals, and thus promotes a division of labour.

Connected with these social contrasts and the distinctive character of individual differences, is another circumstance,—the importance of which has, indeed, formerly been overvalued, but which certainly plays no subordinate part in the progress of civilization,—which is, the emergence of highly gifted individuals from the mass of the people, who as rulers, heroes, lawgivers, transform the position of their people, change its relations with other nations, regulate its internal constitution, expand its horizon in science and art, improve their morals, and direct their attention to nobler objects. Whether these objects are attained, whether the seed thus thrown falls upon a productive soil, germinates, and grows to maturity, or decays, depends upon the people; for which reason the capacity and the character of a whole people cannot exactly be determined from the intellectuality exhibited in individual instances.

To form, however, a correct judgment, we must take into consideration that the great mass occupies almost everywhere a very inferior position as regards civilization, and that it is by individual great teachers of humanity that the progress of the mass is mostly effected. It cannot be denied that a number of discoveries and inventions have also been made among the coloured races, but it probably took them a longer time than the Whites before the people appropriated and applied them. Everything seems to depend upon the right man appearing at the right time. Genius exists in every race and in every period; but there must be a mental susceptibility among the people, and a happy combination of circumstances, in order that the talents of an individual may lead to important results, and have their full effect on civilization. The greater the individual disparity amongst peoples, and the greater the difference in their respective modes of life, the less is it to be feared that important inventions may be lost to society; but they will certainly remain neglected so long as the people occupy a low scale in civilization.

We have already had occasion to observe, that trade and commerce are calculated to stimulate the industry of productive countries, provided their inhabitants possess the desire for foreign products. Trade becomes a greater stimulus to invention and enterprise amongst peoples who are compelled to import necessaries from foreign parts.

Productive countries, *i. e.*, such as support their populations abundantly, are self-sufficient; their inhabitants are not anxious for intercourse with strangers, they do not take the initiative in commerce, but are rather passive in bartering for foreign commodities which appear to them useful or curious. So long as poor countries are ignorant of the abundance existing elsewhere, their efforts may remain nugatory, until some few who had been cast away, return and make known their discoveries to their own people. The insular or geographical position of the country is as influential at the outset as in the development of commerce. In order to take the initiative in commerce, (which is a more powerful lever in civilization than a mere passive acquiescence, but at the same time presupposes a higher civilization), a series of inventions, arts, and contrivances are requisite, in order to overcome the difficulties of transit by land and water, and natural or artificial products, either of native or foreign growth, must be collected for exportation. The observation of natural phenomena, especially of the movements of celestial bodies, becomes essential to the navigator, whilst the agriculturist takes only an interest in the changes of the weather and the seasons. Thus trade stimulates inquiry into the connexion and the laws of natural phenomena; whilst elsewhere it is a religious motive which directs the attention to the motions of celestial bodies, and the gradual production of a calendar. It is unnecessary further to dwell on the variety of impulses to physical and mental activity, directly or indirectly, given by commerce. Though in this, as in many other things, the most obvious inventions and discoveries have been long in being made, and many efforts have remained fruitless; still, these very efforts act beneficially on subsequent exertions, by the stimulus they have given to mental efforts.

The immediate results of trade on the civilization of a trading people are not estimated so highly as the efforts made to establish it. There is no doubt that a knowledge of foreign countries, and their history and manners, expands the intellectual horizon; but there does not seem to result from it a genuine improvement in the mode of life, for everything is viewed from the stand-point of profit. "Commerce," observes Falconer,[1] "renders the people more industrious than agriculture; but they become very selfish, they over-estimate the value of wealth; everything is for sale; they are sober and honest, not from virtue but from interest, and they become timid and unwarlike."

Whether trade and intercourse contribute to raise a savage people partly depends on the commodities interchanged, and also on the parties which carry on the trade. The intercourse with a foreign country may become most beneficial, if it, for instance, receives important plants and domestic animals in which it is deficient, so that now a regular agriculture is rendered possible; or it may become a curse, if the natives are provided with brandy, fire-arms, and similar articles, which lead to their destruction. Where cereals of a superior quality are wanting, an original impulse to a higher civilization cannot be expected: thus at Molucca, and Borneo, New Guinea, the possession of gold and spices, and the foreign trade with these articles, do not lead to any great progress.[2] The commerce which more civilized nations entertain with the natives is generally injurious to the latter. It is known that the Dutch at a former period, destroyed the spices, and even prevented the cultivation of rice in the Moluccas, (excepting the Amboyna, Banda, and some small islands), in order to import rice, so as to render the natives altogether dependent on them, and to force them to labour at the lowest wages for their benefit. We need not refer to the slave trade—this source of the greatest misery—to point out the injury which the intercourse of Europeans has done to the natives of many parts of the globe. The treachery, the excesses, the utter absence of any moral

---

[1] Loc. cit., p. 404.

[2] Crawfurd, i, p. 15.

sense, which Europeans have evinced in their intercourse with the aborigines of every part, have been such that it is utterly absurd to assert, in order to prove the incapacity of certain peoples and savages for improvement, that they have appropriated nothing from the intercourse with civilized nations but their vices. An unprejudiced observer sees in this only the natural consequence of the intercourse of the refuse of European society with primitive nations. Passing by the natural effect of criminal colonies on the natives, it may be observed, that vices are more easily contracted than virtues, even by comparatively civilized beings. To give only one instance, we may mention that the gifted New Zealanders have everywhere descended from their station of proud, though rude, warriors, to become common beggars, in proportion as they came in contact with Europeans. D'Urville[1] says of them, "Though trade may be a potent means of leading rude nations to civilization, it is incapable, in many instances, of effecting it on account of the bad character of the people who first come in contact with them."

Instances of a perfectly peaceable and friendly intercourse, between Europeans and savage nations, are very rare, and belong to a very recent period. Port Essington offers such an instance, having been an English colony from 1839-50, but has since been abandoned. During that whole period, no inimical collision between White and native is said to have occurred. There is another instance of this kind furnished by Brooke in Sarawak, Borneo. Brooke took care that the old laws and customs of the population should, as much as possible, be preserved; he protected them from the oppression of the native rulers, established an impartial court of justice to punish crimes, free trade and labour, and very moderate taxes.[2] The results, however, of these attempts at civilization seem to have been, that the natives of Sarawak, by being freed from oppression, by the diminution of taxes, and the obtaining

---

[1] "Voyage au Pole Sud," ix, p. 134.

[2] Reports of Rajah Brooke's doings have been latterly spread, which do not agree with the above statement; whether they are true or not must for the present remain undecided.

security of life and property, have become lazy, contrary to Brooke's expectation that it would stimulate their industry.[1] Such an expectation is not always realized, since deliverance from oppression and the establishment of order alone do not positively impel man to labour. These impulses, as has been justly observed, arise only when new physical or mental wants are excited, such as can only be supplied by their own activity; it is then that trade may become a lever for the civilization of savage tribes.

If the new wants which arise in a people are in the direction of progress, much has already been gained. Thus, for instance, in Delagoa Bay the natives, although inveterate smokers, preferred being paid for their services in clothing.[1] There are many and striking instances, especially in the South Sea, of progress shown in the proper estimation of commodities. The acquirement of such wants may, however, become injurious if the people do not learn to supply them by their own efforts, and become thus dependent on importation which is irregular. If commerce is to raise a people, it is necessary, not merely that it obtain a knowledge of really useful foreign products, but that it should endeavour to reproduce them, not directly, but indirectly, by increasing their own produce by labour. Next to the opportunity of exchanging the commodities, stand as chief conditions, security for life and property and the possession of a currency in sufficient quantity. Gold, ivory, and the slave trade have not, as Cruickshank observes, been sufficient to raise the Negro on the gold coast; but now flourishing palm oil trade, which annually imports 150 tons of cawris as current coin, will effect much. Similar improvements are now taking place in Senegambia, whence European trade exports skins, wood, palm oil, etc., all which must be gained by the labour of the natives, who are thus habituated to labour and to European requirements.

In investigating the influences upon the civilization and development of various peoples, we have first considered the physical conditions and the accidental events. We have further

[1] Keppel, "A visit to the Indian Archipelago," ii, p. 61, 1853.
[2] Owen, "Narr. of a voy. to Explore the Shores of Africa," i, p. 159, 1833.

reviewed the elements of civilization arising from occupation, mode of life, and social condition, and we have now finally to examine the agents of psychical life chiefly concerned in its development. Religion and knowledge must be considered as the chief elements in this respect.

Whether religion promotes or impedes the progress of civilization and in what proportion, depends in the first place on its nature, and mainly on its adaptation to the intellectual status, and the moral ideas which govern practical life. Where the intelligence is yet undeveloped, there arise the crudest religious notions and the most absurd superstition. Such a religion can only obstruct mental activity and civilization. It has a similar effect when its doctrines have no relation to morality, or when it exercises a depraving influence by authorizing barbarous customs, such as cannibalism and human sacrifices, the assassination of twins, ordeals, etc. We shall here illustrate these relations, chiefly as regards primitive peoples.

We have seen that the original form of all religion is a raw unsystematic polytheism. Man in a state of nature finds himself surrounded by threatening dangers and actual miseries, which he attributes to unfriendly powers who appear to him to be constantly on the alert to impede his progress. That, on the contrary, which regularly and periodically recurs, passes by him unheeded, because, being expected and anticipated, he is not obstructed in his path. He looks thus at nature as a world of spirits; but the notions he conceives as to the nature of these inimical powers depend partly on surrounding nature and the vividness of his imagination, and partly on the special occasions which excite his affections and passions. The interpretation of sensible objects depends entirely on the mental disposition of the individual who perceives them, and the mode in which they act upon him. The heavenly bodies, the elements, plants and animals, even stones, are looked upon as spirits. Thus, for instance, rock-crystal is something sacred in the eyes of the Australians. Leichardt[1] says, that the savage endows glittering stones with beneficial qualities, and so is blood-

[1] Tageb. einer Landreise in Austr., p. 221, 1851.

stone considered, with other minerals, by the Indians of South America.[1] Even the artificial products, such as watches, telescopes, etc., are looked at as possessed by demons. An intelligent Betchuana, on seeing the sea and a ship for the first time, observed that the ship must be an uncreated object, a thing that had come by itself, and had not been made by the hand of man.[2] The instances of Cortez and Cook show that even living human beings have been considered as gods, a delusion which certainly disappears on nearer acquaintance, for man is too commensurable to man: "Æquales sunt qui æqualia contra se invicem possunt; at qui maxima possunt, nimirum occidere, æqualia possunt" (Hobbes). When the ruling family is looked upon as of divine origin, it is not surprising that the ruler should, after his death, or even during his life, be placed among the gods, and be worshipped accordingly, as, for instance, Tamatoa, king of Raiatea.[3] Religions of this kind are characterised by their discrepancies. Every one worships either what he fears the most, or from which he expects the greatest aid in need. There are few general, but many local and individual, objects of veneration, and even the general objects of worship possess at different times a greater or less importance for their worshippers. Faith as yet lays no claim to universal assent; there is an absolute toleration, and it is considered quite natural that other people should have other gods. The endeavour to force upon others his own views, whether concerning religious or other subjects, is altogether foreign to the primitive man, who so highly values personal independence.

In Africa the Christians and Mohammedans only, try to make proselytes, and in America Peru was the only state which did so. On the other hand, foreign gods are easily added to the native ones. Thus the Fantees purchase gods which have acquired a certain celebrity.[4] The gods are put on their trial, to see whether they are more powerful than others, and, if they prove themselves so, obtain preference and a higher rank above

[1] Humboldt und Bonpland, "Reise," iv, p. 334.
[2] Thompson, "Travels and adventures in South Africa," 2nd edit., 1827.
[3] Tyermann and Bennet, "Journal," i, p. 524, 1831.
[4] W. T. Müller, "D. Afrika Landschaft Fetu." p. 55, Hamb., 1676.

other gods. This is, as regards religious belief, in many cases the result of the conversion of such peoples, if peacefully effected. If the religion of the conqueror is forced upon the conquered, the belief in the old gods continues for a considerable time, as they are considered to have been only temporarily defeated and banished by the new gods to caves or distant mountains. The Mexicans shut up the gods of the conquered nations in a separate temple.[1] The facility of the adoption of foreign gods among the native deities and the *evocatio deorum* among the Romans afford similar instances. The gods of the conquered peoples were by the old Peruvians placed in the temple of the Incas.[2]

Hence it is clear that the religions of savages are incapable of promoting civilization, but that, on the contrary, they impede progress by attributing all that is to them unintelligible in nature to the power of spirits, so that the fate of man depends much less on his own exertions than on the changing humours of mysterious, malicious powers. Opposed to them, there remains nothing for man but to do them homage, to flatter them, to enter their service, or (and this also sometimes happens) to over-reach or even conquer them. The most senseless actions, the coarsest immorality are often supported by religious motives, and the purely utilitarian objects which man pursues in relation to his gods contribute to confirm him in his crude egotism.

In this stage of development the thought easily occurs of making sacrifices to the higher spirits; they are first made to take their share in food and any other enjoyment. A further step is to deprive oneself of something, and to sacrifice it to the gods. Among some American tribes the religious feeling is so intense, that they readily give up what is dearest to them, and inflict upon themselves the greatest pain, in order to prove their devotion: hence the vows, the strict fastings, and the self-mutilations on certain festivals. In some places they produce by long fasting an ecstatic condition, attended with dreams and

---

[1] Clavigero, "History of Mexico," translated by Cullen, vi, p. 11, 1787.
[2] Garcilasso, "Hist. des Yncas." Amst., 1737; Acosta, "Hist. delle Indie," Venet., 1596.

visions, in which they are supposed to approach the higher spirits. The young medicine-man, especially, required such an initiation. The chiefs among the Caribs, Mexicans, and Peruvians, who exercised both spiritual and temporal powers, had to undergo similar ordeals.

When nature is thus spiritualised, every little accidental occurrence is attributed to the mysterious action of higher powers, and in them the primitive man sees prognostications. To interpret these becomes an art which requires much study. The want of a mediation with the higher spirits, to interpret their signs, to conciliate them, to take their advice as regards the future, gives rise to priestcraft, and gradually endow it with power and influence in all the affairs of life. As the spirit world is always called upon when human means are exhausted, so its aid is also invoked in the administration of justice: hence the ordeals which are found among nearly all primitive peoples. This fundamental idea is well shown in the doctrine of Indian legislation, in which the proof by ordeals is only admitted where other proofs are wanting. The opinion of Wuttke, that the belief in prognostics and ordeals rests upon some obscure innate idea of fate which is beyond religion, cannot be admitted.

In consequence of this transference of sensible impressions to a spiritual province, the gods are generally located in elevations, or at great distances, on high distant mountains, the clouds, the sky. It is, therefore, very possible that, as Squire[1] observes, among many peoples the first temples were artificial mounds, an imitation of the localities in which they placed their gods. The Mexicans, Peruvians, and Cherokees called their high buildings "Houses of God."[2] Temples properly so called were only built when man himself lived in houses.

If nature is once spiritualised in the manner indicated, so that the spiritual world is not something above or beside the physical world, but contained within it, the idea of the influence of deceased persons on earthly life suggests itself. As Tiede-

[1] "The Serpent Symbol," p. 77, New York, 1851.
[2] Adair, "History of the American Indians."

mann well observes,[1] some idea of sensation is still attributed to the corpse; he is sympathised with, and the dead are still more feared than the living. It is believed the spirit has left the body to wander about, and that it can now assume any shape, can appear in dreams, and torment the living if no honour be shown to it, so that the survivors avoid pronouncing the name of the deceased, from fear that he would hear it, and return. This kind of belief in immortality, which is erroneously confounded with the belief in a transmigration of souls, whilst it is nothing but a belief in spectres and transformation, may have led to animal worship, which, however, as we have already shown, is due to other causes. The worship of some particular animals sometimes arises from a tradition that a tribe had descended from them. The departed souls are by some believed to return to the spiritual world, dwelling near the gods: hence they are buried in places already consecrated to the gods; or inversely, the burial places become sacred by the fact, that they contain the remains of the dead, and thus become the chief places of worship. Such is especially the case where the religious faith is fused with the belief in immortality, when great men after their death are numbered among the gods.

Among many peoples the princes, the rich, and eminent persons only are considered as immortal, as man is believed hereafter to continue to play the same part as during his lifetime. The future is looked upon as a counterpart of the present: the master remains a master, the slave a slave; the common man is considered too powerless to continue his existence. Such men, therefore, who were pre-eminently distinguished in life, and especially where distinctions in rank are well defined, become gods after their decease, and a hero-worship becomes gradually the chief element of religion, when, for instance, as in Polynesia, the nobles and the priests alone claim a divine origin and a relationship with the gods. The deified chiefs become then confounded with the ancient gods, so that it is sometimes difficult to distinguish the latter from the former. Thus Nden-

[1] "Magaz. v. merkw. Reisebescrift." xxiii, p. 47.

gei, the highest god of Fiji islanders, was, it is said, originally a man, and wandered about in the islands. The worship of deceased chiefs is very general in other islands of the South Sea, and constitutes an important element in religion.

The adoption of eminent men among the gods becomes, for the transformation of religious ideas, important in many respects. If man can only imagine higher beings in his own image, idol worship is easily established, especially if deceased persons are worshipped as gods. Nearly all idols resemble the human form, and even the three feet long, irregular-shaped coral piece which, on the King's-Mill Islands, is every month covered with cocoa leaves, and worshipped as the image of the highest god,[1] has some resemblance to the human shape. The reception of human individuals among the gods becomes particularly important in relation to their teachings, which we find in every mythology. They are either considered as incarnations of a god, or as the sons of the highest god, born of a human mother, or a virgin, and miraculously conceived.[2] They be-

---

[1] Hale.

[2] This point recurs under various forms, of which we shall cite a few examples. The legend of the birth of Fohi, in China, runs thus:—Three nymphs descended from heaven to bathe in a river. They had scarcely entered it when the lotus plant appeared upon the garments of one, with its coral fruit. The consequence was that she became pregnant, and gave birth to a son, who became a founder of religion, a warrior, and lawgiver. Father Tachard relates the legend of the birth of Codom, as follows:—Many, many years ago, a virgin in a state of ecstasy, left the society of men, and haunted the most solitary places of the forest, expecting the advent of a god long predicted. One day, when she knelt down to pray, she became pregnant by the sunbeams. On the shores of a lake, between Siam and Camboya, she was delivered of a boy, whom she placed in the leaves of a lotus. She was then translated to heaven; but the boy was found by a hermit, and became a great sage and performer of miracles. Archer, in Corea, is also said to be the son of a virgin impregnated by the sun. Huitzilipochtli, in Mexico, was born by a woman who caught in her bosom a featherball which descended from the heavens (Clavigero, "History of Mexico," vi, p. 6). In a legend of the Apaches, rain caused a supernatural conception: in Tahiti, it was the shadow of a leaf of a bread-tree which Taaroa passed above Hina (Ellis, "Polynes. Resear.," i, p. 326, 1832); the mother of the first Mandan chief conceived by eating the fat of a bison cow (Prinz Max, loc. cit). Other similar instances are related in Ausland, 1856, T. G. Müller, etc. The Chibchar equally attribute a supernatural birth to their heroes (P. Simon, "Noticias de las Conq. de Tierra Firme," ii, p. 13; in Kingsborough, viii). Hence it clearly results that R. Schomburgk ("R. in Guiana," ii, p. 320) wrongly supposes Christian admixtures in the Indian traditions, which, like those of the Maipures and Warraus, speak of the supernatural conception and birth of one of their heroes.

come then the mediators between gods and men, and the benefactors of the latter as the founders of a new religion, the inventors of important arts, the founders of agriculture and social order, and the promoters of civilization. Squier[1] gives as examples, Buddha in India, Fohi in China, Zoroaster in Persia, Osiris in Egypt, Odin in Scandinavia, etc. In the New World belong to this category, Quetzalcoatl in Mexico; Manco Capac in Peru, the founder of Cuzco, sent by the sun; analogous heroes we find among the Muyscas in Yucatan, in Nicaragua, and even among the Natchez;[2] Hiawatha among the Iroquois, the founder of their confederacy; Manabozho among the Algonquins; Tamöi among the Guarayos.[3]

It is by the influence of such heroes that religion becomes an element of civilization, whilst in its natural form it directly or indirectly impedes it. In order to promote culture, it requires a transformation, which, like all psychical progress, is not so much determined by the influence of external natural forces, or by social relations and historical events, as by the influence of pre-eminently gifted individuals, who no doubt, to be successful in their endeavours, require a susceptible and productive field in their own people. No natural religion seems in itself to possess the germ of a higher development conducive to civilization. The mass of superstition which these religions contain suffocates thought; and the exclusive predominance of evil spirits, whilst the benevolent beings are little heeded, deprives them of any beneficial effect which religion should exercise upon moral conduct. It is only in a higher stage of cultivation when man becomes the master of nature, and his moral sense is developed by means independent of a religious source, that he is led to the worship of a good principle. Even the question as regards the variety of surrounding phenomena, and the origin of the world, is not originally raised by man; the idea of a creation does not immediately occur to him, but remains for a long time dormant, or at least confused.

---

[1] "Serpent Symbol;" and Rougement, "Le peuple primitif," ii, p. 108.
[2] Du Prats, "Hist. de la Louisane," ii, p. 324, 1758.
[3] D'Orbigny, "L'Homme Amér.," iii, pp. 12, 23, 1839.

Just as the establishment of a well organized community is not the work of the multitude but of gifted individuals who, either with or without the consent of the people, place themselves at their head,—so can religions be only created by individuals, and imposed upon the masses. As such religions are frequently opposed to old prevailing religious notions, their introduction among peoples in a low state of culture are the more successful if they supply a want, or if their representative is in the possession of sufficient personal authority. If the new doctrines are of native growth, they will, however much they may be opposed to the ancient faith, find their points of attachment in the psychical life of the people, and take root, which can be scarcely expected if they are imported by a people whose history, civilization, and social conditions, differ widely. Islamism and Christianity offer instructive examples in this respect. The first spread in Africa imperceptibly, as it was more intelligible to the Negro, and is more compatible with his culture, so that even in Abyssinia it gains on Christianity; whilst large sums have been spent, and great and noble efforts made, to promote the latter, with but little success.

Next to the historical condition, civilization will depend on the comparative purity of the new religion. A religion may be said to be the purer the less it prevents the development of knowledge, and the more its principles coincide with those of morality. Where faith extends to subjects accessible to knowledge, it becomes superstition, and prevents the progress of knowledge, not merely by establishing false principles as fixed doctrines, but by investing these doctrines with a sacred character so as to render them unassailable. If the religion contains immoral elements, it corrupts the motives of man, confirms him in his errors by placing before him bad ideals, and directs him into paths which estrange him more or less from a higher cultivation.

It is difficult to exactly determine the influence of certain religions on civilization, inasmuch as all peoples at different periods fuse their religious doctrines with other elements of their psychical life, and either abandon or modify the old doctrines. Thus neither the Mohammedan nor the Christian religion has at all times and in all regions produced the same effects. The Mohammedan religion has made the Arabs a people of great historical importance by giving them unity, and rousing their enthusiasm for common enterprises, whilst it was unable to secure its conquests of Babylon and Egypt. This religion is, nevertheless, such an incubus on intellectual and moral progress, that its professors will always remain inferior to Christian peoples. Whoever professes a belief in Allah and the Prophet is acknowledged as a brother. The monotheism of the Mohammedans loses its moral force by their God being only the God of the faithful, to whom He has given the world. Their notion of God does not include the world as a whole, and all mankind as one family; but only a God of the faithful, all the rest being considered as God's enemies, which may be killed or reduced to slavery, and to fight against whom is meritorious. The doctrine of immortality promises sensual enjoyments to the faithful. The belief in predestination may impart submission to fate, but it deadens at the same time every effort, mental and corporeal. "'Tis the will of God," is among Mohammedans not merely an expression of religious faith and resignation, but of superstition. The permission of polygamy, in connexion with the doctrine that women possess no souls and do not enter heaven, leads to an undignified position of the female sex. The prohibition to make images of men and animals, prevents any attempts in the plastic arts. To use knives, spoons, or forks, is considered irreligious by the Arabs in Africa; and the faith in the sanctity of the Koran, which gives rise to a number of superstitious customs, explains why the Arabs in Africa are but little superior in intellectual culture to many heathen peoples. Moreover, the Koran contains many contradictions, by inculcating fanaticism against all infidels, and in teaching toleration. Submission to authority is not inculcated as a religious duty. The Turks, the Syrians, Egyptian Arabs, though they utter with their tongues the most beautiful moral sentences, possess, in fact, but little piety, compassion, or honesty, as they believe they fulfil every duty by their prayers and ceremonies (Burckhardt).[1]

Art usually attaches itself to religion, by supplying the requisites of worship sensibly to represent the religious ideas. The creations of plastic art and poetry frequently give a type to religious notions. This applies both to the forms of individual gods and to the traditions attached to them. It is in this way that gradually a series of less varied mythological persons and legends issue from the original mass of superstition. At the same time, the first attempts at plastic delineations, as we find among rude nations, are used as communications of remarkable events, to which is allied the development of picture writing. Despite these important contributions of art to the progress of culture, we do not consider them as the chief causes which determine civilization as a whole. However great the influence of the arts may be on the forms of life which a high civilization presents, they must, in the inferior stages of development, be rather considered as the products than as the springs of culture, and are hardly capable of effecting the elevation of a people; because the really beautiful can neither be produced nor enjoyed by rude nations, and since the formation of taste becomes only important for the masses in proportion as the sense for the beautiful is already developed.

On the other hand, the progress of knowledge must be considered as the second principal cause to which civilization owes its development and duration. Its effects in this direction are so great that it cannot possibly be over-estimated; for knowledge penetrates all the ramifications of life and makes them dependent on itself, so that the intellectual development of a people is the standard of its civilization.

To what a degree the material welfare of a people depends on its intellectual development lies on the surface. Surrounded by abundance and favoured by nature, we see many peoples

[1] Among those authors who have by experience acquired a knowledge of life in Mohammedan countries, D'Escayrac may be mentioned as an eloquent eulogist of the Mohammedan religion ("Die Afr. Wueste und das Land der Schwarzen"). An impartial review of the lights and shadows of Islamism will be found in "Zeitschrift f. d. Kunde des Morgenlandes," iii, p. 352.

of the tropics lead a miserable life, helplessly exposed to alternate changes, and careless of the future. They support themselves in the most simple and uniform manner from what nature voluntarily offers, or they cultivate the soil with the rudest implements. Their preparation of food is defective, and the aliments are frequently unwholesome. The protection against climate by dress and habitation is neglected; nor does the savage take any measures to secure himself against any external evils.

"Knowledge is power." This is shown by the subjection of nature to the aims of man, and by the application of its resources to social wants. In proportion as man studies his own nature, the scope and inclination of his desires and passions, and the general interests of society, in the same proportion can he succeed in establishing and developing a fixed social condition. In order to overcome the difficulties and dangers which beset social life, a knowledge of the means capable of effecting it must be attained. Here, as everywhere, knowledge must precede the power, unless the development of what already exists is abandoned to mere chance. In order to secure the basis of all social order, the institution of private property, a certain self-control is requisite, which can only rest upon the consciousness, that the limitation of arbitrary power is better than general insecurity.

It is the eating of the fruit of the tree of knowledge which enables us to distinguish right from wrong, and which gives tongue to conscience. Whether this knowledge be in many cases merely traditional, and the conception of morality be only acquired, it is not less true that conscience speaks accordingly. The crude or fine distinctions which conscience makes, its perversity and defects, its singularities, have all their source in the theoretical conception of the condition of man. But on account of the reciprocal effect of all branches of human knowledge, there is full reason to expect that the knowledge of morality and its application will not lag behind where all others become developed, there being a parallelism in the progress of all.

Hence religion experiences a decided reaction from the progress of knowledge. Although a progressive knowledge of nature does not at once destroy the spiritualisation of the sensible world, it gradually limits it. Diseases are no longer considered as the effects of evil spirits, the number of which is gradually lessened, until reduced to one devil. The local gods, also, are considerably reduced. The remaining gods, formerly spectral and capricious, are now differently conceived; they are more spiritualised, and are endowed with a more specific character, their actions have more design, they receive a symbolical signification, so that a connected mythology is established which promotes the plastic arts. The more man is enlightened by the torch of knowledge, and perceives that the ethic-æsthetical interests form the centre of his destination, the more his gods, either from analogy to himself or to his ideals, acquire an ethic-æsthetic signification, until at length their number no longer corresponds with his improved notions of the unity and design of the world, and he abandons polytheism.

These illustrations must suffice to show that it is essentially the development of knowledge which is the moving power, all other forces being secondary. Nevertheless, it cannot be denied that it is attended by some injurious effects. In every branch of human science, ignorance is first replaced by a series of errors which surround certain truths. Though many of these errors may, separately, be harmless enough, they become highly dangerous when they affect the passions of man. The danger and destructiveness of knowledge grows in proportion to its superiority above others. Refined wickedness is frequently the result of intellectual development. Knowledge itself may rouse the passions, by leading to disputes, giving rise to vanity and over-weening pride. Again, every new fact is over-valued, transferred by false analogies to other phenomena, and prematurely made the basis of general theories. Old theories oppose, with the power of inertia, the acknowledgment of inconvenient facts or arguments; and it is often that some false theory seizes the masses after it has been completely refuted: hence the extreme errors between which knowledge in its progress frequently seems to oscillate.

The motives for the development of knowledge lie rarely

in theoretical interests; for these are only manifested in any strength among civilized nations, and even among them it is not so much the desire of knowledge, but the striving after honour and power. Then comes the habit of mental exertion in solving the questions conducive to the progress of knowledge. There is no impulse among rude or primitive peoples to obtain knowledge, which, according to Aristotle, is innate in human nature. It is the practical wants and misery which overcome the natural psychical indolence of man, and induce him to overpower the natural forces. In the course of our investigation, we have had frequent occasion to insist upon this point, and it has always been shown that in the primitive man there is no tendency to progress. The modern idealistic doctrine of the necessary development of the human mind out of itself, is a fiction, which may flatter man's vanity, but which is contradicted by actual facts. There can be no doubt that it is man's thought which produces and preserves civilization; this thought, however, does not originate by itself, nor does it move by itself, nor is it the function of *one* mind, but is the combined activity of all individuals living together, produced by surrounding media, and nourished and matured by the historical events which befall them.

We are far from pretending to have given a history of the development of mankind from the primitive state to that of civilization, or even a general outline of what may be termed the natural history of human society. The attempt to solve this interesting problem would only lead to the same result as obtained by the so-called philosophy of history, namely, the establishment of a model theory, which, considering the great variety and manifold concatenation of the conditions on which the civilization of nations depends, can have no claim to general application. We have therefore confined ourselves to investigating the general motives which lie at the foundation of, and promote culture. Whether the result of such investigation, for the elucidation of the psychological causal connexion as regards civilization, be great or small, this much has been proved, that the various degrees of culture in various peoples depend in a much greater degree on the mode of life, the historical events, and other elements, than on their original mental endowment, which, however, does not exclude the latter, and which possibly, also, may have its influence. The latter supposition is possible, but cannot be demonstrated. The whole course of our investigation has rendered it more probable that barbarism and civilization prevail among all peoples of the earth, and that powerful impulses are required to change their conditions; but that as regards the further development of already partially civilized peoples, there is this circumstance in their favour, that in consequence of the civilization already acquired, the progeny inherit better predispositions than those possessed by their progenitors. And yet we find that even in the higher stages of civilization, it is by single individuals only that the progress in science, art, religion, and social economy is really effected. Even among the rudest nations, such genial natures are not wanting: there is no specific difference of mankind in this respect; but they rarely produce more than a transitory effect.

The question has been frequently asked, in what consists the national character of a people? The preceding investigation has shown that it depends on so many conditions that an exact analysis is extremely difficult. That it is not the race alone which determines it, is proved by there being different nationalities within the same race. It is therefore probable, as observed by Hugh Murray,[1] that the mental peculiarities of peoples are generally more flexible and changeable than the physical characters of the race, and are transmitted with a less degree of constancy. Though it may be admitted, that peculiarities of race exercise an indirect influence upon the national character by the tradition of manners and laws, it cannot be generally asserted that the political or religious institutions determine it, for among primitive peoples we find the latter very similar, and yet the national characters differ widely. These are developed, and become permanent by the

[1] Loc. cit., p. 149.

combined simultaneous or successive effects of all the factors of the physical, social, and psychical life of the respective peoples; and hence it is easily explained that each of these factors, though it may be found in two or several peoples, in consequence of its combination with others which either support or oppose its action, may produce very different effects. As every event and every experience acts differently upon the same individual in different periods of life, and according to different circumstances, so have the same events different effects upon the various peoples. The same climate, the same social position, political constitution, and religion, may produce very different effects on the national character, according to the different periods of development of the peoples; and it may thus occur that what essentially determines the national character in one people may be powerless in another, or produce quite different effects.

From our investigation of the psychological nature of man, we have obtained a result, which, though not strictly proved, admits of but little doubt, namely:—that there exists an extremely gradual variability in the mental development of peoples, which justifies us in considering the greatest differences in the states of civilization as merely different in degree; that the conditions for mental development are essentially the same in all races; and that there is no sufficient reason to assume specific differences among mankind. Are we then, if human nature is everywhere the same, to suppose that the object of its development is one and the same? Are we to imagine that the object of the history of humanity is an essentially uniform civilization akin to our present European civilization, which may once prevail over the whole globe? These are questions which we will just touch upon in concluding our investigations.

Whoever entertains the conviction, that the transition from a primitive to a civilized state neither increases the sum nor the intensity of enjoyments, but only their variety, may put the same value on the various phases of human life, or what amounts to the same thing, consider the values of barbarism and civilization as merely subjective notions. Everyone is pleased with the world in which he moves, and with the fate nature prepares for him; hence the civilized man desires no change in his mode of life, nor does the primitive man desire to emerge from the state of nature. Nature acts equitably towards both; the more our capacity for enjoyment, and the greater its intensity, the more the capacity for suffering increases, as pleasure and pain flow from the same source,—from the possession and loss of the same goods. All the modes of life in human society are equal in the amount of gratification which they afford to man; it is better to abstain from comparing their relative value, and to consider them merely collectively as a grand spectacle in the changes and evolutions in which they take a part.

We might certainly regret the restlessness with which the civilized man strives to improve his position, the efforts which he makes to pursue his object, and the sufferings and the deprivations which he encounters in his pursuit. The desire for a deeper signification of human life would thus be an error,—a mournful product of a perverted culture,—the thirst after intelligence, neither better nor nobler than the thirst for water. The history of mankind would thus only exhibit the melancholy spectacle in which, notwithstanding the greatest efforts, there would only be obtained the common object which nature attains in every animal, namely, a constant sum of enjoyment.

The wonderful design in the construction of separate parts contradicts, however, the idea of viewing the world as an aimless combination of forces. The natural laws sufficiently indicate that the object of nature is not merely the production of the greatest possible sum of enjoyment: although the sum of enjoyment may not be increased by civilization, yet the mode of enjoyment is essentially altered by it. The great value of civilization above the primitive state lies chiefly in this, that it places human life upon a different foundation from that in which it took root. In the natural state it was the individual interest which, in the form of the instinct of self-preservation and sensual enjoyment, acted exclusively on man, whilst in the civilized state the general interests begin to predominate. Enjoyment is in its nature confined to the individual;

but psychical advantages have the tendency to become common right.

The progress of civilization in every stage of development of human society, is mainly effected by labour and the renunciation of immediate enjoyment, for the latter merely consumes and produces nothing. It is on this account that civilization does not increase enjoyment. The prevalence of labour is above all characteristic of civilization; the object of labour is first to make man the master of nature, to overcome it, and to make it subservient to his wants, in order to gain leisure and force for his psychical life, and to secure his existence from the dangers of natural forces. The performances of physical efforts are determined by mental labour, and they become more perfect in proportion as the knowledge of nature extends. But whilst man gradually renders himself more independent of the influences of natural forces, his mental independence grows simultaneously, he becomes master of himself, and learns to shape his individual and social life. The variety and extent of his performances thus grow in every direction. His mental efforts gradually predominate over the physical; but they are not made as having an object in themselves, or as referring only to individual interest, but in order that they may benefit the world, that is to say, all the members of human society, partly by lessening the pressure of external circumstances on the present generation, and partly for the benefit of generations to come. Thus civilization is an incessant labour of all for every individual, not alone for his enjoyment, but for fitting him for an intellectual life,—a labour which can only have its full effect by the coalition of all the external and inner forces of individuals, but which, on this account, at first includes only small and gradually larger circles of society, until at length it connects all humanity by closer moral bonds.

It is in this sense that we look upon civilization as the universal destination of mankind. This is the development which nature designs for man, in which all human beings participate, though the parts which they take in it may greatly differ. We need not investigate here how far the present European civilization corresponds with our abstract notions. If its dark side, which we are too much accustomed to look upon as necessarily evil, is overlooked or under-estimated, and the theory is indulged that all the countries on the globe may become assimilated in manners and morals to Europe, doubts may arise whether such a consummation is indeed so much to be wished for. No one, it is true, now gives any credence to the idyllic descriptions of a golden age; yet the information given by many travellers of the condition of some primitive peoples is too well authenticated to be entirely rejected as fabulous.

Capt. Woodes Rogers, and other travellers of the seventeenth century, describe the natives of Port Natal—who at a later period were almost entirely exterminated by the Zulus—as a people of innocent manners, kind and hospitable to strangers, and as living in a state of ideal happiness. The inhabitants of Chilöe, who neither have nor require physicians and lawyers, living with the Indians (to whom, since 1829, they have ceded their country), in peaceful vicinity, are said to be in a similar blissful state: murder, robbery, debts, are not heard of; drunkenness is only seen among the foreign sailors; doors are not barred; general confidence and honesty prevail.[1] The patriarchal happy life of the colonists of the small island Pitcairn (in the South Sea), now transferred to Norfolk Island, is too well known.[2] To this may be added what Father Garces (as communicated by Humboldt), narrates of his visit to the Indians in the vicinity of Casas Grandes, south of the Rio Gila (1773). They were peaceable agriculturists, cultivated maize, cotton, and gourds, extremely gentle, and living together in the greatest concord. The missionary pointed out to them the advantages of a mission, when they would have an alcalde to administer full justice. The chief replied, "We neither steal nor quarrel, what occasion have we for an alcalde?" East of Surabaya, in Java, in the Tengger mountains, in the

---

[1] Blanckley, in "Journal of the Royal Geogr. Society," iv, p. 351.

[2] Beechey, "Narrative of a voyage to the Pacific," 1831; Bennet, "Narrative of a whaling voyage round the globe," i, p. 44, 1840; Moerenhout, "Voy. aux Iles du grand Océan," ii, p. 283, 1837.

vicinity of the so-called Sandy Sea, there live in about forty villages, the remnants of a people which still profess the old Hindoo religion. They are taller and more robust than the other Javanese.[1] The position and the structure of their houses, in the midst of which stands the sanctuary of bricks, which no stranger must touch, are entirely different from anything else on the island.[2] The chiefs of every village and his assistants are elective. Four priests, intelligent, but otherwise uneducated men, are the keepers of important documents, and the sacred books, written on lontar-leaves, describing the origin of the world, the attributes of the deity, and the forms of worship; they perform the marriages, and sing the hymns. "The people universally declare that adultery, theft, and other crimes are never committed amongst them, and that consequently there is no punishment for them. If an individual commit any wrong, he is reprimanded by the chief of the village, and this rebuke is considered a sufficient punishment for an inhabitant of Tengger. The authorities of the country confirm this. They are almost exempt from crime, generally peaceable, frugal, and industrious; gambling and opium are unknown." The whole population amounts to about 1,200 souls. They live, without exception, in the fairest and richest region of Java. Their language is the present Javanese. Proud of their independence and morality, they do not intermix with the people of the low-lands.

In contrasting these examples with the laziness and vulgarity into which small communities of civilized Europeans have sunk, when far removed from their native country, we are not merely cautioned against the assumption of specific differences between the white and coloured races: but the question obtrudes itself, whether, after all, it would be so very beneficial for all races to partake of our European civilization; or whether there are not certain states of culture, which, though differing widely from ours, may not excel it in their moral aspect by the sum of happiness and well-being they afford.

If we admit that instances of this kind refer exclusively to

[1] Jukes, "Narrative of the Surveying Voy. of H.M.S. Fly," ii, p. 80, 1847.
[2] Stamford Raffles, "History of Java," i, p. 329, 1817.

small populations living in a state of seclusion, we must infer from it that if the main object of human life is happiness and well-being, a break up of nations into small independent communities would be requisite to attain the proper end of the human race. If, further, it be granted that in all the adduced examples a strikingly low psychical condition and a deficiency of mental efforts is clearly manifested, then it may, with regard to our European civilization, be asserted, that it is just to this circumstance that we must attribute the essential cause of the undisturbed happiness of these men, and of man in general, provided that security against external danger, uncorrupted morals, and a consoling faith free from the coarsest superstition, are added to it. But it assumes a very different aspect when we consider the ideas of civilization and development as the destination of humanity.

A superficial glance at the great differences of peoples, and the mighty influences of natural conditions and climates which preserve these diversities, is sufficient to convince us of the little probability that a uniform civilization will ever prevail among all peoples of the earth. Just as the animal and vegetable world offers, in the various degrees of latitude, a diversity which will continue so long as the present condition of our planet remains; so nature seems inclined to preserve a similar diversity in the physical and psychical characters of mankind. It would, however, be unjust to infer from this, as has often been done, that some peoples are by nature intended for civilization, and others for barbarism. Every civilized society, be it large or small, clearly shows that for its existence and development a division of labour, a variety of occupation, are requisite,—all equally necessary, though of unequal intrinsic value. These extremely varied performances must tend to a common object: what individuals are to the state, individual peoples must be to mankind, as a whole; as the former by their special callings supply the wants of the society in which they live, so all separate peoples must gradually take their special positions and functions in regard to mankind at large. For this reason the isolation of small communities, or larger nations, however happy they may be in undisturbed enjoyment, cannot last; for it is their destination sooner or later to be drawn within the vortex of general intercourse, and to be made in some way, by their labour, to contribute to the end and aim and development of society.

Even after this shall have been effected as regards all the peoples of the earth, it is not to be expected that the great differences between the various kinds of labour required by civilization will disappear. Setting aside all minor differences, and keeping in view the chief object of labour, we find that it is physical, social, or intellectual, accordingly as it is directed to physical well-being, the preservation of social order, or the promotion of knowledge. In every people which partakes of civilization, these chief divisions of labour will be represented by different classes, though it does not follow that this is effected in every people in the same manner. Though in every people the group of social arrangements remains generally the same, since social order is not easily transferred from one people to another, we find that some have more regard for the material, and others for the psychical, development of the respective peoples. Thus, among some peoples material, among others mental, labour would predominate, and each would partake of the productiveness of the rest. In tropical countries the material products, in temperate climates psychical productiveness, would predominate.

A high degree of intellectual development, deep thought, and a refined morality seem scarcely compatible with the mental prostration which life in the torrid zone produces in the European as well as in the native. Human art will hardly ever overcome the power of these natural obstructions. Christianity, exclusively directed to the moral elevation of man, finds there for its spiritual doctrines a very infertile soil. An experienced author intimately acquainted with India, Montgomery Martin, asserts, that no Indian has ever become a true Christian, whilst all picturesque religions which much engage the imagination, and possess an eudæmonistic colouring like Mohammedanism, is more homogeneous to the nature of the inhabitants of the tropics, and more intelligible and satisfactory to them than is Christianity. For this reason, and taking into consideration the successes hitherto obtained by the various missions, it appears doubtful whether Christianity will ever, not merely in name, but in spirit, enter the hearts of mankind all over the globe. Our European civilization is, on the whole, too artificial and abstract immediately to attract uncivilized nations: such peoples must first pass through a long series of transitional stages before our culture becomes accessible to them. In order to arrive at it, the vital power and energy of a people must neither have degenerated into idleness and sensual enjoyment, nor have been exhausted by misery and distress; a happy combination is requisite to enable it gradually to encounter difficulties raised by nature and man, but in such a manner, that its power of resistance and its external and internal resources should be adequate, so that the people may emerge from the struggle physically and morally strengthened.

Where the necessary transitional stages, which a primitive people has to pass through to arrive at a higher development, are wanting, it will, after a short apparent elevation, relapse again into the original state, and, as so frequently occurs when primitive and civilized peoples come in contact, the former will unavoidably perish. Civilization may then continue to spread in the habitable world, but it will crush these peoples, for a sudden transition from the natural state to Christianity and European civilization is opposed to the laws of nature. The attempt to effect it resembles the attempt of the ignorant pedagogue, who expects by one powerful effort suddenly to transform the character of his pupil. Civilization must progress slowly, or it will retrograde; the history of revolutions yields the same results in this respect as the history of the missions.

END OF VOLUME THE FIRST.

INDEX.

Abipones, 140, 149, 258, 293
Aborigines, rights, 165
Abyssinians, 45, 210, 325, 326
Acclimatization, 199; of white, 125
Acosta, 184, 370
Adair, 371
Adams, 106
Adiahs, 213
Adultery, 325
Africa, 257, 369
Agassiz, 21, 22, 32, 196, 203, 233, 351
Age, signs of, 114
Agriculture, 336, 353
Aguanas, 219
Aïnos, 42
Alberti, 118
Albinism, 85
Aleutes, 149, 257, 314, 339
Alexander, 118
Alfurus, 221
Algoa Bay, 147
Algonquins, 148, 249, 257, 374
Algerian Arabs, 152
Aliment and mode of life, 34
Allen and Thomson, 131, 133, 143, 212, 213
Allerhand, 258
Amboyna, 365
America, 257
Americans, 144, 238, 242, 255, 306
American lean compared with Englishman, 53
American school of anthropology, 351
American school, 22
American Indians, 61, 145
Amerigo Vespucci, 122
Amock, running, 332
Analogies between nations, 255
Anamese, 304
Anatomy a branch of anthropology, 6
Ancient buildings, 195
Andersson, 278
Angola, 311
Animal heat, 109
Anatomical differences in man, 90
Ancon sheep, 82
Anderson, 55
Andrews, 308
Anthropology discussed in America as a party question, 1; scarcely yet touched upon in Germany, 1; comprises the labours of the zoologist, geologist, linguist, historian, and psychologist, 1; definition of, 3; formerly restricted to the differences between man and animals, 5; formerly included such naturphilosophical subjects as the origin of mankind, animal magnetism, etc., 5; sometimes treated empirically, sometimes philosophically, 5; its empirical definition the one adhered to in this work, 5; includes the anatomy, physiology, and psychology of man on the one side, and the history of civilization on the other, 6; its relations to history, 8
Anthropophagy, 296
Antiquity of man, 194, 285
Apaches, 148, 150, 373
Ape, man compared with, 91
Ape and negro, a certain resemblance between, 100
Appendix to Section II, 144
Apron of Hottentot women, 105
Aquapim, 212
Arab children swim, 88
Arabs, 61, 63, 115, 218, 254, 332, 339
Arabs of Sennaar, 101
Araucaños, 103, 146, 309, 316
Arbousset and Daumas, 137, 171, 186
Archer, 373
Argentine republic, 308
Aristotle, 10, 281, 380
Aristocracy, hereditary, of the mind, 89
Arnauts, 314
Arnoux, 94, 98, 100
Arowakas, 46
Arowaki, 115, 306
Arru islands, 278
Arsenic used to poison aborigines, 167
Artistic talents transmitted, 89
Ashantees, 142, 212, 304
Assuan, 318
Atavism, 168
Athens, 317
Atmosphere, hygrometric state of, 34
Australians, 58, 100, 102, 103, 116, 135, 140, 144, 176, 204, 233, 257, 296, 297, 300, 304, 306, 312, 325, 334, 357
Author's preface, 1
Avare skull, 239
Axe, 309
Aymarás, 216
Azara, 123, 140, 151, 183, 251, 345
Aztecs, 255

Bachmann, 82, 128, 186, 264
Baghirmi, 210
Baily, 313
Baker, 164, 166, 304
Balbi, 245
Baldness, 114,
Baltos, 234
Banana, 331
Bancroft, 319
Banda Islands, 311
Banjarmassing, 249
Baptism, 256
Barabra, 66
Barbot, 218
Barrington, 126, 135, 186, 300, 305
Barrow, 54, 208, 257
Barth, 66, 105, 133, 209, 210, 212, 246, 300
Barthes, 38, 357
Bambarra, 299
Baseler, 147
Baseler, Miss, 163
Basques, 257
Bayadères, 102
Bayard Taylor, 115
Beauty, ideas of human, 305
Beaumarchais, 269
Beard in Negro, 96
Bechuanas, 65, 137, 140, 369
Béclard, 98
Becroft, 213
Bedouins, 63, 156
Bedouin Arabs, 115, 138, 315
Beechey, 122, 147
Bees, 203
Belcher, 50, 121
Bellows, 257
Benguela, food of workmen in, 59
Benin, 142, 242
Bennet, 159, 165, 169, 177, 202, 270
Bennett, 86, 87, 164
Benuwe, 306
Berber, 66
Berbers, 325
Bergmann, 135
Berthelot, 253, 326; Webb and Berthelot, 194
Berthold, 35
Billings, 62, 149
Birmah, 85
Birmese, 304
Bissagos Archipelago, 143
Blackfeet, 145
Black peoples created first 193
Blake, Carter, 107
Bleek, 56
Blindness, hereditary, 85
Blind Children, 142
Blue Nile, 211
Bluish ring round eyes of Mongrels, 178
Blood of Negro, 97
Blumenbach, 28, 29, 30, 35, 38, 39, 42, 55, 107, 168, 191, 207, 218, 222, 224, 232, 234
Blushing, 135
Bodily strength of various nations, 121
Boers, 147, 151
Bogotá, 83
Bonny, 142
Borabora, 159
Borneo, 365
Bornou, 209
Boroanos, 219
Boors at Cape, 138
Borlat, 300
Bory, 15, 23, 38, 102, 226, 228, 233
Bosjesman, 57, 295, 314, 334
Bosnian soldiers, 249
Bosnian soldiers in Nubia, 43
Bosnians, 106, 142
Botanical Provinces, 196
Boteler, 133, 213
Botocudos, 55, 68, 140, 153, 215, 299, 310
Bothriocephalus, 128
Boucher de Perthes, 194
Boudyk, 299, 304
Bowka, 140
Bowdich, 96, 142, 209, 212
Bradford, 255
Bracknas, 252
Brackenridge, 183
Brandy sold to Indians, 152
Brachycephalic, 235
Brass, odour of, 140
Brain of Ape, 91; of Negro, 93
Brain, 312, 316
Brazil, 111
Brazil, mulattos in, 179
Brazilians, 250, 300, 319, 322
Brazilian society, 178
Brahmin children highly gifted, 89
Brehm, 40, 51, 101, 113, 125, 184, 297, 318, 326
Bretons, 101
Bridges, 309
Broad skulls, 236
Broc, 38, 71, 226
Brook, 257
Brooke, 147, 278, 359, 366
Brothertons, 249
Brown, Joseph, 54
Brown, W., 110
Bruce, 45, 210, 218, 326
Brunner, 133
Buccal cavity in Negro, 95
Buchanan, 223
Buckland, 254
Buck goat, 82
Buckton, 117
Buddha, 374
Buenos Ayres, 111, 293, 308, 345
Buffalo, 319
Buffon, 23, 169, 184, 207, 281
Buildings, ancient, 195
Bullams, 211
Bunbury, 105
Burchell, 114, 137, 139, 164
Burckhardt, 43, 69, 139, 140, 377
Burdach, 88, 112, 177
Buriats, feeding on animal food, are weakly, 61
Burmeister, 50, 70, 93, 94, 95, 96, 97, 101, 122, 154, 168, 172, 238
Burton, 105
Burutu, 162
Bush, 142
Bushmen, children precocious, 88
Bushmen, 105, 106, 114, 137, 139, 257, 325
Bushwomen, cerebrum of, 93
Byrne, 59, 166, 167, 316

Cabouret, 178
Cafusos, 174
Cagots in Spain, 86, 193
Cailliaud, 106
Caillie, 134, 299
Caldcleugh, 111, 149
California, 62, 145, 213
California, Upper, 112
Callao, 147
Camanchees, 145

Camel, 388
Camel drivers, 115
Campbell, 172, 257
Canary Islands, 253, 299
Cannibalism, 296
Cantfield, 117
Cape, 314
Cape Cod, 147
Caraccas, 120, 309, 348
Careri, 202
Carians, 348
Caribs, 100, 146, 218, 258, 295, 371
Carimango, 313
Carinthia, 217
Carli, 318
Carne, 99
Carohies, 257
Carpenter, 83
Carrier Indians, 116
Carsange, 257
Carthagena, 258
Carus, 291
Castelnau, 105, 112, 173, 219
Castien, 77
Catholic missionaries, 315
Catinca, 103
Cattle in the United States, 23
Caucasians, 318
Causes of civilization, 341
Cavazzi, 125, 293
Cayowas, 219
Cazegut, 212
Celebes, 51, 147
Celts, 343
Ceylon, 218
Chamisso, 250, 257
Chambon, 177
Chamois of Pyrenees and Alps, 21, 251
Change of colour produced by age, 99
Changos, 251
Chaptal, 341
Characteristics of man, 275
Charleroix, 218, 313
Charruas, 140
Chastity, 297
Cheever, 122
Chenier, 126, 317
Cheras, 301
Cherokees, 243, 371
Chibchas, 373
Children swim in Polynesia, 87
Chile, 146, 172, 257, 309
Chimpanzee and Gorilla; their differences, 32, 91
Chinook, 146
Chinos, 174
Chinese, 238, 242, 245, 304, 317
Chinese in East Indian Archipelago.
Chippeways, 155, 164, 337
Chiriguanas, 46
Choles, 183, 187
Cholores, 154
Chonos children swim, 87
Christians, 369
Christianity, 325
Chronology, 285
Church, Col., 141
Cieza de Leon, 192
Circumcision of girls, 106
Civilized man inferior sensually to savage, 137
Civilization, degrees of, 328
Civilization stationary, 325
Clapperton, 94, 105, 213
Clarke, R., 100, 106, 218, 238, 299
Classification of man, 10
Classification of mankind, 230
Clavigero, 110, 123, 370, 373
Clemens, 130
Click of Hottentots, 136
Climate, 34
Clutterbuck, 166
Cobija, 251
Cochin China, 218, 305
Cocamas, 175
Codom, 373
Cohabitation between Negros and Indians, 154
Colenso, 136
Colour of first pair, 207
Colour and hair distinctions of race, 232
Colour of skin influenced by climate, 52
Colour, deviations in, 217
Columbia, Indians of, 62
Columbus, 41, 140
Combes and Tamisier, 45, 65
Copenhagen, Icelander in, 130
Concepçion, 172
Congenital deformities, 113
Congo negros, 209, 218, 293
Conjunctiva in negro, 94
Conquistadores, 151
Constancy of types, 225
Consumption of food, 115
Convolutions in negro brain, 93
Cook, 369
Cooley, 66
Coppermine Indians, 150
Coral islands, 344
Cordilleras, Indians of, 354
Cordova, 308
Corea, 373
Coreal, 85
Corroados, 145
Cortez, 369
Costa Rica, 251
Coultner, 112
Courson, 340
Courtesy, ideas of, 305
Courtet De Lisle, 79, 222
Cowley and Dampier, 271
Cox, R., 181
Coxcox, 256
Cradle of mankind, 200
Cranial capacities, 261
Cranium, shape of, 78
Cranium, deviations in, 21
Cranz, 255, 298
Crawfurd, 127, 131, 238, 239, 304, 306, 359, 365
Crees, 147
Creeks, 150, 152
Creole, 205, 319
Creoles, 308
Creoles in West Indies become fat, 54
Crows, 145
Crowther, 306
Crozet, 299
Cruickshank, 143, 367
Cuba, 100
Cumbrie negros, 193
Cunningham, 139
Curumbars, 45
Cushions on hips of female Hottentot, 165
Cuvier, 15, 19, 194, 234, 254
Cuzco, 3, 74
Cynocephalus, 92
Czermak, 107

D'Abbadie, 172
Dahomey, 93, 106, 142, 212
Dajakes, 92, 139, 257
Dakota, 242
Dallas, 70, 142
Dalzel, 142
Dampier, 59, 257, 358
Danakils, 175, 306, 318

Dandolo, 96, 213
Danish colonies, 250
Darfur, 183, 208, 292
Darien, 137
Darien, Isthmus of, 85
Darnell, 97
Darwin, 120, 146, 164, 271, 345
Daumar, 138
Dauphiné, 321
D'Avezac, 242, 304
Davis, 184, 214
Dawson, 59, 100, 126, 166
Day, 71, 97, 133, 178, 185
De Barras, 326
Decandolle, 21, 31
Deccan, 134, 325, 343
Definition of species, 17, 18
De Jong, 77
De Hell, 69
Delafield, 255
Delagoa Bay, 367
De la Salle, 55, 251
Delaware Indian, 138
Delawares, 109
Delegorgue, 107, 116, 138, 294, 297, 299
De Lisboa, 71, 179
Demersay, 49, 189
Denham, 105, 209, 210
Denham, Clapperton, and Oudney, 209, 210
Density of population, 349
D'Entrecasteaux, 295
Depons, 302
Derwent river, 315
De Salles, 30, 74, 108, 125, 207, 223, 298, 319, 352
D'Escayrac, 63, 98, 99 115, 138, 213, 315, 377,
Des Marchais, 40, 133, 297
Desmoulins, 23, 32, 43, 108, 196, 226, 233, 265, 305
Desgraz, 158
De Pages, 102, 250
De Pauw, 110
De Smet, 146
Development of nations, 266
Deviation from type, 34
Devil, the negro, white, 305
Dieffenbach, 157, 163, 215
Diet of various nations, 60
Diet, influence on the body, 57
Dieterici, 131
Diseases of man, 124
Diseases, 145
Disinclination for labour, 330
Distinctions between man and brute, 270, 274
Dobrizhoffer, 115, 123, 140, 145, 149, 258, 308
Döhne, 137
Doko, 210
Dolichocephalæ, 235
D'Omalius d'Halloy, 227, 232
Dory, 257
Douville, 106
Dowding, 132, 327
D'Orbigny, 37, 49, 69, 71, 72, 110, 114, 119, 135, 178, 374
D'Orbigny and Troyer, 178
Durand, 47, 143, 212
Dureau de la Malle, 107
D'Urville, 113, 114, 186, 193, 233, 251, 301, 309, 310, 366
Dutch, 249, 365
Dutch Guiana, 177
Dutch and Hottentots, 186
Duttenhofer, 95, 127, 238
Drake, 147, 151
Drunkenness, 315
Duclesmour, 218
Duhaut Cilly, 128, 317
Duméril, 38, 233
Dumont d'Urville, 166
Duncan, 13, 96, 212
Dunmore, 48
Dunmore Lange, 320
D'Unienville, 44, 311, 319
Du Petit-Thouars, 161, 165
Dunn, 146
Duprat, 44
Duprats, 203, 374
Dupuy, 135, 142
Duration of life, 123
Duvernoy, 91
Dynamometer, 116

Ear, lobule of, 86
Ear of Bushmen, 105
Ear in Egyptians, 101
Earl, W., 126, 218, 257, 343
East Indies, 298
East Indies, mortality in, 131
Eastern Carolinas, 306
Eberhard, 198
Ecuador, 250, 313
Edeeyahs, 213
Edward III of England, 315
Edwards, W. F., 76, 189, 227
Edwards, B., 142
Edwards, W. A., 332
Edwards, 76, 171
Effects of climate, 333
Egypt, 340
Egyptian monuments, 25
Egyptians, 326
Ehrenberg, 92
Eichthal, 328
Elphinstone, 45
Ellis, 113, 149, 160
Elmina, 304
Enarea, 45
Engel, 38, 78, 225, 261
English stand tropical heat worse than Spaniards, 129
Epp, 65, 317
Erboul, 50
Erskine, 157
Eschwege, 49, 145, 153, 155, 184, 252
Esquimaux, 115, 121, 140, 215, 217, 218
Esquimaux and Fuegians resemble each other, 38
Esquimaux consume fat, 60, 62
Esthonians, 136, 218
Ethnography, 10
Ethnology, 10
Etruscans, 348
Etzel, V., 116, 173
European, colour varies according to climate, 47
Experience, teachings of, 271
External characters, 226
Extinction of tribes, 163
Extremities of ape, 91
Eyes, deviations in, 217
Eyre, 113, 115, 163, 164, 165, 166, 167, 300

Face of ape, 91
Fakaafo, 272
Falconer, 56, 355, 359, 363
Falkland Islands, 271
Falkner, 146
Fantees, 369
Fanti Negroes, 143
Farnham, 62
Featherstonhaugh, 152
Fechner, 112, 113, 176, 177, 238
Fecundity, greatest known, 41

Fecundity no proof of common origin, 25
Feldner, 141
Fellahs, 301, 318
Fermin, 258
Fernando Noronha, 310
Fernando Po, 213
Fetishism, 303
Fevers, 124
Fick, 38
Fiji, 313
Fiji Islands, 186, 298
Fiji Islanders, 110, 373
Fingers, skin between, 71
Finnish nations, 64
Finns, 221, 253
Finns, their type, 76
Fire, how produced, 257
Fishers, 336
First appearance of man, 285
Fohi, 373, 374
Foissac, 35, 57, 59, 82, 97, 109, 117, 123, 125, 319, 330
Foote, 311
Foramen magnum of ape, 91
Forearm in Negro, 96
Forey, 174
Forrest, 47
Forster, G., 158
Forster, 85, 135, 158, 199, 218
Fox, 41, 157, 162, 163, 205
Fleetness, 118
Flinders, 238
Frankenheim, 322
Franz, 53
Franz Mayer, 112
Frederic I. of Prussia, 84
French, 309
Frère, Abbé, 79
Freycinet, 117, 134, 139, 238, 250, 300
Freyreiss, 153
Frezier, 119
Friendly Islanders, 159
Fronto-temporal union in Negro and Mongol, as in Chimpanzee, 93
Fröbel, 313
Froriep, 39, 238
Froschel, 142
Fulahs, 43, 65, 211, 306
Funes, 183

Gaboon, 209
Gaes, 219
Gage, 149
Gaimard, 157
Galapagos, 271
Galindo, 111
Gallas, 210, 211
Gallatin, 243
Gambia, 157
Garcia, 308
Garcilasso, 110, 184, 370
Gardiner, 60, 296, 309
Gascony, 207
Gauchos, 138, 345
Gemara, 113
Genitals, 154
Genitals in Negro, 98
Genitals (dark) in Mongrels, 178
Genius in every race, 361
Genoux, 309
Geoffroy and Nott, 185
Geoffroy St. Hilaire, 1, 206
Geoffroy, 57
Geographical distribution of human race, 196
Georgians, 216, 261
Gerdy and Lucas, 61
Germans, 316, 320
Germans in Pennsylvania, 52
Giebel, 21, 26, 30, 32, 202, 217
Gillii, 102, 123, 258, 300, 359
Giron, 88, 168
Gmelin, 109, 218
Gobineau, 181, 347
God, belief in, 278
God, knowledge of, and knowledge of human nature (Anthropology) identical, 4
Godron, 30, 225
Golberry, 135, 194, 211
Gold Coast, 142
Gomara, 102, 153
Gorilla, 92
Görz, 124, 131, 181, 187
Gosse, 87
Gouron, 36
Goyaz, 310
Grafenegg skull, 237
Granier de Cassagnac, 179
Grammatical structure, 240
Gran Chaco, 145
Grebos, 212
Greece and Rome, 317
Greek army, 307
Greek athletes, 115
Greenland, 148, 298
Greenlander, 115
Gregg, 150
Grey, 59, 122, 296
Grey hair, 114
Griquas, 186
Guadaloupe, 179, 194
Guam, 250
Guanches, 108, 193, 216, 253, 300, 325, 326
Guanaxuata in Mexico, 41
Guarayos, 374
Guarani, 115, 156
Guatemala, 148
Guatemala, 304
Guaycunas, 153
Guiana, 146, 174, 319
Guiana children, 4
Guinea, 133
Guillain, 131, 326
Gum gatherers of Marensin, 102
Gumilla, 49, 156, 300
Gumprecht, 102, 180
Gunda, 209
Gützlaff, 70, 349
Guyon, 42, 86
Guyot, 331
Gypsy, 254

Hair, dealers in, 103
Hair in Negro, 100; deviations in, 217
Haiti, 100, 250
Hale, 41, 59, 62, 70, 136, 242, 246, 373
Halleur, 304
Hamamwa, 306
Hamilton, W., 94
Hancock, 72
Hands, use of, 137
Hapiris, 119
Hapsburg, house of, 84
Harthann, 221
Harvey, 176
Harriers in Mexico, 82
Harris, 85, 175, 210
Haussa, 209
Hawaii, 160
Hiawatha, 374
Hayti Indians, 190
Head, 120, 138, 345
Head, Negro carries burdens on, 96
Hearne, 145, 150, 155
Hecquard, 95, 137, 142, 209
Heel of Ape, 91
Hekewelder, 114, 155

Heller, 300
Hellespont, 342
Helms, 119, 309
Heusinger, 36, 46, 81, 116, 169
Hereditary transmission, 81; blindness, 85
Herrera, 41, 100, 140, 192
Hessian skull, 216
Hetæræ, 317
Hexadactylous abnormities, 85
Hilhouse, 116
High skulls, 235
Hind, 300
Hindoo mongrels, 178, 223
Hindoo rebellion, 314
Hindoos, 38, 51, 218, 304, 317
Hines, 162
Hips of female Hottentot, 105
History; its relations to Anthropology, 8
History of civilization, developed by the action of four groups of causes—man's physical organization, the psychical life peculiar to each people, surrounding nature, and social relations, 7
History of mankind, 10
History of civilization, a branch of Anthropology, 6
Hobbes, 369
Hodgson, 55, 58, 59, 138, 166
Hodgkinson, 165
Hofacker, 111
Hoffman, 112, 315
Hogs, lice of, 128
Hollard, 26, 93, 94, 95, 108, 215, 226, 341
Holmberg, 116
Hombron, 45, 49, 186, 193, 233
Homicide, 297
Honduras, 148
Hoof, in Hungarian cattle, uncloven, 82
Hornemann, 209
Hoskin, 40, 67
Hoskins, 326
Hoskings, 63
Hotham Bay, 217
Hottentot, female, hips of, 103
Hottentots, 37, 124, 136, 137, 139, 164, 186, 249, 293, 325, 337, 345
Hottentots, consume fat, 60
Howitt, 165
Höven, 238
Huallaga, 154, 175
Huasco, 251
Hudson's Bay, 149
Hueck, 237, 238
Human hair, 42
Humanity: its spirit, equivalent to the spirit of God himself, 3
Humboldt, 41, 46, 69, 129, 132, 134, 140, 147, 156, 179, 202, 298, 318, 333, 338
Humboldt and Bonpland, 68, 103, 107, 123, 146, 194, 251, 252, 255, 331, 369
Humboldt, William von, 245
Hume, 290
Hungary, 327
Hunter, 207, 341
Hunting life, 335, 339
Huntley, 105
Huschke, 69, 79, 94, 238, 264
Hutchinson, 121
Hybrids, 22
Hygrometric state of atmosphere, 34
Hyperboreans, 38, 199

Ibn Batuta, 301
Icelander in Copenhagen, 130
Iothakri, 210
Idrisi, 210
Imlay, 53
Immithlanga, 296
Incas, 184, 370
Indians of the Cordilleras, 354
Indios Mansos, 140
Indo-German nations, 199
Indolence, 295
Infanticide, 163
Infanticide bears no relation to congenital deformities, 113
Influence of knowledge on religion, 379
Influence of respiration on the form of man, 37
Instinct, 271
Intercondyloid perforation, 108
Intermaxillary bone of ape, 91; of Negro, 95
Intermixture of race, 171
Intermixture induces change of type, 229
Intermixture of types, 167
Inviability, 144
Iran, 253
Ireland, 307
Irreclaimable savages, 284
Iroquois, 109, 374
Irving, 313
Isert, 96
Islamism, 375

Jakutes, 62, 115, 129, 149
Jamaica, 129
Jambures, 212
James, 103, 137, 156, 304
Jameson, 254
Japanese, 256
Jargon, the Chinook, 248
Jarrold, 46, 53, 54, 70, 74, 82, 101, 128, 141
Jarves, 122, 163, 202
Java, Bayadères of, 102
Java, 77, 305, 306, 315, 318
Jefferson, 156
Jew, 254
Jewish crania, 224
Jews, 223, 249; complexion of, 47; banished from Portugal, 48; in Berlin, 112
Johnston, 53, 210, 306, 318, 326
Jolofs, 211
Jukagires, 149
Jukes, 297
Junghuhn, 227
Juris, 258

Kabyles of N. Africa, 42
Kabyles, 218
Kaffirs, 125, 136, 208, 257
Kalmucks, 135
Kamschatdale, 149
Kamschatdales, 278, 339
Kangaroos, 165
Kanori, 209
Kansas, 155
Kareles, 76, 227, 253
Kaskes, 187
Katte, 69
Katte, V., 325

Kay, 208, 312
Keate, 137
Keating, 109, 114, 115, 141, 148, 154, 155, 337
Kentucky, 151, 314
Kendall, 68, 148
Keppel, 257, 367
Kessel, 139
Khartoum, 133, 314
King, 102, 257
King and Fitzroy, 87, 119, 158, 251, 304
Kingsborough, 373
King's Mill Islands, 373
Klaproth, 170
Klemm, 291, 328
Knee in Negro, 97
Knight, 82
Knisteneaux, 153
Knox, 135, 185, 205
Kögel, 92, 311
Kohl, 140, 173, 184, 305
Köler, 60, 69, 99, 132, 218
Kolff, 278
Kölle, 133, 137
Kölliker, 98
Kordofan, 51, 141, 208, 271
Korjäks, 215
Kornheim, 175
Kortüm, 348
Koster, 173, 179, 250
Kotzebue, 135, 158, 250
Koujages, 116
Kretschmar, 103, 125, 138, 184
Kriegk, 53
Kruman, food of, 60
Krus, 212
Kru Negros, 293
Krusenstein, 162
Kurds, 64
Kuruglis, 182

Labat, 140, 142, 146, 156, 178, 258, 295
Labillardière, 100, 122, 140
Labour, disinclination for, 330
Lacépède, 38, 40, 207, 233
Ladinos, 148
Lafitan, 153, 257, 318
Lahontan, 109, 121, 154
Laing, 142
Lamarck, 206
Lambert, the porcupine family, 85
Lancerote, 326
Lander, 86, 211
Landolphe, 113
Langsdorff, 83, 102, 162, 301, 314
Language of conqueror replaced that of conquered, 77
Languages, 239
Laplace, 112, 161, 305, 316
Lang, 166
Lapp, 199
Lapps, 118, 156, 227
Latham, 80, 176, 201, 233, 251, 342, 344; man and his migrations, 10; limits of the Negro region, 93
Lascazas, 278
Lassen, 265
Laundresses, 299
Laurence, 135, 261
Lauvergne, 38
Lavayssé, 73, 181, 321
Lawrence, 94
Lay, Tradescant, 250
Lay, James, 46
Leg in Negro, 97
Ledyard and Lucas, 184
Lefebvre, 45, 126, 210
Legendre, 120
Leichardt, 138, 139, 368
Leigh, 126
Leleges, 348
Lenguas, 153
Lenormant, 101
Leo Africanus, 252
Lepouse, Ile, 23
Lepsius, 67, 68, 223
Leri, 122
Lery, 313
Lesson, 54, 61, 103, 113, 139, 159, 215, 221, 227, 238, 333
Le Vaillant, 136, 139, 170, 208
Lewis, 71, 186
Liberia, 311
Lice, 127
Lice-eating, 306
Lichtenstein, 60, 88, 105, 116, 136, 139, 184, 295, 297
Life of primitive peoples, 335
Lifeguards of Prussia, 84
Lima, 49
Liuk, 207
Lion of Africa and Asia, 21
Lip of house of Hapsburg, 84
Lipplaps, 187
Lips of Negro, 95
Lisiansky, 301
Lithuania, 225
Littre, 194
Livingstone, 42, 48, 58, 109, 131, 133, 140, 147, 311
Llama, 338
Llanos, 309
Loango, 358
Lobes of the brain, classification founded on, 79
Logan, 343
Long, 184
Long skulls, 236
Longevity, 123
Longobards, 252
Lopez, 218
Louisiana, 144
Lower Columbia, 141
Loxa, 313
Lucae, 216
Lucas, 32, 81, 82, 83, 88, 168, 170, 172, 176, 184, 205
Lüken, 201, 217
Lund, 195
Lutu, 257
Luzon, 102, 103
Lyell, 37, 72, 82, 169, 179, 215, 333
Lyon, 121

Mac Camn, 345
McCox, 188
M'Culloch, 131
Macauley, 41
Mackenzie, 153
Machacares, 140
Macgillivray, 183
Macousis, 146
Macrocephali, 216
Macrocephalæ, 237
Macapana, 219
Macassars, 157
Madagascar, 112, 218
Madagascans, 256
Magua, 357
Maguas, 149
Magyars, 75, 242
Mahat, 212
Majoribanks, 316
Malabar, 223
Malatza, 223
Malays, 123, 137, 254, 256, 304, 306, 332, 238, 339
Malcolm, 75
Mallat, 123, 182, 251
Mallat, 73, 102, 103, 169
Malta, 254
Man and brute, 273

Man, zoologically speaking, the highest mammal, 8; theologically speaking, occupying a position between God and nature, 8; characteristics of, 275; appears in history a combination of physical and psychical life, 9; primitive state of, 9; specific characters of, 269
Mankind, classification of, 230
Manilla, 249, 253
Manco Capac, 184, 374
Mandans, 155
Mandingos, 142, 211, 299
Mandingo and Guinea negro, their differences, 32
Mankind, cradle of, 201
Maniok, 311
Manabozho, 374
Mandans, 373
Marañon, 146, 219
Martius, 318
Mandshus, 256
Mariner, 127
Marchand, 127
Mandaranes, 209
Mandans, 145
Mandan women, 106
Marquesas islanders, 102
Marital rights, 301
Marrensin, gum gatherers of, 102
Marsden, 257
Matebeles, 360
Maximilian zu Wied, 99, 106, 123, 127
Martin, 243
Marian Islands, 272, 250
Marion, 218
Martius and Dieffenbach, 147
Marcarave, 218
Marchand, 321
Marghi, 209
Mariette, 222
Marriage, 297
Marquesas, 135, 301
Martius, 148
Maroon Negros, 142
Maroons, 142
Mauritius, 250, 311
Maury, A., 194
Matthews, 106, 211, 304
Marriages, prolific, 162
Mariner, 122
Marsden, 102
Maximilian zu Wied, 68, 86, 155, 225
Melvill, 100
Melly, 301
Meigs, 198
Meyer, 107, 237
Mexico, 313; high elevation, 82; mortality in, 132
Meinicke, 162
Measles, 164
Meigs, 225
Melville, 135, 162
Mechanical talents transmitted, 88
Mental and physical qualities, transmission of, 81; endowments, 323; development, 67
Mental condition of nations, 260
Mestizoes, 27, 187, 169, 172, 177, 519; in Paraguay, 180
Meredith, 212
Mexico, 112, 188, 255; miners of, 129
Mexican, 332
Mexicans, 370
Micronesia, 65
Micronesians, vegetarian, 61
Middle-aged persons acclimatise best, 129
Milne-Edwards, 63
Miers, 308
Mindanao, 257, 358
Migrations, 346
Minas Geraes, 173, 195
Mindans, 250
Miners, 120; of Mexico, 129
Minatarrees, 145
Mississippi, 144
Miserable boats, 204
Mitchell, 59, 130, 164
Military standard in France, 63
Mithridates, 234
Monro, 93
Molina, 68, 120, 146
Mollien, 189
Mongrels, 27, 138; viability in, 182; peculiarity of, 167; in Peru profligate, 181; in New Zealand healthy, 181
Mohammed el Touney, 292
Mongols, 121, 199, 215
Mongolians, 255
Mœrenhout, 61, 139, 162
Moffat, 118
Moluccas, 92, 365
Montezuma, 102
Montevideo, 345
Moral sense, 315
Mortality percentages, 131
Morton, 22, 24, 30, 87, 107, 222, 234, 261, 262, 263, 351
Morel and Vinde, 177
Mourning, colours of, 304
Moors, 224
Morse, 148
Mollien, 48, 86, 183, 211, 348, 354
Mofras, Duflot de, 309
Moffat, 255
Monrad, 47, 135
Mohammed el Tounsy, 131, 183, 210
Moore, 305
Moors, 317
Moodie, 118, 136, 165, 316, 345
Mouflon of Sardinia and Asia Minor, 21
Moral bearing of the doctrine of polygamy, 12; degradation, 296
Moody, 124
Moquis, 150
Mosquito, 146
Moxos, 62
Mohammedans, 317, 360, 369
Mohammed Ali, 314
Mozambique, 209
Muhlenfordt, 43, 172, 180, 188
Mühlengeldt, 123
Müller, 98, 106, 107, 108, 216, 221, 225, 227, 245, 253, 334, 336
Müller, F., 23
Müller, W. T., 123
Müller, W., 95
Müller, J. G., 320
Müller, W. T., 369
Müller, W. de, 35
Mulatto more gifted than Negro, 178
Mulattos, 27, 135, 171; sterile, 187
Murder, 297
Mundrucus, 258
Mundy, 135, 312
Mussgu, 210

Mutilations transmitted, 86
Murray river. 166
Murray, Hugh, 294, 381
Muyscas, 374

Nails of mongrel breed, 178
Napier, 249
Nakedness, 299
Nasal bones of Bushmen, 108
Natural objects, worship of, 303
Natahoes, 150
Naturvölker, 292, 306
Nature, healing power of, 126
Naturzustand, 9, 10
Nolengei, 372
Nicaragua, 374
Negritos, 73, 104
Negros, spotted, 86
Negrillos, 104
Negros, 183, 337
Negro, 222, 257; resemblance to ape, 205; mongrels, 311; his black skin, 35; mental capacity of, 15; lighter in advanced age, 99; type, between tropics, 93; physiognomy, 37
Negros, and mulattos, 218
Negros, 169, 208, 211, 225, 250, 296, 326, 339
Negros, longevity of, 123
Negro Portuguese, 250
Negros, mortality of, 133; in New England States, 134; cannot pronounce the R, 135
Negros born in America, 72; improve by contact with Europeans, 72
Negro type not fixed, 213
Negro English, 250
Negro capacity, inferior to white, 267
Negro children run about early, 40
Negros, free, 307
Negro most resembles ape, 92
Negro and ape compared, 143
Negro and ape, a certain resemblance between, 100
New South Wales, children become tall and lean, 54
New Russia, 112
New Zealanders, 114, 215, 299, 312, 366
New Holland, 199
New England States, 134
Newton, 319
New Guinea, 365
New-born Negros light grey, 99
Niagara, 285
Nicaragua, 215, 331
Nilsson, 195
Niebuhr, 253
Newmann, 213
Niger, 213
Niquet, 43
New Spain, 309
New Zealand, 135, 162, 218, 301
New Zealanders, 114, 366
Nile, the ascent of, 213
Nikobars, 357
Nerbudda, 92
Nerves, thicker in Negro, 93
New peculiarities, spontaneous origin of, 80
New Granada, 348
New Caledonia, 278
New Zealand, mongrels healthy, 181
Nott and Gliddon, 22, 24, 25, 30, 88, 172, 184, 188, 189, 195, 198, 222, 225, 228, 248, 263
Nott, 124, 182, 184, 223
Norton, 70
Noah, 256
Normans, 252
Natches, 374
Northern, 333
Nubia, 63, 213, 326
Nukahiwa, children of, 40
Nusard, 32
Nutka, 218
Nuttall, 121

Odin, 374
Odour of Negroes disagreeable, 100, 103
Odshis, 212
Oelsner, Montmerqué, 179
Ojibbeways, 121
Oldendorp, 250
Old Testament, 202
Olivier, 47, 51
Olshausen, 148
Omahos, 145, 155
Omboni, 97, 105, 123, 209, 311
Ompizes, 193
Onibou, 160
Oregon, 146, 248
Original equality of races, 351
Orinoco, 102, 116, 146, 300, 301, 357
Orinoco, Indians on, 68
Orthognathæ, 235
Osage, 121, 156
Os Incæ, 107
Osiris, 374
Osmanli Turks, 75
Othomi, 247
Otomaks, 116
Otter sheep, 82
Otto, 111
Oudney, 105
Ovaglie, 173, 192
Ovambos, 278
Oviedo y Valdez, 103
Oviedo, 113, 127
Owen, 47, 91, 209, 311, 367
Owen, Richard, 128

Pain, exhibition of, 127
Pallas, 217
Paraguay, 145, 173
Paranahyba, 170
Parry, 109, 110
Parchappe, 94, 265
Pallme, 131, 271
Panamá, 147
Park, M., 96, 134, 211
Paiuches, 62
Papuas, 139, 343
Passy, 357
Passos, 183
Patachos, 299
Patagonians, 106
Pavie, 75
Painting and tattooing, 300
Palmo, 92
Parallelism in the animal kingdom, 14
Painted Indians, 305
Pampas, 345
Paraguay, Europeans in, 104; cattle in, 82
Papuas, 193, 221; in South Sea, 218

Parchappe, 262
Parkyns, 126
Parker, 141, 173
Parthian, 253
Parish, 126
Pecari, 83
Pediculus, 128
Pedras, Rio das, 170
Pehlwi, 253
Pehuenches, 100, 219
Penguins, 271
Pelasgi, 222, 348
Péron, 41, 116, 117, 118, 132, 257, 300
Perrin du Lac, 121, 335
Pelvis of ape, 91
Petit, 126, 210
Petermann, 123
Peters, 127
Pelvis, size of, 64
Peuls, 183
Pernambuco, 173
Peru, 146, 338; Indian, 295
Peru, 172, 250, 369, 370
Peruvian skulls, 107, 216
Peruvian thrives at 7000 to 15,000 feet above the sea, 87
Peruvians, 137, 140; their variable complexion, 49
Petit, 126
Pfyffer, 43, 188
Philippines, 169, 188
Philip, 65, 73
Philipps, 238, 263
Physical and mental qualities, transmission of, 81
Philippi, 251
Philip, 141
Philological investigations, 238
Phrenology, its fables rejected in Germany, 237
Physical changes to which man is subject, 34
Physiology, its relations to psychology, 7
Physical investigations, 17
Physiological differences in man, 90
Pitcairns Island, children swim, 87
Pickering, 113, 173, 227
Pigafetta, 123
Pickering, 121, 142, 157, 188, 219, 233, 250, 344, 349
Pigment of Negro skin, 98
Pisang, 331
Plough, 309
Pitcairn, 147
Peyroux de la Condremière, 290
Polyandry, 228
Physiology, a branch of anthropology, 6
Peron and Lesueur, 106
Polynesians, their difference of colour, 41
Polack, 100, 114, 184, 312
Polo, M., 257
Pondicherry, 129
Pöppig, 56, 87, 100, 120, 123, 145, 147, 154, 170, 172, 175, 180, 181, 183, 219, 307, 309
Population, density of, 3
Population, 157
Portlock and Dixon, 155
Portuguese creoles, their complexion, 48
Portland Bay, 166
Polltax, 163
Port Essington, 366
Pouqueville, 76
Pott, 273
Prichard, 261
Potawatomis, 141
Precocity of children, 40
Port Natal, 56
Power, 157
Preserved heads, 163
Prescott, 263
Pfeyffer, 305, 318
Polynesians, 114
Polynesia, 64, 157; no hissing sound in, 135
Plato's Republic, 317
Polar nations, 129
Political conditions, 361
Polygamy, 153, 325; moral bearing of the doctrine, 12
Port Essington, 297, 343
Port Stephens, 166
Polyklet, 217
Polynesians, 144, 160, 343
Porcupine family, 85
Portuguese, 170, 310; degenerated, 65
Pott, 76, 243, 253, 255
Potawatomis, 115, 153
Protestant missionaries, intimidation imputed to them, 161
Property, 276
Primitive state of man, 9
Proportion of male to female births, 110
Protoplasts, 20
Protestant slave trade, 315
Prognathæ, 235
Proctor, 120, 130
Proyart, 86, 358
Pruner, 47, 91, 93, 94, 144, 169, 181, 210, 216
Pre-Celtic population of Scotland, 195
Prichard, 19, 24, 28, 29, 48, 51, 55, 57, 63, 64, 66, 72, 75, 81, 95, 109, 208, 217, 307
Primeval Language, 245
Prince Regent's Bay, 140
Psychical influence, 4
Psychical unity, 321
Psychology a branch of anthropology, 6
Psychical qualities transmissible, 83
Psychological investigation, 259
Prèsort, 42
Puberty, time of, 40
Puberty of girls, 110
Pueblos, 184
Puelches, 185
Puris, 155, 299

Quadroon, 170, 176
Quandt, 128, 153, 258
Quartin Dillon, 210
Quatrefages, 187
Question of the unity of mankind, 11
Quetelet, measurements of, 63
Quetelet, 40, 57, 111, 118, 121, 237
Quetzalcoatl, 374
Quichés, 304
Quichuas, 250, 304
Quintroon, 170
Quioga, 250
Quirus, 218
Quito, 120, 172; elevation of, 37

Raffenel, 47, 86, 95, 133, 173, 183, 212
Races, intermixture of, 171
Raiatea, 156, 399
Rainy months, 133
Rajpoots, 51
Rathke, 87
Raratonga, 147

Rendu, 210
Rengger, 102, 104, 109, 121, 123, 127, 139, 153, 154, 156, 308
Redakins, 152
Reptiles, wide distribution of, 197
Réeke, 111
Religious notions, 369
Religion of primitive man, 302
Remusat, 261
Resiniers of Aquitaine, 102
Respiration, 109
Retzius, 76, 78, 225, 234, 235, 238, 253
Reversion to original type, 27
Reversion no criterion of race, 33
Rey, 75
Riccarees, 145
Richardt, 111
Richardson, 116, 164, 209
Riggs, 242
Riley, 138
Rioja, 308
Rio Janeiro, 251, 309
Ritter, 38, 51, 63, 65, 115, 138, 156, 175, 332
Ritter, C., 340
Rivero and Tschudi, 246
Robertson, G. A., 113, 143
Robertson, G. P. and W. P., 293
Rochet d'Hericourt, 210, 326
Rochon, 218
Rodriguez, 219
Rohillas, 43
Romanic nations, 77
Römer, 1
Roquefeuille, 219, 301
Rose Cowper, 293
Ross, 109, 115, 271, 316
Ross, J., 140
Roth, 135
Rougemont, 257
Rousseau, 289
Rudolphi, 23, 201
Rüppell, 66, 210, 325
Rush, 88, 170
Russegger, 126, 133, 142, 211
Russian peasants, 307
Russo-American Company, 314

Sack, v., 177
Sadler, 111
Sahantin, 242
St. Peter's River, 337
St. Crica, 251, 258
St. Hilaire, S. Geoffroy, 1, 63, 171
St. Hilaire, A. de, 49, 132, 170, 179, 309, 319
St. Thomas, 133
Salt, 65, 210
Samoa, 157
Samoa Archipelago, 272
Samoiedes, 199, 215, 227
Sandwich islanders, 159, 160, 306
Sandwich islands, 297
Sandifort, 101, 224, 238
San Luis, 308
S. Salvador, 251
Sanscrit, 245, 252
Sarawak, 366
Sarmiento, 181, 308
Sartorius, 180
Savage, civilized man inferior sensually to, 137
Savage, 181
Savolax, 76, 253
Say, 103, 109, 137, 155, 156
Scarlett, 88, 218
Scalphunting by White Americans, 150
Schamanism, 255, 303
Scherzer, 189, 251
Schlegel, 197
Schleicher, 75, 249
Schendy, 69
Schiel, 138
Schultz, 238
Schoffer, 156
Schoolcraft, 14, 62, 107, 145, 148, 149, 150, 151, 164, 238, 243, 263
Schomburgk, Sir R., 37, 40, 96, 130, 146, 153, 154, 174, 180, 189, 290, 312, 319
Schön and Crowther, 133
Schoschonies, 62
Schadow, 217
Scherzen, 167
Schmaida, 170, 175, 181
Scruple, 348
Scythian, 253
Sea voyages, 204
Seemann, 15, 62, 140, 187, 217
Selberg, 305, 315, 330
Selisk, 248
Semitic-Phœnician, 348
Semitic, 222
Semple, 184, 188, 348
Senaar, 208, 213
Senaar, Arabs of, 101
Senegambia, 133, 137, 367
Sentences, construction of, 241
Senegal, 214
Senses, perfection of, 137
Sense of shame, 299
Sense of smell in Negro, 95
Sertanejos, 173
Sertajo, 310
Sererer, 300
Serres, 79, 101, 177, 182, 183
Sesamoid bones, 97
Sexual excesses, 297
Shape of the skull, constant to a certain extent, 232
Shangallas, 210
Sheighias, 63
Shorthand, 157
Siah-Posh, 45
Siamese, 304
Siberian tribes, 110
Sicily, 253
Siebols, 172
Sikeliotes, 253
Sikhs, originally Hindoos, 74
Siland, 125
Silliman, 263
Simbura, 313
Simon, Pedro, 219, 373
Simon, 99
Simpson, 47, 148, 163, 257, 336
Singapore, 254
Sioux, 109, 115, 149, 155, 335
Sitgraves, 61
Skeleton of Negro heavy, 93
Skin of Negro, 98
Skinner, 119
Skull, form of, 78
Skull, deviations in, 217
Skull of Negro thick, 93
Slaveholders and slave-dealers, 92
Slaveholders, 315
Slaves well cared for lose their specific odour, 73
Smell, sense of, 140
Small-pox, 164
Small-pox poison, 145
Smith, Hamilton, 118, 142, 185, 192, 261

Smith, 98, 226, 233, 297
Smoking a baby, 305
Smyth, 186, 264, 284, 320
Society, 276
Sokotra, 326
Solimoes, 258
Solomon's Island, 140
Sömmering, 93, 94, 96, 97, 128
Sonnerat, 218
Sonnini, 106
Soreno, 103
Soudan, East, 296
South America, 257
Sowaheili, 254
Spaniards, 250
Sparrman, 171
Sparta, 317
Spanish Creoles, their complexion, 48
Spanish conquerors, 151
Species, signification of, 22
Species, diversity of, 220
Species neither subjective abstractions, nor exemplars, 17; definition of, 17
Specific differences among mankind, 13
Speech sounds, 135
Spix and Martius, 123, 131, 135, 154, 169, 174, 179, 154, 258, 300
Spontaneous origin of new peculiarities, 80
Spotted Negroes, 86
Sprengel, 48
Spurzheim, 88
Squier, 148, 181, 255, 331, 371
Stanhope Smith, 38, 53, 73, 124, 352
Stature of man, acted on by climate, 39
Stephens, 111, 307
Stevenson, 37, 48, 71, 120, 123, 170, 172, 181, 309
Steen Bille, 159, 187, 357
Stewart, 161, 306
Steedman, 299
Steffens distinguished a geological, physiological, and psychological anatomy, 5
Stokes, 59
Strap and twig garment, 301
Strzelecki, 176, 293
Sturm, 83, 168
Styria, 217
Subdivisions of species, 21
Suckling, 163
Sumatra, 102, 257, 306
Sunda Islands, 92
Surinam, 250
Susus, 211, 299
Swainson, 21, 31, 39, 196
Sweat, 104
Sydney, 316
Syphilis, 162, 164

Tachard, 373
Tænia, 128
Tagal, 249
Tahitians, 305
Tahiti, 112, 135, 147, 158, 218, 373, 388
Tailed men, 92
Talcahuano, 309
Tamatoa, 369
Tams, 59, 133
Tanner, 118
Tapajos, 258
Tapeworms, 128
Taaroa, 373
Tartars, 221, 225
Tasmanians inferior to Australians, 116
Tavastlander, 76, 253
Taylor, 134, 158
Taylor, B., 222
Tchuktchi, 215
Tchadda, 306
Teeth of ape, 91; of Negro, 95
Temperament transmissible, 82
Temple, 120, 121
Tente en el ayre, 187
Testament, Old, 202
Tertroon, 176
Tegg, 167
Ternaux, 103, 150, 151, 219
Tertiary formations, 194
Teutons, 343
Thär, 83
Thickness of Negro's skull not exclusively peculiar to him, 100
Thompson, 116, 176, 390, 314, 369
Thunberg, 60, 105, 136
Thomson, 85, 238
Thevenot, 106
Thighs of ape, 91
Thigh in Negro, 79
Thumb, toe of Negro used as a, 107
Thompson, G. H., 168

Tibarenes, 257
Tiedemann, 93, 94, 262
Tierra del Fuego, 58, 119, 223, 293, 304, 325, 334
Tierra Firme, 14
Time of puberty, 40
Tibet, 255
Tiger, 205
Timor, forty languages in, 247
Tibboo, 209
Timani, 211
Timorese, 117, 218, 257, 300
Todd, 53, 176
Toe of Negro used as a thumb, 101
Toes in new-born children, 87
Tozar, 214
Tomat, 211
Tonkin, 218
Torquemada, 218
Toucouleurs, 183
Towaras, 156
Transmission, hereditary, 81
Tropical provinces of Asia, 200
Trémaux, 105
Tropics in East India, South America, and one part of Africa, do not contain blacks, 35
Troyer, 50
Tschittagong, 92
Tscherkesses, 216
Tschudi, 48, 107, 114, 119, 123, 148, 170, 174, 179, 180, 210, 234, 237, 258, 304, 313
Tschego, 91
Tschuvasches, 175, 193
Tschumbulpur, 92
Tschuktsh, 56, 62
Tumbucus, 301
Turnbull, 138, 139, 147
Tunguses, 118, 156, 215, 217
Turkish nations, 242
Turkish army, 307
Turkish rule, 297
Turks, 304, 318, 342
Tupinambis, 122, 313
Turkey, 327
Tucuman, 308
Tuboris, 301
Turco-Russian war, 314

Tupinambis, 313
Types, constancy of, 225
Types of languages, 247
Tyermann and Bennett, 40, 162, 369
Tyrrheni, 348

Ualan, 333
Uanne, 55
Ucayale, 258
Ulloa, 42, 68, 100, 113, 146, 172, 173, 187, 295, 297
Ulster, degeneration of Irish, when expelled from, 57
Unanue, 104, 188
Uncultured peoples, 292
Unity of the human species, 167
Unity of mankind, 143
Unity of mankind as a species, 10
Unity of species, 20
Upper jaw, 95
Usher, 195

Van Amzinge, 15, 185
Vancouver, 159
Vancouver fort, 248
Vandals, their descendants in North Africa, 42
Van Diemen's Land, 140, 199, 295
Van Diemen's Land, natives of, 100
Van der Hoeven, 97
Van der Kemp, 136
Van Hogendorp, 218
Vater, 53, 234
Vei, 137
Velasco, 192, 219
Venezuela, 111
Venezuela, 156
Vertebral column of ape, 91
Vespucci, 156
Viability in mongrels, 182
Victoria Land, 271
Villavicencio, 65
Vincendon-Dumoulin, 158
Vindjha, 252, 334
Violin, sound of, 140
Virey, 38, 208, 233, 265, 304
Virginia, 151
Virgin, 162, 249
Vis medicatrix naturæ, 126
Vocabularies, 240
Vogel, 301
Vogt, 15, 21, 24, 222
Voice, 136
Volkmann, 14
Vollgraff, 188
Volney, 37
Von Glümer, 321
Von Sack, 119
Vrolik, 96

Waddington and Hanbury, 63
Wadai, 210
Wafer, 85
Wagner, M., 152, 182, 252
Wagner, A., 24, 28
Wagner, R., 24, 87, 101
Wagner, 125, 135
Wallis, 218
Waldeck, 102, 137
Wagner and Scherzer, 331
Ward, 72, 120
Wallschägel, 250
Walpole, 163
Warm climate, 201
Wars of extermination justifiable, 13
Washington Irving, 145
Webster, 310
Weerth, 217, 339
Weber, 225
Weber, M. J., 224
Werne, 56, 101, 103, 130, 133, 134, 138, 175, 211, 314, 318, 326
Webb and Berthelot, 300
Web-footed abnormities, 85
Weigl, 148
Weld, 121
Wells, 148
West Indies, 250; mortality in, 131
West, 114, 156
White, 96
White, acclimatization of, 128
Whites, 330
White teeth, 305
Wilkes, 58, 59, 66, 122, 145, 146, 158, 161, 162, 163, 164, 166, 202, 238, 272
Wilde, 195
Williamson, 54, 73, 83
Wilson, 112, 119, 132, 158, 195, 297, 358
Wilson, Professor Daniel, 78
Winnepegs, 148
Winckelmann, 107
Williams, Roger, 121
Winterbottom, 46, 218
Wise, 40
Wisemann, 72
Worcester, 243
Wojgerat, 65
Wotjakes, 218
Worms eaten, 319
Wrestling, 116
Wrangell, 62, 149, 356
Wuttke, 291, 303, 328
Wydah, 106
Wyeth, 62

Xenophon, 257
Ximenes, 140, 304

Yankee type, 52
Yarriba, 212, 218
Yarriba, food of inhabitants of, 60
Yebus, 242, 304
Yellow fever, 124
Yembo, 218
York Sound, 257
Yucatan, 102, 111, 137, 255, 299, 374
Yünnan, 257
Yvan, 187

Zambo, 170, 173
Zambos, 181
Zacatecas, 120
Zambezi, 301
Zarate, 48
Zenaghas, 252
Zeune, 107, 235
Zimmermann, 30, 74, 129, 300
Zoological provinces, 196
Zoroaster, 374
Zuchelli, 315
Zulu Kaffirs, 101
Zulu, 137, 296
Zulus, 294, 299, 360

ERRATA.

Page						
15	line	1 *note* ...	for	Voigt	read	Vogt
26	„	9	„	Holland	„	Hollard
36	„	13	„	2 (reference)	„	1 (reference)
40	„	10	„	Schomburgh	„	Schomburgk
64	„	8 from bottom	„	Inka	„	Inca
95	„	5 „	„	Vollard	„	Hollard
100	„	7 „	„	Penhuenches	„	Pehuenches
106	„	2	„	A monkey	„	An ape
106		in *note* 3 at foot	„	Donville	„	Douville
107		... ...	„	1862	„	1863
111	„	7 from bottom	„	Cumena	„	Cumana
123		in *note* 9 at foot	„	Petermanns	„	Petermann's
131		in *note* 8 at foot	„	Görtz	„	Görz
134	„	8 from top	„	Callié	„	Caillié
134		in *note* 1 at foot	„	Fraissinet	„	Freycinet
140	„	9 from top	„	Firma	„	Firme
140		in *note* 2	„	Seeman	„	Seemann
141	„	9 from top	„	Philipp	„	Philip
143		in *note* 1 at foot	„	Allan	„	Allen
153	„	11 from top	„	Knisteneux	„	Knisteneaux
171	„	14 „	„	Geoffrey	„	Geoffroy
172		in *note* 8 at foot	„	Unanne	„	Unanue
186	„	8 from top	„	Bachman	„	Bachmann
188	„	6 in *note*	„	Unanne	„	Unanue
195	„	13 from top	„	Nilssohn	„	Nilsson
204	„	12	„	Hot	„	Torrid
218		in *note* 1	„	Marcgrav	„	Marcgrave
237	„	11 from top	„	Microcephalæ	„	Macrocephalæ
238	„	19 „	„	Hushcke	„	Huschke
250		in *note* 3	„	Seeman	„	Seemann
301	„	17 from top	„	Mahommedan	„	Mohammedan
302		in *note*	„	People	„	Peuple
371	„	10 from bottom	„	Squire	„	Squier
373		in top line	„	insert *the* before Fiji		
373	„	7 from bot. in *note*	„	Chibchar	„	Chibchas
374		in *note* 2 at foot	„	Louisane	„	Louisiane

CPSIA information can be obtained
at www.ICGtesting.com
Printed in the USA
LVHW040350110522
718423LV00001B/208

9 783375 000929